/2

WHEN SNOW FALLS

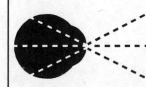

This Large Print Book carries the
Seal of Approval of N.A.V.H.

WHEN SNOW FALLS

BRENDA NOVAK

THORNDIKE PRESS

A part of Gale, Cengage Learning

GALE
CENGAGE Learning®

Detroit • New York • San Francisco • New Haven, Conn • Waterville, Maine • London

GALE
CENGAGE Learning®

Copyright © 2012 by Brenda Novak, Inc.
Whiskey Creek Series.
Thorndike Press, a part of Gale, Cengage Learning.

Thorndike Press® Large Print Romance.
The text of this Large Print edition is unabridged.
Other aspects of the book may vary from the original edition.
Set in 16 pt. Plantin.

LIBRARY OF CONGRESS CATALOGING-IN-PUBLICATION DATA

Novak, Brenda.
  When snow falls / by Brenda Novak. — Large print ed.
    p. cm. — (Whiskey Creek series) (Thorndike Press large print romance)
  ISBN-13: 978-1-4104-5240-5 (hardcover)
  ISBN-10: 1-4104-5240-9 (hardcover)
  1. Family secrets—Fiction. 2. Life change events—Fiction. 3. Large type books. I. Title.
PS3614.O926W46 2012
813'.6—dc23   2012032346

Published in 2012 by arrangement with Harlequin Books S.A.

Printed in the United States of America
1 2 3 4 5 6 7 16 15 14 13 12

To Stephanie Novembri.
Thank you for all the volunteer hours
you've put in on my annual online
auction for diabetes research.
You came into my life at a time when
I really needed some help — and
you've been there for me ever since.

Dear Reader,

Who can resist a story about a woman who isn't sure her mother is really her mother? When I started this book, I couldn't stop thinking about that situation, how it would make my heroine feel — and what she might do to find the truth. It kept me eager to write each day.

Cheyenne has always had her doubts about Anita, has always wondered why certain troubling memories surfaced again and again, especially when it snowed. But given her childhood, she has to wonder if maybe she created a pleasant fantasy in order to cope with reality. Because of her sister, and the duty she feels to the woman who raised her, she vacillates between aggressively exploring her past and shying away from it, especially now that she's established herself in Whiskey Creek and is happier than she's ever been. Part of her doesn't want to rock the boat — but the questions that have gnawed at her for years just won't go away. And if she's ever to answer them, she has to act soon. Anita is dying of cancer. If she doesn't tell what she knows before the end, it may be too late.

That right there was enough to keep my attention — but then Dylan Amos walked

7

onto the scene and added a few complications of his own. I hope you'll enjoy reading all the intrigue as much as I enjoyed writing it!

I'd like to thank Marcy Mostats-Passuello, whose name appears as a character in this book, for her generous support of the Make-A-Wish Foundation.

Because Dylan is one of my favorite heroes (and he has four sexy brothers who will appear in future books), I've had a fabulous Amos Auto Body T-shirt (black with white imprint) designed for those who might like one. You can purchase it and other Whiskey Creek items at www.brendanovak.com. There, you can also find more information about my books and my annual online auction for diabetes research, which happens every May. So far we've raised more than $1.6 million!

Brenda Novak

1

It didn't snow in Whiskey Creek often. But when it did, it took Cheyenne Christensen back to another time and place. Not one filled with picture-perfect memories of warm holidays, gaily wrapped packages and hot apple cider, like the Christmases her friends enjoyed. No, this kind of weather made her feel sick inside, as if something dark and terrible had happened on just such a night.

She wished she could remember exactly what. For years she'd racked her brain, trying to make sense of her earliest memories, to conjure up the woman with the smiling face and pretty blond hair who featured in so many of them. Was she an aunt? A teacher? A family friend?

Surely it wasn't her *mother*! Cheyenne already had a mother who insisted there'd been no one in her life meeting that description.

That didn't mean it was true, however. Anita had never been particularly reliable — in any regard.

"Chey, where are you? I need my pain meds."

Real mother or not, the woman who'd raised her was awake. Again. It was getting harder and harder for Anita to rest.

Trying to shake off the stubborn melancholy that had crept over her when the snow began to fall, Cheyenne turned away from the window. The three-bedroom hovel she shared with her mother and sister wasn't anything to be proud of. She'd put up a Christmas tree and lights, and kept the place clean, but their house was easily the most humble abode in Amador County.

Still, it was better than the beater cars and fleabag motel rooms she'd lived in growing up. At least it provided *some* stability.

"Be right there!" She hurried to the cupboard to get the morphine. After more than a decade, her mother's cancer was back. Cheyenne hated to see anyone suffer. But if Anita hadn't gotten sick fifteen years ago, they might never have settled down, and coming to Whiskey Creek was the best thing that had ever happened to Cheyenne. As guilty as it made her feel, she would always be grateful for the diagnosis that stopped all the shiftless rambling and finally enabled her and her sister to enroll in school. She just wished the cancer that had started in Anita's ovaries had stayed in remission instead of reappearing in her pancreas.

"What are you doing out there while I'm lying in here, suffering?" her mother demanded as soon as Cheyenne walked into the room. "You don't really care about me. You never have."

Fearing there might be some truth in those words, which sounded slurred because she wasn't wearing her dentures, Chey refused to meet her mother's gaze. "I wouldn't be here if I didn't want to be a good daughter," she said, but even she believed it was duty, not love, that motivated her. She held too much against Anita, had longed to escape her for so many years she couldn't remember when she'd first started feeling that way.

Anita preferred her sister, anyway. She'd made that clear all along. Fortunately, Cheyenne didn't have a problem with it. Presley was older by two years. She came first and would always be number one with Anita.

"I did my best by you," her mother said, suddenly defensive.

Here we go again. She brought a spoonful of morphine to her mother's lips. "That might be true," she conceded. But it was also true that Anita's best fell far short of ideal. Until they came to Whiskey Creek, she and Presley had been dragged through almost every state in the western half of the country. They'd gone hungry and cold and been left alone in cars or with strangers for indefinite periods of time. They'd even been forced to beg on street corners or at the entrances to malls when their mother deemed it necessary.

"You never cut me any slack," Anita complained, snorting as she attempted to shift positions.

Determined to preserve the peace, Cheyenne changed the subject. "Are you hungry? Would you like a sandwich or some soup?"

Her mother waved dismissively. "I can't eat right now."

Cheyenne helped her get comfortable and smoothed the bedding. "The meds will make you sick if you don't get something in your stomach. Remember what happened last night."

"I'm sick, anyway. I can hardly keep anything down. And I don't want to put my dentures in. The damn things don't fit right. Where's your sister?"

"You know where Presley is. She works at the casino."

"She never comes around anymore."

That had to be the painkiller talking. Not only did Presley live with them, she watched Anita during the day so Cheyenne could work at the bed-and-breakfast owned by her best friend's family — and as long as Presley didn't have the money to buy dope, she helped out on weekends, too. "She left a couple of hours ago." Already it seemed like an eternity to Cheyenne, and evidently Anita felt the same way.

Growing more agitated, her mother shook her head. "No."

"No what?"

"I haven't seen her in ages. She's abandoned me. I'm surprised you're the one who stayed."

It wasn't so unusual that Chey would be the daughter to come through for her in difficult times. She'd always been the most responsible in the family. She almost said so, but what was the point? Her mother would believe what she wanted. "She'll be here again in the morning." And as soon as she got home, she'd crash in her bed. . . .

"Can you call her?"

"I'm here to take care of whatever you need. Why bother her?"

"Because I want to talk to her, that's why!"

Chey knew she couldn't deal with her mother if she was going to be difficult again. "Calm down, okay?"

"I'm not acting up!" She struggled to sit but couldn't manage it. "Who the hell do you think you are? Where do you think you'd be without me, anyway?"

"That's what I'd like to know." She had a feeling she'd be someplace better. But that was the suspicion talking. She normally didn't say such things. Today, the words rushed out before Cheyenne could stop them. Then they hung in the air like a foul stench.

Her mother blinked at her. Her eyes, though rheumy with sickness, could still turn mean. But she'd lost the power she'd once wielded. She could no longer frighten Cheyenne.

Thank God.

Anita must've realized it wouldn't do her any good to rail, because she didn't let her temper boil over. Her voice became whiny. "You can treat me like this when I'm about to die?"

There was nothing more the doctors could do. They'd prescribed liquid morphine for the pain and Ativan to ease the anxiety, and released Anita so she could spend her last weeks at home. Pancreatic cancer typically moved fast. But Cheyenne didn't think Anita had arrived at her final moments quite yet. "Let's not despair too soon."

"You won't shed a tear when I'm gone."

Hoping to distract her, Cheyenne turned on the TV. "I'll heat some soup while you watch *Jeopardy!*"

Anita caught her before she could walk out. "*I've* always loved *you*. I could've abandoned you, but I didn't. I kept you with me every step of the way, even though it wasn't always easy to feed and clothe you."

Cheyenne pivoted to confront her. "Who was the blonde woman? Someone you used to leave me with?"

Anita grimaced. "What blonde woman?"

"I've told you about her before. I can remember someone with blue eyes and platinum-blond hair. I was with her, wearing a princess dress, and there were presents all around as if it was my birthday."

A strange expression came over Anita's sallow face, one that led Cheyenne to believe she might finally receive an explanation. Her mother knew *something*. But then a hint of the malevolence Anita had just masked sparkled in her eyes. "Why do you keep asking about that stuff? I don't know what on earth you're talking about."

■ ■ ■ ■

Presley Christensen sat in the parking lot of the Rain Dance Casino, smoking a cigarette in her 1967 Mustang. It was cold outside, too cold to have the window cracked open, especially when the heater was busted, but if she wanted to smoke she had little choice. It was against California state law to light up in a public building, and she sure as hell wasn't going to stand outside.

Crossing her ankles beneath the steering wheel, she took a long, calming drag. As a card dealer, she was entitled to a fifteen-minute break every hour, which sounded like a lot but wasn't, not when she was on her feet for the rest of her shift. She had three hours to go and already her back ached. She wished she could earn a living some other way, but there weren't many options available to someone without so much as a high school diploma. She was lucky to have her GED and a job.

"Excuse me."

A man rapped on her window, and she nearly jumped out of her skin. Where had he come from? She hadn't seen anyone approaching. . . .

She locked the door to be certain he

couldn't get in and spoke to him through the gap in her window. "What do you want?"

Several years ago, a woman had been abducted from a casino northeast of Sacramento. Presley hadn't heard of anything like that happening where *she* lived, but it was nearly three in the morning, and she was out in the dark alone with a stranger. One who'd been drinking for all she knew.

He lifted his hands in a calming gesture. "I'm sorry. I didn't mean to startle you. I'm Eugene Crouch, a private investigator." He used a penlight to illuminate the ID he flashed at her. "Are you Presley?"

She wasn't sure whether to answer him. She was afraid the P.I. claim was designed to lower her guard. Her first name was, after all, sewn onto her blouse. "What if I am?" she asked skeptically.

"I'm looking for someone you might know."

"Who?"

"Anita Christensen."

She practically dropped her cigarette. As it was, some ash fell into her lap and she had to brush it away before it could burn a hole in her uniform. What did this man want with her mother?

Considering the way Anita had lived her life, he couldn't have any *good* reason to be looking for her. As the black-sheep daughter of a hard-bitten, broken woman who'd had six kids by as many men, she wasn't likely to inherit money. And, like her own mother, Anita had never been accepted by her extended family, so Presley doubted this man was here to help some long-lost friend or relative reconnect. . . .

Maybe she'd stolen a watch from someone who'd paid her for sex and the police had issued a warrant for her arrest. Or worse. She'd once crashed into a man on a bicycle and driven away from the scene of the accident. She'd been drinking and shouldn't have been behind the wheel. Presley was surprised she'd suffered no repercussions for that. But it'd happened in Arizona and they'd crossed into New Mexico right after.

Presley had shoved that incident into the back of her mind — until now.

This could also be about welfare fraud or tax evasion, she supposed. Anita had done anything she could to get by.

"Say that name again?" She took another drag on her cigarette while trying to decide how to answer.

"Anita Christensen. Used to be Karen Bateman. Went by the name of Laura Dumas before that."

Presley had a vague recollection of being

told her last name was Bateman — maybe when she was eight or nine. But she'd never heard of Dumas. That one must've been before she was old enough to remember. "None of those names are familiar to me." She'd been trained to protect her mother, to assist in whatever con Anita was running. If she didn't, they'd go hungry. Or she and her sister would be abandoned. She was too old for those threats to have the same effect, but old habits and loyalties were hard to break.

"You're sure?" he pressed, obviously disappointed. "You're listed as a reference on a credit card application from years back, in New Mexico. She claimed you were her daughter."

She'd only been sixteen when they were in New Mexico. How had he been able to trace her from there?

"I've never lived in New Mexico." Presley felt no remorse for lying, just an odd sense of panic that this might spill over onto her. Right or wrong, she'd done what her mother had taught her to do.

"Christensen might not be an unusual name, but Presley is," he persisted. "As a first name, I mean."

"Maybe this Anita person liked Elvis as much as my own mother did."

Presley considered herself a pro when it came to misinformation, but he seemed stubbornly unconvinced. "She may have assumed yet another identity," he said. "Would you mind taking a look at her picture?"

"Sorry." She stubbed out her cigarette in the ashtray. "My break's over. I've got to get to work."

Except she didn't dare open the door with him standing there, and he wasn't backing off. She hesitated with her hand on the latch, and that was all the opportunity he needed.

"It'll only take a second." He pulled out an old mug shot, which he illuminated with the penlight like he had his ID. "She's the one on the right."

Presley was too nervous to really look. She knew who she'd see, but with her mother sick and about to die she figured it didn't matter anymore. Whatever Anita had done wrong, cancer was punishment enough. "Never seen her before in my life," she said as her eyes flicked over it.

He held up another picture. "Do you recognize either of these two?"

She nearly told him he had to leave or she was going to call the police on her cell phone, but clamped her lips shut. She did recognize one of the two subjects of *that* photograph. Chey was in it as a very young girl. And something about her struck Presley as odd. Although Anita had looked as Presley would've expected — significantly younger but still unkempt — Chey didn't. Her hair was curled into pretty ringlets tied with a ribbon, and she was wearing a fancy dress with black patent leather shoes.

When had this picture been taken? And why wasn't *she* in it? She couldn't remember a single time their mother had bothered to curl their hair. They'd been lucky to have a comb to straighten out the snarls after several days without a bath.

Not only that, but . . . who was the third person — the pretty blonde woman?

"Ms. Christensen?" the man prompted.

What did this picture mean?

The possibilities terrified Presley. Anita was about to die. She couldn't lose Chey, too. "I don't recognize them, either."

Cheyenne woke to the sound of voices. Her sister was home and, apparently, her mother had survived the night. Chey couldn't say she was glad; she couldn't in all conscience say she wasn't, either. It was just another day.

A glance at the digital alarm clock told her she didn't have to be up for another hour. She rolled over to go back to sleep, but the wary tone of her mother's voice aroused her curiosity.

"Did he say what his name was?"

"One sec." Presley. "I got his card." There was a brief pause. "Eugene Crouch."

"He's a private investigator?"

"That's what he told me, and that's what's written here. Do you have any idea what he wanted?"

"None."

"Do you think he'll come back?"

"I guess he could, but I don't know why he pestered you in the first place."

Although Presley lowered her voice, Cheyenne could still hear. "He's been searching for you a long time, Mom. You have to have *some* idea."

"I don't, unless it's an unpaid speeding ticket."

"Do they go to such great lengths to track people down for that?"

"They put out arrest warrants, don't they? Anyway, whatever he wants, it's too late. Feel free to invite him to my funeral."

"Don't talk like that! You know it upsets me."

Chey tightened her grip on the blankets. That was precisely why Anita did it. To get a reaction. To be reassured.

"You and Chey are the only family I have," Presley said.

"You need to prepare yourself, honey. I won't last much longer."

"I can't go on without you. I can't cope as it is." Presley sounded as if she might be crying. Cheyenne felt bad for her, but she felt even worse about the fact that she experienced no grief — that she was merely waiting for release from the responsibilities that imprisoned her.

Was there something wrong with her? Was she as bad, as ungrateful, as her mother claimed?

"Come here," Anita cooed.

As she pictured Presley falling into their mother's arms, Chey covered her eyes with her hand. She was glad her mother and sister had each other. Maybe Anita deserved more love than Cheyenne could give her. Despite all the differences between her and Presley, Cheyenne cared deeply for her older sibling. Growing up, Presley had been her only friend, her only ally, especially when Anita went on one of her frightening tirades. For whatever reason, their mother's anger had always been more focused on Chey. Once or twice, Anita had become so violent that Presley had been forced to step in.

"So . . . what should I tell that P.I. if he comes back?" Presley asked.

"What you told him already."

"I don't know if he'll buy it a second time. He knows we're related or he wouldn't have approached me. He said you used my name as a reference on a credit card application in New Mexico." Cheyenne heard Presley go on to say that she'd been working at the Sunny Day Convenience store back then and had used that as a reference for her next job. She thought that was how this Crouch had been able to trace her. But then she must've turned in a different direction or buried her face in the blankets because Cheyenne could no longer decipher her words.

Hoping to catch the last of the conversation, she sat up, but that didn't make it any easier to hear. "Presley?" she called out. "What's going on?"

"Nothing," her sister responded. "Didn't mean to wake you."

"Who's Eugene Crouch?"

"None of your damn business, little Miss Know-It-All," her mother snapped. "I'm still kickin'. Until I'm six feet under, I'll handle my own affairs!"

Dropping onto her pillow, Cheyenne counted to ten instead of thinking the same old terrible thoughts about her mother. Where was her control? Her pity?

Meanwhile, Presley spoke up, which siphoned off some of the tension. They'd always acted as buffers for each other, especially with Anita.

"Just some guy I met at work, Chey," she called back.

Her sister had plenty of scary stories about the gamblers who frequented the Indian casino. They could get drunk and far too friendly. Or violent. Presley dated bikers, many of whom were ex-cons, so she had more than a few scary stories about them, too. Cheyenne worried about her safety. What they'd endured as children had affected them so differently. Chey wanted to cling to everything that society deemed normal and admirable. She wanted to forget the past and pretend she was no different from the group of friends who'd provided so much love and support since she started high school.

Presley, on the other hand, didn't resent Anita or how they were raised. She lived fast and loose, a lot like their mother had once lived. The sad part was, Presley was capable of so much more.

"You said it was a private investigator," Cheyenne said.

"So?" Presley responded.

"Why would he be looking for Mom?"

"I figured it was better not to ask."

She had a point. Whatever this man wanted was sure to involve a fair amount of humiliation. Anita had long been an embarrassment to Cheyenne. And that made her feel even more guilt. What kind of child was so ashamed of her own parent?

Maybe it *was* better if they never found out why that man had come to the casino.

2

"Do you think I should ask him?"

Sitting in the passenger seat of her friend's Prius, Cheyenne pulled her gaze away from Joe DeMarco. Together with his father, he owned the only service station in town. He was facing away from them, standing in one of the auto repair bays, while her best friend, Eve Harmon, got back behind the wheel. They hadn't really needed gas, but they left the Gold Nugget B and B in the hands of Cheyenne's kitchen helper to come here as often as possible, hoping to bump into him.

"Of course you should." Cheyenne forced a smile. It wasn't easy to encourage Eve to ask Joe out. Joe might be a relatively recent infatuation for Eve, but Chey had had a crush on him since forever. Not that she'd ever told anyone. She was fairly certain it was the best-kept secret in town.

Fingering the thick, knitted scarf tied

around her neck, Eve worried her lip. "I don't know. . . ."

"What do you have to lose?" Chey asked.

"Face, I guess. I want *him* to ask *me*."

"I once heard Gail say he wasn't interested in a stepparent situation for his girls."

"He only has them every other weekend. And I'd be a great stepmom!"

"That's true, but he's always seen us as his little sister's friends. Maybe he feels he's too old for us. For *you*," she quickly amended.

Fortunately, Eve didn't seem to catch the slip. "He's nice, but . . . sort of preoccupied when I'm around. I can't really get his attention."

As Chey watched, Joe turned, saw her sitting in the car and waved. Instantly, her cheeks flushed hot. That was all it took — a wave. He'd had that effect on her ever since Anita had first carted them into town in her old Skylark. She'd never forget how hungry she and Presley had been that day. While her mother counted out the change they'd scrounged up to buy gas, she'd left Presley, who wanted to stay in the car, and went to the minimart. They didn't have the money for food. She'd just wanted to look, to imagine what it would be like if she *could* indulge in one of the many treats displayed on those shelves.

When it was time to leave, Anita had called her twice. Chey remembered because her mother had then shouted for her to "get her ass moving" and thumped her on the head.

Stomach growling, Cheyenne had dragged herself from the Hostess aisle to the door, where Joe had caught up with her long enough to hand her two packages of the Twinkies she'd been eyeing. Embarrassed because she knew they looked as poor as they were, she'd tried to give them back, but he'd insisted the snacks were past their sale date and he was about to toss them.

It wasn't until she was back inside the car, groaning in pleasure and devouring those Twinkies with Presley, that she'd taken a closer look at the wrappers. The expiration dates hadn't passed. Neither one was even close.

Cheyenne was pretty sure she'd been in love with Joe ever since that day. Or maybe it was a couple of weeks later, when she first saw him at school. He was a handsome, popular senior, she a lowly freshman, when he'd noticed some kid making fun of her ill-fitting dress. He'd immediately walked over and sent that boy running. Then he'd grinned at her as if he somehow saw the sensitive girl, who'd already been through far too much, beneath the ratty hair and secondhand clothes.

"How'd he treat you at the Chamber of Commerce mixer last night?" she asked, picking at her nails so she wouldn't be tempted to look at him again. It had broken her heart when he'd married right out of high school. But then he'd divorced and returned to Whiskey Creek and, at twenty-six, she'd been granted a second chance — not that anything had happened in the five years since.

Eve slid the receipt for the gas purchase into her purse. "He said hello. That was about it."

Cheyenne hated that she was secretly pleased by this report. She wanted Eve to be happy more than anyone else in the world, even if it meant she couldn't have Joe. Eve was like a sister to her, one she could both love *and* admire. Eve's family, the Harmons, had taken Cheyenne in at various points during the past seventeen years. They'd given her a job in the kitchen of the family inn, trained her to cook and let her take over when their other cook moved away. She owed them so much.

Suppressing a twinge of conscience, she attempted to make a joke about the situation. "He should be grateful for your patronage. You come here more than anyone else. He probably wonders what you do with all those bags of chips you buy. He'd be able to tell if you were eating them."

Eve laughed but sobered immediately. "Do you think I'm being too obvious?"

That was hard to tell. Joe was always friendly. He just never called or did anything else to show special interest — in either one of them.

Cheyenne drew a bolstering breath. "Why don't you see if Gail will give him a nudge?"

His sister was part of their clique, a clique that had been friends since grade school — except for her, of course. She was fourteen when they moved to town. Presley had been sixteen.

"Gail would love to see Joe marry again," she added. "Especially someone who'll treat him better than his ex." Gail had no doubt been too caught up in her own life to notice that Eve suddenly had a thing for her big brother. A year ago, she'd married a famous movie star who'd been a PR client and had her hands full coping with all the changes that required.

"She and Simon are in L.A. He's working on a movie."

"That doesn't mean she never talks to Joe."

With a frown, Eve started the car. "No, but . . . I'm not ready to go that far yet."

Now that Eve had aborted her mission to invite Joe to dinner, Cheyenne could relax for the moment. "So you're not going to ask him out?"

"Not right now. Maybe I'll work up the courage later."

Cheyenne nodded. She needed to forget about Joe, finally get it through her head — and her heart — that there was no chance he'd ever return her interest. As long as Eve wanted him, it didn't matter even if he did.

"What are you doing here? It's too cold to be sitting outside."

Cheyenne turned to see Eve, who'd been as busy as she had since their trip to the gas station, weaving carefully through the headstones of the old cemetery next to the inn. "Just thinking."

It was the slowest part of the day, between the morning rush when they prepared a fancy breakfast for the inn's guests and cleaned the rooms, and three o'clock, the time new patrons began to trickle in. She would've run home to check on her mother. She normally did. But this afternoon she couldn't bring herself to make the effort. Presley was there; she'd call if Anita's situation worsened.

Eve's footsteps crunched in the patchy snow. Since her boots were more for looks than bad weather, she watched where she was going until she got close enough to avoid ruining the pretty black suede. Then her eyes cut to the words carved in the closest headstone — also the oldest and largest — as if they made her uncomfortable.

They probably did. They made everyone uncomfortable.

Here lies our little angel, brutally murdered at six years. May God strike down the killer who took her from us, and send him into the fiery pits of hell. Mary Margaret Hatfield, daughter of Harriett and John Hatfield, 1865–1871

"Are you feeling bad that we're planning to capitalize on the mystery of her murder?" Adjusting the scarf around her neck, Eve perched on the garden bench next to Chey.

Eve didn't have to say who *she* was. "Maybe a little." Not only had Mary been born in the home that was now Eve's parents' B and B, she'd died there. Her murder had taken place well over a century ago, but just about everyone in town knew the terrible details. She'd been found in the basement, strangled. There'd been no indication as to who'd killed her.

"Maybe we shouldn't do it."

"We don't have a choice," Cheyenne responded. "You and your parents will lose the inn if we don't do something." If that happened, Chey would be without a job, too, but she could probably get on somewhere else. It was Eve's situation that concerned her. The Gold Nugget meant so much to the Harmon family. Over the years, especially during the past twelve months, they'd dumped everything they had into the business.

Eve hugged herself for added warmth. "I know. I keep telling myself that publicizing a haunting isn't a big deal. It's such an old crime. It just adds atmosphere, right? But . . . we're talking about a girl who died a violent death. Her ghost really *could* be lingering here."

Cheyenne straightened in surprise. "I thought you didn't believe in things like that. I thought you said every rattle and creak could be explained as the settling of an old house."

"Since I'm so often at the inn alone, it's easier to believe that. There's no point in scaring myself to death. But —" Eve met her eyes "— a lot of people do believe in the paranormal."

Chey frowned at the sea of headstones surrounding her. For the most part they were organized in neat rows, but crookedness in certain spots suggested a random beginning. "Do you remember, shortly after we moved here, when my mother got mad because I stayed with you part of the time and with Gail part of the time and I didn't come home for a couple of days? She tied me to that tree." Cheyenne pointed to the big oak in the corner, which was located close to another bench.

Eve grimaced. "How could I forget? You spent the entire night out here. When my father found you the next morning, he was furious that she could do such a thing to her own child. But . . . your mother pretty much wrote the book on how to be a terrible parent."

After that incident, Cheyenne had gone to live with the Harmons for three months — until her mother's cancer took a turn for the worse. Because she hated feeling like a burden on people who shouldn't have to take care of her, and because Presley wanted her to come home, she'd eventually gone back. "At first I was terrified to be trapped in the dark, so close to Mary's grave."

The memories of that warm, summer night often lingered on the fringes of her mind. They were partly what drew her out here.

"But after a couple of hours," she went on, "I felt this strange sort of peace, as if she was with me and didn't want me to be frightened. I even started talking to her." Uncomfortable admitting this, since she'd never told Eve before, she laughed to make herself sound a little less crazy. "I know it was all my imagination, but I've never been frightened of her since."

"You don't feel like you're betraying a friend by using her death or her ghost or whatever in our marketing ideas?"

Cheyenne shook her head. "We could never squelch the rumors, anyway. A good ghost story gets handed down generation after generation."

"But we'll be playing into it," Eve argued. "And do you really think we have to go so far as to change the name?"

Cheyenne studied the Victorian-style building just beyond the black-iron filigree fence that surrounded the cemetery. All the Christmas garland and lights made the inn look magical, but underneath the decorations it needed caulking and paint and some dry-rot repair. New plumbing, too. "Saving the inn will require a total makeover, Eve. The place should get a new name to go with it. That feels like a clean start. And I like calling it Little Mary's. Adding 'Gold Country's Only Haunted Bed-and-Breakfast,' softens the darkness of it."

"My parents don't agree." Eve kicked at the snow.

"Things are different than when they were in charge."

"You mean the Russos hadn't opened A Room with a View," she grumbled. "Still . . ." She sighed. "I can't help feeling bad about using what happened to Mary to book rooms."

"We're trying to save her home." An idea occurred to Chey that brought her to her feet. "Hey, maybe we can save the inn and do her a favor at the same time."

Eve's eyebrows slid up. "What are you talking about?"

"What if we get *Unsolved Mysteries* or one of those shows to come out here and do a segment on Mary's murder, see if they can convince forensic profilers and detectives to take a look at the scene and try to solve the case?"

Eve blew on her hands, then rubbed them together. "How would we even reach the

37

right people?"

"Are you kidding? One of our best friends owns a PR company. If Gail can't get in touch with the producer, I bet her movie-star husband has contacts who could. Simon might even be willing to do a guest spot on the show, to mention that this inn is in his wife's hometown. We'd be a shoe-in if Simon's name was attached."

"I don't want to impose on him, Chey. He already sent us those movie props for our new haunted house theme — not that we'll be able to use them now that we're going with a restoration."

"He won't mind," she said. "It wouldn't take more than an hour of his time. Just a quick cameo appearance. Come on. Getting the B and B on a show like that would be great PR for our grand reopening. We'd blow the competition away. It might also bring Mary some peace." She bent closer to Eve. "Think about it. What if we finally solve the mystery?"

Grooves of concern appeared in Eve's normally smooth forehead. "That would be great, but does it mean we hold off on the renovations until these forensic people have a look?" Now that her parents had retired and left her in charge, her first consideration was, and had to be, how to cover the mortgage payments, especially now that her parents had done all they could to help financially. "Because I can't really do that," she added. "Riley's about the only one, besides you, who isn't going on the cruise on Sunday and part of the reason he's staying is to start the improvements so we can reopen in January."

Eve and five other friends were taking a ten-day Caribbean cruise for the holidays. They were leaving this weekend and wouldn't get back until the day after Christmas.

"We won't have to change the schedule," Cheyenne said. "We're not renovating the basement." No one had ever changed anything down there, which gave her hope that, one way or another, the mystery could be solved.

The darkening sky threatened another storm. Eve stood as she glanced up. "It's a long shot that they'd be able to tell anything after a century and a half."

"A long shot is better than no shot at all. Even if they don't end up solving the crime, we'd get the PR. It's a national show. You can't *buy* publicity like that."

Linking her arm through Chey's, Eve pulled her toward the shelter of the inn. "Okay, fine. We'll see what we can do to get their interest, but not until after I'm back and the holidays are over."

"That should work," Cheyenne said as they walked. "But why aren't you more excited? It's exactly what we need to get the word out."

"You're right. I'm just . . . stressed. It's a great idea. Gail's going to be mad she didn't come up with it first." Eve gave her a conspirator's smile, but it disappeared almost immediately. "How's your mother doing?"

Cheyenne didn't want to dwell on the cantankerous woman who awaited her at the end of each day. She had only a couple of hours until she was off work, hours that would pass far too soon. Then Presley would head over to the casino and she'd be in for another endless night with Anita. "She's hanging in there."

"How much longer do you think she'll last?"

"Who knows? The doctor says it could be a few days or a few weeks."

Eve stopped, jerking Cheyenne to a stop with her. "Maybe I should cancel my trip. I've been thinking of doing that, anyway."

"No." Cheyenne wasn't willing to let Eve miss the cruise she'd scrimped and saved for, the vacation she'd talked about for twenty-four months.

"But what if your mother dies while we're gone? You'd have to deal with that all by yourself." She lowered her voice even though there wasn't anyone around to overhear. "Lord knows Presley's not much support."

"Presley does what she can. And your folks are here. I'm sure they'd offer me whatever I need." The cold was beginning to seep into Cheyenne's bones. Suddenly anxious to get inside, she tugged Eve to get her moving again. "Anyway, I don't think any of our friends particularly want to go to Anita's funeral."

"We're all too angry at her to like her very much," she admitted. "But we want to be there for *you*."

"You are. Always."

"I can't believe the cancer came back, and that she went downhill so fast."

"It's bad timing, what with Christmas and all. But you can't miss the cruise. There's no canceling at this late date. You wouldn't be able to get a refund."

Eve made a sound of impatience. "I had no business spending that money in the first place. If I'd had any idea we wouldn't recover after A Room with a View opened . . ."

41

Chey held the gate as they passed through. "I know. But look at it this way. The money's spent. We have a plan for rescuing the inn. And Anita will probably survive until the new year. She may have her faults, but she's tough. No one could argue with that."

Once they reached the welcome mat, Eve stomped the dampness from her boots. "I wish you were going with us."

So did Cheyenne. But she hadn't even made an effort. She'd known from the onset, when the idea had first been proposed during one of their Friday morning get-togethers at the coffee shop, that she'd never be able to afford the trip. The Harmons paid her what they could, but she didn't make a lot. And either her mother or her sister always needed financial help. "I don't have a birth certificate, remember? I can't get a passport without one."

"We could've gotten a copy of your birth certificate *somehow*."

"Not if my mother can't remember where I was born!"

A roll of the eyes told Chey what Eve thought of that. What mother didn't have this information? "There has to be another way to find it. We just need to do the research."

Cheyenne knew it would be a lot harder

to come up with than Eve imagined. There weren't even many pictures of her and Presley as children. For several years they'd lived out of a car, which made it impossible to collect much memorabilia. Even Presley's birth certificate had fallen by the wayside when, shortly after Anita was diagnosed with cancer for the first time, they'd come back to the motel where they'd been staying to find the manager had thrown all their stuff away because Anita hadn't been able to come up with the payment.

Cheyenne had shared that incident with Eve and the others. But she hadn't told them about the blonde woman in her dreams, how any type of snowfall made her feel bereft, or the suspicions that went along with her earliest memories. Intimating that her mother might've kidnapped her would be a very serious accusation. And she wasn't sure she could trust that the images in her mind were accurate. She needed some sort of proof before she went that far.

"I'll be fine here," she said. "I'm overseeing the renovations for you."

"My folks could've done that. They're not leaving to visit my aunt until February."

Cheyenne slipped into the warmth of the inn and was immediately enveloped by the scent of the expensive pine-and-mulberry

43

potpourri they purchased to impress their guests. "This way they won't have to," she said, but she knew it wasn't going to be easy to face Christmas with all her friends gone, her mother dying and the inn closed for remodeling.

3

Presley sat next to her mother's bed, chain-smoking while watching her sleep. Part of her felt guilty about spewing carcinogens into the air Anita was breathing. She knew Chey would have sent her to the porch if she were home. But it was cold outside, and Presley didn't see how a little secondhand smoke could make any difference now.

The small TV on the dresser droned on in the background. They were supposed to be watching *The Bold and the Beautiful*. It was their favorite soap; they'd followed it for years. But her mother was so drugged she could hardly keep her eyes open. She drifted in and out of consciousness, scarcely aware that Presley was in the room.

Once again, the morphine on the nightstand drew Presley's attention. She'd already taken a swallow of it, but she was tempted to drink more — or head over to the blue shack down the hill where she could buy crystal meth. She had to be careful not to take too much of her mother's supply. The state would provide only a limited amount. The hospice nurse, who came in every Monday, kept a close eye on it, and so did Cheyenne.

Anita moaned, shifting as if she couldn't get comfortable, and opened her eyes. Then she saw Presley and made an attempt to rally. "What's happening . . . on our show?"

She recognized the voices of the actors, knew what she was supposed to be doing even though she'd been asleep for twenty minutes or more.

"Nothing new," Presley replied to cover for the fact that she hadn't really been watching, either.

"Have they shown Thomas?"

He was Anita's favorite. She'd loved that bit about the ecstasy-induced weekend with Brooke and whether or not he'd slept with his stepmother. "Not today." That she'd noticed, anyway.

"What's happening with Ridge?"

"He was kissing his ex-wife before the last commercial." Presley had seen that much, but even if she hadn't, Ridge cheating with his ex was a safe bet. The writers had kept that love triangle going for several seasons.

"If he doesn't choose between Brooke and

Taylor soon, I'll miss it." Her eyes drifted shut. Presley assumed she'd fallen back asleep, but she spoke a few seconds later. "You'd better quit smoking, or you'll wind up like me."

Presley wanted to quit. She remembered how yellow her mother's teeth had been before she lost them to poor hygiene. But now was not the time to fight that battle. She needed all the help she could get just to survive each day. "I will. Later."

"Right." Her mother coughed as she tried to laugh.

"Mom?"

Anita took a deep breath. It was getting harder and harder for her to speak. Sometimes she didn't have the energy for it at all. "What?"

Presley used the remote to turn down the television. "Chey's not home."

"I didn't ask if she was."

"I wanted you to know she wasn't."

Her mother's eyes showed a heightened alertness. She'd noticed the change in Presley's tone. Sometimes they told each other more than they ever admitted to Chey. "Why?"

"Because I'm going to ask you again about Eugene Crouch."

"Don't." Her mother smoothed her thin

gray hair. "It's better if you . . . leave that alone."

"Why? He had a picture."

A grimace added more wrinkles to Anita's heavily lined face. "So?"

"*So*?" Presley repeated. "Aren't you curious where he got it? Who was in it?"

She coughed again. "No."

"Why not?"

"I don't want to . . . hear anything about it."

"Because you already know."

With a grimace, Anita motioned to the TV. "Turn that back up."

Presley didn't comply. She bent over Anita to convince her that she wanted the truth. "What happened, Mom? Who was the blonde woman in the picture? Is she the one Chey keeps asking about?"

Her mother waved her off. "Stop. Just trust me."

"That's all you have to say?"

Her face flushed with the first color Presley had seen in several days. Maybe she realized she hadn't earned much trust, even from the daughter who loved her. "I'm trying to . . . do you a favor," she said, finally meeting Presley's gaze. "Don't ruin it. It's . . . the last gift I have to give you."

"That doesn't make any sense."

"It does! Why make you . . . carry the secret after I'm gone? It will . . . only tear you up inside." She lowered her voice. "Or cost you . . . the one person you've always been able to count on."

The sickening feeling that'd crept over Presley when she'd seen that photo of Cheyenne as a little girl, all dolled up, returned. "She doesn't really belong to us, does she," she said, clutching her hands in the bedding.

Anita's breath rattled as she dragged it in and out of her lungs. "You knew that. You might . . . deny it, but in your heart . . . you knew all along."

"No." Presley shook her head. "We don't look alike because we come from different fathers. That's what you said!"

"That's what you wanted to believe!"

She was right. As much as Presley would rather have denied it, she'd had her doubts. She'd just been unwilling to face them. She'd heard Cheyenne ask about the blonde woman, had listened to her sister describe with longing the many toys she'd once had, the pretty clothes and the full belly, and she'd purposely pretended she remembered no time when they weren't a family. She'd even told Chey, on a number of occasions, that those images had to be from a dream.

"Oh, God," she muttered, and sank down into her chair.

It required considerable effort, but Anita managed to sit up on her own. "Presley, you wanted a sister so bad. I couldn't have another child, but you needed someone, someone besides me. I couldn't be there all the time. I had to make sure we had food to eat and somewhere to sleep. I — It was just the two of us, and every day you begged me for a playmate."

Anita's actions hadn't been entirely altruistic. She'd used her children as much as anything else. But Presley didn't make an issue of it. She was too preoccupied, too frightened by what she was learning. Covering her mouth, she spoke through her fingers. "So what did you do?"

"I got what you needed, that's what."

The drugs Presley had taken made her feel as if her mother's voice was growing loud and then dim. Was this really happening?

Yes. She was pretty sure it was. She'd suspected for a long time. But now that she was confronted with the reality, she didn't know how to react. Was she supposed to be grateful to her mother?

She would've been miserable growing up alone. Cheyenne had provided the companionship that'd made life bearable. Together they'd weathered so much, stood against the world, especially when Anita took up with a man and her daughters became less important to her. Or when Anita went on a drunken binge. Cheyenne had been there to provide love and comfort.

"But . . . what about *her*?" Presley wasn't sure how she managed to speak. It felt as if someone had put a clamp on her tongue.

"What about her?" Anita's eyes snapped with the instant anger that was so typical of her. "She's fine. I took care of her just like I took care of you, didn't I? Why does she deserve party dresses and birthday presents? Why does she deserve to have life any better than you or me?"

Because Anita had stolen her from the family she would've had, and who could say what they would've been able to give her. Didn't she see the injustice in that? "You told her you have no idea who the blonde woman is or why she keeps remembering all those things," she whispered. "She's asked at least a hundred times."

"Well, now that you know, we'll see if you tell her anything different," she responded, and with a bitter laugh that said she didn't think Presley would, she fell back on the pillows.

■ ■ ■ ■

Presley was gone when Cheyenne returned home from work, which surprised her. With Anita in such bad shape, Presley usually waited for Chey to arrive so that someone would be with Anita at all times.

Cheyenne would've asked her mother why her sister had left early, but Anita seemed to be in a drugged stupor. As Chey stood at her bedroom door, looking in, she realized that what she'd told Eve wasn't true. No way could Anita make it until after the cruise. The cancer had progressed too far. She'd already been reduced to a bag of bones beneath waxy skin. She'd grown so small and feeble compared to the woman Cheyenne used to fear, it was a wonder she was still breathing.

Maybe that was why Presley had gone. Watching Anita die a little more each day wasn't easy.

Grateful that her mother was sleeping so she could have dinner and unwind, she headed into the kitchen, where she'd left her purse when she came in. She could smell the pine of the Christmas tree and the cinnamon candles she liked to burn, but those scents hardly cloaked the stale, antiseptic stench of her mother's sickness.

Briefly closing her eyes, Cheyenne drew a deep breath, trying to block out anything unpleasant, and went to the refrigerator. She'd made some beef stew before bed last night, to get a jump on the day.

Presley didn't seem to have eaten any, which worried Cheyenne. Her sister was getting far too thin. . . .

Reminding herself not to dwell on the negative, she spent the time waiting for her stew to heat looking through pictures on the iPhone the Harmons had given her for her birthday in May. She had snapshots of her friends — Riley, Gail, Simon, Callie, Ted, Noah, Baxter, Kyle, Sophia and several others who joined them, although less frequently, on Friday mornings at Black Gold Coffee. They were all going on the cruise, except Gail and Simon, of course, who were in Hollywood, Sophia, who had a daughter as well as a husband, and Riley, who was raising a son and planned to spend the holidays remodeling the B and B. Cheyenne was disappointed to be missing the big trip. The Caribbean sounded like a marvelous place to go. But taking a cruise wasn't something she'd ever expected to be able to do, anyway.

With a faint smile for the fun Eve and the

rest of her friends would have, she thumbed farther back in her album to find the picture she'd been looking for.

There it was — Joe, with his arm around his sister. Cheyenne had taken that photograph at a barbecue last summer. Sometimes he came to the events Gail attended when she was home, but Gail wasn't home all that often. She'd been living in L.A. for more than a decade, ever since she started Big Hit Public Relations. And now that she was married to Simon, she'd likely return even less.

The stew bubbled on the stove, but Cheyenne didn't remove it. She was too taken with Joe's image, although she'd seen this picture a million times. He looked good in his swim trunks, his broad chest and muscular arms bronzed from the sun, his wet hair tossed back off his face. Her heart beat faster as she stared at the contours of his strong jaw, the laugh lines bracketing his mouth and the intelligence shining through his blue eyes. In the past year or so, his hair had begun to recede a little at the temples, but Cheyenne didn't mind. She'd never seen anyone she thought was more handsome.

"Presley?"

Her mother was awake and calling for her

sister. Cheyenne set her phone aside and turned off the burner. "Presley's gone to work," she called back. "I'm in the middle of making dinner. I'll bring you a bowl of stew in a minute."

"I'm not hungry."

She was never hungry anymore. But she had to eat or she'd lose what little strength she still had. "You should try to get a few bites down."

"Did Presley say anything to you when she left?" Anita wanted to know.

Because it was difficult for her mother to make herself heard, Cheyenne hurried to her bedroom to answer. "About what?"

Anita studied her before relaxing. "Nothing."

Cheyenne considered asking why Presley had left early but guessed, from her mother's questions, that she wouldn't know. What did it matter? Nothing had happened. "So . . . will you try to eat?"

"If you want," she relented, a shrug in her voice.

"Good. I'll be right back."

Her cell phone, which she'd put on the counter, rang while she was on her way to the kitchen. Glancing at the display, she could see it was Eve and wasn't surprised. She'd left The Gold Nugget only an hour ago, but Eve called her more than anyone else.

"You'd better not have canceled your cruise," Cheyenne said as soon as she picked up.

"No, although I should," Eve responded with a note of chagrin.

"There's no point. You can't stop what's going to happen."

"But I could help you through it."

"You've already done everything you can. What's up?"

Eve's voice filled with breathless excitement. "I did it."

Cheyenne had opened the cupboard and was reaching for two bowls, but she dropped her hand. What was Eve talking about? "Did what?"

"I asked him out!"

Cheyenne froze. "You mean Joe?"

"Who else, silly? I just . . . worked up the nerve, called him at the station and said, 'I'd really like to get to know you better. Is there any chance you'd be interested in having dinner with me tomorrow?' "

Gripping the edge of the counter, Chey managed a strangled "And what did he say?"

"Yes!" It sounded as if she was jumping up and down. "He was so nice about it. He didn't make me feel uncomfortable at all."

Of course not. Joe was good at making other people feel accepted, regardless of the situation. He'd looked after Cheyenne as a sort of unofficial big brother ever since she'd moved to town, hadn't he? Not once had he treated her as if she was insignificant, like so many of the other popular guys had at first. Although Cheyenne was eventually accepted by the "in" crowd, she felt that Eve had so much more to offer. She came from a highly regarded family. She was beautiful in the classic sense with a slender figure, dramatic widow's peak and shiny dark hair. And she was such a nice person. Chey couldn't imagine anyone not loving Eve.

"That —" Chey had to clear her throat "— that's so exciting. Where will you take him?"

"I think we'll drive to Jackson and have dinner at the Old Milano Hotel."

"The one famous for its prime rib?"

"That's it."

Slumping onto the counter, Cheyenne rested her forehead in her hands. "That'll be romantic."

"Are you bringing me that soup today or tomorrow?" her mother interrupted, calling from her room.

Cheyenne covered the phone. "Give me a minute!"

"I might not have a minute!"

"Is that Anita?" Eve asked.

After making a sound of exasperation, Cheyenne laughed. "Yeah. Pleasant as always."

"I don't know how you do it. I'll let you go, but . . . what do you think I should wear?"

Cheyenne knew Eve's wardrobe as well as her own. They were the same size and often shared clothes. Until Cheyenne became an adult and had her own money, she was the only one who'd benefited from the arrangement. But that was slowly changing. Now it was Chey's turn to give back. Eve had plenty of cute things, but she loved the new dress Cheyenne had found in San Francisco during her last visit. "I've got that pretty Caren Templet I got on sale, if you want to wear it. It would go perfectly with your leopard-print shoes and the black jacket with the fake fur."

"You'd let me borrow that?" Eve said. "You haven't even worn it yourself. The tags are still on the sleeve!"

"I've been saving it for a special occasion."

"Exactly."

She glanced over her shoulder. Her mother was making a fuss. She had to get going. "This *is* a special occasion." She fought the lump rising in her throat. "Wear it. You'll be stunning."

"That is *so* sweet. Thank you, Chey. You are the *best* friend anyone could ever have."

In reality, it was the other way around. If not for Eve, Cheyenne would've run away while in high school — or started using, like Presley. The Harmons had tried to befriend Presley, too, but she was already set on her course, had chosen other friends who weren't a very positive influence on her. Cheyenne owed Eve and her family everything. And it wasn't as if Joe had been hers to begin with. "I'll bring it to the inn tomorrow."

"Do you think he'll like it?" Eve asked with a fresh burst of enthusiasm.

A tear rolled down Cheyenne's cheek. Angry that she could feel sorry for herself when Eve had such an opportunity, she set her jaw, wiped away the dampness and blinked faster to staunch the flow of more tears. "He won't be able to resist you," she said, and believed it with all her heart.

4

Friday morning at the coffee shop was usually Cheyenne's favorite part of the week. She loved sitting around the table with a cappuccino, catching up with her friends. But there was so much on her mind — starting with her mother's worsening health, the fact that Presley was acting strange and was probably on drugs again, and the knowledge that she'd be without the friends who sustained her through the biggest holiday of the year. Then there was Eve's impending date with Joe, which, she was sad to acknowledge, upset her more than everything else. With all of that, she couldn't enjoy herself, even though they had a great turnout today.

Riley Stinson had shown up with his thirteen-year-old son, Jacob, who'd been born the year they graduated from high school. Riley assured Eve that he was ready to begin the remodel on Monday. Sophia

Knox, now DeBussi, had joined them. But thanks to her past and her arrogant husband, who always seemed to be working out of town, she wasn't particularly liked or trusted. Chey thought Sophia came only to see Ted. They'd once been an item, and it was obvious that there were still feelings between them, but at this point those feelings were mostly negative, especially on Ted's side. He seemed annoyed that he had to put up with her butting into his group of friends and rarely spoke to her. This added a level of tension that hadn't existed before, but Sophia had been coming to coffee for over a year. They'd grown used to her presence even if they didn't quite welcome it.

Then there was Callie Vanetta, who owned her own photography studio on Sutter Street, and Kyle Houseman, who'd recently been through an acrimonious divorce. Callie and Kyle had become extremely close of late. Cheyenne sensed it and wondered if they were sleeping together, but they certainly didn't let on if they were. Noah Rackham, a professional cyclist whose twin brother had been killed when the mineshaft caved in on graduation night — Cheyenne would never forget the moment she'd heard that terrible news — and Baxter North, Noah's best friend, rounded out the group.

Without Gail, there were nine. Most were talking and laughing, but today Eve didn't seem to be enjoying herself any more than Cheyenne was. Although she'd come to the coffeehouse walking on air, thanks to her date with Joe, her mood had wilted as soon as the elegant European couple who owned A Room with a View B and B strode in and sat across from their table.

"Ignore them," Callie admonished when she noticed Eve's preoccupation.

Eve lowered her voice. "I can't. They've single-handedly destroyed my family's business."

"It's not illegal to give you some competition," Baxter pointed out. He'd grown up next door to Noah, and they'd spent most of their time together, but they were nothing alike. In keeping with his profession, Noah was athletic, perfectly toned and always tan. He rode outside nearly every day, including the winter. Baxter, a stockbroker who commuted to San Francisco three or four days a week, was handsome, too, but in a suave, cultured way.

"They've been doing more than that," Eve muttered. "They've been *trying* to drive me out of business. That's unethical, even if it isn't illegal."

Cheyenne knew how close they'd come.

She wasn't sure the Harmons would be able to hang on to the inn, despite the remodel and the name change and the plans they'd developed to promote Little Mary's as a haunted house. "They've been undercutting our rates by so much they can't possibly be making any money," she explained. "They're taking a loss every day — a significant one, considering how much they've thrown into restoring that place. They're just hoping to outlast us."

"At which point they'll be the only B and B in town and will recoup their losses," Eve said bitterly. "You wait and see."

"Except they won't succeed in forcing you to close your doors." Riley handed his son some money so he could go to the counter and buy one of the giant muffins Black Gold was known for. "You're about to give people a good reason to stay at *your* place, even if it costs a little extra."

"What?" Eve asked dryly. "A scare?"

"A piece of Whiskey Creek history." Ted pushed his to-go cup aside. "Maybe it'll help that I've decided to tackle Mary Hatfield's murder as the basis for a new book."

"Really?" Noah flipped his hair out of his face as he leaned forward. "You're moving away from fiction?"

"I'll keep up with my current contracts.

The thrillers are my bread and butter. But in my spare time I'd like to research what happened to Mary. See if there's a story there. I've always been curious about it. If I can find enough information to proceed, maybe it'll bring some notoriety to the inn."

"You'd better work fast," Eve said.

He reached over to cover her hand with his. "You're making lots of great changes. Have some faith."

"Everything will work out." Callie tucked her shiny blond hair behind one ear. "But even if it doesn't, you've done all you can. We're leaving on Sunday. Don't let the Russos ruin your trip."

Eve flattened her hands on the table. "I'm sorry. It's just . . . I've tried to talk to them, but they won't listen, let alone show any sympathy."

"It's business," Noah said. "You can't take it personally."

That was easy for Noah to say, Cheyenne thought. His future didn't depend on the bed-and-breakfast.

"There are human beings behind businesses. Eve has always believed that running The Gold Nugget would be her future."

Everyone glanced at one another as if they were shocked it was Sophia who'd contributed this. She and her husband were the wealthiest people in town — not counting Simon, who'd married Gail a year ago. One would think if anyone was going to weigh in on the side of ruthless business practices, it would be Sophia, who'd chosen to break Ted's heart and marry for money.

"The problem will still be here when you get back," Riley said, reiterating Callie's sentiment. "Tackle it then. For now, the inn is *my* baby. You have better things to think about."

He was referring to the cruise, of course. But that wasn't where Eve's mind went. Cheyenne could tell by the smile that broke out across her face. "I do have better things to think about," she agreed. "One of them is dinner with Joe DeMarco."

Cheyenne nearly dropped her cappuccino. Eve had sworn her to secrecy. She'd said she didn't want anyone to know how she felt about Joe, not until she'd had the chance to see if he returned her interest. Did his agreement to have dinner mean that?

"So . . . is this a date?" Callie was instantly intrigued; they all were.

Blushing slightly, Eve rolled back the foil lid of her orange juice. "It is."

Baxter crossed one leg over the other. Although he usually worked at home on

Fridays, he was dressed in one of his hand-tailored suits, signifying he had business in San Francisco. "Since when have you been seeing Joe?"

"Tonight will be our first evening out. But . . . I've had my eye on him for ages."

Cheyenne couldn't look up. She didn't want to meet anyone's gaze, didn't want her friends to realize that she felt as if she'd just been kicked in the stomach. Eve hadn't had her eye on Joe nearly as long as Cheyenne had. But she couldn't say so. Eve's announcement made Joe *hers*, whether he felt the same or not.

"He needs to start seeing someone." Callie put her plastic spoon into an empty yogurt container. "How long has it been since his divorce?"

Noah answered. "I was getting back from my first race in Europe when I heard, so it would have to be four, five years ago."

"The divorce was hard on him," Baxter commented.

Riley's chair scraped the wood floor as he made room for his son, who'd returned with his muffin. "What his ex-wife did would've been hard on anybody."

"I think he's seen a few women over the past couple of years, but no one from around here," Ted volunteered.

"And no one who's as perfect for him as I am," Eve joked.

When everyone chuckled, Cheyenne tried to laugh, too, but couldn't manage much more than a pained smile. She wanted to say she had to check on her mother so she could slip out. But she'd driven over with Eve.

Forcing herself to sit quietly, she pretended the same happy interest the others exhibited as Sophia said how delighted Gail would be, and Ted teased that it was about time the reluctant-to-commit Eve settled on someone. It'd been three years since her last relationship.

Soon talk of Eve and Joe died down, but the next subject didn't make Chey feel much better. Ted told everyone about the tourist information he'd found online. Callie went over what to pack for the cruise. And Eve asked whether or not to buy traveler's checks — all for a trip Cheyenne couldn't take.

When they finally began to disperse, Cheyenne breathed a sigh of relief. Callie had to open her photography studio by ten. Baxter had a long drive to reach his office in San Francisco. Ted was behind on his deadline. They all had work to do. Since this was the last day The Gold Nugget would be open until after the first of the year — not to mention the last day it would operate under its current name — Chey was just as eager to start her day. She couldn't expect her short-order cook to wrap up breakfast alone.

But just as she slid out of the booth, Noah clasped her arm. "What will you do while we're gone?" he asked.

She could tell by his sympathetic expression that he felt bad she wasn't able to join them, so she mustered yet another smile — and prayed it was more convincing than the ones that had come before. "The same. Taking care of my mother."

But with the way things were going she'd probably be burying Anita instead. And to make her Christmas even merrier, she'd most likely have to drag her sister back to rehab.

It was pathetic to drive past Eve's house so many times. Especially because she'd left her mother alone in order to do it. But Cheyenne couldn't seem to stop herself. She had to know what time Eve got home, had to see if Joe kissed her at the door . . . or was invited inside.

Eve lived on her parents' property, but she had her own small bungalow in back, which afforded her enough privacy to be able to entertain a lover. As long as Joe parked his car off the premises, her aging parents would never notice if their daughter had overnight company. When they weren't traveling in the motor home they'd bought when their financial situation still looked good, they went to bed early and, for the most part, let Eve visit them at the main house instead of trudging back to her place.

The fact that Eve would, no doubt, provide a detailed recap of the evening added to the guilt that troubled Cheyenne. They shared everything. But Cheyenne wasn't planning to ask about Joe. She hoped Eve would be so caught up in getting ready for the cruise that they wouldn't have to talk about him. She couldn't continue to pretend approval and support when each word Eve said cut like broken glass.

Besides, she didn't want to see the man she loved through Eve's eyes. She wanted to see him through her own. She'd memorized every encounter they'd ever had, every nuance of his expression, tone and body language. She was hoping that would help her determine whether or not he was excited about Eve or merely being polite. He was nice enough to accept a dinner invitation from just about any woman.

Cheyenne should know how kind he was. He'd always made her feel good, despite the unkempt way she'd looked when they first met or the number of guys in Whiskey Creek who wouldn't date her in the early years. Although Chey had never slept with anyone — Joe was the only man she'd ever dreamed of touching in that way — Presley and Anita had gone to bed with any man who showed interest. The Christensens were barely one step above J. T. Amos's clan, who were always fighting and going to jail or getting busted for dealing drugs. At least the people in Whiskey Creek had learned to differentiate between her and the rest of her family.

She'd been listening to the car radio to pass the time, but the noise made her nervous. Turning it off, she pulled down the tree-lined dirt road that led to the neighbors' farm and stopped just beyond Eve's house. From there she'd be able to tell when a car arrived. If she got out and stood hidden in the shrubs, she might even be able to ascertain what went on at the door.

Five minutes passed before she decided she couldn't invade her friend's privacy out of her own jealousy. Why would she betray the one person who'd brought some legitimacy to her life? Who'd convinced her that she could rise above her situation? Who'd made her whole in a way she'd never been whole before?

With a curse for her own weakness, she started up the Oldsmobile she'd bought from Henry Statham over in Jackson last Christmas and swung it around. But before she could drive out of the lane and onto the paved road, headlights appeared. A vehicle was cresting the hill.

Afraid it might be Joe and Eve and that they'd see her, Cheyenne backed up and switched off the car again. She had to remain hidden by the trees. The Olds was too distinctive; she couldn't hope to drive by them and escape notice.

Sure enough, Chey recognized Joe's white truck as it turned into Eve's driveway, but she'd expected as much. Whiskey Creek was a small town of only two thousand. Not many people lived out here, in the country. With the older Harmons and their farmer neighbors asleep, it almost had to be Eve.

Curving her nails into her palms, Chey watched as the headlights went off. But when Joe and Eve climbed out, she made herself look away. What happened next was none of her business. She had no right to be sitting here, spying like some sort of obsessed weirdo. What kind of friend was

71

she? Eve would make Joe a wonderful girlfriend, lover — even wife. He deserved the best, didn't he?

She waited until they both went inside. Then, sick at heart because of what that might mean, she drove home. She needed some silence, some space.

Unfortunately, her mother called her the second she opened the door.

"Cheyenne? Is that you?"

"It's me," she called back, but hesitated in the small entry. She wasn't sure she could make herself continue into the house. She didn't want to be here, didn't want to see the reality of her mother's condition, didn't want to think about what was coming or when it might happen, didn't want to take stock of the painkiller and know her sister had stolen more.

"I spilled my sippy cup," Anita complained. "I need another bath."

Chey gripped her purse tighter. "No problem. I'll bring a wet washcloth."

"That won't be enough. It was juice. I'm sticky all over. And the bedding . . . it has to be changed."

Squeezing her eyes closed, Cheyenne pressed her free hand to her face. Bathing Anita was so difficult. It took all her strength, despite her mother's dramatic weight loss. And now there'd be two baths in one night?

She imagined Eve lying beneath Joe, imagined how he might be touching her, kissing her, and nearly crumpled to her knees. She'd fantasized about Joe ever since she'd met him, but much more since his divorce. It was her only guilty pleasure.

But now . . . she couldn't even have that, not if he got together with Eve.

"Are you coming?"

The impatience in Anita's voice grated on Chey's nerves. What if she walked back to her car, got in and simply drove off?

Determined to do just that, she whirled around and ran to the street. She'd escape her mother at last — on her own terms — and go find the blonde woman.

She had her keys in her hand and was opening her car door before the rational part of her mind regained control. What was she thinking? She didn't even know where to start looking. She had no name, couldn't associate the blonde woman with any particular city or place. She'd gone to the police before — not here but in New Mexico after she'd turned fourteen. She'd told them she thought she'd been abducted, but they'd insisted she didn't match anyone who'd been reported missing and sent her home.

What made her think she'd get a different reception now?

Besides, she couldn't go anywhere. What would happen to Presley? Who would take care of Anita while Presley had to work? Who would handle their mother's funeral and burial when the time came?

Not Presley. She wasn't capable of holding herself together long enough.

And who would help Eve save the inn?

Hanging her head, Cheyenne stood in the cold, the wind whipping at her hair while she stared at her feet. Not only did she have responsibilities here in Whiskey Creek, she had friends. She couldn't let them down just because Eve was dating the man she loved. She wouldn't be able to live with herself if she did.

With a deep breath, she locked up her car and returned to the house.

"Coming," she called to her mother the moment she walked in, but as she hurried past the full-length mirror hanging on Presley's door, she stopped dead in her tracks. In the dim light streaming into the hallway from her own bedroom, she looked so much like the willowy blonde woman in her dreams she almost thought her reflection belonged to someone else.

5

Joe was the last person Cheyenne wanted to see. Whether he was aware of her aborted attempt to spy on him last night or not, she was embarrassed about her behavior, afraid that he'd see through her, and she didn't want to cope with finding him wearing a big, fat, satisfied smile. She was having a hard enough time soldiering on *without* knowing whether he'd slept with her best friend. She wanted to close her eyes to the whole affair and concentrate on what she had to do to fulfill her obligations today and in the days to come.

But when they nearly collided as she pushed her cart around a corner and down an aisle at Nature's Way, a local, family-owned grocery store between Whiskey Creek and Jackson, she couldn't turn and run in the other direction. That would make her envy and upset even more apparent. So she dredged up a smile and said hello before trying to circumvent him.

"Whoa, where's the fire?" he asked, catching her by the elbow.

With an effort, she kept her expression innocent and friendly. "No fire. I'm just . . ." She struggled to invent an excuse for why she couldn't take a second to talk to him on a Saturday morning. Obviously, she wasn't working. And Presley was home with Anita or she wouldn't be out. "You know . . . busy. Always busy."

He studied her before responding. "Eve said the B and B's closed today."

"It is. But we'll reopen after New Year's. I'm overseeing some remodeling while she's on the cruise." The changes and repairs wouldn't start until Monday. Maybe Eve had told him that, too, but Chey was grappling to fill the silence with something unrelated to the turmoil churning inside her.

"Too bad you can't go with her. I'm sure you could use a vacation." His voice was concerned. "How's your mother?"

Miserable. Fading. Cheyenne wanted to tell him how much more complicated it was to watch someone die whom you resented. How guilt played a bigger role than sadness. How she sometimes longed for a release despite knowing that wishing her

76

mother gone made her a terrible person.

But she hadn't shared those realities with Eve or Presley or anyone. She was afraid of what they said about her, afraid she was even worse than Anita.

I've always loved you. Had she *really*?

"She's hanging in there."

He was studying her so intently, almost as if he was trying to peek beneath the polite mask she wore.

"It's got to be tough." His hand still rested on her arm. She knew he was just being sympathetic. He'd always known when she was having a difficult time. He could sense it, seemed to pay attention to more than most people noticed or cared about. Unfortunately, his touch made her yearn for contact of a different sort.

"Everyone has problems," she insisted as if it was nothing out of the ordinary. But tears welled up, calling her a liar and embarrassing her so badly she jerked away and hurried around him.

"It was fun! He's really easy to talk to, Chey. And so smart. And kind. And —" Eve twirled, sighing wistfully "— handsome. God, is he handsome. Those blue eyes held me riveted the entire night."

Cheyenne was sitting on Eve's bed while

Eve packed for the cruise. At her friend's request, she'd come over to say goodbye before the trip. She'd also brought a bikini and some costume jewelry Eve wanted to borrow. But the conversation had quickly turned to Eve's date with Joe, as Cheyenne feared it would. That was all Eve could think about.

"I saw him at the grocery store this morning." She wasn't sure why she volunteered that. It was irrelevant, a moment she preferred to forget since it had ended so awkwardly. And yet that brief encounter, the memory of his hand clutching her arm and the caring expression on his face, had been on her mind all day.

Eve's eyes lit with excitement. "Really? Did he say anything?"

"About you?"

"Or last night . . ."

Cheyenne fiddled with the strap of her purse. "No. I doubt he realizes I'm aware the two of you went out. And I didn't think you'd want me to bring it up. But . . . you're right, he's a great guy. You two are perfect for each other." Hadn't she said so before? "How'd he like the dress?"

"He said I looked great."

Chey had seen that for herself. "Do you want to wear it on the cruise?"

"No, I've got plenty of clothes for the trip. Go ahead and take it home so you have it while I'm gone."

"How many outfits are you packing?"

Holding a pair of shorts that was supposed to go into her suitcase, Eve sank onto the bed. "I was hoping he'd kiss me. I *almost* leaned in to make sure he did, but chickened out at the last second." She slanted a devilish grin at Cheyenne. "Maybe I should've gone for it."

Eve hadn't heard, let alone responded, to her question about the number of outfits. It had merely been Cheyenne's attempt to divert her, anyway. Chey didn't want to talk about this. It told her that Eve liked Joe more than ever and that last night had gone well. Maybe they hadn't slept together, but Eve was bent on seeing him again, and Cheyenne couldn't imagine any man rejecting a woman as beautiful, caring, sophisticated and intelligent as Eve.

"Wait for him to make a move. He will when he's ready." Was that her true opinion? Or only what served her best?

"Why is it always up to the guy?" Eve demanded. "What if *I* want to kiss *him*?" Her voice warmed. "What if I'd like to do even more?"

Cheyenne wished she could look away

from her friend's face, but she was afraid that might reveal how she felt. "Then . . . I guess you could let him know — if you want to take that risk."

Eve's scowl said she wasn't particularly pleased with Chey's response. "Do you think it would be a risk? Do you think he'd hesitate? I'll bet he hasn't been with a woman in ages. I can't name one he's dated since his divorce."

"He doesn't date women from Whiskey Creek. It's too uncomfortable when things don't work out. That's the danger of seeing someone in your hometown, right? You run into them, and keep running into them, long afterward." The same was true for falling in love with someone who didn't love you back, she thought.

"I get that, but he has to miss sex." She sighed. "I know I do. My last experience was with that guy I met because he stayed at the inn, who wound up being *married*."

Cheyenne remembered what a smooth liar *he'd* been. He'd had a woman with him the first time he'd stayed, but he'd convinced Eve she was only his girlfriend and said they'd broken up. That part turned out to be true — but he still had a wife. "I have no idea how he'd respond if you tried to kiss him. I don't know anything about his private life."

Eve wasn't really listening. She was too consumed by her own thoughts. "I almost wish I wasn't leaving town. I mean . . . there's your mother's health. I should be here in case . . . you know, the worst happens. And now I've started a relationship with Joe that I have to walk away from for two whole weeks." She pinched her bottom lip. "I should've held off until after the cruise to ask him out."

"You were thinking if he turned you down, it would be easier to recover if you were gone, remember?"

She chuckled. "I remember. I should've had more confidence. If only I'd waited . . ."

"He won't forget you that soon." Cheyenne got off the bed to take the shorts and fold them herself. "Did he ask what you're doing tonight?"

She hated herself for prying. She'd promised not to make matters worse by digging for information, especially information that would upset her, but she couldn't help this one question. If last night had been so amazing, Joe could've invited Eve one more time before she left.

"He didn't, but he talked about how much work it is to get ready for such a long trip, as if he was expecting me to be busy."

"Anyone would expect that," Cheyenne concurred, but she wasn't convinced that two people who were really excited about each other would put off getting together just because of *packing*, especially when Eve had had all day.

Still, she had to admit there were a lot of reasons Joe could've decided not to ask Eve out. Maybe he had to work.

As Cheyenne put the shorts in the suitcase and began folding items Eve had yet to gather up, Eve stood and embraced her. "I'm going to miss you. You'll be okay while I'm gone, won't you? I hate that I'm leaving you in the lurch."

"You're not leaving me in the lurch. We've both known this was coming for months and months."

"True, but . . ."

Cheyenne collected the dress she'd lent Eve. "Stop worrying. I'll be fine." Part of her felt she'd be *better* off. She couldn't handle what was happening between Eve and Joe while she felt so vulnerable because of her mother and sister. Two weeks of not having to pretend would give her a chance to get her feet underneath her again. "I'm happy for you. You deserve a vacation."

"You deserve one, too."

"I'll take one someday."

"We'll track down your birth certificate and go to Europe together," Eve promised.

"That'd be fun." She draped the dress over one arm so she could fish her keys from the side pocket of her big bag. "I should head home. Presley has a date tonight."

Eve frowned. "Why does she get to go out while you take care of Anita? You're always stuck at home."

"Someone offered to take Presley to a movie." She wiggled her eyebrows for comedic effect. "I can't say the same."

"I can guarantee it's no one she should be with," Eve said.

That was probably true. But Cheyenne couldn't tell her sister whom to date. It was hard enough encouraging her to stay clean and sober, not to mention employed. "Have a wonderful time," she said, and took the gift she'd bought Eve out of the main compartment of her purse.

"What's this?"

"A send-off."

"Oh, my gosh! How sweet! Can I open it?"

"Of course. But don't be fooled by the fancy wrapping. It's just self-tanner," she said with a laugh. "You'll need it if you plan on wearing that bikini."

"Sad but true." Eve gave Cheyenne another brief hug. "Thank you. As usual, you've come up with the perfect gift."

Cheyenne was almost out of the bedroom when Eve called her back. "Chey?"

"Hmm?" she said, turning.

"I don't know what I'd do without you. You realize that, don't you?"

For the first time in several days, Cheyenne felt good, or at least better. This was Eve. She could give up the man she loved for Eve, couldn't she?

Of course. She'd do anything. . . .

"I know." With a smile and a wave she went home, telling herself that Joe was just one guy among many. Someday she'd find someone else who made her feel the way he did. She had to. Because she couldn't, *wouldn't*, put him before her best friend.

6

"How'd it go last night?"

Joe looked up from the basketball game he'd been watching since he got home from work. His father had asked him about his date with Eve Harmon twice already — earlier today, when they were at the station. Joe had brushed aside the subject both times and didn't have much to add now. "Fine."

"That's all you've got to say? It was fine?"

He returned his attention to the TV. "What were you expecting?"

"I don't know . . . A little excitement maybe? Eve seems like a nice girl."

She *was* a nice girl. Joe couldn't argue with that.

"Do you think you'll go out with her again?" A cabinet banged shut as Martin started dinner. When they were home together, they took turns doing the cooking. They had a few part-time employees at

Whiskey Creek Gas-N-Go who helped out on nights and weekends. Since the station opened at six and closed at midnight seven days a week, they couldn't man it every hour.

"Joe?" his father prompted when he didn't answer.

Apparently, Martin wasn't going to let this go. Using the remote, Joe lowered the volume on the Kings and Lakers. "I don't think so. Why?"

"Why not?" his father countered.

"You know how I feel about getting involved with someone from Whiskey Creek. I made that mistake when I got married." He ran into Suzie's family all over town — her parents, aunts, uncles, cousins. These people, whom he'd once loved as much as his own relatives, no longer spoke to him. They blamed him for the divorce and God knew what else, even though it was Suzie who'd cheated, Suzie who'd tried to pass off another man's child as one of his.

Sometimes he wished he could tell the Petrovicks what Suzie had been like as a wife. He wanted to see the shock on their faces, especially her stodgy old father's.

But he'd never say a word. Not even to Gail or Martin. He'd destroyed the results of the DNA test as soon as he received them in the mail. He'd never told Suzie that he knew. Summer meant as much to him as Josephine. If the truth got out, he stood to lose far more than he already had.

The lid to the trash can closed with a thump. "Then why'd you go out with her in the first place?"

Because she'd taken him off guard when she called and he hadn't wanted to embarrass her. And, ideals or no, he needed some kind of diversion. Lately, he'd been so damn lonely, so dissatisfied. That didn't exactly put him in a strength position when it came to turning down invitations.

"It was just dinner, Dad, not a date." Eve had talked too much and tried too hard, and then she'd nearly tackled him at the door as he tried to leave. But he'd known he wasn't interested in her when he said yes. That made the discomfort *his* fault.

"Right," Martin said with a skeptical cackle.

Swallowing a frustrated sigh — he really didn't want to be grilled about this — Joe turned up the volume. "It's true. You're making too big a deal out of it."

His father raised his voice to compete with the sudden roar of the Laker fans. "You're saying she just wants to be friends."

He slouched lower so he could lean his

head against the back of the couch. "Yeah."

"That's why she stops by to get gas almost every single day and spends fifteen minutes hanging around the minimart hoping to run into you."

The frequency of Eve's trips had given her away. Joe had guessed, long before she'd asked him out. She'd been hinting that she liked him for the past several months. But he couldn't see himself in a romantic relationship with her, couldn't see her as anything other than the chubby little girl with pigtails who'd played Barbies with Gail. "Give it a rest, okay?" he grumbled.

"You got to date somebody."

"Who says?" Finally goaded into dealing with this, he hit the mute button. "*You* don't date. You've lived without a partner for years."

"Because I had you and Gail to worry about, and now I'm too old and ornery to get along with anyone."

He hadn't brought a woman home since Linda left him for her high school sweetheart. Joe had been thirteen when his mother walked out, Gail eight. They'd hardly seen her since. She was still with the same man and by all indications happy, but she wasn't one who liked to look back.

"You don't want to be alone for the rest

of your life," Martin said.

"How can you be so sure?" The first few years after his divorce, being alone hadn't been so bad. It beat the hell out of trying to live with someone as high-strung and volatile as Suzie. He never wanted to go through any of that again. The fighting. The shock of some of the things she said. The betrayal he'd felt when he'd learned about her affair with their next-door neighbor. The sickness that had swamped him when he found out she'd brought the man he'd considered a friend, the man he'd been barbecuing burgers for on Saturdays, into his bed. The sense of failure that'd dragged him down when she finally kicked him out because he was only staying for the sake of the girls. The loss of no longer waking up in the same house as his children. It had been hell.

But his fear of getting involved in another bad relationship was quickly being offset by the downside of his current situation. He was tired of living with his father and sleeping alone. He hadn't had sex with anyone since Deborah Hinz, the woman who'd come from Sacramento to sell him energy-conservation lighting for the exterior of the station eighteen months ago. Even that hadn't been as enjoyable as it should've been. He'd thought there might be some potential there when she'd asked to meet him at a bar not far from where she lived. But when he woke up and realized he'd drunk too much and gone home with her, he beat a hasty retreat. Then he bought the lights she'd been hoping to sell him, even though his father insisted they could find them cheaper, to make up for not wanting to see her again.

"I just need to go to Sacramento or the Bay area more often," he said, and hoped he was right, that getting out and meeting new people would fill the void.

His father's voice was barely audible; he'd stuck his head into the refrigerator to get something out. "How will you meet someone in Sac or anywhere else? At a nightclub?"

"I guess I could join a church group, but doing it for the wrong reasons seems a bit deceptive, don't you think?" The Lakers scored from at least five feet behind the three-point line. "Nice shot," he muttered, and rewound the DVR so he could take another look at that bucket.

"You don't need to leave Whiskey Creek," his father said. "There are plenty of nice women right here."

Martin didn't want to lose both of his kids to other locations. "Like who?"

"Eve Harmon! That's what I've been trying to tell you."

He glanced over to see his father salting
two pieces of fish, which he could smell
from where he sat in the living room. "You
want me to date one of Gail's friends?"

"What's so bad about that?"

He had to explain? "If things don't work
out, loyalty would force Gail to side with
me, since I'm her brother, which could cost
her one of her closest friends. That's not
fair."

His father arranged the fish on the broiler
and slid it into the oven. "You're overthink-
ing it."

"How ironic."

Apparently satisfied that he'd started dinner, Martin came to the living room doorway. "What's ironic?"

Joe shot him a crooked grin. "Most dads
tell their sons not to think with their dicks.
Sounds like you're saying just the opposite."

"Most dads are talking to young boys.
You're thirty-six."

"I left home once — and learned my lesson. Now you're never getting rid of me."

His father must've known he was only joking because he didn't comment. He leaned
against the wall, watching the game while
they talked. "It's time to get back in the

saddle."

"I'm not sure I'm willing to listen to your advice in this area, Dad." He took a pull of his beer. "It's a bit too much 'do what I say and not what I do,' don't you think?"

When his father made no comment, Joe saluted him with the can. "You have nothing to say to that?"

"I guess you got me," he replied, and went back into the kitchen.

With a chuckle, Joe shook his head. His father didn't lose an argument very often. And he never acknowledged it when he did. "Listen, you can relax, okay? I'm fine. Quit worrying."

"There has to be someone you find attractive," his dad called back.

Cheyenne Christensen came to mind. But only because he hadn't been able to forget her since he'd bumped into her at the grocery store earlier, he told himself. He'd known she was going through hell. It had to be hard watching a parent succumb to cancer. But she'd seemed more on edge than usual. . . .

"You think Anita Christensen's going to die soon?" he asked.

"Where'd that come from?" His father was digging around in the freezer. They were probably going to have frozen peas with the fish — a healthy enough choice but not a particularly exciting one. Predictable, boring, safe. That seemed to be the story of his life these days.

"I saw Cheyenne at Nature's Way," he explained. "When I picked up the milk and eggs."

"What'd she have to say?"

Joe cursed when the Lakers went on a 6-0 run. "Not much. Just that she was fine."

"So Anita's hanging on."

"Unfortunately."

"Joe!" The surprise and reproof in his father's voice demanded an explanation, if not a retraction.

"It doesn't sound good to say it," Joe admitted. "But Cheyenne and her sister would be better off."

The stove ticked until a burner lit with the soft, distinctive *poof* of gas. Sure enough, Martin was putting some peas on to boil.

"Since when have you become so interested in the Christensen girls?" his father asked.

"I'm not," Joe replied, but that wasn't entirely true. Presley had never appealed to him. Physically, she was okay, even with all those tattoos. But she had a mouth more suited to a sailor and eyes that gazed out on the world with bitterness and suspicion. If there'd been a few warning signs he'd overlooked with Suzie, Presley came with neon flashers.

But there'd always been something about Cheyenne. His eyes followed her whenever they passed on the street. He couldn't help turning around to catch a second glimpse of her when she came into the station. And this morning . . . he'd felt so protective when those tears welled up.

"Glad to hear it," his father said. "Eve would be a much better bet."

Joe propped his elbows on his knees. "What's wrong with Cheyenne?"

"She's had a hard life. If anyone has the right to carry excess baggage, it would be her. Just look at her sister."

The way his father automatically dismissed Cheyenne bothered Joe. "She's done well, considering what she's been through. Like you said, it's Presley who's out of control. She propositioned me at the Sexy Sadie Saloon a few weeks ago."

"How does a woman do that these days?"

"She said for twenty bucks she'd take me in the girls' restroom and 'blow my *mind*.' "

"I take it you declined."

"I did — and that didn't embarrass her in the slightest. She told me to go to hell and started scanning the bar for her next mark."

"See what I mean?"

"Presley isn't Chey," Joe argued.

"Doesn't matter. You marry the girl, you marry the family."

He understood that concept only too well. But he was feeling contrary enough that his father's disapproval pushed him further into Cheyenne's camp. "It wouldn't hurt to befriend her."

"You've never paid much attention to her before."

"She belongs to Gail's group. And I've been busy."

His father motioned at the clock. "You're not busy tonight. Maybe after dinner you should take a bottle of wine and head over there."

"Maybe I will."

"She could probably use some company."

"No doubt," he said, rising to the challenge. But once he caught sight of his father's grin, he realized that Martin had been manipulating him the whole time. "You think you're so clever," he complained.

"It's not hard to lead someone right where they want to go," he said with a laugh. Then he nearly drove Joe crazy whistling as he finished making dinner.

No one ever came to the house, unless it

was one of J. T. Amos's sons, looking for Presley. Sometimes Presley partied with them down at their place, which was a rambler along the river half a mile away. Since it was nearly eight o'clock on a Saturday night, Cheyenne felt confident it had to be one of them — confident enough that she wasn't the least concerned about her appearance. She'd already scrubbed her face so she wasn't wearing any makeup. She wasn't wearing shoes, either — just a pair of holey jeans with a sweatshirt. She'd stand behind the door, tell Dylan, Aaron, Grady, Rodney or Mack that Presley was out for the evening, and be done with it.

But it wasn't the Fearsome Five, as they were often called. Cheyenne couldn't believe her eyes when she saw Joe standing on her rickety porch. She hadn't even realized he knew where she lived.

"Hey." He offered her a grin that made her stomach flip-flop. "Looks like you're in for the night."

She resisted the urge to raise a self-conscious hand to her messy bun. Did her hair look as bad as she thought it might? She could feel wet tendrils clinging to her face. "Yes. I, um, I'm not planning on going anywhere. I mean, I can't. Presley's out. I have to stay with my mother."

"That's what I figured." He lifted the bottle he carried in one hand. "Would you like to have a drink with me while you do your caretaker thing?"

She blinked several times before finding her voice. "Did you come to talk about Eve?"

"Eve?" he repeated.

"She's crazy about you, you know. I'm sure you've guessed what with all the trips we've made to the gas station." She laughed, hoping to appear less off balance. "And . . . she's *so* great. You wouldn't want to lose out on someone like her."

A strange expression flitted across his face. "Thanks for the encouragement. I think she's nice, too. But I'm not here to talk about Eve."

He didn't indicate whether or not her words had surprised him. Of course they hadn't. He couldn't have missed the way Eve kept singling him out. She wasn't nearly as good at hiding her feelings as Cheyenne was. She'd never had to hide anything because she'd never really feared anything. Besides, she'd asked *him* out. That made her interest quite obvious.

"Is this about . . . earlier, then? This morning? Because I'm okay." She cleared her throat. "I didn't mean to make you feel sorry for me. *Again.* That's sort of the history of our relationship, isn't it?" She managed a self-deprecating chuckle, but he didn't join in.

"I feel bad about what you're going through. That's not the same as pity." He lowered his voice as if confiding a great secret. "Having a drink with me isn't any sort of betrayal, Chey."

This was the first time he'd ever called her by the shortened version of her name but it seemed natural. No doubt he'd often heard Gail refer to her that way. "Right. Of course it isn't. I didn't mean to suggest it would be."

"So . . . can I come in?"

She thought of her Charlie Brown Christmas tree. She'd taken all her good ornaments over to the inn — what few she owned. Would he find her place as pathetic as he did her situation?

Maybe. But she couldn't be so rude as to turn him away. He meant too much to her. And the fact that he was seeing Eve shouldn't stop them from being friends. He'd made that point already.

With a nod, she stepped aside and allowed him to enter. As he did, she breathed in the outdoorsy scent that clung to him. Normally, she could smell oil and gas from the station, too. But not tonight. He was freshly showered and wearing a sweater, jeans and boots, unlaced enough to make them comfortable and fashionable. He didn't have the style her friend Baxter did — no one in Whiskey Creek had the style Baxter did — but Cheyenne liked the way Joe dressed. She liked everything about him.

That was the problem.

"Have a seat." She gestured at the kitchen table. She was afraid he'd choose the spot with a hole under the cushion if she directed him to the couch. She hadn't invested much money in household furnishings or the house itself. There didn't seem to be any reason to. It was just a rental. She didn't plan on staying after Anita died; she wasn't even sure what she and Presley would bring with them when they moved. Presley might insist on keeping a few things, but as far as Cheyenne was concerned, there were too many bad memories attached to all of it.

She put a couple of cheap wineglasses on the table. "Go ahead and pour. I'll be right back."

After checking on her mother, who was — *thank God* — asleep, she put on a bra and returned to find Joe holding a glass of wine while standing in front of the Christmas tree.

"The one at The Gold Nugget is a lot prettier," she said. "I promise."

"At least you have a tree."

"You don't?"

"Not yet. My girls keep bugging me to put one up. Maybe I'll do it tomorrow."

"I thought decorating might cheer my mother up."

"Does she still have the strength to come out here?"

"Every once in a while." She'd hoped it would be comforting for Presley, too, who was having such a hard time coping with Anita's decline.

He motioned to the empty fireplace. "Mind if I start a fire?"

"No." She showed him the woodpile at one corner of the porch, then put on Enya's Christmas CD while he coaxed a couple of logs to light.

"That'll ease the chill a bit," he said as he dusted off his hands.

She hadn't realized it was cold. She was so nervous about other things, the temperature of the house hadn't even made the list. "Feels good."

"You *look* good," he said. "Really pretty."

Cheyenne's heart skipped a beat. "You've got to be kidding."

"No. I like you this way."

When their eyes met, she was afraid he'd see how much his compliment pleased her, so she turned her attention to the glass of wine waiting for her on the table. "How's Gail doing?" she asked as she walked over.

"Great. She's happy." He smiled distantly, as if picturing his sister, then sobered. "I hope to hell Simon continues to treat her right. You know the kind of temptations he faces in Hollywood. He could have his pick of women."

"He'll be true to her. He's as much in love as she is. Besides, he'll have you to answer to if he doesn't."

He grinned at her teasing. "Damn straight. That's my little sister."

She tried the wine and liked it. "Do you remember the boy you grabbed by the shirt-front and tossed to the ground when I was a freshman?"

"No." He seemed genuinely surprised. "Why would I do that?"

"Because he was making fun of my dress."

"Sounds like he deserved it."

"It was a pretty ugly dress," she admitted with a laugh. "*Everything* about me was ugly back then."

A contemplative expression came over his face. "That's not how I remember it."

"Yeah, well, you're like *my* big brother, too."

He paused with his glass halfway to his mouth. "Is that how you see me?"

She didn't know how to answer. *Yes* would be the safest way to go. But it was also a lie. So she did what she could to avoid a direct reply. "I mean, you've never looked at me very critically."

"I can tell when someone's attractive, Chey."

Her mouth went dry. "Of course you can. T-take Eve, for instance. She's beautiful, don't you think?"

His eyes never left her face. "Why are we talking about Eve again?"

"She's my best friend."

"I know. And she likes me. I get that." He changed the subject as he glanced away. "Do you have any playing cards?"

She had several packs. Before her mother had gotten too sick to manage a game, they'd often played hearts to distract her from the pain. "In the drawer."

"Any chance I could challenge you to a game?"

"Which one?"

"Poker?" he suggested with a shrug.

How long did he plan to stay? "Sure. But . . . what will we bet?"

"I'll wager dollars toward oil changes and car repairs. Considering what I found when you brought your Olds in last time, it could use some work."

"It could. But what will *I* wager? I help run a B and B, so . . . cooking and cleaning?"

His smile shifted to one side. "I'll settle for some Christmas cookies and tree decorating the next time my girls are in town."

"Why settle? You could have cooking, cleaning *and* decorating." She smacked the cards on the table. "*If* you win."

"I plan on winning," he confided. "But that would still be settling, since it isn't what I'd ask for if I could have anything."

This took Cheyenne by surprise. "What would you ask for?"

He glanced at the sprig of mistletoe Presley had tied to the light fixture over the table. "Peace on earth," he said with a wink. "So deal."

7

He was flirting with her. There was no question about that. Cheyenne just didn't know why. Was he trying to cheer her up? Was he interested in becoming closer friends? Had he stopped by because he'd told his sister that she'd started crying in the grocery store and Gail had asked him to?

He didn't reveal what he was thinking or feeling, but they talked and laughed and laughed and talked until it grew late. By the time he yawned and said he should go, Cheyenne had lost a lot in tree decorating and cookies, and he wasn't willing to let her attempt to win it back. All she could do was claim that one day of her baking and tree trimming services was worth an eight-hundred-dollar credit.

"You must be one hell of a Christmas decorator," he said.

"I am." She waved toward her only example. "Don't let that fool you."

"I'll suspend my disbelief, for now. You can prove yourself next Saturday."

"That's when your girls are coming?"

"That's when. But we should pick up the tree tomorrow, before all the good ones are gone."

"*We*?" She corked the wine bottle since he'd declined a refill.

"I don't want to buy something you wouldn't be interested in decorating."

Eve would, no doubt, find this arrangement odd if she heard about it. That made Cheyenne hesitate. As much as she wanted to spend time with Joe, she had no business doing it. "I'm easy to please."

"Then why don't you ever date?"

She shuffled the cards. "Nice segue."

"I thought so."

"How do you know I don't?"

"We live in Whiskey Creek, remember? If you were seeing someone, I'd know about it. Everyone would."

That was true. So she began searching for excuses. "I've been too preoccupied."

"That's it? That's all you've got?"

She tried not to laugh. "I was seeing John Kovinski there for a little bit."

"Not *Mr.* Kovinski, the school principal . . ."

" 'Fraid so."

"When was this?"

She pretended she had to think about it, although the answer was on the tip of her tongue. She didn't see any point in letting him know that she marked the events in her life by how they corresponded to his. "While you were married." She forced herself to throw in, "I think," even though she was as positive as she could get.

"That was five years ago!"

"I don't get out much."

"Not to mention he's like . . . twice your age," he added with a grimace. "Gail once dated a much older man, too. What's the appeal?"

"Safety. Security. Companionship."

"So no threat."

She chuckled. "Maybe."

"I must've missed the news that you were seeing him."

Because the relationship hadn't gone anywhere. They'd dated three times, and made out once. That wasn't much for even the nosiest people in Whiskey Creek to gossip about.

Joe finished the last of the wine in his glass. "Who else have you dated?"

She put the cards back in the box. "I've been preoccupied, like I said. Who have *you* dated, Mr. DeMarco?"

"Too many girls to count," he teased.

"Who's there?" Her mother's voice, cracked and pleading, came out of the bedroom. "I need my meds! Cheyenne? Presley? Bring me my morphine! Hurry!"

Joe jumped to his feet as if this sudden intrusion into their conversation had startled him. "She okay?"

The distress in her voice could be more than a little unnerving, especially for someone who wasn't used to it. "Yeah. Don't worry."

"Is there anything I can help you do for her?"

"No, I've got it." She took her mother's painkiller from where she'd hidden it behind the refrigerator.

"That's where you keep it?" he asked with a perplexed expression.

Because of Presley. But she didn't want to go into that. "For the moment."

"Okay." He didn't question her further. "I'll put out the fire while you tend to her."

She'd expected him to leave. She could only imagine how uncomfortable he felt now that Anita was awake. But her mother was so impatient she had to postpone their goodbye and he seemed willing to wait. "Calm down, Mom, I'm coming!" she called, grabbing a bottle of water in case

Anita was thirsty.

"Where's Presley?" her mother asked as soon as Cheyenne reached her bedside.

"On a date."

"I heard two voices."

Cheyenne ignored her obvious disappointment. "She's not home."

"Someone's here!"

"*I* am," Cheyenne insisted.

"Besides you."

"No. No one." She didn't want her mother interacting with Joe. That he'd seen her situation at home was bad enough.

"I need to be moved. I can't —" Anita gasped for breath "— if you could slide me over a bit and . . . turn me on my other side. My hip is aching."

Cheyenne tried to do what she'd been asked, but her mother cried out. "You have to pick me up! You can't shove me!" she shouted, then started moaning and weeping.

Afraid that Joe would hear, Cheyenne lowered her voice. "I wasn't shoving. I was doing it the way I always do." The only way she knew how. She wasn't strong enough to lift Anita as easily as Anita wanted.

"Presley, come help your sister!" her mother called. "Hurry! She's killing me!"

"Presley's not home."

"Yes, she is. I heard her. *Presley?*"

There was no doubt Anita was in pain. Cheyenne could see it in the hollowness of her eyes. But Cheyenne knew her mother was also being purposely difficult. She wanted Presley, and this gave her an excuse to demand her other daughter's attention.

"Mom, please," she said, but a sound at the door told her the noise had succeeded in drawing Joe to the room.

"What is it?" he asked.

Cheyenne could tell he wasn't sure whether or not he could enter but wanted to help.

With a sigh, she tucked the tendrils of hair that'd fallen from her loose bun behind her ears. "My mom needs to be moved over and onto her right side."

"I can do that." He crossed to the bed and lifted her as though she weighed nothing.

Anita was so surprised to see a man in the house she didn't complain. But she didn't leave it at "thank you," either. "Are you sleeping with my daughter?" she asked as he straightened the blankets. "Has someone finally taken her virginity? God, I hope you banged her good. She needs it. Maybe she won't be so critical of the rest of us once she finds out what she's been missing."

Cheyenne's face flushed hot but she

ignored her mother's vulgarity. "Thanks," she told Joe. "I'm sure she'll be fine from here on."

Also ignoring what Anita had said, Joe mumbled a polite good-night and let Cheyenne walk him to the door. "That isn't true, is it?" he asked when he'd stepped out on the porch.

"What?" Cheyenne said, but she knew. She just wasn't sure how to respond.

"That you've never slept with anyone?"

She didn't need his shock to tell her how unusual she was. These days, there weren't many thirty-one-year-old virgins. Her lack of a sex life wasn't a subject she wanted other people talking about. But she couldn't hide who she really was, not from Joe. "Yes."

"Why? Are you waiting or —" he rubbed his neck as if searching for the right words "— has something happened that's made you unwilling to . . . be touched in that way?"

He obviously knew a great deal about her background. She probably had Gail to thank for that. Maybe Eve, too. There was no telling what they'd discussed at dinner last night. "A truck driver gave my mother twenty dollars to let him fondle me once."

When Joe's jaw tightened, she put up a hand. "But it stopped there and he isn't the reason I've . . . held off. Growing up, I wanted sex to have some meaning. I've been waiting for the right time and place." The right man.

"I see." He nodded.

"Besides, we live in a small town." She smiled, hoping to lighten the tone of the conversation. "I have a reputation to protect."

"The threat of gossip doesn't stop everybody."

She wondered if he was alluding to her sister. "I guess it doesn't."

"Good night, Chey."

He was halfway to his truck when she called after him. "Why'd you come, Joe?"

He slid his hands in his pockets as he pivoted to face her. It was so cold that she could see his breath misting in front of him, but he didn't seem to be in a hurry. "I could say my father suggested it."

"Why would he do that?"

"He doesn't think I get out enough."

"But . . ."

"The truth has more to do with Eve."

"Which means what?"

"I figured if she was going to make her move, I'd better be sure there isn't something between you and me. Every once in a while, I've sort of wondered . . . what if?"

She hadn't expected him to be so frank. Suddenly a bit weak in the knees, she grasped the pole that supported the porch. He was considering her *now*, of all times? Why couldn't he have acted on that "what if?" a week ago? "And? What did you decide?"

"That we should see each other again."

"I can't," she said. Not now that she knew he wasn't merely being nice or looking for friendship.

He smiled. "You have to. You owe me, remember?"

Joe drove around town for fifteen minutes before finally turning toward home. He doubted his father would still be up. Martin was an early-to-bed, early-to-rise kind of guy. So was he, since he had to work such long hours. But he'd felt so unsettled since leaving Cheyenne's that he wouldn't be able to sleep. He'd gone to her place expecting to feel what he'd felt when he was with Eve. Respect for her as a person. A certain amount of admiration for her pretty face. The hope that they could maintain a friendship. But ultimately nothing that moved him, nothing that made him regret not asking her out before. He'd convinced himself that the spark he felt whenever Cheyenne was around was no more than curiosity and sympathy for everything she'd had to endure.

But their time together hadn't felt nearly as platonic as he'd envisioned.

He could tell that she hadn't been wearing a bra when she came to the door. She'd gone and put one on right away. But the gentle sway of her breasts as she moved in those first few seconds had reminded him that it had been a long time since he'd felt a woman's soft body beneath his, especially a woman he *wanted* to make love to.

Those weren't the kinds of thoughts he'd been anticipating in conjunction with his little sister's unfortunate friend. When he let his father goad him into visiting her, he'd figured it was better than staying home or going to Sexy Sadie's and milling around with the same old crowd.

Or . . . maybe he'd been lying to himself from the beginning. Maybe seeing Cheyenne as a desirable woman instead of a pity project was what he'd been hoping to avoid by keeping his distance from her in the first place.

A honk broke into his thoughts. Riley Stinson sat in his beat-up Explorer, idling at the light next to him.

Joe rolled down the passenger window. Riley was another of his sister's friends, but Joe liked him as much as Gail did. Although most of Joe's buddies from high school had moved on, as he'd originally done, the people in her group were still as tight as family.

"I don't usually see you out so late," Riley called above the rumble of their engines.

"Just checking to make sure the station's locked up." Joe wasn't sure why he lied. He supposed he felt a little funny about seeing Cheyenne after going to dinner with Eve last night. Also, he knew that Cheyenne would appreciate the discretion.

"Everything okay?"

Someone had broken in after-hours about three years ago and looted the minimart. Whoever it was had taken all the alcohol, cigarettes and condoms. But there hadn't been any trouble since. "Fine," Joe replied. He *had* driven past the station, but only because, in a town this size, it was unavoidable. "What about you? What're you up to?"

"Heading home."

"From . . ."

"My folks." He covered a yawn. "I fell asleep there a couple hours ago."

"Where's Jacob?" Riley had gotten a girl by the name of Phoenix pregnant while in high school. She'd always been a little different, definitely offbeat, but no one could've guessed she was capable of murder. She ran down the next girl he showed interest in and went to prison before the baby was even born. Riley and his parents had had Jacob since birth, when the authorities had shuttled the infant out to them.

That story had been the talk of the town back in the day. It was the most sensational thing to ever happen in Whiskey Creek — except for the cave-in at the old mine, which had killed Noah Rackham's twin brother right about the same time.

"I let him sleep over. I have to repair a roof first thing in the morning."

"Doesn't he usually go along and help if he's on break?"

Riley, a contractor, was already teaching Jacob how to build and fix houses. As Jacob grew older, the two acted more like good buddies than father and son.

"I told him he could spend the day with Grandma and Grandpa tomorrow."

"They getting ready for Christmas?"

Riley grinned. "He has cooking, decorating and going shopping to look forward to."

Joe could tell Riley was glad to be off the hook. "How does Jacob feel about that?"

"He wanted to come with me, but I told him it would make Grandma happy to have him stay. The bells and whistles of the holidays are very important to my mom." His tone suggested he didn't quite understand, which made Joe smile. He didn't see the point in some of the tacky decorations he saw, either. Putting up a tree just meant it had to be taken down. But he knew that was being too practical and was willing to do whatever it took to keep his girls happy.

The light had turned green twice already, but there wasn't anyone behind them so they didn't feel any pressure to drive on.

"How's Gail?" Riley asked.

"Happy. Busy doing Simon's PR and managing the other publicists at her firm. They have a star-studded list now."

"Simon's got another new movie coming out, I hear."

Joe checked his rearview mirror again. Still clear. "Another blockbuster. This June."

"I've been meaning to call Gail. I want to tell her I got a Christmas card from Phoenix."

Leaning forward, Joe turned off his stereo. "Does she write you often?"

"She sends letters to Jacob all the time but I don't pass them on. There's no way I want to nurture *that* relationship. I rarely hear from her myelf, though."

"Why do you think she sent the card?"

Suddenly pensive, he frowned and tapped his steering wheel. "She gets out this summer."

Another car came motoring up from behind, forcing them to move on.

"Good luck with that," Joe called.

"Thanks. I might need it," Riley said with a wave.

A noise alerted Cheyenne to the fact that she was no longer alone. Presley came stumbling into the kitchen, squinted at the clock, then groaned. She acted as if it was far too early to face the day, but it was eleven-thirty. "Where are you going?" she mumbled through a yawn.

Cheyenne had been up, doing some cleaning, since six. "A friend wants my help picking out a Christmas tree," she said as she rinsed her coffee cup.

Her sister started for the fridge, then stopped and winced as if that much movement hurt her aching head. "What friend?"

"Does it matter?" Cheyenne took two ibuprofen tablets from the cupboard and handed them over.

Presley wrinkled her nose. "This the best you can do?"

She wasn't getting anything stronger. Not from Cheyenne. "That's it."

Obviously exasperated, her sister popped them in her mouth, pulled the orange juice from the fridge and drank out of the jug.

Cheyenne scowled at her. "Seriously? You can't get a cup?"

"Too late now," she said as she put the juice back. "And do you have to talk so loud? What's wrong with you today?"

The keys to the Olds were lying next to her purse. Cheyenne grabbed both. "Nothing."

"Something has you bugged. You're in a shitty mood."

Because Cheyenne had been up most of the night, trying to talk herself into canceling. A loyal best friend would've refused to go anywhere with Joe. But she kept telling herself that nothing was going to happen. She'd pay off her poker debt while Eve was gone, so Eve would never even know about it, and that would be the end of it. What was so bad about buying and decorating a tree with a friend's big brother?

"I'm in a hurry," she said. Joe had called to say he'd pick her up at noon, but she'd insisted on dropping her car just outside of town. From there, they'd go to Jackson. Most of her friends were away. They'd had to be up long before dawn to get to the airport by eight. But still . . . No way did she want anyone she knew to see them together.

"What's the rush?" Presley rubbed her temples. "Christmas is two weeks away."

Cheyenne didn't answer. She was too busy pulling on her coat and scarf.

"And I thought all your friends went to the Caribbean," Presley added, slouching against the counter.

"Not *all* of them," Cheyenne said.

"Who's left?"

Anxious to get out of the house, Cheyenne didn't even glance at her. "Riley's still here."

"You're getting a tree with Riley? That's what has you so worked up?"

"Nothing has me worked up." Realizing that she'd forgotten to note the amount of morphine she'd given their mother in the log, she searched for a pen and wrote down the information. "How was your date last night?"

Presley scowled. "I've had better."

"What movie did you see?"

"We skipped the movie."

"So what did you do?"

"He took me back to his place."

Tossing the pen aside, Cheyenne whirled to face her. "That's it? You had sex?"

She shrugged. "He wasn't a *total* cheapskate."

"Meaning he provided the drugs and alcohol."

No response.

"Why do you settle for so little?" Cheyenne knew the intensity of her words and expression would bother Presley, but she couldn't help it. She wanted her sister to be happy and that didn't seem possible if her sister continued down the same road as Anita.

"You have fun your way. I'll have fun mine," she said, shuffling back to bed.

Cheyenne watched her go, then checked the clock. If she didn't leave now, she'd be late.

She felt a hint of misgiving as she reached for the door handle. She even pulled her cell phone from her purse and stared down at Joe's number.

Call him. She could tell him no, put an end to whatever they'd started last night.

Her finger hovered over the button. But she'd been waiting for the chance to spend time with him for far too long.

"Today and the next Saturday with his girls. That's all," she promised Eve, and walked out.

8

Cheyenne had the creamiest-looking skin Joe had ever seen. He'd noticed before, of course, but as they wandered through the Christmas-tree lot in Jackson, with the cold adding a tinge of pink to her cheeks, he realized she was even prettier than he'd given her credit for. She was interesting, too. She saw the world so differently from the women he'd dated in the past.

"What about this one?" he asked. They'd finally arrived at the corner of the lot where St. Nick's displayed their best and most expensive trees. Joe had been searching for this section all along. He knew finding it would make the decision an easy one. But Cheyenne wasn't convinced. She scrunched up her nose as she inspected the ten-foot-high blue spruce with the $150 price tag.

"What's wrong?" he asked. "It's perfect."

"That's just it," she said with a sigh. "It's *too* perfect."

This surprised him. "How can a Christmas tree be too perfect?"

"Anyone with enough money can buy a tree like this. An expensive artificial tree would be, technically, even *more* perfect — no branch out of place and that sort of thing. The challenge is to take something that has serious flaws and make it beautiful." She turned in a slow circle, inspecting the options around them before pointing at a specimen that had been shoved off to the side. "What about that one?"

He couldn't believe it. She'd chosen the ugliest tree he'd ever seen. Whoever owned the lot obviously agreed with him because it bore a clearance tag that read, Only $35!

To humor her, he went over and tried to stand it up straight. "You're kidding. Look, it has a broken branch."

She didn't move on as he expected. "I can see that."

"What about all the gaps and holes along the bottom, where it should be the fullest?"

"We can use garland and decorations to fill that in."

Was she trying to help him save money? Show him how thrifty she could be? "Why mess with it? What you'd save on the tree itself, you'd spend on decorations."

"Maybe. But bringing out this tree's true

beauty would be a worthy challenge. Then it wouldn't have been chopped down for nothing."

A lot of trees were going to be wasted. He couldn't save them all. But he supposed it was refreshing that she wasn't demanding the best money could buy. She saw value in a tree that had been tossed aside and rejected by everyone else who'd already come through.

"Now I understand why you picked the tree you did for your own house," he joked.

She gave him a guilty-as-charged expression. "It would've been wasted, too."

"I see." He wondered how his girls would react. At eight and ten, they were still pretty young. Maybe they wouldn't notice the tree's imperfections. "You think you can make it look decent?"

"With enough lights and ornaments, we can make any tree look decent."

This woman was quirky. Of course, her background and situation would make her a bit different, but he'd never thought he'd like those differences as much as he did. Suzie had known nothing but safety, security, love and praise. She'd been so terribly spoiled that she couldn't settle for the attention of just one man; she'd had to have the attention of every man in their social circle.

Cheyenne, by contrast, had no compulsion to be the center of attention. She'd grown up living on the fringe, saw beauty in the unconventional.

"Or . . . maybe you'll like that other tree better," she said, suddenly second-guessing herself. "Get the nice one, if it suits you."

He glanced between the two options. He'd automatically chosen the expensive, seemingly perfect Christmas tree when he'd fallen in love with Suzie. He'd been young, too young to marry, but he'd never questioned that she'd be a wonderful wife. Maybe it was time to try a tree that hadn't been placed in the best corner of the lot, one that'd had to struggle just to survive.

It was an interesting thought. One worth considering. "I'm fine with this one," he said, and motioned to the employee who'd been trailing them through the lot. "We'll take it."

The young man's eyebrows went up. "Seriously? Dude, we were about to throw that tree out."

"Now you don't have to," Joe said.

With a shrug, the guy waved to a coworker wearing a Santa hat and, together, they muscled it off the lot and into the bed of

Joe's truck. Joe was just paying the thirty-five dollars when he turned to say something to Cheyenne and spotted a man standing in line he'd hoped never to see again.

"Hey, that you, big guy?"

A jolt of alarm shot through Cheyenne when someone recognized Joe. She assumed the person lived in Whiskey Creek, which meant Eve might hear about them being together. But when she looked at the handsome, blond-haired man who'd come up behind them, she realized she'd never seen him before. At that point, she would've relaxed — if Joe hadn't stiffened.

"Lance." He gave a slight tilt of his head, but there was no warm smile, no pleasure Cheyenne could detect in meeting this person.

The man seemed oblivious to Joe's negative reaction. Or he was too interested in whatever he could learn to let the lack of welcome bother him.

"I can't believe it!" He slapped Joe on the back. "It's been years, buddy! What are you doing here? You can't be living in Jackson. . . ."

Joe accepted his change and shoved it in his pocket without counting it. "No, Whiskey Creek," he responded, and stepped out of the way so they wouldn't hold up the line that had formed.

When Cheyenne moved with him, Lance's eyes cut to her. "This your new wife?"

"Actually —"

The cashier interrupted. "That'll be eighty-five dollars," he said, waiting for Lance to pay.

Lance handed him some cash but never took his eyes off Joe. "Last I heard, you were still single."

"That hasn't changed." Joe didn't explain what Cheyenne was to him, but he performed a perfunctory introduction. "Chey, this is Lance Phillips. He was my —" he seemed to be picking his words carefully "— neighbor when I lived in Sac."

"Nice to meet you," she murmured.

As Lance shook her hand, Cheyenne got the impression he was sizing her up, wondering if she and Joe were romantically involved. Deciding whether or not he found her attractive enough to be considered a good catch. "They call you Chey?"

"Yes. It's short for Cheyenne, Cheyenne Christensen."

"My pleasure." His gaze lingered on her, then shifted back to Joe. "How are your girls?"

A muscle twitched in Joe's cheek. "You're

asking *me*? You probably see them more often than I do these days."

Lance blinked several times, obviously taken aback. "Not anymore. Suzie didn't tell you? We moved here shortly after you, er, left."

"You're kidding."

"No."

"Who's *we*?"

"What do you mean?" He laughed awkwardly. "Me, Maddy and the kids, of course."

"So Maddy stuck with you."

The cashier handed Lance his change.

"Yes," Lance said, losing some of his false cheer. "Things got a little rough, as you know, but then we found out she was expecting and decided we had too many reasons to hang on to our marriage. That child turned out to be the little girl she always wanted," he added, attempting another smile.

"A girl," Joe repeated.

"Yes."

A strained silence followed. It felt to Cheyenne as if Joe had just suffered a blow of some sort. She'd watched him for too many years not to recognize when he was upset. Something about this conversation, this person, was all wrong. Maybe they'd once been neighbors, but Joe had no liking or respect for Lance. Was he one of the men rumored to have slept with Suzie? Gail had mentioned infidelity, and Cheyenne couldn't imagine anything else making Joe act like this.

"Congratulations," Joe finally said, the word so dry Cheyenne wondered how it hadn't turned to dust in his mouth.

"We named her Madeline, after her mother. She's been a real blessing." Lance talked fast, as if doing so might carry him into friendlier territory. "Came at the perfect time."

"For you, maybe. I don't see how a pregnancy forcing Maddy to give you another chance could've been a blessing to her."

All pretense of camaraderie disappeared. "I've apologized, Joe." Lance shoved his hands in the pockets of his worn jeans and hunched forward in his wool pea coat. "I don't know what more I can do."

"You can quit pretending we're friends," Joe said, and guided Cheyenne away.

Cheyenne could hear Joe's labored breathing as he marched to his truck. With his hands curved into fists, he walked so quickly she could barely keep up.

"Why do you hate that guy so much?" she asked once they'd both climbed inside the cab. Although she had her suspicions, she had no idea if she was right.

He gazed at her, but she was fairly certain he wasn't seeing her. His mind was somewhere far away. When he came back to himself, he seemed almost startled to realize she was in the truck with him.

"I'm taking you home," he said. "This was a mistake."

Presley stared down at Eugene Crouch's business card. All his information was there — his name, the name of his agency, his P.I. license number and his email address. She could contact him easily, right now while her mother slept, with a phone call or an email, and put an end to the mystery of the blonde woman.

She owed her sister the chance to assume her rightful identity, didn't she? The chance to have the respectable family she'd always longed for. Those ringlets in Cheyenne's hair, the expensive party dress and the pretty shoes suggested she'd come from a very different situation than the one in which she'd been raised, a far superior situation —

"Presley?" Anita called. "Where are you? Aren't you going to turn on our show?"

It was Saturday. Their soap didn't air on

weekends, but the meds were making Anita's brain so fuzzy she could no longer keep track of the days. Presley hated that as much as she hated everything else about what was happening. Her mother was no longer the strong, dominant personality she'd once been; she'd been reduced to a helpless stranger.

"Where are you?" Anita demanded.

Presley couldn't bring herself to answer. She continued to lean on the kitchen counter, Crouch's card in one hand, her thumb passing absently over the embossed lettering.

It didn't give an actual address. She didn't even know where he was from. New Mexico? Here? Somewhere else?

Regardless, there was enough information that she could contact him. Should she do it?

If not, she had to at least tell Chey what she suspected his business with them to be. Not telling would be unfair, almost as unfair as what Anita had done in the first place.

But what would Chey do when she found out they weren't even related? That she was and always had been better than her mother and sister — as good as the group of friends she'd admired for so long?

Would she go back to her original family?

Embrace what could have been?

If so, she wouldn't want the one person who reminded her of everything she'd lost tagging along. Maybe she'd even begin to blame Presley. In a way, she had the right. It was Presley whose pleading for a playmate had instigated the events that had changed Cheyenne's life. If not for Presley, Anita wouldn't have bothered to take on a second child. Half the time she hadn't wanted either one of them.

"*Presley!* Why won't you answer me?"

Anita's voice had turned into a panicked sob. Presley had to go reassure her. But she wanted to make a decision on this first. Constantly dwelling on it, having Crouch's card in her pocket, was driving her crazy.

She picked up her cell phone but couldn't bring herself to dial. Cheyenne was the only person she had in the world, the only person, besides Anita, whom she loved. If the truth came out, Cheyenne would have no reason to stay with her. Resentment would eventually overtake any good feelings she had, and that would be the end of what they'd known as sisters. Presley was too realistic about her own shortcomings to believe she was the type of sibling Cheyenne would cling to.

Anita was dying. Soon, their mother

would no longer have any effect on Cheyenne's happiness. That meant Cheyenne didn't need to know about Crouch or the years that had come before. It was too late to undo what had been done. Even worse, it might make Cheyenne more miserable to realize what Anita had stolen from her.

"Should I tell her, Mom?" Presley suddenly cried out.

Silence met this question. With all the medication, and considering that they hadn't discussed Crouch since right after she'd met him, Presley thought her mother would ask what she was talking about.

But Anita didn't need clarification. In a lucid moment, she called out, "You're a fool if you do."

Her mother was right, she decided. God help her but she couldn't tell Chey. "I'm sorry," she whispered. Then she took out her lighter and burned Crouch's card in the sink.

9

Cheyenne didn't know what to make of her two hours with Joe, but the minute he dropped her off at her car and drove away, she felt instantly relieved. Nothing had happened.

She also felt terribly disappointed for the same reason. Which made no sense at all. She'd known they could only be friends; she wouldn't be able to live with herself if she let it go any further.

"So get over him," she muttered, and got into her Oldsmobile. She still owed him a day of tree decorating with his girls, but doubted he'd collect. She'd convinced him to buy that damaged, ugly tree, and now he was on his own with it. Whatever had possessed him to come over last night, and invite her to join him today, had fizzled. After that ambiguous "mistake" comment, he'd scarcely said a word to her, and she'd instinctively known not to push him.

"It's *fortunate* that he's backing off," she told herself. "You don't want to be the kind of friend who'd sneak around on Eve." No one had come through for her like Eve and the Harmons.

She checked her phone. Afraid she might accidentally dial one of her friends, who would then be able to overhear her and Joe, she'd turned it off when she left the house earlier. But, hoping for some contact from Eve to bolster her resolve, she powered it up again.

As she'd expected, Eve had sent her a series of text messages.

Layover in Minneapolis two hours long. Argh! Going to grab a bite with the gang.

Ted is in rare form. Kept us entertained on the plane. Baxter is sulking — who knows why. Callie and Kyle are sitting together — another clue that things between them might be more serious than they're letting on. Noah spent the flight completely zonked out. Can't believe I chose him for my seat partner. Sure feels strange leaving you behind. Everyone says so. We should have done more to get you on this trip!

How's your mom?

Fine, Cheyenne texted back. We're both fine. But she wasn't entirely sure. Anita wasn't long for this earth. And being the object of Joe's attention, even for such a short period, had made the yearning she felt for him that much more poignant.

What would it be like to feel his bare skin against hers? She'd never experienced that kind of sensation, but she'd dreamed of it often enough. And he was always the man in her dreams.

Gently banging her head against the steering wheel, she groaned, then forced herself to sit up and act like an adult. She'd get through this the way she survived everything else — by taking it one day at a time.

She started to drive home but when she reached Whiskey Creek and the road leading to the dilapidated string of homes tucked away by the river, she couldn't make herself turn. If she went back, Presley would come up with some excuse to take off, and Cheyenne would once again be left alone with Anita.

She needed a longer break. So she crept down Sutter Street at ten miles per hour, trying to enjoy the Christmas decorations strung on the historic buildings and converted Victorians. As in so many other gold-mining towns of the 1800s, the storefronts of Whiskey Creek had a quaint charm, with multipaned windows, antique lettering, old-fashioned streetlights hung with wreaths — at least in December — and Western board-walks.

When she passed the huge, decorated tree in the park, where the city council had recently erected a giant statue of a man panning for gold, she stopped and got out.

She was staring up at the angel poised at the very top, her thoughts a million miles away — on Eve and Joe, on the P.I. Presley had mentioned to her mother, on the reno-vations that were to begin tomorrow — when a voice intruded.

"Enjoying the fresh air?"

The question came from behind her and had a sardonic edge.

When she turned, she saw a man leaning up against the cinder-block building that housed the public restrooms. With his face cast in the shadow of the overhang, she couldn't immediately tell who he was. It took her a second to identify the voice, but her memory eventually came up with a name.

She was looking at one of the Amos boys. Dylan, the oldest. "It's a bit chilly." She assumed the conversation would end there. Presley knew the Amoses; she didn't. But he spoke again.

"Who let you out of the house?"

"Excuse me?"

Propping one foot against the wall behind him, he lit a cigarette, which illuminated his face. "Presley said you never go anywhere."

"That's not true."

He paused before taking another drag. "She also said you're too uptight to have any fun."

"Why would she tell you that?" Cheyenne couldn't imagine the Amoses talking about her at all. She was as different from them as night from day, and that was apparent long before any conversation.

"I promised her that if she'd bring you along someday, I'd show you a good time. But she said you wouldn't let me, that you'll probably remain a virgin till you die."

Rumors about her lack of sexual experience had circulated through town before, along with plenty of speculation on whether it could be true. But she was surprised he'd confront her like this. "My personal life is none of your business."

He blew out a mouthful of smoke. "Doesn't stop me from being curious."

"You can't believe everything you hear. Presley must've been high when she said that. Which doesn't make her particularly reliable." She wasn't sure why she'd dignified his remark with a response, except that she didn't want him poking fun at her innocence.

"I gotta take what I can get."

She shot him a frown. "What's that supposed to mean?"

"She's the only person we have in common," he said with a shrug. "Anyway, she's always high when she's at our place. That's why she comes over. She's looking for a party. And my brothers are more than happy to give her one."

Cheyenne continued to grimace. It didn't help to have her worst fears confirmed. "As I thought."

"You blame us for your sister's addiction?"

He'd obviously picked up on her tone.

"You could be a better influence."

"It's not *my* job to set her straight. She makes her own choices."

"I'm not happy about the drug use."

"Duly noted." A laugh rumbled from deep in his throat. "Your lack of approval changes everything."

Stung by his flippant remark, she reacted angrily. "I hope no one's taking advantage of her while she's there. Because if I find out that's the case —"

"You'll what?" He shoved away from the wall to move closer. He wasn't bad-looking, but he wasn't particularly good-looking, either. He had a wiry build with broad shoulders and plenty of muscle, apparent even beneath his denim jacket and jeans. She couldn't find fault with his body. It was his face that bothered her. With an abundance of angles, cruel, dark eyes and a jagged scar on one temple, he looked . . . dangerous. The fact that he was reckless and had a history of getting picked up by the police only added to her sense that it was smarter to keep her distance.

"I'll do whatever I can to protect her," she said, folding her arms to appear more resolute.

"Relax. Nothing's going to happen to Presley at my place," he told her. "But, like I said, she makes her own decisions. And there isn't anything either of us can do about that."

When he continued to advance on her, she glanced around. It was three o'clock on a Sunday. She could reasonably expect to find other people in the park, even on a cold afternoon, like this one. A few dog walkers, if nothing else. But they were alone and being alone with Dylan Amos made her uncomfortable. He had a powerful presence that encouraged others to give him a wide berth. No one wanted to cross the Amos boys, especially the biggest and baddest.

But Cheyenne was in no mood to skitter away. "Are you the one she sleeps with when she's there?"

He stopped a foot or so shy of her. "Me? No. I've never been interested in Presley."

She narrowed her eyes. "Are you suggesting there's something wrong with her?"

With a laugh at how quickly she'd grown defensive, he shook his head. "You can say what you want about her but I can't? Is that it?"

"She's *my* sister."

"She's also a lost soul. Deep down, I think you agree with me."

"And you're not?"

He gazed at the end of his cigarette. "We aren't talking about me," he said.

"Maybe we should be. Who are you to point a finger at anyone else?"

He took a long drag before flicking away the ashes. He looked like such a badass with that scar and slightly crooked nose. "You're the one making judgments. But it's nice to see you've got some spunk. After what you've been through, that surprises me. I'm impressed."

She hadn't been trying to impress him.

She'd rather he gave her a target. She had to play nice with everyone else — her friends, her sister, her dying mother. It wasn't fair to behave any other way. But there were moments when the rage and frustration she'd known all these years threatened to consume her, made her want to rant and rave and throw whatever she could lay her hands on. She felt that way now, as if she was on the brink of letting all that negative emotion spew out.

He seemed braced for the worst, like someone poking a rattlesnake with a stick to see if it would strike. Of all the people in Whiskey Creek, she thought he could take it if she unleashed her rage. But she didn't. They were virtually strangers. She had no right to go after him any more than anyone else.

"No comment?" he prompted.

"You don't what to hear what I have to say," she said, turning away.

He tilted his head to be able to look her in the face. "Why not?"

"It's not polite."

"Far as I'm concerned, polite is boring."

"Fine." She met his gaze. "I want to slug somebody, okay?"

Dylan didn't draw back in horror. He didn't laugh at her, either. "It's a wonder you haven't done that by now. I doubt anyone would blame you." He leaned in to tweak her chin and lowered his voice at the same time. "But take it from me, sweet pea. There are better ways of working off frustration."

She knew she should let it go at that, but spoke before she could stop herself. "Such as . . ."

He grinned. "You ever want me to show you what it's like to have a man in your bed, you know where to find me."

Taken aback, Cheyenne blinked. She'd never spoken directly to Dylan Amos before, not more than a hello when they passed at school over a decade ago — or maybe a nod of acknowledgment when they bumped into each other on the street. She resented him and his family for adding to the problems of her already confused sister and did whatever she could to avoid them. So this was essentially their first conversation. Had he really just propositioned her out of nowhere? "You don't actually think —"

"That you'd give me a chance?" Smoke curled from his nostrils. "Why not? Joe certainly isn't stepping up."

Cheyenne felt her jaw drop. How did he know she cared for Gail's brother? "What makes you think I want anything from Joe?"

She'd quickly masked her surprise in an effort to keep up the charade, but he wasn't buying her act.

He squinted through the smoke drifting lazily up from his cigarette. "It's hard to miss, for anyone who's really looking."

Why was *he* looking? "I don't understand."

Suddenly, the intensity on his face disappeared behind a mask of indifference — his usual expression. "Forget I said anything."

Tossing his cigarette on the cold, icy grass, he stubbed it out with his boot and strode away. But she couldn't let what he'd said go at that. She jogged after him, catching him before he could reach the parking lot. "Wait! How did you know? Did Presley tell you about Joe? Has *she* guessed?"

When he turned, those cruel eyes swept over her — except, up close, they weren't all that cruel. They actually held enough blatant appreciation to send a tingle down her spine, and for the first time she understood why Dylan Amos appealed to so many women. It wasn't necessarily his looks; it was his raw sexuality, excess energy and fierce pride, combined with a certain amount of unpredictability.

"*Well?*" she said.

"I would guess she doesn't, since she's never mentioned it," he said. "Does that make you feel less exposed?"

He turned to go again and she grabbed his arm to stop him. Then she realized she was touching him and released her hand. "So how is it that *you*, of all people . . ."

She never finished the question. She didn't need to.

"Maybe I've been watching you a little closer than anyone else." With that he crossed to his motorcycle, which, she wasn't surprised to see, he'd parked illegally.

"Why would you bother?" she called out.

"Why do you think?" he replied. Then he pulled on his helmet and started his bike, leaving her staring after him as he turned around and opened the throttle.

10

"What do you know about Dylan Amos?" Cheyenne asked. She and her sister had been watching TV for the past hour. Presley planned to go out later, but it was only ten o'clock — early by her standards. The parties she attended didn't get started until eleven. Normally she'd be hard-pressed to find one on a Sunday. Even the Amoses had to work during the week. They ran their own collision repair shop just outside town. But it was getting so close to Christmas there was a party almost every night.

"He's beyond sexy," Presley responded. "Why?"

Chey pretended to be absorbed in studying her hands. "You have a thing for him?"

"Doesn't everybody?"

"Not that I've heard."

"Maybe he isn't popular with *your* crowd. But all the women *I* know want him."

Chey refused to speculate on just what

type of woman that would be. She preferred not to acknowledge that her sister was one of them. "You've slept with him?"

Presley screwed up her mouth, apparently puzzling it out. "I don't *think* so."

Chey felt her eyes widen. "You don't *know*?"

"How would I? I don't always pay attention to everything that's going on."

Sometimes Presley was far too honest. . . . "That really scares me, Pres."

"Letting go feels good. You should try it sometime."

Cheyenne wasn't that self-destructive. She'd just decided to drop the subject — her encounter with Dylan was odd and nothing she needed to spend time thinking about — when her sister spoke again.

"What makes you ask about Dylan? You hate the Amoses."

"I don't *hate* them," she said. "I don't even know them."

"You never want me to go over there."

"Because their parties are notorious for sex, drugs and alcohol, any one of which could land you in deep trouble. In short, the Amos brothers are thugs."

"They're *fun*. And I can take care of myself."

That remained to be seen. She hadn't

done such a brilliant job so far. Her inability to make wise decisions kept Cheyenne playing the heavy. "So . . . which of them *have* you slept with?" she asked.

Presley grabbed the remote and paused the program. "Why the sudden interest?"

"I ran into Dylan earlier, at the park."

"And?"

"Nothing, really. He surprised me by saying hello. I didn't think he even knew my name."

"He definitely knows your name. He asks about you all the time."

Cheyenne tucked her hair behind one ear, trying not to stare at Presley. "Why would he do that?"

"You intrigue him."

"*Me*?"

"Yes, you. Every other woman he knows would spread her legs for him in a heartbeat. But you're hard to get, aloof. You treat him like he's not good enough."

"*That's* how I come off?"

"To the Amoses you do. They don't understand that you're just trying to get out of this shit hole, change your life. Anyway, I've already told him he doesn't have a snowball's chance in hell of getting in your pants. You'd think he'd forget about it."

Cheyenne scowled at her. "That's a crude

way of telling him I wouldn't be interested."

Presley rolled her eyes. "You should've been born in a different era. Or to a Quaker family. Sometimes I wonder where the hell you came from."

Her sister had said similar things in the past. Cheyenne had never taken them literally. But the fear that suddenly flickered in Presley's eyes, as if she'd just said something she wished she could retract, made Cheyenne feel that maybe this wasn't a throwaway statement.

"What does that mean?" she asked.

Jumping to her feet, Presley threw the remote on the couch. "Nothing. I have to go."

"Before we finish *Alaska State Troopers*?"

"I've seen enough."

"But you love this show."

"It's getting late."

"Pres!"

Her sister must've heard the serious note in her voice because she stopped and turned. She'd also hunched in on herself as though she was expecting the worst, which set off another alarm in Cheyenne's head.

"What's wrong?"

"Nothing. What makes you ask that?"

Her behavior. "You haven't heard from that private investigator again, have you?"

"No."

"What was his name? Something like Couch . . . or Crouch?"

She waved a dismissive hand. "I don't even remember."

"You have his card."

"I tossed that. No point in keeping it. Mom won't be around long enough to make right whatever she did wrong — or to be punished for some old mistake."

They'd had to increase the dosages on Anita's meds again. She'd been unconscious for the past few hours. "That's true, but . . . shouldn't we at least see what it's about?"

"We'd be foolish to dig up the past."

"You're convinced it's bad?"

"What else could it be? Has there ever been a surprise like that you thought was good?"

No. Definitely not.

Cheyenne shrugged, effectively ending the conversation, and Presley disappeared into her bedroom. When she returned twenty minutes later, she had on thick eyeliner, deep red lipstick and a low-cut blouse with a pair of tight-fitting jeans that left no detail to the imagination. There'd once been a time when Presley was chubby. But those days were gone. If anything, she bordered on too thin. Cheyenne knew her drug use had a lot to do with that.

"Are you going back to the Amoses'? Or somewhere else?" Cheyenne tried to make her tone more conversational than parental, but she knew how the question sounded.

"Does it matter?" she asked, obviously irritated.

"I'd like to know where to look for you if you don't come home."

She gave a dramatic sigh. "I might stop by to see what the Amos guys have going. Don't know if I'll stay."

Her sister's perfume was so strong it burned Cheyenne's nostrils. "Will you be stopping by alone?"

"No. Carolyn from work's planning to hang out with me. We might also go to the Devil's Lair in Jackson."

So she'd have company. That was good news, at least.

Cheyenne turned off the TV. "I worry about you, Presley," she said. "You're two years older than I am. Don't you think it's time to settle down?"

"Don't start," she snapped, and hurried out the door.

Silence fell like an anvil once the door banged shut. Cheyenne told herself she should use this opportunity to get some sleep. She hadn't slept well last night. She'd been too busy wrestling with her conscience over Joe. But she was too listless to go to bed this early.

Leaving the TV off — it was no longer capable of holding her attention — she went into the kitchen and poured herself a glass of the wine Joe had left behind. If only her friends weren't gone. She could've had one or more of them over. Eve often came by to keep her company on the long nights she had to babysit her mother. Sophia and Riley were in town, but Sophia had a husband and a daughter, and Riley had his son, Jacob. She couldn't imagine that the two of them would want to come over and hang with her, not when they had to be at the inn first thing in the morning.

She eyed the phone. She wanted to call Joe, ask him what had gone wrong at the tree farm, why that guy had upset him. Was it related to his divorce as she'd guessed?

Regardless, she had no business breaking down whatever barrier had sprung up between them. That barrier was keeping her safe from herself.

You ever want me to show you what it's like to have a man in your bed, you know where to find me.

Dylan's words ran through her mind, as they had several times since the park. She had no intention of taking him up on his offer, but she had to admit she was curious about what it would be like to finally sleep with a man. She was also beginning to wonder if she was waiting for something that was never going to happen. . . .

Maybe holding off was an excuse not to take the risks that came with getting that close to another human being. Maybe she was so fearful of being categorized as a whore, like her mother, that she was determined to remain above *any and all* accusation, so determined she wasn't leading a normal life.

Or she was as damaged as her sister and was simply reacting to it differently.

That could be it, she thought, but at least *her* response to what she and Presley had been through wouldn't lead to rehab or leave her open to an STD. Her sister didn't even know if she'd slept with Dylan!

Cheyenne shook her head at the craziness of that. But then her gaze drifted to her cell phone and she decided to go ahead and make a call. She wasn't sure where it would lead. It would probably be a terrible mistake. But at least diverting herself in this way would insure that she kept her distance from Joe.

■ ■ ■ ■

Cheyenne had expected to hear a lot of noise in the background. Music, possibly some raucous laughter. But that wasn't the case. When Dylan answered, she could hear him perfectly. A dog barked. Probably one of the two he had with him most of the time. That was it.

She almost hung up as soon as he said hello. But she knew caller ID had already recorded her number. Chickening out would be more embarrassing than saying what she'd devised as her excuse.

"Dylan?"

He went silent, as if the sound of her voice took him completely off guard. The fact that she'd called him surprised her, too.

"It's —" she drew a steadying breath "— it's Cheyenne. Christensen."

"I only know one Cheyenne, Cheyenne Christensen. What can I do for you?"

"I'm sorry to bother you, but . . ." This wasn't going as smoothly as she'd intended. It was one thing to try to keep her mind off Joe; it was another entirely to contact a virtual stranger just because she'd run into him at the park and thought he might be able to ease her loneliness.

"I don't mind," he said, putting the onus of the conversation back on her.

She swallowed, her throat dry. "My sister told me she was coming over again tonight."

More surprise. "You're welcome to come with her, if you want," he said, guessing at the reason behind her call.

That was nice, at least. "I can't. I have to stay here with my mother."

"What about that Mostats-Passuello woman? Doesn't she come over and sit with her sometimes?"

Marcy was a nurse who helped out from time to time. But she had a family. "Once in a while."

"Call her."

"I can't call her this late!"

"So . . ."

"So I was hoping you'd . . . that you'd . . ." Suddenly what she'd rehearsed — *I was hoping you'd look out for my sister while she's there* — promised to come across as so lame she couldn't bring herself to say it. This wasn't the first time Presley had gone over to his place, and he'd already said nothing would happen to her there.

Face burning, she decided to end this as quickly as possible. "Never mind. I shouldn't have interrupted you," she said, and hung up.

"That was colossally stupid." She groaned, pacing back and forth in the kitchen. For all she knew, he was with another woman. "What was I *thinking*?"

She'd been thinking that he was a lot more attractive than she'd given him credit for. That she'd gone long enough without knowing what it felt like to make love to a man. That it didn't matter if she called Dylan, just as long as she didn't call Joe.

But she'd made a fool of herself.

"I'm an idiot," she murmured, and forced herself to go to bed.

Almost two hours later, the doorbell rang. Cheyenne dragged herself from sleep and checked the clock, but it took a moment for the time to register. Two. Who on earth would be at her door in the middle of the night?

She listened to see if the noise had disturbed her mother. But there was no other sound. Anita was so drugged she could probably sleep through the apocalypse. And, apparently, Presley wasn't home yet. That, however, wasn't unusual.

Hopefully, her sister was okay. . . .

Climbing out of bed, Cheyenne grabbed the fluffy robe Eve's parents had given her years ago and shuffled to the front door in matching slippers. There, she peered out the peephole. Then she pressed a panicked hand to her chest. Although the image was somewhat distorted, she recognized the tall, dark figure who stood leaning against the railing.

Dylan.

Cheyenne's heart began to pound so loudly it reverberated in her ears. What was he doing here?

She'd called the devil, and now he'd come calling on her.

"Oh, boy, oh, boy, oh, boy," she breathed, flicking her hands. Did she dare open the door? Would he go away if she didn't?

She hesitated, watching him. He was smoking. She could see the glow of his cigarette.

He waited patiently for a couple of minutes. Then he put out his cigarette and straightened, addressing the door as if he could see her quaking behind it. "Are you going to answer or not?"

Before bed, she'd left the porch light on for Presley, but she'd turned on the living room light when she got up. He knew she was there. It wasn't as if her mother could respond to a visitor.

Should she let him in?

She couldn't decide, didn't know what

she'd say once he was inside. She hadn't consciously committed to *seeing* him. She'd just given in to whatever weakness had made her react to the way she'd felt in the park.

"*Go*," she whispered. But when he stepped off the porch to do just that, she unlocked the dead bolt and poked her head out.

He turned at the sound, stopping a little beyond the circle thrown by the porch light. She wondered if he'd been drinking. He'd been doing *something* in the two hours since she'd called him. But he didn't seem drunk, wasn't at all unsteady.

"Aren't you going to say anything?" she asked when he merely stared at her.

"What do you want me to say?"

"I don't know." Acute anxiety made it difficult to talk. She was shaking, too. Why, she couldn't explain. He hadn't taken so much as a step toward her.

Then she realized how cold he must be. He was wearing the same Levi's jacket he'd had on earlier with a pair of jeans. The worn denim hugged his body in all the right places, but it didn't provide much protection against thirty-degree temperatures.

"Would you like to come in?"

"Is that why you called?"

Not in her conscious mind. She could

never admit it, not even to herself. But she knew she hadn't phoned him to ask if he'd look after her sister as she'd pretended. She'd been hoping he could fill the gap her friends had left. He seemed like a safe substitute. He wasn't part of her circle, wasn't close to anyone who was, and he wasn't likely to judge her. Not only that, but she was pretty sure he could keep a secret. He didn't do a whole lot of talking — about anything. It was other people who talked about *him*.

She shoved back her hair, combing her fingers through it so she wouldn't look like a hag after tossing and turning in bed. Then she breathed deep and swung open the door.

He didn't chuckle at her transparency or taunt her for giving in, as she thought he might. In fact, he said nothing as he walked past her. It was almost as if he was a bit nervous himself.

His gaze cut to the tree, then skimmed over the rest of their threadbare furnishings. But, unlike with Joe, Cheyenne felt no need to apologize for what she lacked. Dylan wouldn't look down on her for her background or her impoverished circumstances. There was something liberating about feeling like an equal, just as there'd been something liberating about standing at the park, knowing that if she acted badly, he wouldn't necessarily regard her as a bad person.

For a second, she was afraid he'd wait for her to come up with some small talk and couldn't think of anything. As much as she must've wanted this — or why would she have called him? — she hadn't rehearsed what would come next.

She owed him an explanation for her unexpected behavior, didn't she?

Probably. But she was grateful he didn't demand one. He reached behind him and turned off the light, plunging the room into semidarkness, with only the porch light filtering in from outside. Then he extended his hand to her.

Cheyenne thought she must be dreaming. Except she couldn't be. If she was, she'd be with Joe and not Dylan Amos.

"Chey?" The vulnerability in his voice told her he was afraid she might reject him. Apparently, he wasn't quite as cocky as he'd seemed at the park.

Butterflies rioted in her stomach as she stared at his outstretched hand. She dared not touch him, but she couldn't bring herself to ask him to leave, either. She stood locked in indecision — until he gave her more encouragement.

"It's okay. I won't take it too far."

"How far is too far?" She heard the breathless quality in her own voice but, at the moment, couldn't seem to speak normally. Her pulse was racing so fast it was making her dizzy.

"Any further than you want to go," he replied. "You call the shots."

She wasn't convinced she could rely on that promise. But if he was dangerous to women, she would've heard about it by now. Her sister went over to his place all the time. When he got in trouble with the law, it was for speeding, fighting, possession of unregistered firearms, setting off illegal fireworks — misdemeanors that suggested he had problems with authority, not women. He'd never been picked up for anything sexual in nature.

"I'd hate to get you excited and then . . . you know, bail out." She swallowed hard. "But I don't know what I want. I'm not even sure why I called you. It took me over an hour to get up the nerve."

"I wondered. But I'm not asking for any kind of commitment." He crooked his fingers, coaxing her. "Why don't we start with a simple kiss?"

A kiss sounded innocuous enough. She wanted to kiss him, didn't she?

Slipping her hand in his, she allowed him to tug her forward. But when his arms went around her, bringing her up against his body, she nearly balked. She didn't know this man. The solid muscular frame, the hair that fell to his shoulders, the eyes that watched her so closely — it was all foreign to her.

But *any* man would feel foreign to her. She hadn't been on a date since Joe's divorce. The last guy she'd kissed had been twenty-five years her senior and had asked permission.

Dylan seemed cautious, as if he was trying hard not to spook her, but he wasn't tentative. He knew what he wanted and was working on the best way to get it.

"You smell like Christmas trees and cigarette smoke," she said as her cheek brushed his.

He rubbed his lips against her ear as he spoke. "I'm sorry. I should quit."

For his health, he should. But he'd misinterpreted her comment. "I don't mind the smell," she admitted. "My mother smoked until recently. Now Presley does. I'm used to it."

"Your mother is . . . where?"

Although he was taller by at least six inches, she fit nicely against him. "In her

161

room. Asleep."

Tilting her head back with both hands, he looked down at her as though he wished he could read her mind, understand her intent. She recalled her earlier opinion — that he had cruel eyes — but they didn't seem cruel tonight. A soft, liquid brown, they held a world of sensual promise, which he began to fulfill when he brought his lips to hers.

Cheyenne didn't resist. The contact felt surprisingly natural, considering how little they knew each other. She liked the feel of his mouth, firm yet soft, moving on hers, so much that she leaned closer and parted her lips.

He groaned as their tongues met, sending a wave of awareness through her that weakened her knees. When she answered with a similar sound, his arms tightened until she could feel his erection against her abdomen.

They'd barely touched and yet they were already getting swept away. It felt as if they'd been waiting for this moment their whole lives.

She slipped her hands into his hair, let the silky strands slide through her fingers. She couldn't taste any alcohol — just spearmint, as if he'd eaten a breath mint on his way over.

"That's it," he murmured as she kissed

him harder. "I can give you what you want."

As he trailed kisses down her throat, his hands found their way inside her robe. She thought he'd immediatcly go for her breasts. They tingled with the desire to be touched. But he slid his palms up her back instead, perhaps to make sure that she was comfortable with such intimacy.

"I've wanted to feel you against me for years," he said.

She didn't know how that could be true. She'd pretty much ignored his existence. But whatever they'd felt before didn't matter. Right now she was drowning in desire, so much so she feared her legs wouldn't have the strength to support her if he let go.

When his hands finally found her breasts, Cheyenne gasped and covered them with her own. A gratified smile told her he took that for the encouragement it was. Kissing her again, he bent her slightly back, then dropped his head to suckle her through the silky fabric of her nightgown.

"Oh . . . that feels amazing," she whispered. How could he bring her to a state of arousal so quickly, so easily? She'd felt nothing but mild affection for Principal Kovinski when they made out after their last date. If not for her fantasies about Joe she would've feared she was frigid. Never had she been tempted beyond her ability to re-sist.

But the fire burning through her veins left no doubt that her body was as healthy and normal as anyone else's. Maybe she was a little late in embracing her sexuality, but the need building inside her was already turn-ing to an expectant throb between her legs.

She wanted to feel Dylan inside her.

It was a shocking revelation, so shocking that she pulled back.

He seemed reluctant to let her go. He stared at her as if he couldn't make himself turn away, but he did — and without com-plaint. When she realized he was leaving, that he thought she'd stomped on the brakes, she caught him by the shoulder.

"No!" she said, and started yanking off his jacket.

She sensed his surprise that he'd misread her intent. Or maybe he was surprised by her sudden aggressiveness. It wasn't like her to be so forward. But she couldn't seem to rein herself in.

Fortunately, he didn't hesitate. He shed his coat. Then he pulled his thermal over his head.

She'd known he had tattoos on his arms. She'd seen them before. There were more on his chest. She couldn't tell what they were in the dark, couldn't see clearly enough. But she didn't really care. Being able to feel him was all that mattered.

As he tossed away his shirt, she explored the sinewy contours of his chest and arms with her hands and mouth. It was insane, inexplicable, but she wanted to do things to him she'd never imagined before, and he didn't seem to mind. She could hear the change in his breathing, knew he was feeling the same crush of excitement.

Then she glanced up and saw the stubborn set to his jaw and realized he was trying to retain control of the situation. "What?" she said.

"This is hard to believe," he explained, but he closed his eyes and dropped his head against the wall when she found his nipple.

"Why?" she murmured against the wet spot she'd made. She was too absorbed to manage a conversation. She didn't want to *think*, anyway. She just wanted to get rid of the rest of his clothes, to feel more of his supple skin.

"You never let *anyone* touch you."

"So?"

"Why me?"

"I don't know."

Apparently, that wasn't an acceptable answer. He grasped her shoulders to stop her long enough to pay attention to what he was saying. "Tell me this isn't a game, that you're not playing me. Tell me you're not going to dangle yourself in front of me and then, at the very last second, shut me down."

Before, he'd acted as if he'd have no problem accepting a refusal at *any* point, if that was what she chose. But his ambivalence was long gone. The spark created by that first kiss had changed everything.

Struggling with the power of her emotions, she bit her lip as she considered his words. "Have you slept with my sister?" It was the one thing that made her uncomfortable, the one thing that threatened to ruin her enjoyment. She couldn't let what she'd started go to its natural conclusion until she knew.

"I told you I haven't." His voice was harsh with need, adamant. "*Ask* her."

Cheyenne didn't want to admit that she'd tried. It didn't matter. He was convincing.

"It's actually been a while since I've been with *anyone*," he added.

"Why?" The way she heard it, he had a new girl every weekend.

"Hit-and-runs get old after a while."

"You seem interested enough now."

"This is different."

She wasn't sure why. Maybe it was because

he couldn't resist relieving her of her innocence. "But you've got a condom, right?"

"I've got a few."

"Then tell me how much you want me," she said. "Tell me I'm the one who makes you hard."

He didn't sound as if he had to pretend. "It's true. I've wanted you for years. Virgin or no. Makes no difference to me."

Was she really going through with this? She'd spoken to him for almost the first time earlier today. Now he stood shirtless in her living room, his hair mussed from her hands, his eyes feral and hungry. And instead of being frightened, repulsed, too uninterested or too shy to continue, all of which she'd experienced with other men, she found him absolutely irresistible.

Maybe she was no different from her mother and sister. She craved physical intimacy with a man she had no emotional commitment to. But she'd been holding back the demands of her body for so long, she didn't seem capable of doing it any longer. Already she was pressing into him, couldn't seem to stop grinding her hips against his erection. It helped that she didn't have to be anyone other than who she was. With this man, she could be completely naked, literally and figuratively, and yet feel safe. He was even aware of her feelings for Joe.

But he still seemed unconvinced that he could trust her, as if he just knew it couldn't be this easy. "Are you sure you want *me*?" he asked. "You won't change your mind? Or regret it later?"

She couldn't promise she wouldn't regret her actions. She had no idea how she'd feel in the morning. But she wasn't going to change her mind. It made no sense that Dylan would be her first — but why not? Eve didn't have dibs on him. Neither did Presley. As far as Cheyenne knew, no one did.

"Sometimes you have to take a chance," she said, and led him to her bedroom.

11

It didn't hurt. Cheyenne had been warned that penetration would be painful the first time. But maybe that was for younger women. Or she'd simply been too drunk on hormones to feel the pain. It didn't matter. What mattered was the pleasure she'd been able to experience, the fact that she could enjoy sex like other women.

"That was incredible," she said as they slumped, exhausted, against the pillows.

"It took a while, but we got there."

She mustered a tired smile. "Because you wouldn't give up."

"I was the only one who knew what was waiting for you."

"I don't think that's supposed to happen during a girl's first time."

"I couldn't see any reason for you to miss out. It just takes figuring out what you like and doing it long enough."

She used her arm to wipe the perspiration

from her forehead. "You certainly figured it out."

"Not immediately. But . . . like I said, we managed it in the end." His teeth flashed when he raised his head to grin at her. "And it was worth the effort, right?"

"It was definitely worth the effort," she agreed with a laugh.

"I'm glad you cooperated. You're far more responsive than I expected. I thought you might be too self-conscious to climax." He rolled over to face her but didn't touch her. "I'm glad I was wrong."

With other guys, she'd been too self-conscious to even get *naked*. But not with him. She wasn't sure what made the difference. "It was time to get the deed done."

"Good thing you got *that* over with."

She laughed at his sarcasm.

"So . . . what?" he asked. "Did I just hit you up at a weak moment or . . ."

He wondered why she'd chosen him after waiting so long, but she couldn't explain. She hadn't figured out the reason herself. "Who knows?" She pulled up the sheet and rolled onto her side, to face him as he was facing her. "Maybe I was tired of being a freak."

He lifted a sweaty tendril of hair off her cheek.

"What?" she said when she noticed the way he was looking at her.

"Being a virgin doesn't make you a freak."

"At thirty-one?"

"Okay, maybe a little bit of a freak," he teased.

She rose up on her elbow. "How many women have *you* slept with?" she asked but then fell back and raised her hand before he could speak. "Never mind. Don't answer that. It's none of my business."

When he didn't comment, she opened one eye so she could see his expression.

His mood seemed to have sobered. "I'm clean if that's what you're worried about."

They'd used the condoms he'd brought, anyway. Fortunately, he'd been prepared, as if he'd guessed the reason behind her call — before she even knew. "Good information to have."

Her mother's voice yanked her out of the euphoria that had descended. "Chey? Cheyenne? Where are you?"

A wave of panic that maybe Anita had overheard them, that they'd given themselves away, brought her crashing back to earth.

Dylan, sensing her reaction, seemed concerned. "Everything okay?"

She forced a smile. "Fine. But I — I have

171

to go take care of my mother. I'm sorry."

"Don't apologize."

"It's awkward timing."

"Trust me, it could've been worse."

She laughed at his meaning. "True."

"Anyway, I admire you for the sacrifices you make for her. I know your sister hasn't helped as much as she should."

Dylan Amos understood how heavy a load she'd been carrying — and sympathized? That said he was more intuitive and understanding than she'd expected. She was beginning to think she'd been wrong about him in a lot of ways. That frightened her, but she couldn't say why.

Suddenly, she wanted him to leave. "Thanks for . . . for everything," she said as she got up. "I hope that's the right thing to say in a situation like this. I haven't had any practice at pillow talk."

"There's no manual."

"Good point. So then I'll say . . . I appreciate your time . . . and your . . . skill with women."

That was a send-off if ever there was one. She wasn't starting a relationship — she was in love with Joe. But he didn't move. He watched her from the bed, as naked and still as a Greek statue. "With *women?*" he repeated dryly.

"Yes. You know how to make sex as . . . exciting as everyone says it should be. That was . . . great. Really great. I'll give you an endorsement if you ever need one."

His tone went flat. "I'd be flattered if you weren't basically telling me to get lost now that we're done."

This wasn't ending as smoothly as she'd hoped, but she'd never had sex with anyone and wasn't sure how to wrap up even an isolated encounter. She'd made that clear, hadn't she? "Like you said, there's no manual. I'm not trying to offend you. I'm just . . ." She was a little panicked by what she'd done, but she didn't think it would be very polite to say that, so she went for something she thought he'd be able to understand. "I'm afraid my sister will come home and see your bike out front."

"Would that be so terrible?" he asked. "Presley certainly isn't someone who could find fault."

She pulled on her robe. "Maybe not, but we live in a small town."

"I'm aware of that."

"Then you know the gossip a lapse like this would cause if she happened to mention it to anyone else."

"That's what it was? A lapse?"

"Other people would see it that way," she

said to avoid answering more directly.

"Who cares? What can they do? *Talk?*"

"Yes. I realize it wouldn't hurt your reputation, but it could do permanent damage to mine." And her reputation was all she had, the only way she could differentiate herself from her mother and sister.

"So . . . being with me would cheapen you."

She blinked at him. "*Sleeping* with you, yes. Don't say it like I'm acting superior. That isn't the case. I've grown up on the same side of the tracks as you have."

He got out of bed and began jerking on his clothes. "Yeah, but I'm not ashamed of it."

"Maybe you didn't have a mother who hooked for a living."

"You're right." His eyes grew flinty; she could see the shine to them, even in the darkness. "I didn't have a mother at all, at least not for long."

Cheyenne should never have brought this up. His life had been as difficult as hers. When his mother took an overdose of sleeping pills and died only five or six years after Mack was born, his father started drinking and, according to all the rumors, he was one mean drunk. Cheyenne was a sophomore, Dylan a senior, when J.T. knifed a man in a bar and went to prison. It was Dylan who'd dropped out of school to take over the family's auto body shop, Dylan who had cared, all these years, for his four younger brothers. His father was still incarcerated.

"I'm sorry." She took a shaky breath. She was out of her element, or she wouldn't have been so insensitive.

His lips, which had kissed her so tenderly just minutes before, twisted into a snarl. "I'm not looking for your pity."

"Then what do you want from me?" she asked softly. "I thought I already gave it to you."

He shook his head. "I don't want anything more. Why would I? You're committed to someone else. Someone who doesn't give a shit about you, by the way."

She winced at the harshness of his words but he spoke the truth. "I've been in love with Joe since I was fourteen, Dylan. Whether or not he returns my interest doesn't seem to make any difference, although I wish it did."

"Fourteen, huh?" He zipped his jeans but didn't button them before putting on his boots. "That's pretty tough to compete with. I don't know what the hell *I* was thinking."

When he chuckled without mirth, she got the impression he was kicking himself for coming over, and she wasn't sure how to react to that. She'd never imagined that *he* might regret being with *her*. Judging by some of the wild stories she'd heard, women were merely toys to the Amos men, interchangeable.

"I'm sorry," she repeated. His shirt was in the living room, where they'd left it earlier. She wanted to get it for him. He looked far too good without it, even now that she was thinking clearly. But she held back. "I never dreamed you'd take this seriously, not when you have so many other women to . . . to sleep with."

He pushed his hair out of his face. "Yeah, well, I guess I was lying when I said it'd been a long time. Or . . . maybe I'm not as shallow as you choose to believe."

Cheyenne felt helpless in the face of his disappointment. She could see how her words and actions came across. She'd taken too much for granted. She'd used him without a thought about how that might make him feel because she'd assumed he was using her, too. "I'm not accusing you of being *shallow*. I thought you'd be satisfied with getting . . . you know . . . lucky, that's all. From what I've heard —"

"Just because you hear it doesn't make it true," he broke in. "The people who spend so much time talking about me don't even know me. And I won't live my life trying to please them. Whiskey Creek's fine, upstanding citizens would never accept me even if I did."

"You're the one who made the offer in the park!" she snapped, finally rallying. "It wasn't as if *I* propositioned *you*."

"Thanks for the reminder. It's always good to know I can blame myself when I do something stupid."

She felt like he'd just slapped her. "Why do you have to blame anyone? We had fun, didn't we? Can't we leave it at that? I mean, we barely know each other —"

"We've known each other for seventeen *years*, Cheyenne."

"We've never hung out together! So this can't really matter that much!"

Suddenly, he was the implacable, indifferent man she'd seen around town wearing a sardonic half grin as his gaze trailed after her. "It doesn't. It doesn't matter at all. Call up Joe tomorrow and see if he can satisfy you any better. Maybe you'll decide this actually sucked."

"I already said it was good. I —"

"Who's there?" Her mother, voice ragged

with weakness and pain, interrupted. "Presley? Cheyenne? Where are you? I've yanked out . . . my damn catheter."

Dylan waved her out of the room. "Go take care of her."

Cheyenne felt she had no choice but to do exactly that. She couldn't leave Anita lying in a bed soaked with urine. "Wait here . . . so we can talk, okay? Let's not end the night like this."

"If you wanted to end it better, maybe you should've held out for someone who was on your list of possibilities."

She swallowed hard. "I — I don't know what to say."

"You don't have to say anything."

"Don't go away mad." This wasn't the memory she wanted to carry with her from her first time. Everything had gone so well, until now. Somehow, she'd miscalculated, had no idea *she'd* been on *his* list of possibilities.

"Just . . . hold on, okay?" She could convince him to be her friend, if only he'd give her the opportunity, she thought as she hurried to fix Anita's problem. But she heard his motorcycle roar to life while she was still in her mother's room and knew, as the sound dimmed, that he hadn't bothered to wait.

■ ■ ■ ■

"You're quiet today." Riley bent to get a better look at her face. "You okay?"

Cheyenne glanced up from the computer in her small office off the inn's kitchen. "I'm fine, why?"

She'd come to research some recipes and create a whole new menu for when they opened in January. The printer would take a week, maybe longer over the holidays, so she wanted to get the process started. But in the four hours she'd been at the B and B, she'd accomplished nothing. While Riley and his son made a racket enlarging the bathroom on the second floor, she'd been replaying every second of her time with Dylan.

Even now, hours after the big event, she couldn't help blushing at the memory of the words he'd whispered, telling her how beautiful she was, how good she felt, how much he wanted her. Then there was the memory of his strong hands on her thighs as he guided her movements the second time they'd made love. That was when she'd really relaxed and begun to enjoy herself.

She wasn't sure whether to be embarrassed or relieved that she'd finally dispensed with her virginity, mortified or grateful that she'd chosen Dylan to be the one. Allowing him to remove her clothes, and removing his, was completely out of character for her. She felt she should regret it. And yet . . . regret played no part in her reactions. At least not yet.

Why? He wasn't the man of her dreams, but once she'd led him into her bedroom, she never considered backing out. She couldn't have, even if she'd tried. She'd been too caught up in what he was doing to her — and what she wanted to do to him.

Was it normal to desire a stranger like that? Someone she wouldn't ordinarily date?

She'd never found Dylan particularly handsome. She went for the uncomplicated type, the all-American athlete, like Joe. But she had to admit that Dylan was . . . raw and edgy and quite magnetic.

Riley clicked his tongue. "There you go again."

"Excuse me?"

"You're staring off into space."

She forced a laugh. "I'm sorry. I've got a lot on my mind."

"I don't want you to be sorry. I want you to be okay. I promised Eve I'd look after you."

Chey folded her arms. It was a protective

gesture designed to create a buffer between her and someone who knew her well enough to be able to tell when she was lying. "And you're doing your job."

He wiped the demolition dust from his arms as he responded. "No, something's wrong. I can tell. We've been friends almost since you moved to town, remember?"

She glanced at his son, Jacob, who'd come up behind him and seemed to be awaiting her answer as if he was one of her close friends, too. Even if she'd been tempted to tell Riley about Dylan, to see if he thought she'd screwed up as badly as *she* told herself she had, she couldn't say in front of a young teen that she'd had sex with Dylan Amos. Since Riley had asked her what was wrong in his son's presence, he obviously had no clue how private the real problem was. But then, he knew she wasn't seeing anyone, so he had no reason to suspect it might deal with her sex life.

"I didn't get much sleep," she mumbled.

He frowned in sympathy. "Your mother's getting worse, isn't she?"

With a sigh, Cheyenne rubbed her eyes. Anyone would think she'd be completely preoccupied with her mother's situation. Instead, she'd chosen last night to invite a man she barely knew into her bed. "That's

181

part of it." *Only one part, and not the biggest . . .*

"You don't have to stay here today. I've got the architectural drawings. We know what we're doing. If we run into a problem, I can call you."

"I realize that. But . . . I have things to do." She looked around the six-by-eight office, with its wainscoting and custom cabinetry. This place was her refuge; she didn't want to be at home.

"Dad, can I have a soda?" Jacob asked.

He'd been asking all day, but he always got the same answer.

"No, soda's full of sugar," Riley said, and sent him out to the Explorer to get a power saw.

Once his son was gone, Riley came closer and lowered his voice, which alarmed Cheyenne. For a second, she thought maybe he'd seen her with Joe yesterday, or he'd stopped by late to check on her, and found Dylan's bike in the drive.

"You've never heard anything . . . strange here, have you?" he asked. "You don't *really* believe the inn could be haunted."

She'd heard plenty of strange noises. Some seemed to have no logical explanation. But they didn't frighten her. When she was here alone, she talked to Mary like she had that night in the cemetery. She figured if Mary was around and could hear her, maybe it would bring the girl some peace to be acknowledged. And if Mary's ghost wasn't lingering, there wasn't anyone around to take notice of her actions, anyway. "A few. Why?"

"It's unnerving, don't you think?"

"What have you heard?"

"A door at the end of the hall swung shut just after we arrived. I went to see who was there, assuming it was you, but the room was empty."

"You might also see some billowing drapes."

"You mean when the windows aren't open."

"Exactly."

"That's some crazy shit," he said, shaking his head. "But . . . I guess both could be explained by the draftiness of an old building. You've never actually *seen* anything, an . . . apparition or . . . or something besides billowing drapes or a closing door, have you?"

"No. But I've heard a girl weeping."

His eyes widened. "You kiddin' me? Why haven't you ever said so?"

She shrugged.

"Is it loud?"

"Loud enough. And sometimes Mary whispers to me."

He crouched to get on an even level with her. "*No . . .*"

"Yes."

"What does she say?"

She lowered her voice. "That anyone who stays here isn't safe."

He gaped at her for several seconds before he realized she was teasing him. Then he cocked his head to one side, slapped his leg and stood. "Very funny."

She laughed as she checked behind him to be sure Jacob hadn't returned. "How well do you know Dylan Amos?" she asked.

"Not well. But I've heard a few things." He shook some dust from his hair. "Dude's had a hard life. Why?"

"Does he do drugs?"

"No idea. His brother's been busted for dealing meth, but I heard Dylan kicked his ass for it the last time."

"Dylan gets into trouble, too, doesn't he?"

"Mostly for fighting his brothers' battles. He's fiercely protective. Why?" he repeated. "Presley still hanging out with the Amoses?"

Cheyenne felt grateful that she could nod; she also felt a bit guilty, knowing her nod would be misleading.

"That can't be good."

"It's not. But she claims Dylan is different from the others."

"Could be."

"If that's the truth, why does he have such a bad reputation?"

"He's all those boys have had by way of a parent. Could be he's taking the blame for whatever goes on over there, whether he deserves it or not."

She bit her lip as she considered this. "Ever been to one of their parties?"

"Years ago."

"What was it like?"

"Their place isn't bad. It could definitely use a woman's touch, but it's cleaner than you'd expect and functional. Somehow Dylan's managed all these years."

Jacob returned with the saw. "Got it, Dad!"

Riley hooked his kid around the neck and gave him a fatherly squeeze. "Good. Let's get back to work, chief."

Jacob headed upstairs but Riley hesitated. "What are you doing for Christmas?"

Cheyenne had already turned back to her computer. "Just taking care of my mother. Presley's got to work. She agreed to a couple of extra shifts over the holidays to get time and a half."

"That'll make a nice paycheck."

"I hope so." The way her sister went through money, she needed all she could get. Chey still wasn't sure how she'd be able to afford the funeral expenses once Anita passed away. Fortunately, the state was paying for her mother's medical care.

"Why don't you come to dinner at my folks'?" he asked. "No one can cook a turkey like my mom."

She smiled to show her gratitude, but she doubted she could get anyone to stay with Anita on Christmas Day. Marcy Mostats-Passuello would want to be with her own family.

Cheyenne would feel too guilty leaving, anyway. "I'll make myself something to eat. No worries."

"The invitation stands, in case you change your mind."

She smiled. "Thanks."

He turned back again. "Are you *sure* you're okay? There's nothing wrong?"

Cheyenne felt as if she had a scarlet *S* for *slut* tattooed on her forehead. But she denied feeling anything out of the ordinary. "No. Why?"

He didn't explain. He scowled as he said, "You'd let me know if you needed me?"

"Of course."

With a nod, he left and she released her

breath. But then her cell phone rang. She expected it to be her sister, asking Cheyenne to pick up some food on her way home. It couldn't be Eve or any of her friends. Their cell phones didn't work out of country.

But it wasn't Presley; it was Joe.

12

He was back. Presley couldn't believe it, but as she peered out the peephole she saw Eugene Crouch. He'd found their home! What a way to start the week. . . .

Feeling slightly drugged from sleep — it was his knock that had awakened her — she leaned against the front door, wondering what to do. Her first inclination was to act as if she wasn't home so he'd go away. But she was afraid that would only make him come back at a time when he might run into Cheyenne.

If that ever happened, Cheyenne would never forgive Anita. And she'd never forgive Presley for lying. Now that Presley had made the decision to keep her mother's filthy secret, she had no choice but to stick to what she'd already said.

Heart pounding, she hurried to Anita's room. Her mother was asleep so Presley couldn't warn her to stay quiet. She could only pray that Anita wouldn't choose the next five minutes to wake up and start shouting for one thing or another.

"God help me," she muttered as she returned, without so much as a robe, to the living room. She didn't care if Mr. Crouch saw her in the sweatshirt and boxers she'd slept in. She wanted to get rid of him as fast as possible.

Cracking open the door, she squinted against the blinding sunshine as she peered out. "You *again*?"

He didn't seem pleased to see her, either. Obviously, he'd hoped for better results than what he'd gotten at the casino. "I'm sorry. I'm still trying to locate —"

"Someone I don't know. I remember." She rested her head against the doorjamb. "What was her name?"

"Anita. Anita Christensen. Although that's not her only name."

She scratched her head. "Right. There were others. None of which I recognized. I got that, but apparently you didn't."

He studied her closely. "I have a court document giving this as her address."

A fresh wave of fear swept through Presley. "What kind of court document?" she asked, but was still pretending it couldn't apply to them, still playing her role.

189

He pulled a file out of his briefcase and showed her a Summons and Complaint from a bill collector who'd sued her mother for nonpayment of a credit card three years ago. It wasn't dissimilar to others Presley had seen through the years.

Her mind raced as she pretended to read it. He wouldn't believe her if she said that document was in error. In trying to track down Anita, he'd bumped into her twice. Obviously, they had some connection.

So what now? She couldn't let him in — or could she? Presley wasn't sure how he seemed to know Anita had taken Cheyenne, but would it be possible to convince him she no longer had any association with the child in that picture? It had been a long time. They could've parted years ago, when Cheyenne turned eighteen and became an adult, if not sooner.

"Well?" he said.

Presley cleared her throat. "Fine." She used a grudging tone. "I'm sorry I lied to you. Anita is my mother. But . . . she's dying of cancer. I didn't see any point in letting another bill collector come after her when she's on her deathbed. I'm sure you can understand why I'd feel protective."

His expression didn't say he understood; it said he didn't believe her. "She's dying."

He might as well have added, "Yeah, right."

"Yes."

"Of cancer."

She nodded. "Any day now."

"Listen, I'm not a bill collector. I'm looking for a little girl named Jewel who was —" he tempered his voice as if he was unwilling to make an actual accusation "— seen in your mother's company twenty-seven years ago."

Jewel. Was that Cheyenne's real name? Jewel what? Presley wondered, but she tried to appear unaffected by this information. Although she'd initially felt some sorrow for Chey's other family, her first family, she felt nothing but anger and panic now. If they didn't back off, she'd lose her only sister. And *she* certainly needed Chey more than they did. They'd lived without her this long. . . .

"I was six then," she said. "I don't remember any little girl suddenly appearing. But . . . I'm not lying about my mother's health. You can see for yourself if you want."

He straightened. "I can?"

"Why not?"

"When?"

Gripping the doorknob so hard she couldn't feel her fingers, she glanced behind her, into the house to take a quick survey of what he might see. "Right now."

His eagerness was as apparent as his surprise. "That'd be wonderful. I'd very much appreciate the chance to talk to her. Thank you."

Presley motioned toward her bare legs. "Give me a minute to get dressed."

"No problem. Take your time."

Forever polite, she thought, and shut the door. Then she hurried from room to room, looking for pictures of Cheyenne. They didn't have many. Just one on the mantel of Chey with her friends and a few in Chey's bedroom, which he wasn't going to see.

She dropped and broke the picture frame on the mantel as she took it down, but she didn't have time to clean up the glass. Leaving it, she shoved that photograph and all the others under Cheyenne's bed before closing off that part of the house.

After pulling on a pair of sweat bottoms, she ran to her mother's bedside. "Mom, wake up," she said, jiggling her arm.

Anita moaned but didn't open her eyes. "What? Ow! Don't shake me. Are you here with my meds? I need morphine. I think you missed my last dosage. The pain's terrible. . . ."

Presley had slept through her alarm over an hour, but she counted that as a blessing.

Now Anita might be coherent enough to convince this man that they no longer had any contact with the child he was searching for.

Maybe his appearance at this particular moment wasn't a bad thing. Maybe it was a golden opportunity to put this frightening issue behind them for good.

"Listen to me." Presley squeezed her hand. "I'll get you all the morphine you want. You'll soon be high as a kite. But first you have to help me."

Anita's eyes opened. They were glazed with pain, but she seemed to understand the urgency in Presley's voice and manner. "Wh-what can *I* do? You see me here . . . good for nothin' . . ."

There was no time to waste. She didn't want Mr. Crouch to get suspicious while waiting on their doorstep, not after she'd gained a bit of trust by offering to prove her words. "That P.I. — Eugene Crouch — he's at our door."

"*Now?*"

Thank God she was lucid. "Yes! I told him you didn't live here but he had proof. So this is what we're going to do. I'll show him in, and you'll tell him that Cheyenne ran away when she was sixteen and you've never seen or heard from her since. Only you're not going to call her Cheyenne. Cheyenne is now my best friend, a roommate who helps me take care of you and pay the rent, if that name comes up. Do you understand?"

When she didn't seem to be tracking what Presley was saying, Presley's panic leaped to a whole new level. "Mom! I need you to think straight. Please do your best. Five minutes. Can you give me five minutes? Can you fight the pain? Tell the man I bring in here that the girl you stole ran away years ago. Will you do that?"

Her tongue wet cracked, dry lips. "I'll . . . try," she said, and groaned as she closed her eyes.

"Try. She'll try," Presley muttered to herself, and hoped to hell trying would be enough.

When she returned to collect Mr. Crouch, she found him sitting patiently on the porch in the old kitchen chair she used to smoke. He picked up his briefcase and stood, smoothing the wrinkles from his slacks before following her inside.

"If your mother is as sick as you say, I'm sorry to intrude," he said.

She didn't respond. Her heart was in her throat. She shut the door and waved for him to cross the living room.

He trailed after her, glancing around, taking note of everything he saw. She hoped she hadn't missed some detail that would give her away, but she couldn't imagine what that might be. It'd been at least twenty-seven years since the picture he'd shown her was taken. Chances were he could run right into Cheyenne and not recognize her.

When Presley ushered him into Anita's room, he frowned to find her every bit as badly off as he'd been told. This type of illness could not be faked. Anita was so pale, so feeble, Presley wondered if he saw *any* similarity to the woman he'd been looking for, especially now that she had no teeth.

"Mom, this is Mr. Crouch, that P.I. I told you about."

Anita opened her eyes but didn't speak. Presley hoped she'd been saving her strength — and that she hadn't already forgotten what she was supposed to say.

Clutching his briefcase with both hands, Mr. Crouch approached her bed. "Ms. Christensen?"

Again, Anita gave no response, but she didn't deny her own name, and he must've recognized her, because there was a hint of satisfaction in his demeanor.

"I've been searching for you for a long,

long time," he said.

She showed no surprise.

"You've already guessed why," he added.

Anita nodded.

"Where is she?"

"Gone." Her mother's voice, when she finally used it, shocked even Presley, it was so weak.

He froze. "Gone where?"

Presley dug her fingernails into her palms. There wasn't much she could do now — except trust her mother to lie as well as she always had.

Anita struggled for breath. "Who can . . . say?"

Sensing Mr. Crouch's disappointment, Presley almost applauded. Her mother deserved an Oscar for this performance.

"What happened to her?" he pressed. "Where I can find Jewel?"

Anita pulled the blankets higher. "I don't . . . know."

Shoulders slumping, he set his briefcase on the chair by the bed. "Why not?"

"She . . . ran away. Haven't . . . heard from her since."

Presley feigned distress. "Mom, what are you talking about? It was *Connie* who ran away just before we moved here, when we were in Bakersfield. Connie, remember?

Not someone named Jewel." She turned to him. "I'm afraid she's not making any sense. My sister ran away. My mother must be confused. The meds do that sometimes."

"No." He gripped his forehead, rubbing his temples. "I don't think she's confused."

Presley stared at him. "Excuse me?"

He opened his mouth, then hesitated. The compassion that flickered in his eyes made her feel bad for misleading him. With her mother dying, he didn't want to tell her that the person she'd always believed to be her sister really wasn't.

"It doesn't matter now," he said. "If you could just . . . tell me the name she was using when she left. Was it Connie Christensen?"

Anita spoke up. "Who knows? She had a —" gasp, rattle, breath "— boyfriend. A no-good loser named Ben. Ben Sumner. For all we know —" gasp, rattle, breath "— she married him. Or she picked a name out of a hat . . . so we wouldn't . . . be able to find her."

His lips thinned. "That's unfortunate."

When they didn't comment, he tried asking a few more questions — the names of the cities where they'd been living before "Connie" left, if they had any idea where she might have gone, if she had any tattoos or piercings that could help identify her. He even asked about dental work and broken bones, as if he planned to check the morgues for every Jane Doe.

This guy was nothing if not thorough. But telling him part of the truth was making him believe they were telling him the whole of it. Presley knew from her mother's example that it was the best way to lie.

They said she had a mermaid tattoo covering most of her midsection, and a scar on one arm from falling into a tub of scalding water when she was six. They said she'd pierced her nose and dyed her hair black, creating an image about as far from the real Cheyenne as they could get. And when he was finally satisfied that he'd obtained all the information he could, they lied again by accepting his card and promising to call if they ever heard from her.

Cheyenne didn't answer her phone. It was Joe. Again. This was his second attempt in the past thirty minutes. According to his earlier message, he wanted to apologize for his inexplicable behavior yesterday. But she'd ignored his first call and intended to ignore this one. She had her own inexplicable behavior to worry about, preferred to forget that they'd ever played cards or shopped for a Christmas tree. She'd drifted into dangerous waters there, but now that she had her wits about her, she was going to be very careful not to make any more mistakes.

She waited until the call transferred to voice mail, then checked to see if he'd left another message.

Chey, Joe again. Listen, like I said before, I'm really sorry about yesterday. That guy . . . I didn't explain but . . . my ex-wife and he . . . well, you've probably guessed the situation by now. He was part of the reason for my divorce. But that's my problem, not yours. Please forgive me and say you'll let me make it up to you. I'd like to take you to that Victorian Christmas event going on this week.

She imagined wandering through the streets with him, enjoying the lights and music and the various foods sold by street vendors. There'd be roasted chestnuts and spiced apple cider and smoked turkey legs. Artists and crafters would be selling their wares. She looked forward to A Victorian Christmas every year. The celebration started in Sutter Creek, then moved to a new town in Gold Country every night before ending in Whiskey Creek.

She would love nothing more than to go with him, but . . .

Closing her eyes, she let her head fall into her hands. She couldn't do it. On Saturday she'd told him she was a virgin. On Sunday, she'd slept with Dylan Amos, a guy who just happened to proposition her in the park.

She wasn't good enough for someone like Joe. He was better off with Eve.

Her phone rang again. This time it *was* Presley, so she answered.

"Hey," her sister said.

"What's up?"

"I was just wondering when you might be getting home tonight."

Cheyenne checked the time on her computer. It was almost eight. Riley and Jacob had brought her some takeout from Barry's Burgers and left two hours ago. "Don't know. Why? I thought you didn't have to work."

"I don't. I wanted to tell you there's no rush. If you'd like to go out, you know, do something fun, I'll take care of Mom."

"*Really?*" Cheyenne didn't mean to act so surprised, but Presley abandoned Anita whenever she could. Cheyenne cut her some slack because she knew Anita's decline was harder on her sister, but she was sure there were times Presley said she had to work when she didn't.

"Really. She's having a good night and so am I."

"I'm . . . glad to hear it."

"So what will you do?"

Cheyenne had no idea. Riley and Jacob were beat after putting in nearly twelve hours of exhausting physical labor. They were planning to be back by six in the morning, so they were probably hoping to get to bed early.

"I'll stop over and say hello to Eve's parents. Then I'll drop by Sophia's. If her husband's out of town, maybe she'll want to watch a movie with me."

"You've got a pretty good chance of Skip being gone. He's always gone."

"Because he's such a big deal, right?" Cheyenne smiled. They made fun of Sophia's husband all the time. He was so full of himself. But he was pretty adept at making money. He traveled the world, raising funds for various venture capital partnerships. Almost everyone in Whiskey Creek invested with him. If they had enough money. He'd never give anyone who lived in the river bottoms a second of his time.

"A legend in his own mind," Presley replied.

Covering a yawn, Cheyenne leaned back. She hadn't realized how tired she was, but it made sense, given how little sleep she'd had last night. "Thanks for looking after Mom, Pres. I appreciate the break."

"No problem. Have fun."

After they hung up, Cheyenne drummed her fingers on the desk, trying to decide whether or not she'd really go to Sophia's. She was tempted to call Joe back. She was also tempted to call Dylan. She felt terrible about how things had ended, wanted to apologize to him as Joe had apologized to her.

But she'd be better off to leave both men alone.

She powered down her computer, gathered up her purse and turned off the lights.

A creak from above made her pause, but she didn't go to investigate. She knew she wouldn't find any reason for it.

"Good night, Mary," she said, and smiled as she let herself out.

Dylan sat in front of the television, his two dogs — a chocolate lab and a golden retriever mix he'd rescued from the local shelter five years ago — at his feet. But he wasn't paying much attention to the MMA match his brothers had rented on pay-per-view. He liked cage fighting as much as they did. In the early years, when he'd first taken over his father's business and it wasn't making enough to support them, he earned extra money by competing. Now he occasionally went to the gym in Jackson, but he didn't fight. Training just gave him a way to stay in shape.

He should've been more interested in what he was seeing but, thanks to his visit to Cheyenne's house last night, he'd had to work at the shop for twelve hours on virtually no sleep and didn't have his usual energy. The only thing that kept him from drifting off right there in his recliner was the hope that Cheyenne's sister would show up. He was eager to hear whether or not Cheyenne had let anything slip. How was she today? Had she told Presley she'd finally slept with someone? Or was she still determined to keep it to herself?

Probably what he wanted to know most was: Did she regret what they'd done?

"Want a cigarette?" Aaron held out a pack of Marlboros, but Dylan shook his head. He hadn't had a smoke all day.

"No, I quit."

"You *what?*"

"I said I quit." He knew how damaging it was to his health. He wasn't sure why he'd ever started, except that, once upon a time, cigarettes had given him something to do with his hands when he felt like throwing punches. The nicotine calmed him. Back then, he'd figured smoking was the lesser of two evils. But he was beyond needing that crutch — wasn't he?

"Since when?" Aaron asked.

Mack, Grady and Rod stared at him, too. Even the dogs, Shady and Kikosan, pricked their ears forward.

"Since today."

Rod paused the TV. "What brought this on?"

"Maybe I don't want to get lung cancer, okay?" He didn't know why they had to make a big deal out of it.

They glanced at one another as if he'd just said he was moving to the moon.

"What the heck?" Grady said. "You just had me buy a whole case at Costco."

Dylan didn't want to be reminded of that, and he didn't want to be questioned about his decision. "So? Aaron smokes."

"Only once in a while," Rod said. "And only when *you're* having a cigarette."

"Then we'll throw the damn things away. Nobody *has* to smoke them."

Shady barked, obviously sensing the shift of emotions in the room.

"It's just kind of sudden," Grady said. "That's all."

"And it's because they're unhealthy?" Now Rod was getting into the act.

Dylan gave him a disgruntled look that warned them all to back off. "That's right."

Aaron, of course, didn't back off. He leaned forward. "But they were unhealthy when you started."

"So you're going to give me the third degree?" He preferred not to smoke anymore. So what? It *was* bad for his health. But that wasn't all. He couldn't see Cheyenne with anyone who smoked. Certainly no one in her crowd lit up, except her mother and sister — both people she didn't respect. He couldn't dismiss that, or the fact that she'd mentioned the smell last night, although she'd claimed it didn't bother her. He just didn't want his brothers to know it had taken a woman to make him quit, hated to admit it even to himself. He was stupid to care about Cheyenne. Until yesterday, she'd never paid him any attention. She'd been too busy chasing Joe, thought he was so much better.

So why had she given *him* her virginity? Why not Joe? Dylan couldn't imagine any available male turning her away. She could easily have chosen another man. But she hadn't, and he couldn't regret taking what she'd offered him. There were moments he wanted to believe he wouldn't waste any more time or energy on a woman who'd counted him out before really giving him a chance, but . . . he'd make love to her again if only she showed interest. He couldn't lie to himself about that.

"Fine," Aaron said.

Mack shrugged. "I'm glad. I've been at you for months."

"Then that's why," Dylan grumbled. "For you."

The volume on the TV went up, the dogs lay down and the MMA fight continued. But as the minutes slipped away with no one coming to the door, Dylan finally asked his brothers what he wanted to know. "Presley coming over later? Or does she have to work?"

"No clue," Mack responded, eyes glued to the TV. He obviously didn't care one way or another. Like Dylan, he'd never found Cheyenne's sister appealing. It was Aaron who liked her. They'd been sleeping together for the past several weeks. Dylan thought they might be drifting toward a relationship. Aaron invited her over often enough, but it could be hard to tell what he was thinking. Aaron had been the most difficult of his brothers to raise. He was always getting into trouble.

"Aaron? You heard from her?" he asked.

Aaron glanced over. "Who?"

"Presley."

"No. Why?"

"I thought she might be coming over."

"Haven't talked to her."

The fight on TV ended with a knockout. That might've been exciting except it happened far too soon to satisfy the eager crowd who'd gathered in the living room.

"That sucks," Mack complained.

Rod snapped off the TV. "I don't care if Nero's had a dozen knockouts. He's a pussy. I can't believe he went down so easy. He had the guy in an arm bar, for hell's sake, and allowed him to escape."

"That fight was all hype," Grady agreed.

Aaron unfolded his long body and rose to his feet. "Forget the fight. The night's young. Let's go over to Sexy Sadie's and see what we can find."

"You 'find' a fight, I'm not coming to save your asses," Dylan said.

Mack turned toward him. "You staying here?"

Dylan nodded as he petted Kikosan, who'd stuck her snout into his lap. "You're on your own tonight," he said, but at twenty-one, Mack was the baby of the family, more like a son than a brother. If he got into trouble, Dylan would go through hell or high water to get him out and everyone knew it. As far as that went, he felt just as strongly about the others, even Aaron, who'd caused him so much grief. "Keep a level head."

Grady nudged his foot. "Come with us, Dyl."

"Naw, I'm beat," he said, but as soon as they were gone, he found the energy to go outside and walk with the dogs to the edge of the clearing, where he could see Cheyenne's house. He wanted to catch a glimpse of her driveway, see if her Oldsmobile was there, but it wasn't.

13

It wasn't quite eleven when Cheyenne started home. She'd spent the evening with Sophia, watching a movie, talking, eating — doing whatever she could to distract herself from thoughts of Joe or Dylan. She got the impression that Sophia was as lonely as she was. At least, she'd welcomed the company. Cheyenne wished she could rely on having Sophia for companionship over the rest of the holidays, but she and her daughter were flying to Hawaii in the morning to meet Skip, who was having his parents join them on Oahu.

"Must be nice." She imagined warm, sunny beaches as she turned toward the river bottoms. But she wasn't truly jealous. After several hours in Sophia's presence she felt more like herself than she had in days, which was why she felt so surprised when she drove past her own driveway.

A half mile farther down the road was

Dylan's place, a brick house with a big yard, two dogs that must be in the house because they weren't out and several old oak trees draped with the mistletoe that grew naturally in their branches. His lot sloped down to meet the river behind it and included several outbuildings — a shed, a chicken coop, a workshop and a barn. She'd never seen the barn for herself, but she'd heard Presley talk about the gym they'd set up in there.

Cheyenne knew she'd have to deal with Joe at some point. He was the brother of one of her best friends and circulated among the same people she did. It was rude — beyond rude — to ignore his calls. She'd already decided she'd speak to him in the morning, assure him she wasn't upset and politely decline his offer to go out.

But Dylan was a different story. There were no expectations between them. She could return to her regular life and forget him. He'd given her that option when he left without finishing their conversation. She doubted he'd ever contact her again.

If only she didn't feel so terrible about the way she'd brushed him off . . .

Frustrated by her vigilant conscience, which wouldn't let her rest until she'd apologized, she parked on the road in front of his place.

The house was dark. At first she thought she'd come too late, everyone was asleep. Dylan's Jeep sat in the garage with his motorcycle parked beside it. She could see both vehicles because the garage door was up. When they were home, they rarely bothered to close it, probably because they came and went so often. But then she noticed that Grady's SUV was gone and guessed that some, if not all, of the Amoses were out.

What should she do? Forget about seeking any kind of resolution and go home?

No doubt, but she preferred to get this behind her. So she called Dylan's cell to ask if he'd stop by on his way past her place, or maybe talk to her on the phone.

"Hello?" He sounded groggy when he answered, which told her he hadn't gone out with his brothers. She'd awakened him.

"It's me."

He took a breath she could hear. "That's the only reason I answered."

"I thought you were mad at me."

"That doesn't mean I haven't been hoping you'd call."

His deep voice brought back every sensation she'd experienced when he was in her bed.

"I'm, um . . ." She fought the sexual awareness flowing through her, along with the intimate memories. She didn't want to cause herself more problems. "I shouldn't have called so late. Would you rather we talked tomorrow?"

There was a brief pause. "That depends."

"On what?" she asked, but she already knew the answer. She could tell by his tone.

"On whether or not you really just want to talk."

She told herself to apologize and be done with it. She should not accept the invitation in his voice. But the words stuck in her throat. Desire had come out of nowhere and easily overtaken remorse. "I'm sitting in front of your house."

"Does that mean what I think it does?"

Leaning her head against the headrest, she closed her eyes. "Yes."

"I'll meet you at the door," he said, and hung up.

He was waiting for her when she reached the stoop. Wearing nothing but a hastily donned pair of jeans that were neither zipped nor buttoned, he held back the dogs so she could come in, and she realized in an instant that she found him even more attractive tonight than she had before.

How had she missed his appeal? His face was so much more intriguing than other men's, so rugged. . . .

"I told myself I was coming to apologize about last night," she whispered as she slipped past the dogs.

"But . . ."

"I could've done that earlier, on the phone. I didn't need to come traipsing over here after eleven."

He shut the door. "This isn't about the 'I'm sorry' part of last night."

"What's it about?" She really wanted to know. She'd never imagined she'd be having an affair with Dylan Amos. That was her sister's territory. Or so she'd thought.

"The other part," he said. "This way."

He turned, but she didn't follow. She remained in his front entryway, with his dogs. "I don't want to use you, Dylan. I'm not that kind of person. I can't understand why, after so many years, I'm suddenly making these choices. But . . ."

"What?"

"Touching you again, having you touch me . . ." She met his dark eyes and lowered her voice. "It's all I can think about."

"Then it's fortunate for you that I'm having the same problem." He held out his hand.

This time she didn't hesitate to take it. She was cold after being outside. And she knew, from experience, how warm his body would be.

"What about your brothers?" She glanced apprehensively toward the darker reaches of the house.

"They're gone," he said, and forced his dogs to stay outside his bedroom as they went inside.

Dylan's room smelled slightly of cigarettes, but the scent of his cologne and his . . . shampoo? . . . was much stronger.

She wanted to take a minute to look around, to see what Dylan was like in his own space, but he didn't give her a chance. He didn't even turn on the light before pulling her into bed with him.

"Can a person become an addiction?" she whispered as he stripped off her clothes.

"You think you're already addicted to me?" Once they were both naked, he urged her onto her back and threaded their fingers together as he kissed her.

"It feels that way. I couldn't wait to see you again. I've just been passing time all day."

He smiled as his mouth moved lower. "Sex is new for you. Once you find out that any man can give you what you want, the spell will be broken."

She wasn't so sure. But she didn't argue. His mouth had found her breast and his fingers were sliding down. Once they reached their intended target, she couldn't even think, let alone talk.

A weak winter sun struggled to breach the cracks in the blinds as Cheyenne opened her eyes. She rolled over, confused and unable to remember where she was. Then the memories of Dylan and what they'd done last night came pouring back.

She was still in his bed!

Sitting up so fast her head swam, she blinked away the last vestiges of sleep and turned to see if he was wrapped up in the bedding beside her.

He wasn't. Still, she wasn't alone in the house. She could hear the tramp of footsteps, as well as male voices, in what would probably be the hall and kitchen areas.

Pulling the bedding up to her chin, she waited to see if he'd return. She was naked and felt vulnerable because of it, but she didn't want to get up. She was afraid he'd open the door at the wrong moment and one of his brothers would be standing beyond him. Not only that, but somehow, letting him see her in the light of day felt different than in the dark of night.

Was he with his brothers, getting breakfast?

There was a towel draped over the knob of the bathroom door. It hadn't been there before — she would've noticed when she used the bathroom during the night — and dampness in the air told her someone had recently showered. She guessed Dylan was dressed and ready for the day. . . .

Catching a glimpse of herself — eyes wide, face white, hair tangled — she shook her head. She'd made her first mistake worse by coming back for more. And then she'd spent the night with him, which compounded the problem.

She would've left hours ago, but she'd been far too comfortable tucked up against Dylan. She'd kept thinking, "I'll go in a minute," but the next thing she knew, it was morning.

"You're screwing up," she told herself. She was eager to drag on her clothes and rush out, but she wanted to run into Dylan's brothers even less than she wanted to run into him. Mack, Aaron and the others had to be wondering why her car was sitting in front of their house.

Actually, by now they'd probably guessed.

Burning with embarrassment, she leaned over and grabbed her purse from the nightstand so she could check her phone. It was eight-thirty. But the time wasn't all that caught her eye. Between four and six, she'd received numerous calls and text messages from Presley. Her sister had worried when she didn't come home.

Too bad she'd had her phone on vibrate. Otherwise, it might've gotten her up and out of bed.

She almost called Presley back, then decided to wait. Maybe she could tell her sister she'd stayed at Sophia's, but not if Aaron ratted her out.

Deciding she had to make a move, she relinquished the blankets and hopped out of bed to search for her panties. But they weren't on the floor with the rest of her clothes. She found them tacked to the corkboard above Dylan's desk, along with a note.

She was slightly mortified at the sight but had to chuckle at his sense of humor.

Have to work. Help yourself to anything you want.

D

His voice wasn't among those she could

hear in the kitchen. Had he already left the house? If so, she wished his brothers had gone with him. It sounded like they were getting ready, but she hated feeling like a prisoner in Dylan's bedroom.

She dressed, then paced while she waited, careful not to make noise. When her phone went off, she would've pressed Ignore. She didn't want to speak for fear of drawing attention, but caller ID indicated it was Dylan.

"Hello?" she whispered, huddling in the corner with her face turned away from the door.

"You awake?"

"I am now." The pique in her voice revealed that she wasn't particularly pleased to have slept so late, which elicted a laugh from Dylan.

"You were dead to the world. I hated to disturb you."

"You should've told me you were leaving!"

"We've been up late the past two nights. I felt you could use the sleep."

She lowered her voice even further. "Your brothers are still here."

"Don't worry, they'll be joining me at the shop soon. Then you can duck out."

"I'm sure they've already seen my car, but it would still be embarrassing to run into them as I tiptoe out of your bedroom."

"Actually, they haven't seen your car," he said.

"Excuse me?"

"That's why I'm calling. I wanted to tell you that I moved it behind the barn."

"*When?*"

"After you fell asleep."

It bothered him that she didn't want anyone to know they were seeing each other. He took it as a slight — he'd made that clear when she'd been afraid Presley would see his bike — and she couldn't blame him. Yet he'd taken her keys off his desk and gone out in the cold to remedy the problem in the middle of the night? "That was nice of you. *Really* nice. Thank you."

"Keeping you in my bed was worth it. Have a good day," he said, and disconnected.

Their time together had been incredible, even better than the hours at her place. She had to admit that much. Practice helped . . .

"You're an interesting man, Dylan Amos," she said as she wandered around his room, which was surprisingly clean and well-organized. There were a few articles of clothing he hadn't hung up, but no dust, no dirt and everything smelled fresh.

She examined the bits of paper and receipts tacked to his corkboard. Names and numbers of both men and women. Flyers announcing MMA tournaments. A few pictures of him at the lake with his brothers or some buddies. Before and after photos of various cars he must've repaired. His GED.

When she saw that, she checked the date on the certificate and realized he'd gotten it only a year ago. She wondered why he'd bothered with it. He'd been running his own business since eighteen, and it seemed to make enough to support them all. They certainly had plenty of toys, from motorcycles to Jet Skis to four-wheel drives, and no one was rushing off to work someplace else.

"Come on, we're late!" someone shouted. "Old Man Murphy wants his car today. We don't get it done, Dylan's gonna pound our asses."

She smiled at that. Then she saw a framed picture on the opposite nightstand and walked over to have a look. An attractive woman of maybe twenty-five, with long dark hair, held a young Dylan on her lap.

Sobering, Cheyenne picked up the photograph and stared at the faces of mother and son. They looked so much alike. They had the same coloring, the same pouty mouth. She smiled again, thinking about how much she enjoyed kissing that mouth. What would he have been like had his mother lived? And what about his father? Did they have a relationship?

The front door slammed, jarring her out of her thoughts. At last, she was free.

Putting the picture down, she waited until she heard the motors of two different vehicles flare up and grow dim. Then she hurried out to find her own car behind the barn.

As soon as Cheyenne let herself into the house, Presley came out of her bedroom. "*There* you are," she said, sounding put out.

Self-conscious and guilty, Cheyenne crossed to the kitchen. "Hi. Sorry about last night. I would've called but I zonked out."

Her sister trailed after her, stopping at the table when she proceeded to the fridge. "Where? That's the question."

Cheyenne wasn't sure whether or not she'd gone looking for her. She doubted Presley would have checked the Amoses', even if she did. She'd probably gone in the other direction, past Sophia's and maybe even the Harmons'. "Over at Eve's place."

"I thought Eve was on a cruise."

She rummaged around as if hunting for something to eat, but she wasn't particularly hungry, just trying to avoid facing her sister and meeting her gaze. The fact that she and Presley seemed to have switched roles didn't escape her. "She is."

"So what were you doing there?"

Cheyenne took out a boiled egg and cracked it, using a paper towel to catch the shell, since she didn't want to risk clogging up the garbage disposal. "I stopped by to get a dress I lent her, turned on the TV for a few minutes and fell asleep."

"Oh." With a yawn, Presley collapsed into a seat. "You really had me going there for a while. I searched all over for you."

Fortunately, she didn't ask to see the dress, because it was already hanging in Cheyenne's closet. "You didn't bother Sophia, did you?" She added salt to her egg. "She had an early flight to Hawaii."

"When I couldn't find you, I called over there, but no one answered. So I drove by and, of course, your car wasn't parked out front. It wasn't at Riley's, either."

Cheyenne looked up. "You left Mom alone?"

"I had to. I was afraid something had happened to you."

Breathing a sigh of relief that Presley hadn't managed to find her, Cheyenne took a seat at the table. There was just one more thing that concerned her. . . . "You didn't call the police or anything, did you?"

"No." Presley frowned, watching her eat. "I don't like involving the police in our business, so I thought I'd wait a little longer. I was actually wondering if maybe you ran away." She laughed uncomfortably. "Lord knows I've been tempted on occasion."

"I wouldn't leave you, Pres."

"*Really?*" she said.

Surprised by her insecurity, Cheyenne reached across the table to squeeze her hand. "Of course not. We're sisters, right? We stick together."

"Yeah, sisters."

Cheyenne could barely hear her. She leaned closer. "Is something wrong?"

"No. Just don't scare me like that again, okay? I was so worried."

Cheyenne gave her a pointed look. "Now you know how *I* feel when *you* don't come home."

"That's usual behavior for me. I work nights. I go out often. It's not usual behavior for you."

"There's no excuse for being inconsiderate."

"I know. I'm sorry." She brushed her hair out of her eyes and stood up to get a drink. "By the way, Joe DeMarco came by last night."

Cheyenne twisted around to see her. "He did?"

"Yeah."

"What'd he want?"

"He asked for you."

"And you told him . . ."

"That you were probably at Sophia's."

Her stomach knotted but she forced herself to swallow what was in her mouth. "What time was that?"

"Almost nine."

Cheyenne *had* been at Sophia's then. Thank God. "Did he say what he wanted?"

Presley returned with a glass of milk. "No, but he seemed disappointed you weren't here." She gave Cheyenne a suspicious grin. "You're not seeing Gail's brother, are you?"

"No." Cheyenne shook her head. "Eve's dating him. We're just friends."

She grinned. "Lucky Eve. He's *cute*."

Cheyenne didn't want to be reminded of that. "He's a nice guy."

"He told me to have you call him."

"I will. How was Mom last night?" Cheyenne held her breath, hoping Presley would take the bait, and felt another wave of relief when she allowed her to change the subject.

"Fine. She woke up for a few minutes and we chatted. But mostly she slept."

Nothing new there. Cheyenne was about

to throw away the paper towel she'd been using so she could take a shower and head over to the B and B when she noticed a shard of glass on the floor. "Did something get broken?"

"Oh!" Presley's expression turned sheepish. "I was going to tell you about that."

"What?"

"You know the picture of you, Eve, Gail and some of your other friends in Tahoe? The one you had on the mantel?"

"Yes . . ."

"I accidentally dropped it. But don't worry. I'll get you another frame."

Cheyenne glanced at the fireplace. Sure enough, her picture was missing. But everything else was there, even some Christmas ornaments that were far more fragile. "What made you pick it up in the first place?"

"I was . . . dusting. What else?"

Rocking back, Cheyenne blinked at her. "Wow, what got into you?" she said with a laugh.

"I dust. Sometimes."

"No, you don't." She laughed harder. "And you never offer to stay with Mom."

Presley stared down at her hands, which were busy digging at her cuticles. "I guess I just realized how much you mean to me, and that I haven't been the kind of help I should've been. I want to do more. I want to give you a reason to love me."

Apparently, Presley was in a much more serious mood than Cheyenne had realized. "Stop. I do love you and I always will."

Her sister smiled but, for some reason, it didn't reach her eyes.

14

Steam was beginning to fill the bathroom, but Cheyenne let the shower run and stood in front of the mirror. She hadn't inspected her body in a long while. There hadn't been any point. She was the only one to ever see it. But now . . . now she wanted to put herself in Dylan's shoes, to determine whether or not she was really as attractive as he made her feel.

She wasn't too impressed with her own assets. In her opinion, several of her friends were prettier. But she wasn't bad. At five foot nine, she was fairly tall — long and lean. Since Anita was the opposite, she assumed this genetic endowment came from her father, whoever he was. Or her old memories were what she feared. Her breasts were a C, the size most women seemed to want, or not far from it. And she'd been told through the years that she had nice legs.

She could use a tan, she decided, but it

was the middle of winter so a guy couldn't expect too much there.

Maybe she should cut her hair. Or start lifting weights. Dylan was certainly toned.

She could get a tattoo. . . .

Suddenly, she wanted a drastic change, wanted to break out of the constraints that held her back, try new things, take a few risks.

But she wasn't sure how to do that. She had her mother and sister to worry about, and would need to help her sister even after her mother died. She didn't earn a lot of money. She lived in a small town and couldn't see herself leaving the friends she'd made. Not only that, but her reputation would probably always mean a great deal to her. So how would she ever step away from being dutiful and responsible and . . . boring?

Apparently, *part* of her wanted to break out of her cocoon, and part was afraid to emerge as anything other than what she'd been.

"Chey?"

Presley was calling her.

Grabbing a towel, she wrapped it around herself and opened the door to find her sister standing on the other side. "Yes?"

"Mom and I figured out what that P.I.

wanted."

"You did?" Because of her involvement with Dylan, she'd all but forgotten about the man who'd approached Presley, looking for Anita.

"Remember that hit-and-run in New Mexico?"

"How could I forget it?" she said with a grimace. She was eleven when her mother had mowed down that cyclist, old enough to understand the terrible ramifications of Anita's actions but not old enough to do anything about it. After that day, she'd had nightmares, could still remember the sound of their car hitting the metal of that man's bike. But she'd never spoken of it. She didn't want to speak of it now.

"They want to charge her with vehicular manslaughter."

Cheyenne sagged against the door. "He *died?*"

"So it seems. They've been looking for her ever since."

"We should turn her in."

Presley's chin snapped up. "*What?*"

"I mean it." Their mother had skated out of every mistake. Anita always ran, pointed a finger at someone else or manipulated the system. She'd been conning others her whole life, wreaking havoc and never cleaning up the messes she created, and Cheyenne was sick of it. She'd been sick of it for as long as she could remember.

"What good will *that* do?" Presley asked.

"It'll give the victim's family some closure. She should've called the police that day."

"She was drunk! They would've taken her to jail. And then what? What would've happened to *us*?"

Cheyenne had no answer. Anita was all they'd ever had. Even the few friends Anita had made passed in and out of their lives very quickly. And she had no roots. What she did have, always, was a reason she couldn't do the right thing, why she was justified in doing the opposite.

"She's *dying*, Chey," Presley said.

"Exactly." Cheyenne hitched her towel higher. "We need to hurry."

"I can't believe you! That would affect us more than her. Do you really want to deal with something so negative? To live in the shadow of it? We had nothing to do with her drinking and driving. Anyway, Mom's last days are hard enough. In case you haven't noticed, she's in horrible pain. If you want her to suffer, you can feel confident that she is."

Want her to suffer? Cheyenne didn't want anyone to suffer. But sometimes she did crave justice, just as her mother's victim probably did.

She pressed her forehead to the wall as her sister walked away. Why couldn't Anita have been someone she could be proud of?

Presley stood inside Anita's bedroom, listening to Cheyenne's shower. She should've left the Eugene Crouch issue alone. She'd already sent him off with a story he seemed to accept, hopefully never to return. Why had she decided it would be so smart to put Cheyenne's curiosity to rest, as well?

"What . . . are you doing?"

She turned to see that Anita was awake. "Kicking myself."

"Why?"

Because she'd gone one step too far. "I made a stupid miscalculation where Cheyenne's concerned."

There was a long silence, but when she looked up, she saw that Anita was still watching her closely. "What . . . does that mean?"

"It means she's angrier than I realized. And one day . . ." She wiped her sweaty palms on her sweats.

"One day?"

"I'm afraid of where it'll lead."

Anita's eyes closed but reopened a second

later. "She doesn't know . . . about Crouch."

"No." Presley didn't want to share with her mother what she'd just told Cheyenne. She and Anita had never spoken of the hit-and-run. It was something she preferred to forget; she wished she hadn't brought it up to her sister.

"You'd better . . . hope she never learns."

"Whatever happened in the past is over," she insisted, and prayed to God it was true.

Before dialing Joe's number, Cheyenne locked the door to her office. She could hear Riley and Jacob working upstairs. She doubted they'd come down, but didn't want to be interrupted if they did. She preferred a few minutes of privacy to tell the man she'd wanted since she was fourteen that she couldn't see him again, even while Eve was out of town.

Especially while Eve was out of town.

His cell rang three times before he picked up.

"Finally," he teased. "I thought maybe you weren't going to allow me to apologize."

She could hear sounds from the service station in the background. Obviously, he was at work. "You don't have anything to apologize for. I understand how seeing that guy would throw you. It's fine."

"He took me by surprise, but that's no excuse."

"Considering what you told me in your message, he had a lot of nerve, expecting you to greet him like a friend."

"We *were* friends, once. That's what makes it hard. But it's been years. I shouldn't have let him get to me."

"Seeing him was a shock."

"Thanks for being so understanding." He covered the phone to tell someone he'd be just a minute. Then his voice deepened. "Does that mean you'll give me another chance?"

She hauled in a deep breath. "I wish I could, Joe. I — I've had a crush on you for years," she said with a weak laugh. "I'm sure you're aware of that."

"No, I wasn't," he said in astonishment.

"I guess I'm better at keeping a secret than I thought."

"You're certainly better at it than Eve."

He was joking again, trying to ease the awkwardness, and that offered the perfect segue. "Speaking of Eve. She's . . . great."

Silence, then, "She *is* great."

"She's also my best friend," Cheyenne continued. "And now that she's interested in you, my hands are tied. I don't . . . I don't want to see her get hurt."

"I admire your loyalty. That's rare these days. But —"

"And I definitely don't want to be the person to hurt her," she broke in.

There was another long pause. "You're saying even if I'm not interested in Eve, you don't want to get involved with me."

That was really her only choice. And yet, she knew it would be so much easier to forget her dark, sexy neighbor if she could throw herself into a relationship with Prince Charming instead.

Too bad it wasn't possible. She'd been unsure and overwhelmed when Joe showed up with that bottle of wine — unsure and overwhelmed enough to let him in — but since then she'd received an education. Thanks to Dylan, she now understood how quickly attraction could ignite. "I can't."

Her honesty seemed to take him off guard. No doubt he'd been expecting a simple "no problem," and a commitment to have dinner with him. Instead, she'd told him how long she'd yearned for his attention — and then refused to see him.

"I'm sorry to hear that," he said.

"I'm sorry to say it," she responded. "You're one in a million." With a wince, she hit the end button. Then she sat in her chair and stared at the picture of her and Eve taken while they were visiting Baxter in San Francisco earlier in the year.

"Friendship means a lot," she reminded herself. Ignoring the sadness she felt for what might've been *at last*, she finished booking the internet reservations that had come in over the past couple of days.

Since his divorce, Joe hadn't been eager to jump back into the dating pool. Bumping into the person he suspected to be the father of his youngest daughter, just as he was starting to feel that secret was safe, hadn't helped. It'd reminded him why he'd sworn off women to begin with, how complicated and painful romantic relationships could get, especially when there were children involved.

But spending the rest of his life alone wouldn't be much of an improvement. And Chey seemed like a woman he could trust. The telephone call he'd just had with her confirmed it. Suzie would've put herself above her friend without thinking twice. He had no doubt of that. Suzie believed she was the only one who had a right to be happy.

"Hey!"

Joe turned to see his father holding open the door between the minimart, where Martin had been working the register, and the auto-repair bays, where Joe had been overseeing the automotive end.

"We've hit a lull in here," Martin said. "Can you watch the store while I grab us a sandwich at Stacked?"

"Sure."

"What do you want?"

"Hot pastrami."

"You got it."

Grateful to know he had a few minutes to himself, without worrying about being interrupted or overheard by his father, Joe called his sister in L.A. Since he was interested in one of her friends, he figured he should probably get her permission and maybe a little advice.

"Don't tell me this is my big brother, whom I rarely hear from unless *I* call," Gail said when she came on the line.

Slightly embarrassed, he passed into the store. She was right; she was better at staying in touch. "I hope you're not holding a grudge."

"And I hope that one day you'll start doing your part. What's up? I might hear from you occasionally, but *never* in the middle of the day, which makes this call a bit suspect."

"I must want something, huh?"

"Exactly. Is everything okay? Is it Dad?

Are you two getting along?"

"Everything's fine. How's Simon?"

"Simon's a handful. But I knew he'd be a handful when I married him."

She sounded happy, and that made him feel optimistic, as if some marriages, even a high-risk marriage, could work. "I bet he's busy."

"Actually, he's so excited about the baby he hardly leaves my side."

Joe reorganized the candy near the register and threw away an empty box. "What's the latest?"

"We still don't know whether we're having a boy or girl and we don't want to find out until the baby's born."

"Only two more months to wait. What does Ty think of having a brother or sister?"

"He's as excited as his daddy. He wants to name the baby Elmo."

"Yikes."

"Nothing could be worse."

"Hard to believe you're almost at the naming point. You were barely showing when I saw you last."

She laughed. "I'm definitely poking out now."

He asked about her PR company. She said it was thriving. He asked about Simon's latest film. She said he'd insisted on a hiatus until their Lamaze classes ended. He asked when they might come to Whiskey Creek. She said they were hoping to visit soon. Then the conversation slowed, and her tone took on a playful note. "Okay, enough chitchat. You had a reason for calling me. What is it?"

Dexter Jones, a locksmith who lived in town, pulled up to get gas. Joe kept an eye out in case he needed help, but Dexter was paying at the pump.

"There's a woman," Joe said.

"A woman," she repeated.

"Yes."

"Someone you like?"

"I think so."

"I've been waiting a long time for this," she said gleefully. "Where'd you meet her?"

"Right here in Whiskey Creek." He wiped down the coffee area. "You know her, too. Quite well."

"I know almost everyone in Whiskey Creek. Who is she?"

He stopped cleaning up. "One of your closest friends."

Her silence seemed to come from surprise more than anything else. "Which one? You've never shown much interest in my friends, not romantically."

"Because they were too young for me."

"They haven't closed the gap, Joe," she said with a laugh.

"You know how it is. Now that we're older . . . somehow those years don't matter like they used to."

"I see." She sounded excited. "So are you going to tell me who we're talking about?"

He was about to, but she cut him off before he could.

"Wait — let me can guess. You like Eve, right? Callie mentioned that she's been talking about you lately —"

"It's not Eve. But you're getting close."

"*Callie?*"

He watched Dexter fiddle with his phone while waiting for the pump to fill his tank. "Cheyenne."

"That's wonderful! There's no one better than Chey. She's more reserved than the others, which is why I didn't think of her right away. She's *definitely* different from your ex."

"That might be the attraction," he said dryly.

"I approve. Wholeheartedly."

"You don't mind?"

"Not at all."

He waved to Dexter, who returned the wave and drove off. "Then maybe you can talk her into going out with me."

"Why would I need to talk her into that? You've already asked — and she turned you down?"

"It's a little more complicated than you might expect." He told her about Eve's invitation to dinner, and how often she'd been coming by the station.

"Cheyenne's a very loyal person, Joe. I don't think she'll relent, not if there's a chance of hurting Eve."

"But I'm not interested in Eve. And I've never led her to believe otherwise. I accepted her dinner invitation but knew almost immediately that she wasn't my type. I didn't kiss her or touch her. It doesn't seem fair that she's standing in the way."

"I get that, but . . ." She made a clicking sound with her tongue. "It's a tough situation. You're asking Chey to risk losing her best friend. I don't have to tell you what her life was like growing up, or why she feels so bonded to Eve."

"No, but Eve's gone for another week. I don't see why I can't get to know Cheyenne. Maybe the attraction will fizzle before Eve even comes back. I'd like to explore the possibilities, see if there's anything there."

"Right. Okay." She paused again, as if thinking it through. Then she said, "I'll do what I can to help."

The bell over the door jingled. Twelve-year-old Shelley Brown, who walked over from her house a block down the street practically every day, entered the store and headed down the candy aisle.

Joe gave her a welcoming smile before turning away and lowering his voice. "Which means what? You're going to *call* her?"

"I'm going to have *Eve* call her — and give her blessing."

"Eve's on a cruise. You won't be able to reach her."

"I will if I call the boat."

He grinned, even though she couldn't see him. "I think the power of being Mrs. Simon O'Neal is going to your head."

"I can't say I don't enjoy the fringe benefits of having a powerful husband."

"You're spoiled," he teased.

"At least I'm good to my big brother. Give me a couple of days."

Dylan couldn't think of anything except Cheyenne. The shop was the busiest it'd ever been — there were always more collisions in the winter, due to the wet roads — but he kept looking at the clock, wishing the time would go faster. He wanted to see her again, even though he wasn't sure she'd be interested in seeing him. She openly admitted that her heart belonged to Joe, and Dylan could certainly understand why she'd be attracted to him. Although they didn't socialize, he and Joe referred business to each other quite often, worked on a lot of the same cars. Joe or one of his mechanics did the engine work; Dylan or one of his brothers did the bodywork. Joe seemed like a decent guy, a *respectable* candidate.

"What's wrong with you today, man?" Aaron's paint mask was hanging around his neck as he came into the office from the warehouse section in back.

Dylan glanced up from his computer. He was pricing parts so he could prepare bids for the three vehicles that'd been towed into his front lot this morning. Or at least he was pricing when he could focus. For the past few seconds, he'd just been staring at the screen. "What do you mean?"

"I stood right there in the doorway, talking to you."

Dylan hadn't heard a thing. He'd been too preoccupied. "I'm tired," he said by way of excuse.

"You went to bed before we did."

But his brothers had probably gotten more sleep. "Tossed and turned." *Among other things*, he added silently and covered a yawn. "What do you need?"

"We've got a problem with the paint on Hal's Suburban."

"What kind of problem?"

"It's grainy. Don't know what's going on."

"The surface must not have been clean and smooth to begin with."

"Mack did the prep work. And he's the best collision-repair technician we've got. Isn't that what you always say?"

"He's good."

"He's also your pet, which hardly makes you an objective judge. But in this case, you're right. The grainy paint isn't his fault."

Dylan heard the jab in those words. Aaron had long been jealous of Mack. But Dylan didn't want to get into it. They'd already had an argument this morning over a job Aaron had to redo because it didn't meet Dylan's standards. "If it's not the prep work, there must be dust in the paint booth. Which one are you in today?"

"The big one, but I used it yesterday, too, with perfect results."

"So did you check the sprayer?"

"Everyone knows better than to put chemicals in the sprayer. I think we just got a bad batch of paint."

Dylan pressed his fingers to his temples. This was the last thing they needed when they were so backed up. "Fine. I'll call the supplier."

"You should call Hal, too. He won't be happy to hear we've got a problem. He needs his Suburban."

Dylan already knew they were under pressure, trying to get everyone's car fixed before Christmas. "That reminds me . . . how are we coming on Murphy's Cadillac? We'll have to discount the price if we don't get it done on time, and we're not making much to begin with." That was Dylan's fault. After the number of years he'd been running Amos Auto Body, he rarely underbid a job. But he'd gotten some bad information on the parts needed to fix the Caddie, and it was his policy not to go back on the customer.

"Rod's dealing with Murphy's car. You'll have to check with him." He dropped some change in the soda machine, took a Pepsi and walked out.

Once he was gone, Dylan crossed the lobby and stood by the door his brother had just used. He could see Aaron through the small window, talking to Grady, who was at the sanding station. Aaron wasn't looking good these days. The weight seemed to be falling off him. He was staying up all night and coming to work stoned, which was why,

Dylan figured, he'd screwed up that other job.

Dylan had already threatened Carl Inera, the guy he suspected of supplying Aaron. Carl was so scared of Dylan he jumped every time Dylan saw him. Carl also swore up and down that he hadn't sold Aaron so much as a ten-dollar bag of pot in months.

But Aaron had to be getting his dope from somewhere.

Dylan feared it was Presley.

The phone pealed, and he caught it on the fourth ring. "Amos Auto Body."

"Dylan? This is Joe, over at the Gas-N-Go."

Dylan stiffened, even though he'd never had that kind of reaction to Joe before. "What's up?"

"We've finished replacing the wiring harness on Beverly Hansen's BMW. How should we get it back to you? Do you want me to have it towed over, or did you want to pick it up on the flatbed?"

"I'll send Rod with the flatbed," he said.

"Perfect. I appreciate the business."

Dylan wanted to ask him if he was seeing anyone. He couldn't help hoping that a girlfriend would make Cheyenne forget about Joe. But they weren't good enough friends for such a personal question. And he knew, even if Joe *was* dating someone else, it might not make a difference. Cheyenne had it in her mind that Joe was the one she wanted, and she wasn't about to consider other options. Dylan couldn't see her ever giving him a shot. He and Joe were too different. "I'll get you paid."

"I know you will."

After they hung up, Dylan almost called Cheyenne. He'd been tempted to do so all day, just to hear her voice, to ask if maybe she'd like to grab a bite to eat with him later.

But if she didn't even want her sister or his brothers to know they were seeing each other, he doubted she'd be willing to go out in public. So he ignored the impulse and got back to work.

15

"Mom?" Cheyenne leaned close to her mother's bed.

Anita opened her eyes. The painkiller Cheyenne had given her a few minutes earlier had taken effect but hadn't yet dragged her into a sleepy stupor. For the moment, she could think and speak almost normally.

Cheyenne wanted to take advantage of that opportunity. "Can we talk?"

"I don't like the tone of your voice," Anita responded, but she sounded more strident than she had in a few days.

"Why not?"

"Because I can tell you're gonna badger me about the same old stuff. It's getting old, Chey. There isn't anything more I can tell you."

"I don't believe that, Mom. I want you to try, once again, to remember where I was born. That isn't asking too much. You know

Presley was born in San Diego, right? She could track down her birth certificate, couldn't she?"

Lines of impatience created deep grooves in Anita's forehead. "Where is Presley?"

"It's midnight. She's at work. You know that. She won't be home until morning."

"She's left me to your mercies?"

"She always leaves you to my mercies. So don't act as if that's unusual. Anyway, it doesn't have to be this hard," Cheyenne said. "Just answer the question."

"Your friends are already on the cruise. It's too late for you to go. So why are you at me for your damn birth certificate *again*?"

Cheyenne examined the face of the woman who'd raised her, searching for some sign of weakening resolve or evidence that she was hiding something. "Because I want to find out before it's too late to ask!"

Her mother's eyelids slid closed. Fading out was her way of avoiding a confrontation. Cheyenne had tried to talk to her about this again and again, especially after Anita got sick. Tonight it felt as futile as ever. She was defeated before she even started. But time was getting short. She couldn't continue to let Anita put her off or she might never learn the answers.

The problem was, she couldn't *force* Anita

to talk. Particularly since her memories of the blonde woman and the canopy bed and the pretty dolls could be merely the wishful imaginings of a girl desperate to escape a harsher reality. Maybe she'd made up the place where she had nice clothes and plenty of food, where she felt loved and safe and happy. It was possible. Anita had accused her of that before. And Presley didn't remember anyone like the woman she described.

"Mom! You're still awake. You can answer me."

"I have answered you!" Her eyes flew open. "I've told you time and time again, you were born in Wyoming. Where do you think I got your name?"

She might have gotten the name from Wyoming. But Cheyenne wasn't born there. She'd written to every county in the state. Each clerk had responded with a letter stating that no female Caucasian child of her age, with the name Cheyenne Christensen, was on the rolls. "It wasn't Wyoming. I've checked."

Anita didn't have her false teeth in today. Unless she was eating, she hardly ever wore them anymore. The dentist who'd created them had done a decent job — he donated one afternoon a week to pro bono work for the poor — but she'd had them a long time and hadn't taken any better care of them than her real teeth. Because of her sunken mouth and the ravages of cancer, she looked seventy-five instead of fifty-five. "Someone else knows more than your own mother does?"

"Wyoming shows no record of me having been born there."

"Then the records are screwed up. That happens sometimes."

"Or you were too drunk to realize where you were when you went into labor." That had happened, too — monumental events occurring when her mother wasn't in a position to remember them.

"I've never pretended to be a saint." She shrugged. "If you'd rather blame it on me, go ahead. I'm too sick to stand up for myself."

Cheyenne curved her fingernails into her palms. "Don't start playing the martyr. I just want the truth. *Please.*"

"I'd tell you if I could, but I can't, so you might as well accept it. I don't know what else to say, except that we don't always get what we want."

Cheyenne came to her feet. "I deserve a few basic facts about my own life. Wanting to know where I was born is *not* being self-ish."

"It isn't? What about your sister?"

"What about her?" They were nearly shouting, but Cheyenne couldn't bring herself to care.

"All you can talk about is some blonde woman and a fancy house where *you* had a fancy bedroom and all kinds of toys. She isn't part of that picture. Neither am I. It's like you've imagined a place where we don't exist. How do you think that makes *us* feel? I know you don't care about me, but what about her?"

Her mother had hit her where she was most vulnerable, disarming her, as intended. That was how Anita always won these arguments — by making Cheyenne feel as if she was being egotistical, or delusional, or callous toward her sister.

Maybe Anita was right. Maybe she was all those things and worse. She'd spent the past two nights having sex with Dylan Amos, hadn't she? She knew he wasn't the type of man she wanted, that she could never settle for someone who reminded her so much of everything she'd rather forget. Yet she was eager to go back to him, to let him convince her that her happiness wasn't as immaterial as it sometimes felt.

"Never mind," she said, and stalked out of the room. She shouldn't leave her mother alone in the house. But she couldn't force herself to stay. Dylan had given her a taste of freedom, a way to cope with the hurt and anger. She couldn't wait to see him again.

Promising her usual responsible self that she wouldn't be gone long, she grabbed her coat and hurried out the door.

Fortunately, he lived just down the street.

After Cheyenne called his cell phone, Dylan met her at his front door. He did so quietly, without speaking, because his brothers were at home asleep. It was the middle of the week. She felt bad about waking him. He got up early and worked hard and, thanks to her, he hadn't had a proper night's sleep in three days. But when she whispered that she could go back home if he was too tired to see her, he simply hooked his arm around her neck and guided her into his bedroom. It wasn't until they'd made desperate, frantic love that he asked her if something was wrong.

"No, nothing." She was lying on her back, still trying to catch her breath, and so was he. The last thing she wanted to think about was what he'd just helped her forget.

He drew a deep breath; she heard him

exhale. "There's *something* different about you tonight."

"I was upset. That's all."

"I could tell. About what?"

The physical outlet he'd made possible had siphoned off the worst of it. "Nothing you need to worry about."

"Is it your mother?"

She laid her head on his chest so she could listen to his heart. It was still beating faster than normal. She'd been more aggressive tonight, demanded more intensity and stamina than before, which he'd wordlessly provided. "Do we have to talk about it?"

His fingers slipped through her hair. "Not if you don't want to."

"I just . . . just let me feel you, okay?" She kissed his chest. "That's all."

"I'm right here."

Solid. Warm. Responsive. She couldn't complain about how Dylan made love. She couldn't imagine anyone doing it better. He touched her with just the right amount of confidence and familiarity, was especially sensitive to the give-and-take that made it mutually rewarding and was willing to bestow pleasure even in nonsexual ways. Tenderness seemed to come more naturally to him than she'd ever dreamed it would. Besides all that, she liked the smell of him, the sound of his voice, the fact that he could make her feel so darn *content*.

"Where did you park?" he asked.

"In front."

"Why didn't you pull behind the barn?"

"Because I can't stay. Presley's at work."

"I should've come to your house."

"No, I needed to get out."

"But . . . can you do that? I mean . . . with your mom the way she is?"

"It should be okay if I'm not gone too long."

He let her lie on him for several more minutes. Then, when she got up, he did, too. She assumed he was going to use the bathroom, but he dug something out of the pocket of his jeans and held it out to her.

It was too dark to see clearly. They hadn't turned on any lights. "What's this?" she whispered.

"A key." He put it in her hand. "That way you can come over whenever you want."

She shook her head and gave it back. "No, sorry. I can't accept that."

He stood there, watching her. He seemed completely unconcerned with his own nudity, but then, he didn't have any reason to be self-conscious. She'd just left Dylan's bed and already she wanted to touch him again, to climb back under the covers and go to sleep with him instead of returning to the reality of her own life.

"Why not?" he asked.

She'd offended him. She could hear the hurt pride in his voice. "I'm not the type to — to keep doing this," she explained.

"Doing *what?*"

"Running off in the middle of the night to have sex with —" she tried to come up an ending to that statement that wouldn't be unkind "— with some guy I've never even gone out with."

"We could fix that," he said. "I could take you to dinner."

She thought of all the people who might see them together, and how quickly the news would spread. This was Dylan. Everyone would assume she was sleeping with him — and they'd be right.

She wasn't ready to deal with the backlash that would cause, not when there was already so much going on in her life. Every person she knew — except maybe Presley, who'd finally feel vindicated — would tell her she was a fool to get involved with a man like this. He'd cheat on her, break her heart, offer none of the safety and security she'd been searching for her whole life.

Her friends, when they returned, would think she'd lost her mind.

"It's hard for me to find time for . . . for dating with my mother so sick."

He said nothing. No doubt he'd read her response for the excuse it was. So she added a weak, "But . . . I'll call you if I get the chance."

No response. She'd been getting dressed as they spoke. He just watched her pull on her sweater and shoes and didn't try to stop her when she hurried past him without so much as a goodbye kiss.

He was done with her, Dylan decided. It was stupid to let Cheyenne keep coming over. He couldn't believe he'd actually been willing to give her a key to his house!

He'd always been too impetuous. But his heart was a difficult thing to subdue. And besides that, he wasn't sure how much of her behavior to ascribe to the hell she was enduring. He kept thinking she just needed more time to sort out her thoughts and feelings, to get to know him and realize he could give her everything Joe could.

Even if she never came to regard him that highly, she'd have to recognize the spark between them, wouldn't she? He'd never experienced this sort of chemistry with anyone else. When they made love, it was like . . .

He didn't even know how to describe it.

She sensed the same thing he did. He could feel her shake when she touched him, hear her sigh and gasp. Mechanical sex wasn't like that. He'd had enough experience to tell the difference, but she hadn't. Maybe she thought making love was like this with any partner. He'd told her that other guys could give her the same thrill — but only because he wanted her to choose him for more reason than that.

"Dylan, what are you doing in the flower section?"

Blinking, he shifted his attention from the roses he'd been contemplating to Mack, who'd gone to pick up some hamburger. He'd said he'd get the buns and a few deli items and that they'd meet up at the register, but then he'd noticed the small flower section.

He'd never paused here before. He wasn't sure why he'd done it now. Maybe he *wanted* to buy Cheyenne flowers but he wouldn't be foolish enough to do it. She didn't want that kind of thing from him; she wanted it from Joe.

"Nothing." Embarrassed by the impulse, he turned away.

His little brother was looking at him like he'd gone crazy. "Where're the buns?"

Dylan rubbed his face. "I'm on my way."

"You're not yourself these days," Mack complained. "What's going on with you?"

"What do you mean?" he asked as they headed to the deli section together.

Mack sent him a worried glance. "You're preoccupied, quiet."

He supposed that was true. He'd finally found someone he really wanted in his life. And he was sure that — just like the mother he'd prayed to keep, and the father he'd tried so hard to reclaim from alcohol — he was destined to lose her, too.

Cheyenne didn't let herself go to Dylan's that night or the night after. She worked all day at the B and B Wednesday and Thursday, watched her mother and tried to keep herself occupied with videos and computer games. She was afraid he'd call her and knew she'd go see him if he did, but the phone never rang. Maybe that was why, on Friday, after Riley and Jacob left, she broke down and called him from the office.

Her heart seemed lodged in her throat by the time he answered. Her emotions were such a mixture of embarrassment and chagrin over her wanton behavior, disappointment that she didn't seem to be the person she'd always thought she was, and desire to return to his bed that she couldn't seem to get her bearings anymore. She felt pulled apart, restless. Most of all, she wanted to come out of this tailspin knowing they were friends, that he didn't hate her. Regardless of his reputation, she liked Dylan; there was no denying that.

He picked up but didn't give her a chance to speak. "Damn, do I need to educate you in everything?"

"Excuse me?" she replied, taken aback.

"It's only eight o'clock. Booty calls are supposed to happen later. Otherwise, word might get out that you've lowered your standards enough to sleep with me."

Cringing, she opened her mouth to respond, but he'd already hung up. She should've called him before. She needed to explain that she was trying to get back to the Cheyenne Christensen she recognized, that her behavior had very little to do with him. He had to be wondering what the heck he'd done wrong. After spending three nights in a row together — that last night she'd nearly torn off his clothes — she'd rejected the key he'd offered her and then he'd heard nothing.

He could've called *her.*

She tried to justify her behavior that way, but . . . considering *she'd* pushed *him* away, he really couldn't be the one to call, and she knew it.

"Shit," she breathed, and tapped herself on the forehead with her phone. What was going on with her? Had she ever been more lost or confused?

Not since before coming to Whiskey Creek . . .

She told herself not to call him back. But she knew she wouldn't be able to relax until she'd made at least one more attempt to soothe any feelings she might've hurt — so she tried again.

"*What?*" he said.

He'd answered at the last second, right before the call could transfer to voice mail. "I'm sorry, Dylan. I'm *really* sorry," she said, and hung up so he couldn't beat her to it. Maybe if she didn't act as if she expected his forgiveness, or anything else, he wouldn't think so badly of her and they'd both be able to move on.

After checking to make sure that Presley would stay with Anita for another hour, she left her car at the B and B and walked a block south to Just Like Mom's for a bite to eat. She wasn't hungry. The anger she'd heard in Dylan's voice seemed to be ricocheting through her head. She felt sick inside. But she ordered a bowl of chicken noodle soup and some coffee. She didn't care that it was too late for caffeine. She wouldn't be able to sleep, anyway. Ironically, it'd been even harder to wind down on the nights she'd made herself stay away from Dylan than on the nights she'd seen him. It required that much effort to fight the impulse to return.

She'd become instantly addicted — that was the only way to describe it. She was acting like Presley, always searching for her next hit.

But when he'd handed her that key, as if he assumed what they were doing would continue, it had scared her to death. She couldn't get involved with anyone like him on a regular basis. As soon as Anita died, Cheyenne was moving out of the river bottoms, away from the Amoses and the memories of her past. She'd rent a cute little house in town, maybe even one with a white picket fence, and forget it all — her dreams of the blonde woman, the nightmare of being raised by Anita and the fantasy of Dylan.

So fate seemed almost too cruel when Dylan and his brothers filed into the restaurant. Especially when he did a double take on seeing her by herself in the corner booth.

16

After that initial moment of shock, Dylan ignored her. It made Cheyenne feel even worse, but she wasn't sure how else she expected him to behave. *She* was the one who'd let him know that their relationship wasn't something she wanted to take public. So he was treating her the way he'd treated her before — as if they were basically strangers.

That didn't make it any easier to sit and wait for her food when he was right across the restaurant, however. She told herself not to look over, but every few seconds her eyes naturally gravitated toward him.

With that scar on his face, his crooked nose, which had probably been broken in a fight, and the wary air he carried like a battle shield, she knew most people would consider him the least attractive of the Amos boys. They were all tall, strong and dark-haired, with rugged features and expressive mouths, if not perfectly straight teeth. But they were also reckless, undisciplined and unpredictable. As far as she was concerned, that made them emotionally undependable, too.

Tonight Dylan had on a pair of holey jeans and a distressed leather jacket, which he took off because the restaurant was so warm. At that point, Cheyenne couldn't help admiring the way his Amos Auto Body T-shirt stretched across his chest. It reminded her how well the rest of him was put together. Maybe other people wouldn't find him as attractive as his brothers, but she found him more so. There was something about the way he smiled, the way there seemed to be all kinds of things going on in his head, far more than ever passed his lips. . . .

It could even be his attitude that attracted her. He acted as if the whole world could go to hell, that he'd do exactly as he damn well pleased. Sometimes she felt like ignoring public opinion, too. But she'd always been too scared of ending up friendless — and possibly worse off than she was now.

The waitress brought her a basket of crackers and said she'd be right back with the soup. But Cheyenne was hardly listening. Just looking at Dylan made her throat go dry, because she knew what that mouth, those hands, felt like. And she wanted more.

Taking a sip of water, she tried to change her focus to the Christmas music on the sound system, but Elvis's "Blue Christmas" came on and that certainly didn't improve her mood. She was feeling lonely enough already. So she played a video game on her phone. And when that couldn't distract her, she got up and went to the restroom, where she stayed as long as she could, trying not to make it obvious that she'd abandoned her table just to escape being in the same room with Dylan.

When she returned, he glanced up at her. Their eyes locked, and she felt such a terrible hunger, she knew she couldn't stay. Dropping a twenty on the table, she left the soup and coffee the waitress had delivered in her absence and walked out, not even bothering to wait for her change.

It was all Dylan could do to remain seated. He wanted to go after Cheyenne. He was back to feeling sorry for her, wondering if he'd hoped for too much, demanded too much. She was going through hell right now and couldn't handle a relationship, especially one that had flared into existence so fast and so unexpectedly. He was the first man she'd ever slept with. She was probably overwhelmed on top of everything else.

He could have some empathy, couldn't he?

He could, and he did. Those emotions held him hostage. But, empathy or no, he couldn't chase her down. His brothers would ask too many questions, and he still wasn't sure which way his relationship with her would go, whether or not he wanted them to discover how he felt.

He sat and he ate, even though he could hardly taste his food. Then, as soon as he got home, he climbed on his bike without telling anyone he was leaving and went to find her.

He knew she wasn't at her place. He'd checked when they passed by a few minutes earlier. So he headed into town.

It didn't take long to locate her car. Her Oldsmobile was parked at the bed-and-breakfast where she worked.

Leaving his bike parked near the cemetery railing instead of pulling into the lot, he strode to the front stoop and tried the door.

It was locked. But he could see a light burning inside.

"Chey?" he called as he pounded on the door.

There was no answer.

"I know you're in there."

When she didn't come, he went around to the back. The light he'd spotted in front streamed from a room off the kitchen. "Cheyenne!"

Another light snapped on and she appeared, but she stood well away from the door, as if she couldn't trust herself to go any closer.

"Are you going to let me in?" he asked.

She covered her eyes with her hands, then dropped them and stepped forward. He heard the bolt slide back before she poked her head out. "What do you want?"

He didn't move toward her but he told her the truth. "I want *you*. I think you know that."

He meant what he'd said on a deeper level than she'd probably taken it. But when tears filled her eyes, he told himself that if only she'd ask, he'd give her more time. She just had to show him . . . *something* that would let him believe she might someday look at him the way she looked at Joe. "What do *you* want, Chey?"

"I don't know, but . . . whatever it is, I can't keep seeing you."

That wasn't the answer he'd been hoping for. But it was the one he'd expected.

"I can't handle the risks of being in a

266

relationship right now," she added.

He'd had the same thought — that this was bad timing for her — while he was at the restaurant. And yet, he could see how his friendship, attention, maybe even his love, could help her, now more than ever.

How could she miss that they were perfect together? He knew she felt something when she was with him.

She was fighting the attraction. But that was her choice.

"Right. Okay." Stepping forward, he cupped her face in his hands. He meant only to give her a simple kiss, a tender moment to remember him by. A farewell of sorts. But the touch of their lips caused a sudden change in them both, and they immediately fused together. He doubted he could have made himself pull away even if he'd wanted to.

Fortunately, she didn't seem any more willing to let go. She wrapped her arms around his neck and, when he lifted her off her feet, wrapped her legs around him, too. Then he carried her inside, and she barely managed to kick the door shut before unbuttoning his jeans.

He was inside her in seconds, without a condom, without anything. They had most of their clothes on. He felt a desperate urge to convince her, to get her to acknowledge that they had a chance at something special.

How could this *not* lead to more? She affected him like no other woman ever had, made him want to take care of her, protect her.

But he knew he wasn't going to change her mind. She'd decided against him before he'd even touched her that first time. So he brought her to a quick and powerful climax, somehow gratified that he could do it almost effortlessly, and decided that would be his goodbye.

Fastening his jeans, he left without a word, and this time he told himself he'd never give her the chance to reject him again.

When Cheyenne saw Eve's number on her caller ID on Saturday morning, she couldn't believe it. Eve had said she wouldn't be able to call until she returned to the States, but there were still four more days of the cruise.

Although relieved and excited — it'd been a rough week without her best friend to help steady her — Cheyenne was also a little worried. Had something gone wrong?

Forgetting about the reason she'd been up late, tossing and turning, she scrambled to hit the talk button. "Hello?"

"Chey?"

"Eve! Where are you?"

"Martinique."

An island in the Caribbean, one of their stops. "So how are you getting phone service?"

Eve had to be using her cell, or her number wouldn't have shown up on Cheyenne's screen.

"I decided to get an international plan."

"Why would you do that? You'll be home in a few days."

"Because I wanted to talk to you."

Cheyenne sat up. "Is everything okay?"

There was a brief silence. "It is on this end."

"Everything's fine here, too," she said. And what wasn't okay could wait. She didn't want to ruin Eve's trip. "My mother's still fighting."

"So I've heard."

"*How*?" Cheyenne asked in surprise.

"Gail called the ship from L.A. yesterday. Can you believe that? She can track anyone down."

"But . . . *why* would she? She couldn't call when you got back?"

"No. She needed to reach me."

"Because . . ."

"She had something to tell me about Joe."

Cheyenne tightened her grip on the

phone. "That's good, then, right? He must've spoken to her about you."

"He did, but it wasn't what I was hoping he'd say."

"What do you mean?" Cheyenne could hear the uncertainty in her own voice.

"Chey, stop pretending," Eve said. "I know, okay? I know he wants to date you. And I know you turned him down because of me."

Stunned at being so suddenly exposed, she tried to come up with something that would soften Joe's rejection. "He just doesn't realize how great you are."

"But he realizes how great *you* are. And if you're interested in him, too, I don't want to stand in the way."

How should she react? Should she continue to deny her feelings? Or finally tell the truth? She didn't want to hurt Eve. "I'm sorry."

"For . . ."

"For not telling you a long time ago."

There was a slight pause. "So it's true? You like him?"

She fell back on the pillows. "I wish I didn't."

"I can't believe you sat there and encouraged me, even lent me your best dress to go out with him!"

"He'd never shown any interest in me. I figured you'd have a much better shot."

"Why? That's crazy! You obviously have no idea of your own appeal."

"I don't want to lose our friendship."

"Silly, you won't lose our friendship. You won't lose anything. Go out with him. No need for us both to be deprived." Eve attempted a laugh, but Cheyenne heard the strain in her voice and felt bad about it. She could tell this wasn't easy.

"You're being very generous, but I don't think I could —"

"Go out with him, Chey!" Eve interrupted, her voice more strident. "Don't miss this chance to see if someone as wonderful as Joe might be the right man for you."

"That'd be too weird," she argued. "You and I . . . we wouldn't be able to talk about him. And I'd feel like a slimeball if we ever ran into you."

"We'll get over that stuff, work around it."

"What if we don't? What if it changes our relationship?"

"If you think Joe means more to me than you do, you have no idea how much I care about you."

That statement brought tears to Cheyenne's eyes. "That helps."

"It's true."

Cheyenne swallowed around the lump in her throat. "I have something to tell you."

"What's that?"

As the memory of Dylan pressing her against the wall last night came back to her yet again, Cheyenne curled onto her side. "I've been seeing Dylan Amos."

Eve's response was fast, loud and immediate. "You can't be serious!"

She covered her head. "I'm afraid so."

"What do you mean, you've been *seeing* him?"

"In truth —" she lowered her voice on the off chance that Presley was awake "— I've been sleeping with him."

This met with shocked silence. "I've only been gone a week," Eve said when she finally responded. "When did that happen?"

"The first time?"

A gasp. "How many times have you been with him?"

Cheyenne pressed her palm to one eye. "Four nights out of six."

"God, that scares me to death! Are you using protection?"

"Yes." Except for once, but she didn't add that. She'd already counted the days, knew it wasn't a dangerous time of the month.

"I can't *believe* it."

Cheyenne had expected Eve to be

272

shocked. She'd complained about her sister hanging out with the Amoses for too long to get any other reaction. But now that she knew Dylan better, she also felt somewhat defensive of him. "He's not as bad as you think."

"Cheyenne, he's not what you're looking for. Don't you remember him getting into fights all the time at school? Being kicked out? Being hauled off to jail for disorderly conduct or setting off illegal fireworks or resisting arrest?"

"Of course, but . . . he was a lot younger then. I get the impression he's settled down."

"Funny, I don't get the same impression. He looks like he's part of a biker gang."

Cheyenne liked the way he looked — tattoos, scar and all. She figured that was part of the reason she couldn't seem to refuse him. "You don't think he's handsome?"

"I think he's dangerous. How did you two hook up in the first place?"

Scooting lower in the bed, Cheyenne pulled a pillow to her chest. "I ran into him in the park last Sunday."

There was some noise in the background. It sounded as if Baxter or Noah was asking Eve for details on their conversation. "Wait till I get off," she said.

"Don't tell anyone!" Cheyenne cried. "What happened with Dylan is between us."

"Of course. I'll make up something. But now I'm even more convinced you should go out with Joe. He's the kind of guy you need, Chey, not —" she lowered her voice "— not Dylan. Dylan will chew you up and spit you out."

Cheyenne couldn't remember when she'd seen Dylan with a woman. But until last weekend, she hadn't paid that much attention to him, other than to lump him in with Aaron, who was so bad for Presley. "Dylan actually seems sort of . . . sensitive," she admitted.

"Come on, don't get mixed up with him. You've never wanted your sister to go over there. There has to be a reason. Maybe Joe can help you get out of this."

Eve did seem to be relieved by that idea. But . . . what if Dylan's reputation wasn't the sum total of who he was? What if he'd changed?

Thinking of the desire that had left her helpless when they'd had sex at the inn, Cheyenne massaged her forehead. "But it'll feel disloyal being with Joe, knowing you like him, too. I can't do it."

"Cheyenne, you've never had anything in your life worth hanging on to. I want you to have this."

"I have you," she said softly.

"And that won't change," Eve said. "I want you to make me a promise."

Cheyenne knew where this was going, but she asked, anyway. "What kind of promise?"

"Stay away from Dylan. Don't see him again."

"Tell me Baxter and the others can't hear you."

"No, they're dickering with a street vendor."

"Good. Anyway, I don't think Dylan does drugs or anything else that's too bad. I'm beginning to wonder if he's sort of taken the blame for everything his brothers have done."

"You can't be that generous, Chey. Your whole future could hinge on this decision. Please? Will you forget Dylan and go out with Joe? *For me?*"

Cheyenne wasn't as excited as she thought she'd be by the prospect of dating Joe. That came as a surprise. What happened to all those angst-filled evenings when she'd passed him on the street and hoped he'd linger? Or when she'd waited outside Eve's house just last Friday?

He was still the same guy.

Somehow *she'd* changed.

"I have your blessing?" she asked.

"Of course you have my blessing," Eve replied.

She should be elated. So why was it Dylan's face that appeared in her mind every time she imagined herself in a man's arms? How had he replaced Joe in her fantasies so quickly?

"Chey?" Eve said. "You're going to stay away from the Amoses, right?"

"Right." She agreed because she'd come to the same conclusion. She had to be smart, choose wisely, or her life would never improve.

"And you'll go out with Joe?"

"If that's what you really want."

"It is. Gail's going to have him call and ask you to the Victorian Christmas celebration tomorrow night."

"Okay." She sat up and peered at her closet. "What should I wear?"

"It'll be cold so . . . I'd go with your pea coat, furry boots and that knitted beanie. It looks great on you."

"Good idea." She sighed. "I wish you were here."

"Me, too. I can't believe you finally lost your virginity and I wasn't around to hear about it."

Cheyenne wasn't sure it would've happened had Eve been home. Feeling so alone had made her vulnerable.

"So? What'd you think?" Eve asked, her tone taking on a positive note. "Was it good?"

Cheyenne smiled. "Dylan might have his issues, but . . . he's definitely talented in bed."

Eve laughed. "Somehow I don't doubt it. From what I've seen of him, he's got quite a body — and a wickedly sensual mouth. But a good body doesn't necessarily equate to a good husband. You want a relationship that'll give you something worth hanging on to, don't you? You want a family."

She definitely didn't want a broken heart. "Eventually."

"Then go to the Victorian Christmas celebration with Joe and see where it leads."

Considering what she'd done, it probably wouldn't lead anywhere. "Don't you think I should wait a few weeks? I was just . . . intimate with Dylan."

"Are you and Dylan *together*?"

"No!"

"Then forget about it. Sex means nothing to the Amos brothers."

Cheyenne wasn't convinced that was entirely accurate. Eve didn't know them. But there was no point in arguing while they were on a long-distance call. Aware that their time was limited, Cheyenne felt pressure to let Eve go. She didn't want her to wind up with a big phone bill. "But what about Joe's perspective on it?" she asked. "Surely he wouldn't want to go out with me if he knew I'd just slept with Dylan."

"He has no claim on you yet. Just don't see Dylan while you're seeing Joe and it's all good."

Cheyenne didn't feel comfortable with that. Sunday was too soon. But she supposed she might as well take the opportunity she'd been offered. Maybe Joe could help her forget Dylan. Apparently, she needed *something* to make that happen because she wasn't having any luck forgetting him on her own. "Okay, but I'm going to tell him. I have to be honest."

"*About Dylan?*"

"Yes! It's only fair."

"No way! You can't tell *anyone* about Dylan. What you've done is no one's business but yours. Forget him and move on. So you've had a sexual relationship. Most women have had several by the time they're thirty-one. Put it behind you. Maybe it was ill-timed, but it was . . . a fling, nothing more."

She fidgeted with the edge of her blanket.

"He wanted to give me a key to his house."

"That's not a commitment."

It'd sort of felt like one — or at least, a step in that direction. It told her he wanted to continue seeing her. And that he wasn't worried she might run into another of his love interests in the night.

"I have to go," Eve said.

Cheyenne drew a deep breath. "I know. Have fun. Wish I was there."

"Me, too. Although it sounds like you've been having more fun at home."

"Stop already!" she said with a laugh.

Eve laughed with her. "I'm just so shocked!"

"Don't make me sorry I told you."

She was teasing and knew Eve could tell because she kept laughing. "I won't."

Chey said goodbye and almost hung up, then pulled the phone back to her ear when she realized Eve had one last piece of encouragement.

"Joe's twice the man Dylan is. You'll see."

He certainly fit the profile of the perfect candidate. He was all she'd ever wanted.

But she was afraid that being with Dylan had changed her in some way, that now she wouldn't be satisfied with anyone else.

17

Cheyenne had planned to go in to work for a couple of hours. Although he had no help, since Jacob was spending his Saturday at a friend's house, Riley was there. But she'd overslept and, because of that, had decided to restructure her day. She didn't really need to go to the inn. There was plenty of time to get ready for the grand reopening. And it was the holidays. With Christmas right around the corner, she had shopping and wrapping to do.

She was just finishing breakfast before heading to the closest mall in Sacramento when her sister wandered into the kitchen.

"Thought I heard you."

"Sorry. Was I louder than usual?"

"No, I wanted to catch you before you left." She squinted at the clock on the wall. "Wow, it's after noon?"

Cheyenne swallowed the last of her frosted wheat cereal. "Yeah. I'm not going to work today. I've got some errands to run before Christmas."

A strange expression came over Presley's face. She folded her arms and leaned against the wall.

"Why are you looking at me like that?" Feeling awkward and immediately aware of the secret she was keeping — also known as Dylan — Cheyenne set down her spoon.

"What's going on with you these days?" Presley asked.

She drew her eyebrows together to add another degree of believability to her act. "Nothing. Why?"

"You've been different since your friends left. Everything okay?"

Breathing a sigh of relief, she got up and put her bowl and spoon in the dishwasher. For a second, she'd worried that her sister was going to call her out on their tempting neighbor. "Fine."

"You sure?"

Cheyenne slipped on her coat, which she'd draped over a chair. "Yes."

"Because Aaron told me something last night that has me a little confused."

Now she was nervous again. "*Last night?* I thought you were working."

"I was. I stopped by his place on my way home."

"What did he have to say?" She didn't want to ask. She was afraid Dylan had told his brothers about their romantic liaison. It would certainly be a fitting revenge. . . .

"That he saw Dylan's bike here last weekend."

"*Here*?" she echoed. She didn't know what else to say. At least Dylan hadn't blown the whistle.

"In our driveway."

Cheyenne pretended a sudden preoccupation with putting on lip gloss. He'd only been here for a couple of hours but, apparently, that had obviously been long enough for someone to notice his motorcycle. It was a miracle no one had spotted her car at his place on Monday — although he lived even farther from town, and not many people had to go by his place in order to get home. Except for Carl Inera, the ones who did wouldn't be up and about that late.

"Do you know why?" Presley asked.

Cheyenne met her gaze. "Maybe he stopped by to see you."

Presley's eyebrows shot up. "In the middle of the night?"

"Sometimes you're home."

"I wasn't on Sunday." She shoved off from the wall and moved closer. "You're not seeing Dylan Amos, are you, Chey?"

Cheyenne's stomach tightened, which immediately made her regret eating. She couldn't tell anyone, other than Eve, that she'd been with Dylan, especially Presley. She believed her sister would never do anything *intentionally* to hurt her, but she could get high or drunk and let the secret slip. Or she could use Cheyenne's association with Dylan to justify her own selection of friends. Cheyenne was afraid that if Presley didn't break away from the people she'd been hanging out with and quit using, she'd wind up dead.

She planned to lie, but she couldn't do it quite as blatantly as the situation called for. "He came by and we talked a little, okay?"

"You talked."

She fished her keys out of her purse. "That's right."

Presley sauntered closer. "So . . . will you be *talking* again?"

"I don't think so."

"You're not interested in him?"

This time she didn't qualify her response, because she so desperately wanted what she said to be true. "No, not at all." She started out the back door, since she'd parked her Oldsmobile in the carport, then hesitated. "How'd he get that scar on his temple? Do you know?"

Presley opened the cupboard and pulled out the Cheerios. "A bunch of guys jumped Aaron at a bar over a comment he made, or money he owed or . . . something. I can't remember exactly."

"And Dylan got involved?"

"You can't mess with one of his brothers and not expect Dylan to jump in." Silverware rattled as she opened the drawer. "He put two of those guys in the hospital. But he came away with a piece of glass from a broken bottle in his temple. Aaron once told me if it'd gone in another fraction of an inch, Dylan would've been blinded."

"So he's as good at fighting as we've always heard." Their high school had been abuzz with the news of Dylan dropping out of school to take over his dad's business. He'd grown even more infamous when he'd become an MMA fighter shortly after.

"Apparently. He won a lot of matches." She poured milk on her cereal. "The way Aaron tells it, after their dad went to prison, getting in the cage was the only way Dylan could keep a roof over their heads."

"He had the auto body shop."

Presley held the cereal box so she could read the back of it and spoke between mouthfuls. "Yeah, but his dad wasn't the same after their mother died. He'd let the business fall to crap. It took Dylan several years to build the shop into what it is today."

So Dylan deserved the credit for that. "He's a survivor." She was talking more to herself than to Presley, but her sister glanced up.

"He can be gentle, too. Especially with Mack. Aaron's always complaining about the way Dylan babies Mack."

Cheyenne straightened. She was afraid to hear the answer to this question, but she had to ask it. "Does Dylan do drugs?"

"He's partied over the years, but . . . he doesn't anymore. He might have a beer or two. That's about it. We tease him that he's getting old." Presley's grin faded, and she narrowed her gaze. "You *are* interested in him, aren't you!"

"No." Cheyenne shook her head.

"Yes, you are! I can tell! I think you should go out with him. He's not as bad as everyone says."

Just having her sister recommend him was enough to scare her off. She knew Presley would find it hilarious if Cheyenne were to fall for one of the guys she'd always warned her against. But Presley seemed genuinely excited by the idea. And Cheyenne could understand that, too. It meant Cheyenne would finally like something Presley liked.

"He's not my type, Pres."

"How do you know?"

"I just do."

"No, you don't. You've never even been around him." She held her spoon midway to her mouth but seemed to have forgotten about eating. "I have the night off. You should go over there with me."

The car keys were beginning to cut into Cheyenne's hand, she was holding them so tightly. "Why would I do that?"

"Because you should see what he's like — at least enough to realize what you're turning away."

"I've seen what he's like."

"No, you haven't, or you wouldn't be asking *me* about him. Get to know him. Don't make your decision based on gossip. You hate it when people judge you because of me and Mom."

That got to her. But what would Dylan think if she suddenly showed up at his house with her sister?

"He wouldn't want me there," she said. Not after what she'd told him last night. She'd felt his resolution, the sense of finality when he'd left her at the B and B.

"Are you kidding? I'm sure he'd love it. If not, he can tell you to leave."

"And who'll watch Mom?"

"What about Marcy?"

"She hasn't been here in weeks. Mom's gotten a lot worse since then."

"She's a nurse, Chey. I think she can handle it."

"But it's the holidays!"

"Won't hurt to ask. I bet she'd be willing. She said we could call her anytime we need a break. You know she really wants to help. Or we can call hospice and see if they have anyone to suggest."

"I don't know. . . ."

"For God's sake, take a risk! You always play it so safe."

Because she had to compensate for the rest of her family! Their behavior forced her to the opposite end of the spectrum.

But Presley had a point. If Marcy could watch Anita, maybe she should at least learn enough about Dylan to make an informed decision. Otherwise, how could she say Joe was really the better choice?

"Fine."

Presley blinked in surprise. "*Really?*"

Cheyenne could guess what her friends would say. They'd warn her to stay away from Dylan; Eve already had.

But *she* was the one who'd have to live with her decision. "Really."

■ ■ ■ ■

Dylan was in a terrible mood. He blamed it on an argument with Aaron at work and the fact that Saturday was their busiest — and therefore his most stressful — day. But he usually managed just fine regardless of the challenges he faced at the shop. And he doubted he would've gotten into it with Aaron in the first place if he'd had a little more patience.

It was Cheyenne. She was driving him crazy. He'd told himself he wouldn't speak to her or touch her ever again. Yet that was all he wanted to do. Thoughts of her — her lips parting when he kissed her, her body arching into him as he cupped her breast, her soft gasp when he touched her in a way she particularly liked — intruded no matter what he was doing or how hard he tried to distract himself. Sometimes he even thought he could smell her perfume.

It didn't help that he hadn't used any protection at The Gold Nugget last night. She could be carrying his child. He wondered how she might react to that.

He wondered how *he'd* react to it.

Maybe what he was going through served him right. He supposed he was due for a little poetic justice. He'd never fallen hopelessly in love. He'd made fun of other guys who'd let a woman get the best of them, found it funny that they could no longer think straight. That they were so willing to sacrifice their pride, so willing to act like idiots, drooling over women who didn't want them.

He'd promised himself that would never be him. Until now it'd been easy. He still wasn't sure quite where he'd gone wrong. He'd been traveling through life quite comfortably — had pretty much hit cruise control after conquering the problems of the past decade — and then he'd run into Cheyenne in the park and the earth had dropped away.

But he wasn't going to give in and see her, wouldn't allow her to manipulate his emotions. He didn't care how much his self-denial made him suffer. At least he'd suffer on his own terms.

"Shit, Dyl, you look like you're ready to hit somebody," Mack said as he climbed into Dylan's Jeep so they could head home for the day.

Dylan *wanted* to hit somebody. He needed an outlet for the tension coursing through him. But it wasn't until Mack pointed it out that he realized he'd been glowering, and that he had a death grip on the steering wheel. Forcing himself to ease up, he smiled ruefully. "Hard day."

Mack shrugged. "Was it? Seemed about the same as any other day to me."

"Aaron and I got into it again." He tried to fall back on that, but Mack kept him honest.

"You and Aaron get into it all the time."

Dylan let the engine idle as he waited for Aaron, Grady and Rod, who were in Grady's Explorer, to pass through the gate ahead of them. He always left last, so he could lock up. It was a ritual. "I'm worried about him."

Mack sighed. "I know."

"Where's he getting it?" Dylan rolled through the gate, then stopped so he could go back and fasten the padlock. But he paused for Mack's answer before getting out.

With a scowl, Mack stared after his brothers. Dylan didn't need to explain what "it" was. "I have no idea."

"It's not Carl."

"I don't think so."

Dylan could tell Mack felt torn. He didn't want to narc on one brother to another. But Dylan didn't want to play the role of parent, either. It was just that he had no choice.

He'd been thrust into that position, and because he loved his brothers, he didn't have the luxury of handling it any other way. He'd tried being cool, letting Aaron cope with his own problems. That wasn't working.

"You'd tell me, though, right?"

Mack pinched the bridge of his nose. Then he dropped his hand and turned to face Dylan. "Yeah. I'd tell you."

"What about Presley?"

"She could be bringing it."

"So what do I do about that?"

"I guess you'll have to have a talk with her."

Dylan put the Jeep in Park and opened the door. "Yeah, I guess I will," he said, but they both knew the risks. Once Aaron found out Dylan had gotten involved, there'd be another fight. And this time, Aaron could very likely leave. He'd come close to it before.

If that happened, they might lose the grip they had on him and he could drift away for good.

Cheyenne was so nervous she almost backed out.

"Come on. You said you'd go," Presley whispered.

They were in the bathroom, where Cheyenne was just finishing her makeup. Marcy had already arrived to take care of Anita and might be able to hear them in the kitchen, so they were keeping their voices down.

"He's not expecting me," she said.

"He doesn't have to be expecting you. This is casual. We're just going to drop by and say hello, see what they're doing."

"We hired a nurse. How is that casual?"

"Maybe we wanted to go out together for a change."

That brought up a subject Cheyenne didn't want to broach — the fact that they rarely did this sort of thing, that they lived in separate worlds, except when they were at home. So she didn't point out how unusual that would be. "It'll be awkward to show up out of the blue."

"It'll be fine. Come on."

With a final look in the mirror, Cheyenne sighed. She'd committed herself. She'd even bought a new pair of jeans and some boots. Presley wouldn't let her back out. "I'm glad we have a chance to go out as sisters," she said, trying to bolster her conviction. "We've been playing tag team for so long."

Presley smiled. "Exactly. See? There you go. We'll drive to Sacramento and catch a movie if the Amos boys are busy. You may not even see him."

A movie, any movie, sounded relaxing by comparison. And yet Cheyenne knew she'd be disappointed if they had to resort to plan B. Dylan had been on her mind all day. Some of her memories of him were quite erotic, but she wasn't going to get physical with him again. She wanted to start over — at the beginning this time — to figure out what kind of man he really was. "Let me grab my coat."

It hadn't snowed for a week, but the weather report said another storm was on its way, so they drove over in Presley's Mustang instead of walking.

"You okay?" Presley asked, giving her hand a squeeze before they got out.

Cheyenne could see a number of vehicles in the garage, the drive, the side yard. It looked like everyone was home, including Dylan. His Jeep and his bike were parked in their usual spots. "Are you sure you don't want to go straight to the movies and skip this part?"

Presley chuckled. "Nice try."

After taking a second to gather her resolve, Cheyenne followed her sister across the lawn to the front door. Then she stood there, biting her lip, trying to alleviate the anxiety.

Mack answered their knock, amidst the barking of Dylan's dogs. "Hey, Presley." His eyes shifted to Cheyenne. Cheyenne thought she saw some surprise there, but he covered his reaction with a nod of acknowledgment.

"Aaron around?" Presley asked.

"He is." He stepped to one side. "Come on in."

He showed them through the house Cheyenne had previously seen from the entryway and only in the dark. But the impressions she'd gotten seemed accurate. There weren't a lot of decorations, very few pictures and memorabilia. The Amoses had what most men would consider the basics — a big-screen TV, plenty of other electronics, a comfortable couch and several recliners. There was even a Christmas tree in the corner, one that looked and smelled freshly cut. It had the usual stand, but no ornaments or presents to go with it.

Someone had lit a fire in the fireplace, which made the house several degrees warmer than her own. Cheyenne appreciated that, because her hands felt like blocks of ice. She also appreciated the smell of wood smoke. It was a scent she associated with Christmas.

The dogs seemed to remember her. They followed her, tails wagging, to lick her hand. She bent to pet them, eager for the distraction, since there were three Amoses in the living room — Mack, Grady and Rod — who'd quit watching whatever they'd been watching to stare at her.

Dylan wasn't in the room. Cheyenne could tell immediately, even though the only light came from the TV and fireplace and what spilled over from the hallway and kitchen.

Aaron was getting a beer out of the fridge. "Hey," he called when he saw them. "You brought your sister."

Presley dragged her forward. "I told her you guys wouldn't mind a little company." She grinned meaningfully. "I also told her you were always a good time."

His lips, lips that looked so much like Dylan's, hitched up on one side. He spoke to Presley but never took his eyes off her. "What kind of fun is she after?"

Cheyenne cleared her throat and spoke up, so she wouldn't seem as uncomfortable as she felt. "Just getting out of the house works for me. I don't need a lot."

He nodded toward the TV. "Good. Because I'm not sure the movie we rented shows much promise."

"What is it?" Presley asked.

"That new horror flick — *The Haunting.* We just put it in if you want to watch."

One glance over her shoulder told Cheyenne that the Amos boys hadn't taken her unexpected appearance in stride the way Presley had said they would. They remained in their seats, but one of them had paused the movie, and they were all gaping at her as if she was an asteroid that had just come crashing into their house.

"Sure," she said. "I'll give it a chance."

"Where's Dylan?" Presley asked.

"Right here."

Cheyenne turned to see Dylan walking around the corner from the direction of his bedroom. He had wet hair; he must've gotten out of the shower a few minutes ago. But he didn't look like he was about to leave. He was dressed in a black V-neck T-shirt, jeans and house shoes.

"Great!" Presley smiled broadly. "My sister was hoping you'd be home."

The heat of a blush crept up Cheyenne's neck as their eyes met. Presley had just announced to the whole room that Dylan was the reason she'd decided to tag along tonight; Cheyenne wasn't used to being so transparent.

"You know Chey, don't you?" Presley said.

A muscle moved in Dylan's cheek, indicating the presence of some strong emotion, but Cheyenne had no idea *which* emotion. He probably thought she had a lot of nerve after last night. "I've met her once or twice."

Presley helped herself to a beer. "She wants to watch a movie with you," she said. Then they all settled in the living room, in whatever seats were left, and started the movie at the beginning. But it wasn't long before Aaron pulled Presley away, into one of the back bedrooms, leaving Cheyenne alone with Dylan and the rest of his brothers.

18

Cheyenne couldn't concentrate on the movie. It was as if she could feel every breath Dylan took — even though she'd sat as far away from him as possible. He hadn't said she should sit closer. He hadn't said much to her at all. She got the impression that he was skeptical of her presence, couldn't quite figure out what she was doing.

She was glad he wasn't assuming she'd changed her mind, because she wasn't sure her being there held that much significance. Like she'd told Presley, she was just getting to know him. She wasn't making any promises or commitments, wasn't thinking past a platonic friendship.

For one thing, she'd already agreed to go out with Joe, if he asked her. For another, she felt as though she was at a crossroads, about to enter a new phase of her life, and the decisions she made now would determine her happiness more than ever before. Letting Presley persuade her to come here was a way of making sure that if she walked away from Dylan, she wouldn't regret it later. That was all.

When the movie ended and Presley still hadn't returned, Cheyenne felt even more awkward. It wasn't as if she could get up and leave. Presley had driven; she had the keys.

Cheyenne was considering how to escape gracefully — she could say she had to go, then walk home despite the cold — when Mack suggested they head over to Sexy Sadie's.

"Come with us," Grady said, appealing to her.

Cheyenne's first impulse was to refuse. But Dylan was looking at her, his eyebrows arched in challenge, and she knew he thought she was unwilling to be seen with him in public.

So she said yes.

"Great." Grady smiled and nudged Mack. "Go get Aaron and Presley. But have them drive over separately, since we have to take two cars, anyway. We'll go in my Explorer."

Mack hurried off to do what he'd been told, and the others went to get their coats. Only Dylan stayed behind. His eyes narrowed for a second. But then his lips curved into a victorious smile, giving Cheyenne the impression that she'd just walked into a trap.

Things were looking up. Dylan was surprised they'd reversed so quickly, but it was good to know he hadn't lost his ability to tell when a woman was interested in him. Maybe Cheyenne was playing it safe, but she hadn't completely decided against him. That meant he had a shot.

He just had to be careful, let her come to him.

The music was loud and the bar crowded, but he'd been to Sexy Sadie's so often that it felt like home. They ordered drinks — he paid for the first round — then made their way to the back corner to play some darts. This wasn't a place Cheyenne frequented. He suspected the upwardly mobile group she hung out with visited the trendy clubs in Sacramento, if they ever pulled themselves away from worthier pursuits long enough to make the drive. Sexy Sadie's was a down-and-dirty honkytonk, or as much of one as there was to be found so far from the Deep South.

Dylan had heard the band before and liked them. They played a wide range of music — country, pop, even some blues.

Their group found a table in the corner. Then he watched Cheyenne lose a game of darts to Mack. Although he caught her watching *him* whenever she thought he wasn't looking, she seemed to gravitate toward his youngest brother. He guessed she felt safer with the baby of the family than she did with him.

"I'll take you on," he told Mack. Usually, he didn't play darts, and if he did it didn't matter whether he won. He found pool more of a challenge. But tonight he concentrated on winning because he wanted to take control of the game.

Mack knew exactly what Dylan had in mind. After he lost, he winked as he relinquished his darts and went to the bar for another drink.

Dylan played Rod and Grady, overlooked Aaron because Aaron always offered him more competition than the others and he didn't want to risk losing before he could get to Cheyenne. To be polite, he first asked Presley if she wanted the challenge, but she motioned toward her sister. "Play with Cheyenne. That's what you're after, anyway. Aaron and I are going to dance. But before we do —" she pulled out a twenty "— I'm putting this on her."

"Did you see her play Mack?" Dylan asked.

Outraged, Cheyenne elbowed him in the ribs. "So I had a bad game! I'm usually a lot better than that."

"Sure you are," he said. "I'm just saying your sister might not want to put money on it."

"I can take you," she insisted.

He stepped up to her and grinned when she didn't back down. "You think so?"

She lifted her chin. "I'm certain of it."

"*How* certain?"

She dug through her purse and slapped another twenty on the table. "Certain enough to put up my own money."

Leaning so close he could smell her perfume, he lowered his voice. "I was hoping you might put up something I'd be more interested in winning."

"Like?"

"Dinner. Tomorrow night."

"Nice," Presley said. "He's direct. I like a man who knows his own mind. Now my money's on him."

Cheyenne could also appreciate a man who wasn't afraid to go after what he wanted, who didn't play games or pretend. Dylan seemed fearless in that regard, which somehow reassured her. If he knew what he was doing, maybe being attracted to him wasn't so risky.

But then she reminded herself that they were talking about one of the Amos boys — the ringleader, no less — and that he had a history of going from one woman to the next. Just because he made her feel special *right now* didn't mean his attention wouldn't wane in a few days or weeks. It could be that she was just the latest in a long line of women who'd caught his eye, that he liked the challenge she presented.

"So what do you say?" he asked.

She pursed her lips. "Depends."

"On . . ."

"What *you're* putting up."

"What do you want?"

She studied his face as she considered her answer. She'd made a similar bet with Joe over their card game. He'd offered automotive services. Dylan could probably have provided that, too. But she wanted something more meaningful. "Twenty honest answers."

This seemed to throw him. "To what questions?"

"Whatever I ask," she said, grinning.

He finished his beer. "Give me a sample."

She laughed at his sudden reluctance.

"They'll be tough."

"Personal?"

"Very."

"*Painful?*"

"Possibly."

With a grimace he picked up his darts. "Good thing I don't plan to lose."

Cheyenne was determined not to lose, either. And she didn't.

"You hustled me!" he complained when she won it with a bull's-eye.

"My mother used to manage a pool hall."

"*What?*"

"It was one of the few jobs she kept for longer than a week. We stayed the whole summer, the summer before we moved here."

"So you were . . . what? Fifteen? Sixteen? That's not old enough to hang out in a pool hall, not if they serve alcohol."

"I was fourteen and Presley was sixteen, and they definitely served alcohol. But we lived in a one-bedroom apartment on the second floor. My mom slept during the day, while the place was closed. We weren't allowed to turn on the TV, because the noise would wake her. And we weren't allowed to leave the premises because she didn't want to worry about us getting into trouble. So we'd let in the boys who lived next door and play darts and pool with them all day." She took a sip of her beer. "Told you I was good. You just chose to believe what you *think* you saw."

"So you threw the game with Mack?"

"I could tell you were watching." She shrugged. "Fortunately, Mack was good enough to make it look easy."

"I'll never be able to trust you again," he said with mock outrage.

"Soon I'll know your deepest, darkest secrets. Frightening, isn't it?"

He grew serious as his eyes searched hers. "What will you do with that knowledge?"

A glance at the others told her they were preoccupied and no longer listening. "Decide whether or not I want to get back into bed with you."

He finished her beer. "You already want to get back into bed with me," he said with a sexy grin.

They danced. They laughed. They stayed out late. Cheyenne was a little tipsy by the time Dylan brought her home. He'd stopped drinking after one beer and those few swallows he'd had of hers. Although he hadn't made a big deal about becoming the designated driver, hadn't even mentioned it, she suspected he'd taken on that responsibility to make sure they all got home safely.

He was used to caring for people, she realized. He was good at it, probably because he'd been doing it most of his life. She wondered if his brothers knew how lucky they were that he'd stepped up and been able to fill their parents' shoes. *She* understood the value of what he'd done for them, because she'd never had anyone to give her that kind of care and protection.

She wished Presley was home so they could talk, but her sister was still with Aaron. No one could find them when it was time to leave. Cheyenne worried about what they might be doing, afraid they'd gone off to get high. But she didn't want to think about that right now. She was still engrossed in the afterglow of a wonderful evening.

"How is she?" she asked Marcy as she walked in.

A middle-aged mother of five, Marcy was sitting in the living room reading a book, which she slid into her purse. "Fine. It's been quiet around here. I've written down all the times she woke up, was fed and received her medication."

"Great. Thank you." Cheyenne reached for her wallet so she could pay Marcy and found a note in her purse. Presley had written something on a napkin from the bar.

She didn't take the time to read it. She wanted to send Marcy off first.

"I'm available over the rest of the holidays, if you need me," Marcy said.

"We'd feel too guilty bothering you when you should be with your family."

"I'm happy to help out here and there. You need a break every once in a while."

"Thanks for the offer. I'll keep it in mind." Cheyenne walked her to the door. Then she locked up and returned to the sofa, where she read her sister's brief message.

I love seeing you have a good time. So does Dylan. He's crazy about you. I can see it in his face.

P

Smiling, Cheyenne leaned her head back as she remembered various parts of the evening. Although Dylan had accompanied her to the door, he hadn't kissed her good-night. She'd wanted him to, but in another way she was glad he intuitively knew better than to resume anything physical. She liked the friendship they were establishing. It was a better starting place, a far less frightening approach to including him in her life, whether as a friend . . . or more.

Her phone rang. She glanced at caller ID

and laughed. "Hello?"

"I'm ready for one question," Dylan said.

"Just *one*?" On the drive, when she'd suggested he start to fulfill his twenty-answer debt, he'd scowled and put her off.

"I prefer to handle it over time," he replied, which was what he'd said then, too.

"What if I go easy on you at first?"

"Then you could get two."

Covering herself with the throw blanket she kept on the arm of the couch, she pulled up her feet. "Have you ever been in love?"

"That's supposed to be an *easy* question?"

"It's not?" It was certainly one she was dying to know the answer to. His name had been connected to a lot of different women over the years, but she'd never heard about a steady girlfriend. That didn't mean it couldn't have happened. She hadn't been paying much attention, especially since Joe returned to town.

"How is that easy?"

"Yes or no will handle it."

"But I'm not sure what the truth says about me."

She pictured him standing inside her front door as he had that first night. She no longer saw the scar at his temple as a defect. It was just part of him, and it added character to his face. "Give it a shot. I'll tell you what it says about you, or at least my interpretation."

"Never been in love," he admitted. "Until recently, my life's been almost entirely devoted to survival." He hesitated. "So what do you make of that? Are you now assuming I *can't* fall in love? That I'm not capable of it?"

"I'm assuming the people you've loved, so far, are your brothers."

"Not a bad thing," he said, verifying her response.

"Not a bad thing at all."

"Okay, I'll let you ask one more."

She planned to choose wisely. There was so much she wanted to learn about Dylan Amos, and he wasn't easy to know. In her opinion, that was why he was so misunderstood. "What do you want most out of life?"

It took him a few seconds to respond. "I'm not sure," he said when he answered. "I guess . . . success. No, more than that. Balance. What do you want?"

"Freedom," she decided.

"What kind of freedom?"

"Freedom from my past. Freedom from all the questions and suspicions."

"What questions and suspicions?"

She inhaled deeply. She'd never told

another soul, except her mother and Presley, about the memories that didn't seem to fit the life she'd known. But there was something about Dylan that made her trust him. Maybe that was because they'd slept together. She'd already shared a deeper intimacy with him than anyone else, and he'd kept that secret by hiding her car behind the barn so his brothers wouldn't see it and by treating her as he had tonight, without too much familiarity, when they were with others.

Or maybe she trusted him because he'd been through enough to understand certain nuances that would be lost on Eve or Callie or Gail — or any of the guys she hung out with, for that matter. Although her friends had each suffered tragedy and faced difficulties, some more than others, they'd always been affluent, popular, attractive, well-liked and secure. They didn't have to wonder who they were and where they came from. Even Dylan didn't have to do that. But Cheyenne was willing to bet he could relate to her pain and confusion better than anyone else.

"I have these memories." She told him how empty and odd she felt when it snowed, about the blonde lady and the birthday party and the pretty room with the canopy bed. "I have no idea who that woman is, but she was significant to me, you know? I can *feel* it, deep in my bones. It's almost as if . . . as if I *miss* her."

"Have you asked your mother about it?"

"Of course."

"And?"

"She says she's never met anyone like the person I describe. She accuses me of making it all up. She says I think I'm too good for her and Presley, so I've created this fantasy to explain why."

"Is there any proof that Anita might not be your mother?"

"None. Except she can't even tell me where I was born."

"What does it say on your birth certificate?"

"What birth certificate?"

"You don't have one?"

"None of us do. My mother didn't bother to hang on to stuff like that. And what we did have got thrown out."

"How did you and Presley get into school?"

"One of the men my mother was with for a brief period years ago knew how to make fake IDs. She had him make us each a birth certificate. We used it to get into school wherever we went — when we attended, which wasn't often — but he wasn't very good. It's a miracle they accepted it."

"They probably didn't look at it too closely."

"No one did. She'd hand them a bad photocopy, and they'd chalk up the imperfections to that, I guess. Then she'd tell them that getting immunizations was against our religion, and we were in."

"Where were you born?"

"My mother says in Wyoming. That's why she named me Cheyenne. But I wasn't born there. I've checked."

"So . . . you think she might've stolen you from someone else?"

It sounded crazy to hear her suspicions spoken aloud. Already, she regretted sharing what she had. The alcohol had loosened her tongue. But now that she'd revealed her doubts, she figured she might as well admit the truth. "I've always wondered."

"That would explain why you look nothing like your sister."

"My mother, *if* she's my mother, says we come from different fathers."

"Obviously. Presley's father was Hispanic, wasn't he? But you're saying you might not be sisters at all?"

Guilt for suggesting such a thing suddenly overwhelmed Cheyenne and she rubbed her face. "Or my mother's right. Maybe it's all some weird attempt on my part to pretend I belong somewhere else, somewhere better. Forget I said anything."

She added a humorless chuckle, but he didn't seem willing to drop the subject quite so easily.

"What do you know about your father?"

"Nothing."

"Not even his name?"

"My mom claims she met him at a bar. They went to a motel together. He was gone less than an hour later. I'm sure she wasn't sober." She drew the blanket higher. "Touching encounter, right? You see why I might've been tempted to create a prettier picture."

"Children are stolen every day," he said. "Some are found, some are not. Those who aren't, if they're alive, have to go somewhere, grow up somehow. Considering your mother, and what you know her to be capable of, it's at least as likely that you *didn't* dream it up."

It felt great to have some support, someone else suggesting she might not be crazy for suspecting the worst, especially since Presley had discounted those memories as much as Anita had.

"Have you gone to the police?" he asked.

"Once."

"And?"

"If I *was* kidnapped, my case wasn't as widely publicized as Jaycee Dugard's, that's for sure. They couldn't match me to any missing persons."

"There could be plenty of reasons for that."

"I know. We traveled a lot, were always on the go. That could've been one of the reasons. When I went in, it'd been ten years, which is a long time, so that didn't help, either."

"Not all police departments communicate as well as they should. Or they didn't back then. And there are thousands of missing children."

"Exactly. It feels futile."

"Maybe it's not."

"In any case, what *I'd* like most in life is to either forget the blonde woman — or answer the question of who she is."

"I doubt you'll be able to forget her."

"You're saying my only choice is to answer the question."

"That's what I'm saying."

"Even though I don't have any way to figure out what my original name was, or if my birthday is really my birthday?"

"You could go back to the police. Keep trying."

"I wouldn't want to do that here, wouldn't want the whole town to know that I think I might've been abducted. They've heard enough about our family as it is. I'm an adult now. Maybe I should just . . . let it go." Because she had no idea what she might find and whether or not the truth would be worse than not knowing. What if the perfect childhood she thought she remembered wasn't as perfect as she thought? What if her real family had given her away, to Anita, someone who had no business raising a child?

She'd always wondered if that might be why the police hadn't been able to match her with a missing person. It could be that her original family never filed a report.

"You could go to Sacramento. They have a bigger department and might be in a position to do more for you."

Sacramento was the closest metropolitan city. It made sense to go there. "Maybe I will. Someday. Anyway, enough about me. I think you owe it to me to answer one more question."

"You already stumped me with question number two."

"But I'm the one doing all the revealing. I haven't told anyone else what I just told you, so . . . I'd appreciate it if you wouldn't say anything. The possibility really upsets Presley, for obvious reasons."

"What happens between us stays between us. Regardless of what it is."

He sounded so firm in that commitment she felt a little better about having gotten involved with him. "Thanks. So . . . for your last question of the evening, what are the tattoos on your chest? I know you have some but it's always been too dark for me to make out what they are."

"I'm going to save the answer to that one."

"For . . ."

He lowered his voice. "Someday when you'd like to come over and see for yourself."

Was right now too soon? Suddenly, Cheyenne wanted to be with him. She craved the pleasure he could give her, could already feel her body growing warm and ready in response. But tonight she felt more than a physical reaction. She longed for the companionship and support he offered, too. And that frightened her. It said making love with him would be different this time. It would be deeper, richer — and involve some level of commitment to establishing a relationship.

"You scare me," she admitted.

"In what way?"

"In every way."

"And Joe doesn't?"

Joe didn't have the same reputation. Except for the period when he was married and gone, she'd watched him closely for seventeen years. He seemed both familiar and predictable. And his connection with Gail added a layer of security Cheyenne didn't get with Dylan. Gail adored her brother and would certainly know if he wasn't emotionally reliable or capable of maintaining a relationship. "Joe has never been picked up by the police."

"Neither have I — not for a few years."

"That makes you safe?"

"That means I've had my problems but I've grown up."

"I see. But I'd have to take that on faith."

"You're not a safe bet, either, sweet pea. I'd be taking my own risks."

"What do you mean?"

"You're in love with someone else. Am I going to have to worry about you wanting Joe every time we're together? Is he the one you think about when we make love?"

"No!" She hadn't thought of Joe in that way since Dylan had hijacked her life. Which was odd, given how often she'd fantasized about Gail's brother before. "Even now, when I close my eyes and

31

imagine a man touching me, I see only you."

"I'm willing to work with that," he said. "I can prove myself."

He seemed pleased to have the chance, and that made her smile. There was more she could've said — like how hard it had been to take her eyes off him tonight, how every incidental touch had created an amplified response, how she burned for his hands on her body this very minute. But she knew her defenses were already crumbling too fast.

"Does that mean you'll finally go out to dinner with me?" he asked.

He was nothing if not persistent. She laughed. "Fine. When?"

"Tomorrow night."

The night she was supposed to go out with Joe. But he hadn't called to ask her. "You want what you didn't win."

"*Win?*"

"At darts, remember?"

"I want a lot more than that," he growled.

Her breath caught at the admission. He did something to her, something that made her heart pound and her nerves tingle. She worried that she wouldn't be able to resist him even if she somehow realized, knew without a doubt, that she was making a mistake. "I've never met anyone like you.

You're so . . . frank."

"I don't want to lose out just because I didn't have the balls to make my intentions clear."

She could appreciate that — but it also made her fear that he might be the type to fall *out* of love just as quickly.

If she took the gamble, how would she explain to her friends that she was dating Dylan Amos? They were the family she'd never had, the people who'd pulled her through the past seventeen years. Was she a fool to completely disregard their advice and concern?

They'd come home from the cruise and freak out when they heard. But Dylan was like a drug she'd tried in their absence. All she wanted to do was take another hit, return to that place of euphoria only he could take her.

She wouldn't be the same when her friends saw her again. Would she be able to meld this new relationship with the ones she already had?

The hope was there, but she was afraid her friends, especially Eve, would never really accept Dylan. Certain they had to save her from heartbreak, they'd unite against him.

Fortunately, she had a few days before she

had to deal with their reaction. She'd give herself that much time to see where this was going. . . .

"I'm in for dinner," she said, "but . . . we won't be sleeping together afterward. If we're going to take this seriously, I want to get to really know you first."

"You've got seventeen more questions," he said. "Better make them count."

19

"So what did you think?"

Cheyenne rose up on her elbows and squinted to make out the blurry shape on the edge of her bed: Presley. "What time is it?" she mumbled, but her voice cracked and she had to clear her throat to get all the words out.

"Does it matter?"

"Maybe not to you." She twisted around to find her alarm clock. "*Five!* God, that's early, especially on a Sunday, which is usually my only day to sleep in. What are you doing?"

"I want to hear about Dylan."

With a groan, Cheyenne fell back on the pillows. "Did you just get home?"

"A few minutes ago."

"Where have you been?"

"Hanging out with Aaron."

That didn't provide much information. Cheyenne wanted to relax — at least her sister was home safe — but she couldn't avoid the fact that Presley was high. Now that the sleep was beginning to clear from Cheyenne's head, she could tell by her sister's too-loud voice. "What are you on?"

Presley's gesture was irritable. "Don't worry about it."

"I *do* worry about it. All the time."

"I'm fine!"

"You need to get off drugs, Pres. Go back into rehab if you can't stop on your own."

She hopped off the bed. "You sound like Dylan."

"He said something to you?"

"Tonight he told me Aaron and I are heading down the wrong road. He asked me not to bring drugs to the house, said Aaron's getting in over his head. But I don't know why Dylan's blaming me. Aaron has plenty of ways to get what he wants. It's not like I'm his pusher. I share with him. He shares with me. That's all."

"So that's where your money's going."

"He pays for his share, and when he pays I deliver."

Then Dylan was right. "That's got to stop!"

"It will. Soon."

After Anita died. Once she figured out a way to cope. But Cheyenne feared whatever she was taking would have too strong a hold on her by then. Dylan was obviously worried about Aaron, too. But five o'clock in the morning probably wasn't the best time to force the issue.

Cheyenne took a deep breath. "Have you checked on Mom?"

"No, I haven't. Sometimes I'm just . . . too afraid to go in there."

"I'll do it." Cheyenne swung her legs over the bed, but Presley stopped her.

"How did it end tonight? With Dylan?"

"He brought me home about one."

"That's it?"

"That's it."

"No bumping and grinding? No wet kisses or wild orgasms?"

Guilt welled up, along with the heat of a blush, making Cheyenne glad it was dark. "No."

"How disappointing."

Cheyenne rolled her eyes. "Actually, he's taking me out tomorrow night — if you're available to stay with Mom."

"I was scheduled to work, but Carolyn can cover my shift. She's looking for more hours to help with the cost of Christmas."

"You're sure?"

"Positive. She asked me if I had any she could take."

323

"So you'll do it?"

"Of course."

Cheyenne studied what she could see of her sister's face. "How well do you know Dylan?"

"We've been friends a long time."

"Not close friends."

"No, but I've seen a lot of him."

"Do you think he's someone I can trust?"

"I think he'd be good in bed. Why does everything have to be so serious with you?"

"Because I don't want to pay the price of screwing up my life!"

Sobering, Presley glared at her. "You're such a killjoy."

"Choices have consequences, Pres. That's not my doing."

Her hand went to her stomach. "I need to tell you something."

A prickle of unease ran down Cheyenne's spine. "What's that?"

"I might be pregnant."

Unease instantly turned to nausea. "*What?* And you're still doing *drugs?*"

"It's not for sure. I'm just late, that's all."

Oh, God. "Whose baby is it?"

"*Whose do you think?*"

She seemed offended by the question, but Cheyenne had to ask. Sometimes Presley went home with total strangers she met at the casino. And there was that date last weekend. "Aaron's?"

"Of course. He's the only one I've been with recently, at least without protection," she added under her breath.

Cheyenne didn't know what to say. Her mouth hung open as she tried to absorb this news.

"Never mind." She waved Cheyenne off with a grimace. "It's not your problem. I'll take care of it myself. It's not the end of the world, you know?"

"Meaning . . ."

"I'll get an abortion."

Whether or not to end a pregnancy wasn't something Cheyenne was prepared to consider — for her sister *or* herself. She raked her fingers through her hair. "Does Aaron know about the possibility?"

"No. There's no reason to tell him. He won't want it. He's no more ready for a child than I am."

Cheyenne swallowed hard. "You need to tell him."

"No."

"But maybe you're wrong about him not wanting it. Maybe —"

"Trust me, the Amoses are *not* the marrying kind. So if you like Dylan, watch out. Whatever you do, don't expect a commitment," she said, and left.

Knees suddenly too weak to carry her to Anita's room, Cheyenne sagged onto the bed. She'd already had sex with Dylan without birth control once. It'd happened so fast she hadn't thought much about it, other than to assure herself that it hadn't been when she was ovulating.

But, even so, there was a chance. . . .

Was she letting herself drift down the same turbulent stream as her sister?

The fear that welled up said she was. What was she *thinking*, agreeing to see Dylan? If they got involved, it would never culminate in the kind of relationship she wanted. Presley had warned her as clearly as Eve. And, unlike Eve, Presley would know.

Which was why, when Joe called midmorning to ask her to come over and help him decorate the tree they'd bought together, she said yes.

It was also why she called Dylan as soon as she hung up with Joe and broke their date.

Eve had scrimped and saved for this vacation for months. She'd thought she'd enjoy it more than she was. But she'd decided that two weeks was too long to be gone. She couldn't wait to get home.

"What's wrong with you?"

Turning away from the sun glimmering off the azure ocean, Eve faced Callie, who was lying on the lounge chair next to hers. They were out of port, so they were spending the morning at the pool on the top deck of the cruise ship. "What do you mean?"

"You've been so quiet the past few days."

She shifted the elastic on her bikini to make sure she didn't end up with two different tan lines. "I'm worried about Cheyenne."

"You called her, didn't you?"

"Yes . . ."

"Didn't she sound okay? You said her mother is still alive."

"She is." For a change, Eve's concerns didn't pertain to Anita.

Callie slid her sunglasses up to the bridge of her nose. "I'm *so* glad. I've been afraid she might pass away while we're gone. We really should be there when it happens."

"I know." Eve had two brothers, but both were significantly older and lived elsewhere. Cheyenne was the sister she'd never had. If not for the love she felt for her best friend, she probably would've resented the fact that Joe preferred her. As it was, she was sort of excited that Cheyenne might finally have found a man who'd love and appreciate her the way she deserved.

"So . . . is it Joe?" Callie asked.

Eve anchored her hair behind her ears to stop the wind from whipping it around her face. "No. I just wish I hadn't announced to the world that I was interested in him. Then I wouldn't have to keep explaining that I'm okay. You know how I feel about Chey. She's never had anything. I can take this on the chin for her."

"You're a true friend." Callie reached out to squeeze her arm. "I guessed you'd feel that way."

"I'm more disappointed than hurt," she said. "Joe and I went out to dinner *once*, and it was at my invitation. It's not as if we were engaged."

Callie made a face. "At this rate I wonder if any of us will ever get engaged."

"I guess we're late bloomers. Only Kyle's been married. And Gail. She hit the jackpot."

"Sophia, too."

Her eyes drifted to the pool, where the guys were swimming or hanging out along the edge. Again, Eve wondered about Callie and Kyle but knew better than to ask. "Sophia's married. She didn't hit the jackpot, though."

"True. Skip's a jerk."

"But he *is* rich."

"Doesn't matter. She's miserable."

Eve wiggled her toes, admiring her new pedicure. "And she doesn't count, anyway."

"Why not?"

"She wasn't part of our group in high school. She had her own posse and made good use of them, remember? They were your classic 'mean girls.' "

"I think she's changed."

"Maybe. Maybe not. I'm glad she couldn't come on the cruise. Ted hates that she keeps hanging around."

They could see small splashes as Ted swam laps. "Do you think it's because he still has a thing for her?"

"He'd kill us for even suggesting it, but . . . I wouldn't be surprised. Maybe he's got a string of women coming to his place. It's certainly romantic up there. But I don't get that impression, so . . . he might be holding a candle."

"What about you and Kyle?" The words popped out before Eve could check them.

Callie yawned and stretched. "What about us?"

"You seem to be pretty close."

"We are. I helped him through his divorce from that crazy bitch he married."

"You're not sleeping together. . . ."

With a scowl, Callie tossed a towel at her. "No!"

Eve knocked it away. "You sure?"

"I'm positive! It's strictly platonic. I wouldn't want to be with him while he's on the rebound, anyway."

That qualified her response, and made Eve wonder even more, but she didn't push it any further. She could tell by Callie's reaction that it would be pointless. She'd only get more protestations of friendship.

"There *is* some romantic tension in our little group, though," Callie said, settling back in her chaise.

"Involving . . ."

She lifted her sunglasses. "Baxter."

Eve adjusted her chair so she could sit up a little straighter. Callie couldn't have picked a friend who surprised her more. "Baxter and who else?"

"Never mind." After retrieving her camera from the table between them, she took several shots of the guys in the pool.

"Don't do that!" Eve protested.

"*Take photos?*"

"Throw out a hook and then yank it back. Tell me what you're thinking."

"I shouldn't." The camera whirred with a series of rapid-fire shots.

"But you want to."

Callie put her Nikon back down. "I want someone to tell me I'm wrong."

"Then . . . let me try."

She rolled to the right, so their friends in the pool couldn't see her mouth move or hear her voice. "I think he's in love."

Eve blinked in surprise. "With who?"

There was another long pause.

"*Callie* . . ."

Callie cupped a hand around her mouth as if the steps she'd taken weren't enough to insure their privacy. "Noah."

"*No.*" Eve shook her head. "You're not saying . . ."

Obviously uncomfortable, she frowned. "I'm saying *maybe*. That's all. I mean, haven't you noticed the way he looks at Noah? It's almost as if . . . as if he worships him!"

Baxter tended to brood, but she'd never attached *that* kind of significance to his moods. Now she wondered if Callie could be right. If so, he had a reason to sulk because she couldn't see Noah getting together with any guy, even him. "But . . . if he's gay, why would he hide it from *us*? He knows we'd love him just as much."

Callie raised an eyebrow. "*We* would. But Whiskey Creek is a very conservative town. His parents would be mortified. And what about Noah? The second Baxter comes out, he loses the man he loves, who also happens to be his best friend."

Shading her eyes, Eve regarded Callie's tormented expression. "That's too sad to contemplate."

"And if it's true, which one of them will stay in the group?"

"We would never, ever pick."

"Yet they *both* couldn't join us at the coffee shop, or anywhere else, for that matter. They wouldn't feel comfortable."

Eve reclaimed the towel she'd thrown. "I can't believe it. You're . . . you're stereotyping, that's all."

Callie blanched at the accusation. "Am I?"

"Yes! Baxter is suave and well-dressed and has better taste than the rest of us. He might also be a little more . . . *emotional*. That doesn't make him gay."

"Okay."

The fact that she backed off merely made the seed she'd planted sprout more quickly.

"I mean —" Eve smoothed out a smear of sunblock on her left thigh "— he and Noah grew up next door to each other. They're best friends — almost siblings — like Chey and me —"

"No." Callie broke in. "*Not* like you and

Chey. The older they get, the more friction there is between them."

Eve supposed Callie would know before she would. She captured expressions and nuances through the lens of her camera that others missed. She'd been taking pictures of the trip since they flew out of Sacramento.

Keeping up one hand to block the sun, she took a closer look at what was going on in the pool. While Ted swam laps, Kyle floated on his back near the far corner, talking to Noah, who was sitting on the edge, dangling his feet.

She had to admit that Noah was attractive. Broad-shouldered and long-limbed, he had smooth, bronze skin that rippled over all that biking muscle. But Eve wasn't convinced there was even a possibility of Baxter's being in love with Noah — until her eyes cut to the table where Baxter was reading a book. Although far from conclusive, the way he was looking at Noah made her uncomfortable. "You really think . . ."

"I don't know," Callie responded. "I'm afraid for Bax, that's all."

"And Noah. He'd be hurt, too. Maybe he doesn't want to sleep with Baxter, but he loves him."

"They'd both lose."

"Baxter's dated his share of girls," Eve

pointed out, hoping to disprove their suspicions.

"That doesn't mean anything. A lot of gay guys date or sleep with women, or have at some stage in their lives."

Eve felt her discomfort grow. "I hope you're wrong. Baxter doesn't have a chance with Noah. Noah's as straight as a guy can be."

Callie leaned over to drink her smoothie. "You see what's at stake."

"God . . ." She let out her breath slowly. "I guess that would explain why Bax hasn't ever had a serious girlfriend."

"Or left Whiskey Creek, even though his business is in San Francisco."

"Maybe Noah's the reason he's been such a bear on this cruise, too."

"Noah's been on a roll, hooking up with one woman after another."

"While Baxter has to sit there and watch." Eve doubted they would've noticed this if they hadn't spent a week together in such close quarters. At home, they were too wrapped up in their own lives to be aware of something that well hidden, but on a cruise ship, there were only so many places to get a break from one another.

"I have the impression that Noah senses things aren't quite as they should be," Callie mused. "The way he's been acting with women . . . it's not like him to be so indiscriminate. In fact, he's always been too picky."

"Maybe they do love each other and are fighting it." Eve was determined to consider all options. "If Bax is gay, Noah could be, too. Maybe he's not as straight as we think. How would anyone know?"

"We wouldn't. Not until they were ready to tell us. We just have to pray that whatever happens doesn't rip our friendship apart."

"No kidding." And she'd thought watching Joe date her best friend would be hard. "We're *all* jinxed when it comes to love," she grumbled.

"Except Gail," Callie reminded her.

"How many people can expect to get that lucky?"

Callie shrugged. "Maybe lightning will strike twice."

It just wasn't the same. Cheyenne knelt in Joe's living room, sorting through the ornaments he'd hauled out of the attic. She wanted to see what Christmas decorations he had that might match the new ones they'd bought at the hardware store on the way over. The process was going well; she thought he'd have a nice-looking tree when they were done, despite the challenges she'd created in picking the one she had. But she could definitely tell that the excitement she'd felt in his presence only a week ago — the night they'd played cards together — was gone.

Her fears had been confirmed. Sleeping with Dylan had changed her. Maybe it had even *ruined* her.

"You going totally with gold and white?"

"What?" She turned to look up at him. He was as attractive as ever, standing there in his well-worn jeans and crew-neck sweater. She could still admire his physical attributes. They just didn't do the same thing to her they'd done before — which was crazy. He had a perfect, all-American athlete kind of face. No scars. No long hair. No chip on his shoulder except, perhaps, whatever resentments remained from his failed marriage. He didn't walk around with the "I could do some serious damage" air Dylan exuded. Not only did he have all of that going for him, but Cheyenne had wanted a relationship with Joe for half her life.

How could it be that he'd finally, *finally* asked her out and she'd . . . lost interest?

It couldn't be, she decided. She wouldn't let it. She knew he was a dependable, good-hearted guy. She was going to trust her head and not her heart — or whatever other part of her body might be making its wishes known.

"Are you sticking with gold and white?" he repeated. "Or would this work?" He held out a red-and-white-striped ornament that clashed terribly with everything else she'd selected.

"I'd like to be polite and say it would be fine, but . . ." She shook her head. "Sorry."

He chuckled at her honesty. "Now you know why I needed you."

"Your girls could've helped you do this. Maybe they would even have preferred it."

"I'm trying to impress them. They called me Scrooge last time they were here. Said if I'm going to have any Christmas spirit at all, they'd have to get the decorations out and put them up for me."

"And this will prove them wrong?"

"I'm hoping. I'm also hoping it'll demonstrate my good taste."

She pointedly eyed the ugly ornament he'd pulled out from the pile of other, far better possibilities, and they both laughed.

"At least I can put the angel on top." He dragged over a stepladder that wouldn't have been nearly tall enough had she used it. "Makes me good for something."

"You're good for a lot more than that."

When he smiled, she began to feel a bit better. Joe reminded her so much of Gail. How could she not enjoy every minute of his company?

She could and she would. He might not be *the* man she should marry, but he was the *type* of man. And if she didn't date the right type of man, she'd fall in love with the *wrong* type.

Thank God she'd caught herself before walking into a disaster. There was no telling what being with Dylan would've led to.

Briefly, she touched her stomach and hoped it hadn't already led to trouble.

"Nice," he said when they were finished and he turned on the tree lights.

She stood back to admire their work. "Not bad."

"Considering what we started with."

For some reason, she thought of Dylan's tree. He needed help decorating, too. It was completely bare. No angel. No ornaments or tinsel or lights. For a second, she wondered why he'd even bothered to put it up.

Maybe one of his brothers did.

On second thought, she doubted it. Most likely Dylan had dragged that tree inside for their sakes. They were getting too old to care about that sort of thing, but catering to

Christmas was probably a habit by now, seeing as he was the only Santa they'd had for the past fifteen years.

"Ready to go to the Victorian Christmas celebration?" Joe asked.

"I am." Scolding herself for thinking of Dylan yet again, she finished putting the extra ornaments away and accepted Joe's hand.

20

The tree in the park was lit by thousands of tiny lights and the choir members positioned beside it, dressed in Victorian garb, carried candles. Against the backdrop of winter's early dark, the lights and candles made a beautiful sight as the choir sang the traditional carols. Until that moment, when she stood listening to an a cappella rendition of "God Rest Ye Merry, Gentlemen," Cheyenne hadn't thought much about the meaning of Christmas. She'd merely been going through the motions, putting up decorations because it was expected, especially at the inn. But tonight she felt the Christmas spirit.

She had a lot to be grateful for, she realized as she looked out at the faces of those who'd gathered to celebrate. She'd found a home and people she loved here in Whiskey Creek. Joe was part of her community and her circle of friends. She had so many fond memories of him from high school, not only of the times he'd stood up for her but many others — watching him play football, spying on him when she went to Gail's, giggling when he caught them and chased them down. He'd been the perfect big brother and that made him the perfect teenage crush. That meant he'd also provided hours of pleasurable fantasy. But somehow the sexual element of those dreams had been lost. Right now she felt nothing more than friendship for Joe.

Friendship was a start, she told herself. Maybe they could build on that foundation. She certainly didn't want to give up too soon. Any girl would be lucky to be involved with him; he wasn't someone to be passed over lightly.

The choir director, in top hat and tails, asked the audience to join in on the final number. She sang "Silent Night" along with Joe and the others, but her mind wandered. And, of course, it went right back where she didn't want it to go — Dylan.

She didn't have many memories of him from high school. She hadn't been around him all that much. To some extent, she'd purposely kept her distance. He'd been such a troublemaker. And the good people of Whiskey Creek made a big deal of showing their disapproval when it came to trouble-makers. He'd started acting out *after* his mother died and his father crawled into a bottle, and that should've triggered more understanding. It probably would have, if he hadn't been so darn unfriendly, rejecting both pity and help, so prickly and angry all around.

Then his father had stabbed that guy and Dylan's world had gone from bad to worse. Yet, somehow, he'd gotten through it. Maybe he hadn't done a *perfect* job of behaving and demanding that his brothers behave, but he'd taken on a monumental task. Not many others would have attempted, at such a young age, to raise four siblings. But if he hadn't accepted the responsibility, his brothers would've been split up and parceled out to foster homes.

Cheyenne admired Dylan for keeping his family together. She wondered why more people couldn't see past the typical signs of rebellion, couldn't figure out how special he must be to have pulled it off.

Maybe the people of Whiskey Creek were still a little nervous about the Amos boys because they hadn't quite been tamed.

"Should we get some cider?" Joe asked

"Sounds good."

He took her elbow to help her avoid colliding with a teenager who darted away from his friend. Those who'd been listening to the carols were wandering off, moving in the direction of the food and craft vendors. As they followed, Cheyenne adjusted her beanie to keep her hair out of her eyes and blew on her hands. Her fingerless gloves made a nice fashion statement, but she was beginning to wish they were more practical than cute. The temperature seemed to be dropping fast. The weather report said they should expect more snow before Christmas. She wouldn't be surprised if it started tonight.

"You cold?" Joe paused to chafe her hands. It was a gallant thing to do. But then he kissed her knuckles, and that was a little too intimate for her comfort, especially in public.

She was just trying to decide out how to pull away while making it look natural when a patch of black leather caught her eye. Startled by the realization that she recognized the jacket and the man wearing it, she glanced over to see a pair of familiar dark eyes in a face that could suddenly have been hewn from stone.

For a second, Dylan couldn't breathe. He hadn't been happy when Cheyenne canceled their date, but he'd told himself not to over-react. She spooked easily. He felt confident that, with time and effort, he'd be able to win her back. Because of her past, she wanted a secure future even more than most people did, so he figured he'd do what he could to prove himself reliable.

He'd even been thinking of buying her a Christmas present. He doubted she'd ever been given much. Presley had told them stories of Christmases past that had made his heart ache for what their lives must have been like — the strange men who came around when they were children, the lack of a home, the embarrassment of having a mother like Anita, the hunger and the desperation. Not to mention the way she treated them, as if they were a burden to her. He wanted to give Cheyenne something unexpected and extravagant, something she'd never even dare to want. So, much to his brother's irritation, he'd been dragging his feet every time they passed booths that featured the types of things a woman might like. He'd been particularly tempted by a pair of emerald earrings.

But seeing her with Joe let him know that her call telling him she couldn't see him tonight had a deeper reason. She hadn't gotten scared. She'd sampled what he had to offer, found it lacking and chosen someone else — Joe, the one person he had no chance of competing against.

As their eyes met, her lips parted slightly. Obviously, she hadn't expected to run into him. But then his brothers clued in to the fact that she was with another man and rallied around, heading him off as if they feared he might confront her or Joe. Or maybe they were just trying to ease an awkward situation. In any case, Joe didn't seem to notice anything amiss. He greeted Dylan the second he saw him, like he always did.

Dylan swallowed hard. He couldn't muster a return smile. At the moment, the acting that required was beyond him. But he managed to dip his head before his brothers more or less escorted him away.

Aaron had something to say. Dylan could sense it. He kept looking over but, fortunately, remained silent. He seemed to know better than to express whatever he was thinking. They all did. Dylan didn't want sympathy, theirs least of all. He'd never been able to show them any weakness. It would only frighten them, make them worry that he'd give way to his own pain like their father had.

Falling silent, they picked up the pace,

moving past the displays, which now seemed corny with all the costumes and glittery decorations. Apparently, his brothers had lost interest in A Victorian Christmas, too. Dylan wasn't sure why he'd come in the first place. He'd let his brothers talk him into it because he hadn't wanted to sit home alone and brood.

"Let's go get drunk," Aaron suggested with a "screw her" air.

"There are plenty of women at Sexy Sadie's." Mack added this, for Dylan's ears only. It was the closest anyone came to outright telling him to forget her. Mack had always been able to get away with more than the others. When they were little, and they wanted something they thought he'd refuse them, they'd send Mack to ask for it.

And Mack was right. There were plenty of other women. So why hadn't he listened to his instincts, which had told him all along that making a play for Cheyenne would be reaching too far above him? Until recently, she'd always treated him as if he was no one she'd ever consider.

But now that he'd been with her, he couldn't seem to settle for anyone else.

Cheyenne felt a measure of relief as Joe drove off. The Christmas spirit she'd been feeling had faded the instant she bumped into Dylan. For the rest of the evening, the look on his face had haunted her, making it impossible for her to enjoy herself and awkward when it came time to say good-night to Joe. He'd walked her to the door and leaned in as if he might kiss her, but she'd given him a fleeting smile along with her thanks and fled inside.

Thank God he was gone. Now maybe she'd have a few minutes to try to sort out why she felt so sick inside. If Joe was really the better choice, why was her heart being so rebellious? Why, when he'd invited her over for Christmas dinner, had she told him she wasn't sure she could make it?

With a sigh, she dropped her purse on the kitchen table and sank into a chair. The house was dark and quiet. Presley didn't usually go to bed so early. But Cheyenne figured she had to be sleeping — until she realized she hadn't seen her sister's Mustang in the drive. She'd been too preoccupied with her own problems for that detail to register as soon as it should have.

A peek outside confirmed it. No Mustang.

Had Presley gone? Why would she do such a thing after assuring Cheyenne that she'd be home to look after Anita?

Afraid she'd done just that, and more than

a little apprehensive about the reason, Cheyenne poked her head inside her sister's room. "Presley?" she murmured, hoping to find her in bed, despite the missing car. It wouldn't be the first time she'd left her car somewhere and hitched a ride home to avoid a DUI.

There was no answer. Leaving the door open to use the light from the hall to see the shapes of furniture and other obstacles, Cheyenne waded through the clothes on the floor to the bed.

"Presley?" She patted the blankets, searching for something warm and solid.

The bed was empty. After flipping on the light, she saw her sister's comforter balled up in the middle; there was no one inside it.

Once again weaving through the mess on the floor, she hurried to check on their mother.

Anita's room was just as quiet, just as still. But it smelled terrible. Much worse than normal.

A chill ran up Cheyenne's spine when she called her mother's name and got no response. Thanks to the powerful opiates she was being given to handle the pain, she often slept too deeply to answer. Cheyenne wasn't sure why it disturbed her so much tonight except that . . . the smell wasn't right.

Holding her breath, she listened for the sound of Anita breathing.

Silence . . .

"Mom?" she whispered.

Again, no answer.

She stood in the dark for several long seconds, waiting, listening, gathering her nerve. Some small animal scampered over the roof — probably a squirrel or a raccoon — but she heard nothing other than that.

Anita was dead. Cheyenne knew it before she moved any closer. She just couldn't seem to figure out how to feel about it. Her mother's passing wasn't the immediate release she'd expected.

The sick feeling that'd sat in the bottom of her stomach since she'd seen Dylan grew much worse, along with a general sense of revulsion. Where was Presley? Why hadn't her sister called? Cheyenne had carried her cell phone all night, just in case.

The answer became apparent when she turned on the light.

The voice that woke him was reedy.

"*What?*" Dylan said into his phone. Impatient and unhappy about being awakened, he was letting it show, so it didn't surprise him when the line went dead. Since that was what he'd intended, he told himself he didn't care. He knew who'd just tried to reach him and he had absolutely no reason to call her back.

Except . . . she hadn't sounded like herself. Was something wrong?

"Doesn't matter. Not my problem," he grumbled, and chucked the phone onto the floor.

He lay there for several minutes, staring at the ceiling and refusing to call her back. Cheyenne had made her choice. She'd chosen Joe. Although what had happened between them had felt serious, special, she'd never taken it that way.

But the memory of her voice got under his skin, made him wonder why she'd sounded so panicked, so flustered, so faint. . . .

With a curse, he got up and retrieved his cell. It didn't matter how hard he fought the impulse. It wouldn't go away.

She'd better have a good reason for bugging him, he thought as he dialed. But if she did, he didn't get to learn what it was. She didn't answer. After several rings, his call transferred to voice mail.

I'm sorry, I'm not available right now . . .

What the hell was going on?

He hung up, but when he tried to call her two more times without any luck, he couldn't pass off what he'd heard as inconsequential. What if something terrible had happened? Angry and disappointed though he was, he knew her mother was dying of cancer. So he shook off the last vestiges of sleep, pulled on a pair of sweats, a heavy coat with no shirt and some tennis shoes and hurried out.

Thanks to his motorcycle, he reached Cheyenne's place in a matter of minutes.

Her Oldsmobile sat in the drive, but that didn't mean anything. She'd been out with Joe. Was she home? She had to be if she'd called *him*. But no one answered his knock. And when he went back to calling her cell, that didn't do any good, either. Her voice mail picked up again and again.

"Cheyenne?" He pounded on her door. "You in there? It's Dylan. Open up."

Pressing his ear to the wood, he listened for sounds from inside but heard nothing.

"*Cheyenne*? Where are you?" He might've called for Presley, too, but her car wasn't in the drive. He guessed she was at work.

After crossing to the living room window, he peered in — and was shocked to see Cheyenne. She was sitting at the kitchen table, holding her head in her hands.

He banged on the window, but she didn't move, didn't turn, didn't answer.

Heart pounding, he jogged around the house. He knew the back door was flimsier than the front. It was locked, too, but he didn't ask Cheyenne to open it. He kicked it in. Only then did she lift her head long enough for him to see the tears streaming down her face.

The hospice worker had told Cheyenne to contact Anita's doctor when Anita died. Together they'd gone over the proper procedure. They'd even talked about how to determine whether or not she was really dead, as if someone had to be told that having no pulse meant her heart had quit pumping.

But the reality wasn't anything like what Cheyenne had expected. At this moment, the only person she felt safe reaching out to was Dylan. Maybe she'd been trying to convince herself that Joe was the more reliable man, but she hadn't even considered calling him.

"I'm sorry," she muttered. "I — I shouldn't have bothered you. I know what you must think of me after . . . after tonight. And it's late. I'm sorry . . ."

He took her chin, looked down into her

face. "Shh . . . Tell me what's wrong."

She squeezed her eyes closed. Remembering what she'd seen in her mother's room nauseated her.

"Did your mother die?" he asked gently.

She nodded. Anita was gone, all right. Two days before Christmas. While all of Cheyenne's friends were in the Caribbean or spending the holidays elsewhere.

His voice came to her again, just as gently. "But you expected that. She had to go sometime. And she was in a lot of pain. Now she's in a better place. She no longer has to suffer."

She wondered if he really believed that, about Anita and his own mother. *Was* there a better place? And were both mothers in it? Anita had always eschewed religion, insisted it was man's way of trying to exert control over the lives of others.

Cheyenne, however, had often attended church with the Harmons. She liked the structure it provided, the peace and tranquility. So as terrible as she knew she was for even thinking it, she couldn't imagine there were heavenly choirs of angels waiting to welcome Anita into heaven. Anita would rob them all blind if they didn't watch themselves.

"Do you hear me?" he said when she

didn't react. "Do you want me to call the hospice nurse or . . . or her doctor or someone?"

Finally, she focused. "No."

"Why not? Would you like some more time with her? You can have a few minutes to say your final goodbyes, if you want."

She was surprised he'd said that. He knew how strained her relationship with Anita had been. Actually, maybe that was why he'd suggested it. Perhaps he understood that the strain also made this situation much more complicated. "That's not it." Her voice sounded rusty, as if she hadn't used it in a long while. She almost didn't recognize it.

"Then what is?" His eyebrows rumpled as he awaited her answer.

She started rocking back and forth. "I have to decide."

"On . . ."

"What I should do."

Putting his arms around her, he spoke into her hair. "You should contact the hospice nurse or the doctor, like I said. Or maybe the coroner."

"No." She pressed her face into his shoulder.

"Why?" he prompted, pulling back to see her face.

"We can't call anyone," she said. "Not yet. I have to think it through."

"Think *what* through? You told me she's dead, Chey."

Her eyes latched on to his. "But it looks like P-Presley killed her!"

21

Dylan stepped inside Anita's bedroom and turned on the light. He guessed Cheyenne had turned it off to hide what she'd found or as a subconscious way of blocking out reality.

The stench made him grimace. It smelled like Anita's bowels had emptied on her death. But that wasn't what concerned him. The lamp that had been knocked off the nightstand suggested a struggle of some sort. So did the unnatural position of Anita's body. And there was blood on her face from her nose, as well as blood on the pillow lying next to her.

He heard Cheyenne come up behind him. "What do you think?" she whispered.

He thought what she did, but he didn't want to say so. "Have you tried to reach Presley?"

"Several times. Before I called you. She's not answering."

"What was going through her head?" he murmured as his eyes once again circled the room.

"I don't know. She could've been high, not in her right mind. Sometimes they fought. An argument could've triggered it. Or maybe it wasn't like that at all. Maybe Presley was just tired of seeing her suffer."

"But chances are good she'll be prosecuted for murder. Mercy killing is still considered killing. They could decide to make an example out of her. If we call the police . . . who knows what might happen."

"She needs rehab, not prison."

Unable to tolerate the sights and smells any longer, he stepped out in the hall and called Aaron on his cell.

Aaron sounded sleepy when he answered. "What the hell, Dylan? Why are you waking me up? It isn't time for work. It's . . . shit, it's the middle of the night!"

Dylan didn't apologize. He was too focused, too affected by what had happened. "Cheyenne's looking for her sister. You haven't seen or heard from Presley, have you?"

"You mean the Cheyenne who's now going out with Joe?"

Although Dylan felt his jaw tighten, he ignored the jab. This had nothing to do with who was seeing whom. It was tragic and serious and no one deserved to face such circumstances alone. "Just answer the question."

"We talked briefly earlier." His contrite tone implied that he knew he'd gone too far with the Joe comment and, possibly, regretted it. "Got into a fight on the phone," he added. "Haven't heard from her since."

So it had been a bad night for both of them. "What was the fight about?"

"Does it matter?"

"It might."

"I don't give a shit. That's none of your business."

Dylan wrestled with his temper. No one could get him angry faster than Aaron with his damn belligerence. "Aaron —"

"What?" he cried. "Don't talk to me like you're Dad, because you're not. There're only three years between us."

"Then when are you going to start acting your age?" he snapped. "When are you going to start taking life seriously?"

Silence. Then, "If this is why you called, I'm hanging up."

"Don't."

More silence. But at least there wasn't a click. Aaron knew Dylan wouldn't put up with too much disrespect, not after everything he'd done for the family.

Dragging a hand through his hair, Dylan tried to set aside their personal differences. "Listen, I don't want our shit to get in the way of this. We can fight any day. Right now we have to find Presley. And you might know something that'll help."

Aaron didn't respond immediately but eventually Dylan heard his brother draw an audible breath. "She wanted me to come over. She was having a hard time being alone with her mother. She said Anita was making gurgling sounds. It was freaking her out."

Dylan winced at the mental picture. "And?"

"And I wouldn't. Why the hell would *I* want to listen to that?"

There was more anger and belligerence in these words, but Dylan knew it stemmed from the guilt he felt for not being able to support her. Aaron could act like a jerk, but he wasn't as bad as he made himself sound. He *couldn't* face what Presley had asked him to do. Aaron had been the one to find their own mother when she took her life. Since then he'd refused to go anywhere near death. Wouldn't walk into a cemetery. Wouldn't attend a funeral.

"So . . . what? She hung up?"

"Yeah. I got a dial tone. Never called her back." He hesitated as if wrestling with his conscience. "Why? What's wrong with her?"

"We don't know yet."

"Then why the big alarm?"

"Her mother's dead."

"It's about damn time."

Dylan's hand tightened on his phone. "*That's* all you've got to say?"

"What else am I supposed to say? The woman had terminal cancer."

"You could show a little empathy, for Chrissake!"

"You'd rather she continued to suffer?"

"Quit twisting my words."

"There's a lot more that's twisted here than just your words. But maybe I'm the only one who can see it. Anyway, you're right. I don't care," he said coldly. "I quit caring about anything years ago, and I'm damn glad."

With that, he hung up.

"What'd he say?"

This time, Dylan hadn't heard Cheyenne's approach. He stretched his neck, trying to cope with his own emotions. "Basically, he said he needs some serious help, more than I've ever been able to get him."

"In what way?"

Cheyenne's burdens were heavy enough.

Doing what he could to control the disappointment and worry he so often felt when it came to Aaron, he put more energy into his voice. "In the same way your sister needs help. They're angry and striking out at the world, and the world's just going to strike back."

"Is there no helping them?" she whispered.

"Not until they decide to help themselves." That reality, that lack of power, nearly drove him mad.

She wrung her hands. "What did he say about Presley?"

"Not much. She called earlier, wanting him to come over, but . . ." Dylan couldn't bring himself to repeat what his brother had said. He couldn't present Aaron in such a poor light; he knew that no one else would understand why he'd reacted the way he had. "It was late, and he was already in bed."

"Does he have any idea where we can look?"

Dylan thought he could guess. "She likes Sexy Sadie's." He shot her a look. "She also goes to Carl Inera's a lot."

"To buy drugs."

He nodded.

She rubbed her face as if she was so tired she could hardly think. Then she seemed to gather her energy because she headed into the living room. "I'll go there."

He hurried after her. "No. You stay here."

Her gaze darted toward the bedroom where her mother lay dead. "I don't want to."

"I don't blame you. But Presley might return. We wouldn't want to miss her. I'm not sure she's in a state to handle what needs to be done now that your mother's passed."

Although she blinked rapidly, he saw no tears. "Okay."

"I'll find Presley and bring her home," he said. "Then we can hear what happened and decide what to do."

"So I wait here."

"That's it. That's all you can do."

When he stepped outside, soft flakes of snow fell to the earth. With no wind to buffet them, they lighted gently on his face and coat. A few got caught in his lashes. It didn't snow that often in Whiskey Creek, so it always felt remarkable when it did. He stared up at the sky. "It's snowing," he murmured.

Cheyenne didn't sound pleased when she responded. "Figures."

As soon as Dylan left, the house fell silent.

Cheyenne stood at the window, watching his glowing tail lights as he drove toward Carl's. Then there was nothing to see but the black night with the white flakes drifting peacefully to earth.

She rubbed her arms, trying to compensate for the terrible chill that had invaded the house. She'd never felt so alone. Or maybe she had. When she was ten, her mother had left her on the corner of a busy street, holding a sign that said Hungry. Mom Out of Work. Although she was standing in an area teeming with people — it had been at the biggest mall in Walnut Creek — she'd never felt so isolated. She'd nearly jumped out of her skin when a man grabbed her wrist to put a few quarters in her palm. And she'd been utterly humiliated by the narrow glances of the less compassionate.

Ironically, they'd had a right to feel so skeptical. Her mother hadn't bought food with that money. She'd purchased a bottle of vodka and drunk herself into a stupor, then passed out in their car while she and Presley rummaged for food in a McDonald's Dumpster.

Cringing at the memory, she turned away from the window. "You're gone," she said to Anita, even though she knew Anita was no longer there to hear. It felt so strange, so surreal that her mother wouldn't be calling out in a few minutes. Anita would never be able to manipulate her again — with guilt or the desire for love or the natural optimism that had kept Cheyenne hoping her mother would change.

Nor would Anita be able to reveal where Cheyenne was born. She'd taken her secret, if there was one, to the grave.

Moving back into the kitchen, she glanced at the calendar. December 22. No, it was after midnight — well after midnight. It was the twenty-third. That was the date that would appear on Anita's death certificate. Within a week or two, her mother would be buried in the same cemetery as Mary, where Anita had once forced Cheyenne to wait out a long, anxious night tied to a tree.

That seemed ironic, in a macabre way, but Anita had made Cheyenne promise not to have her cremated. She'd always been afraid of fire, said she couldn't abide the thought of it even in death.

Cheyenne wished that coping with the details of the funeral and burial would be all she had to worry about over the next few days. She didn't mind missing Christmas. Living without the holiday cheer she'd come to expect since moving to Whiskey Creek seemed minor. It was her sister she worried about.

Did Presley kill Anita? What would happen to her if she had?

Cheyenne couldn't imagine a punishment worse than the toll of Presley's own conscience. Presley, for all her confusion and dependence on drugs, loved Anita. But that would hardly provide her with a defense.

After retrieving her cell phone from the kitchen table, Cheyenne checked her call history as well as her text messages. She'd received nothing from Presley, even though she'd tried to reach her several times.

"Come on, Pres." Closing her eyes, she pressed her knuckles to her mouth. She wasn't sure how long she could put off calling the doctor or the hospice nurse.

Nerves stretched taut, she began to pace. But the anxiety only grew worse. She had to do something, had to get Anita out of the house —

The doorbell rang.

Surprised and a little panicked, she brought a hand to her chest. She doubted it was Dylan. He'd only left fifteen minutes ago. She was afraid the police were at her door, maybe with Presley. Had Presley turned herself in — or gotten picked up for something else and confessed?

She hurried across the living room and peered through the peephole.

It was Aaron. His hair stood up, as if he'd just rolled out of bed, and he was unshaven. The "prettiest" of the Amos boys, he had a face that could be on billboards for Armani or Calvin Klein — very classic and sculpted — but he was also the most difficult to deal with. People steered clear of him if they could. He hadn't even dressed for the weather. He shivered as he stood there in a T-shirt and jeans, shoving his hands in his pockets while he waited.

She opened the door. "Yes?"

"Where's Dylan?"

"Out searching for Presley."

"Then why won't he answer his damn phone?"

Maybe he didn't want to talk to his brother. Their last conversation hadn't seemed to go very well. "I couldn't tell you."

He sent an apprehensive glance into the house. "So you haven't found her?"

"Not yet."

"Where's he looking?"

"He went to Carl Inera's and Sexy Sadie's. That's all I know."

He kicked a pebble off the porch. "Fine. I'll go check out a couple places myself."

"You might want to put on a jacket first."

"I'll survive."

He was halfway to his truck when she called him. "Aaron?"

Clearly reluctant to be detained, he looked back at her.

"Do you care about my sister?" Cheyenne couldn't forget the sound of Presley's voice when she said she might be pregnant. Maybe she'd taken a test and found out for sure. Maybe that was what had started this whole night heading in the wrong direction.

"I don't know if I'm capable of caring about anyone," he admitted and left.

Cheyenne was fairly certain that Presley cared about him. Presley might even be in love with him. Her poor sister had never had much. She hadn't been blessed with the same kind of friends as Cheyenne, had lived without the stability they brought. Presley had hung on to Anita instead, who was no anchor. And drugs. And now a man she'd never be able to rely on, either.

Saying a silent prayer to the God Eve and her family worshipped, asking for forgiveness in case she was about to do something He'd find terribly wrong, she drew herself up straight and closed the door.

She'd come to a decision, one she might live to regret. But, like anyone else, she could only follow the dictates of her own conscience.

By the time Dylan started back to Cheyenne's, he was exhausted. He'd looked for Presley every place he could think of — even a few he doubted she'd ever gone. He'd visited the Indian casino where she worked, as well as another one that was farther away. He'd navigated the narrow road leading up to the old mine where they used to party in high school, even though the roads were slick and dangerous. He'd dragged Carl Inera from his bed and accused him of selling her dope, which he denied. And he'd bumped into Aaron, who was making the same rounds. They'd found no trace of her. As a last-ditch effort, they'd driven through the streets of Whiskey Creek for an hour, attacking the search from opposite ends of town and going as slowly as possible, checking every parking lot, alleyway and side road for her car.

He hated to return to Cheyenne without some idea of what had happened to her sister, but there was nothing more he could do, short of contacting the police. And he preferred to avoid that, given the situation, at least for now.

He'd called Cheyenne three times in the past half hour to see if she'd heard anything, but she hadn't picked up. He hoped that meant she'd fallen asleep. She needed the rest. It made him feel better to think she wasn't agonizing over every minute he was gone. Maybe Presley had returned and they were both home safe.

But when he arrived at Cheyenne's house, he didn't see Presley's car. He saw the coroner's van, a squad car and another vehicle — an Acura.

"Oh, shit," he muttered, and parked beyond the drive so he wouldn't block anyone in.

Aaron had been following him. He pulled up alongside Dylan's Jeep. "You're staying here?" he called through the passenger window.

"I'm staying here."

Aaron shook his head. "Sometimes I wish I could be you. You always know what you want. And you know how to get it."

That wasn't true. Dylan had been denied as much as Aaron had, maybe more. But Aaron didn't give him a chance to respond. He gunned his truck and shot past as if he couldn't get away from Cheyenne's fast enough.

"If you only knew." Dylan shook his head.

The front door opened before he could reach it, and two guys he didn't recognize emerged, carrying Anita's body on a stretcher. A sheet covered her, but he glanced away. He didn't want to see so much as a finger or a toe. As it was, the sight he'd encountered in the bedroom would stay with him for the rest of his life.

The men, startled by his unexpected approach, looked up as he stepped out of their way. "You part of the family?" one asked.

"I'm a friend of Cheyenne's."

"Glad someone's here. She's inside."

His stomach churned at the thought of what she'd endured in his absence. Were they taking pictures to document the scene? Were the police now looking for Presley?

He knew how he'd feel if it were Aaron. . . .

As soon as he stepped inside, out of the snow, he could hear voices coming from Anita's room, but his steps grew heavy when he reached the hall. He didn't want to go anywhere near where Anita had died — or been killed. Aaron wasn't the only one who had a problem with death. Dylan, too, had seen his mother before the ambulance took her away.

"Will you be okay here alone?" the sheriff asked.

From his vantage point just outside the room, Dylan could see that Cheyenne was busy cleaning. The soiled sheets had already been stripped from the bed.

"I'll be fine," she replied.

"What time does your sister get home?" This came from a middle-aged brunette.

"Sometimes she stays overnight with a friend."

Dylan found this an odd reply. He found their acceptance of it even odder.

"I wish you could've got in touch with her," the woman said. "It would've been nice if she'd been able to say her final good-bye. It'll be so much harder for her to come home to an empty room."

Cheyenne rolled several hospital gowns into a ball. "She knew it could happen anytime."

"Of course, but . . . still."

"Her phone must be out of battery," Cheyenne explained. "Or she's so deeply asleep she can't hear it. I'll talk to her as soon as possible."

The woman sighed. "I guess that's all you can do, short of searching for her, and the roads are too slick for that tonight. You don't want to go out in this weather."

"No."

"I'm sure Presley will check in tomorrow." She moved closer to Cheyenne, forcing her to stop bustling around long enough to be embraced. "I'm so sorry for what you've been through. It was heartbreaking to watch. But I hope I was able to help you out, at least a little. That's our goal with hospice."

Cheyenne looked fragile, as if she might shatter beneath the slightest touch. But Dylan figured her pale face would seem normal to them. She had, after all, just lost her mother.

"Of course," she told the nurse. "You were great. I don't know what I — *we* — would've done without your support."

"I'm glad." The nurse touched her arm. "Your mother is in a better place."

Cheyenne ducked her head. "Right. I know. I agree." She was speaking softly, respectfully, but Dylan could tell she wanted them to leave. The Whiskey Creek Police Department contracted the sheriff's department to cover any 9-1-1 calls they couldn't respond to, and any that came in after one in the morning, so these were county folk, not from Whiskey Creek. They had no idea what kind of person Anita had been or the mixed emotions Cheyenne was likely to experience.

"I suggest you get some grief counseling," the woman added, a touch of lecturing in her voice. "You and your sister. What you've gone through has been very traumatic, and it'll continue to be difficult for several months, maybe longer."

Dylan allowed himself a wry smile. That was easy advice to give, but grief counseling wasn't free. He knew. There'd been nothing and no one to help his family.

"I appreciate your concern," Cheyenne said. "And . . . we'll do what we can."

The sheriff made a point of checking his watch. "Look at that. It's almost six. Do you think you can sleep? I'll sit and watch TV in the living room until your sister returns if you'd like. I don't want to leave you here alone."

Cheyenne kept tightening that ball of hospital gowns, adding a set of extra sheets that had been sitting off to one side, clean and neatly folded. "That's very nice. But there's no need. Thank you, though."

"I *can't* leave you —"

Dylan cleared his throat, attracting their attention for the first time. If they'd heard him come in, they hadn't reacted. They'd either been too engrossed in what was happening or they'd assumed he was one of the men removing the body who'd come back in for some reason, maybe a glass of water. "I'll take care of her."

"Is this . . . a friend?" The nurse's eyebrows, drawn by a black pencil, nearly hit her hairline.

Cheyenne looked so relieved to see him he almost went over to her, even though the room was already crowded. "My neighbor," she said. "I'll be in good hands."

That statement was spoken with conviction, which confused Dylan. He'd just concluded that she wanted Joe. But if that was the case, why hadn't she called Joe? Why wasn't Joe here? Because he lived farther away? Because she felt more at home with someone she considered beneath her and she didn't want Joe to be part of this terrible process?

The sheriff squinted at him as if his long hair and leather jacket implied that he couldn't be trusted, but there were lines of fatigue in his stern cop face. No doubt he was eager to head home to his family. His shift was probably about to end. "Call if you need anything," he told Cheyenne.

She nodded and kept up with the platitudes and thank-yous until she'd walked them out.

When they were finally gone, she locked the door and turned to face him.

"Any chance you'd be willing to start a fire?" she asked.

"Of course." He didn't question why. He

guessed what she wanted to do and whole-heartedly supported it. He also guessed what she'd already done and knew he would've done the same.

While the flames were beginning to lick at the logs he'd brought from the porch, she carried in a bundle from out back.

"Where'd you hide that?"

"In the shed." The plastic bag contained the bloody pillow and some of the bedding he'd seen earlier that hadn't been in Anita's room when he came back.

She shoved it in the fire. Then she piled on the hospital gowns, towels, washrags, extra catheters and other hospital supplies, even her mother's regular clothes.

"Are you sure you want to get rid of all that?" he asked when she threw in hair-brushes and combs and makeup bags and jewelry.

"Yes," she replied with absolute certainty, and stood back to watch it burn.

22

"You get some sleep," Dylan said. "I'll sit out here until Presley returns."

Cheyenne couldn't believe he was willing to stay. Not after seeing her with Joe earlier. She knew that incident had made an impact on him. Although he'd been kind, he hadn't touched her since they took away the body and she could tell he didn't plan to. "What about the shop?"

"I'll call Grady, have him open."

"Can your brothers manage without you?"

"They'll be okay for one day."

She twisted her hands in front of her. Suddenly, she didn't seem to know what to do with them. "You found no sign of Presley?"

"None."

She'd guessed but had to ask. Where had her sister gone? Could she have driven off the highway and down a ravine in that old car of hers?

Cheyenne feared that might be the case.

She even worried that Presley might've veered off the road intentionally. Drugs made people do things they otherwise never would. The possible pregnancy might've been too much, coupled with Anita's decline and —

Refusing to continue that thought, she changed the subject. "Aaron came by while you were searching. Did he find you?"

"Yeah. He did what he could to help."

"I think Presley might be in love with him."

"I get that impression."

She wondered whether or not to tell him about the baby. He hadn't been too complimentary of Presley when they'd first talked in the park so, in the end, she didn't divulge her sister's secret. It felt like too great a breach of trust. He already knew more than he probably should about the night Anita died.

The memory of going into her mother's room made her feel queasy. "Do you think I'm terrible for . . . for hiding what Presley did?"

His eyes were steady on hers. "No."

"I just couldn't see . . . couldn't see getting her into trouble when Anita was days away from dying, anyway. That's no excuse, but —" But she couldn't figure out how else to handle the situation, how to remain on stable, moral ground and still love and care for her less-than-exemplary family. "I'm sure she just . . . snapped or . . . or she was on drugs or . . . *something*. She loved Anita."

"We don't know what happened. You had to give her the benefit of the doubt. Otherwise, you would've had to trust the system and I don't think that's any more reliable than she is."

True, but it didn't bode well that Presley hadn't even called to explain. Cheyenne was afraid she'd lost both her mother and her sister on the same night. "I hope she's okay."

The sympathy in his eyes made her crave his arms around her. She felt so cold, so estranged from the regular world. She knew he could be the anchor she needed. He'd done it before, although she hadn't wanted to acknowledge his profound effect on her. She wished she could ask him for that physical comfort now, but a divide stood between them that hadn't been there before. And she was to blame for it. She'd made him question everything he'd felt when they were together. Suddenly, he was as leery of her as she'd always been of him.

"I'm sure she is," he said.

She stared down at her phone. How could so much have happened since Eve left? The holidays were never easy. She had too many troubled memories of Christmases past, had learned very early that there was no Santa. But this Christmas was harder than it had been in years.

"Get some rest," Dylan said again, and sat down.

She swallowed hard. "About earlier, at the Victorian Christmas —"

"Let's not go into that, okay?"

"We should talk about it." She *wanted* to talk about it, to tell him how she felt, but the hope she'd seen in his face earlier, when they were at Sexy Sadie's, was gone.

"There's nothing to say. We've both gone through too much. If we hook up with anyone, it needs to be someone who's trusting and consistent and hasn't screwed up in the past. I understand that. Joe's perfect for you."

Cheyenne could hardly breathe. She'd been through hell tonight. But, somehow, this cut the deepest. The moment she thought Joe might kiss her had clarified everything, showing her that what she felt for Dylan wasn't to be taken for granted. It wasn't mere attraction. Joe was better-looking. He'd always wanted to be a family man, so he was also a safer bet. She should've been thrilled to have his interest, especially after all the years she'd wanted it.

But being in *Dylan*'s arms felt like finding home. Maybe he was as battle-scarred as she was, but he understood her and her past. She'd never had such an affinity with anyone else.

She opened her mouth to say so but couldn't imagine he'd care. She'd done everything she could to choke off what had blossomed so unexpectedly between them. "Right. Of course. I'm sorry," she said, and went to her room.

Presley was halfway to Los Angeles before she realized where she was. Even then, she stopped driving only because she was out of gas. Her car had begun to sputter a few miles back as the sun peeked over the horizon, finally ending what felt like the longest night of her life. Now the Mustang wouldn't go at all.

She'd taken Interstate 5, a long expanse of highway intended for travel between California's bigger cities. Unlike Highway 99, which also connected Sacramento and Los Angeles, gas stations were few and far between. It wasn't as if she was close to an exit, either. Music blaring, she'd passed the last one without even thinking about it and didn't know where the next one would be.

Neither did she care. She had nowhere to go. She just had to keep moving — like when she was a child and they'd gone from rest stop to rest stop, begging fellow travelers for enough change to buy something to eat.

As she got out of her car, she heard the deep blast of a semi's horn and stumbled back. The sudden whoosh of air that accompanied it washed over her, whipping at her hair and clothes. She'd almost walked right into certain death.

Dazed, she stared at the double-trailer the semi was towing, watching the dirt eddies swirl in its wake and wondering if she would've felt it had she been hit. Maybe she would've escaped the pain of her life in the blink of an eye. . . .

What was she going to do? Where would she go?

She had no idea. But the effect of the meth she'd smoked hours ago was wearing off. She had to find a way to get more. That was all she was thinking about when, minutes later, another trucker saw her walking on the side of the road and pulled over to see if she needed a ride.

Cheyenne's phone woke her. She had it on vibrate, but as restless as she felt, that was enough to jar her from sleep. Blinking, she rolled over and grabbed it. She wanted to believe it was Presley calling. But she knew before she could clearly see caller ID that it wasn't her sister. The name started with an R.

Riley. He was probably at the inn.

"Hello?" She was doing her best to come to full wakefulness, but she felt like she was buried beneath a thousand pounds of sand. To her own ears, she also sounded like it.

"Hey, what's up? I didn't wake you, did I?"

He must be wondering why she hadn't checked in with him over the weekend. She'd told him she would.

She burrowed into the pillows. "What time is it?"

"Nearly two. I thought you'd be stopping by. I need to show you how the paint's turning out in the central foyer. I don't think it's quite what you and Eve had in mind."

"Um . . ." She shoved a hand through her hair. It was so difficult to switch gears and focus on work. Everything else came crashing down on her — Anita's death, her sister's possible culpability and subsequent disappearance, and bumping into Dylan while she was with Joe. "It happened last night," she said simply.

382

"What happened last night?"

"My mother's dead."

He fell silent. Then he sighed. "Eve's going to feel terrible she wasn't here."

"I know."

"I'm sorry. I can't replace Eve, but I'll be right over."

The door opened and Dylan appeared. Obviously, he'd heard her voice. "I've got to go," he whispered. "There's a problem over at the shop."

She didn't want him to leave, but she'd already asked him for more than she had a right to. She covered the phone. "There's been no sign of Presley?"

"No."

"Okay. Thanks for staying with me."

He nodded and closed the door.

"Who was *that*?" Riley asked.

"My neighbor."

"Which one?"

"Dylan Amos."

"*Really*?"

She couldn't help bristling at the inflection in Riley's voice. "Yeah. He lives down the road so he kept me company after they took my mother away. Why are you so surprised?"

"It's hard to imagine Dylan Amos being sympathetic enough to support you."

It wasn't hard for her. Maybe he didn't look all that respectable, but he'd *always* protected the people he cared about. "He's actually . . . not what everyone thinks."

"What is he, then?"

She hadn't completely decided. But she knew he was a lot better than he'd been given credit for. "He's nice."

"I'll take your word for it. If he ever asks, tell him I think he's nice, too."

He was teasing. "Stop it," she said with a reluctant laugh.

"I'm not going to get in *his* way."

She smiled at Riley's exaggerated tone. "He would never hurt you."

"He won't if I don't cross him. Anyway, I'm coming over."

"No, don't." Even though she felt drugged, she forced herself to sit up. "My sister's gone missing. I have to go out and find her."

"Shit."

"Exactly."

"She didn't react well to the news, huh?"

Cheyenne didn't correct him. "Something's up."

"I'll help you look for her."

"What about work?"

"What about work? I happen to have an in with the boss. I'll be there in ten minutes."

■ ■ ■ ■

"Can you go in this direction first?" Cheyenne asked.

Riley glanced at her. After making a big deal about the dark circles under her eyes, he'd insisted on driving. "You want to go *away* from town? Why? What's down there, besides a dead end?"

The Amoses, for one. Cheyenne wanted to believe that Aaron would've told his brother Presley had contacted him. But the truth was she didn't really trust Aaron. Given that he was also on drugs, he wasn't the most reliable person in the world.

She supposed she didn't fully trust Dylan, either, because she was also eager to see if he'd gone to the shop as he'd said — or if he'd just wanted to escape her place. "She has friends down this way."

"What *kind* of friends?" he muttered as if only sketchy people lived on the river bottoms.

Normally, Cheyenne wouldn't have thought anything of encountering such a sentiment. She basically agreed with it. Today, however, his attitude irritated her. "Not everyone down here is a lowlife," she said. "*I* live here, don't I?"

Her mother had also been a river bottoms

resident, and Anita definitely fit the stereo-type, but he didn't point that out. "Of course not. Sorry."

She didn't answer. She was too busy scrutinizing Dylan's house. She'd never really looked at it in the light of day — and certainly not through the eyes with which she was seeing it now. It was as well-maintained on the outside as it was inside, she decided. She saw no frills, no flower beds or Christmas wreaths or welcome mats, but she didn't see the broken-down cars, or castoff tires and batteries that characterized so many of the other homes in the area, either. Someone had recently repaired the fence and the house had been painted, probably last summer.

Dylan's Jeep was gone. That made her feel slightly better, although she didn't want to think about why. But there was no trace of her sister's Mustang.

She had Riley stop so she could get out and trudge around back. She planned to check the barn where Dylan had hidden her car that one night, just in case. She had no idea why her sister's Mustang would be in that spot, but she had to start somewhere.

There were no hidden vehicles, no signs of Presley at all — just some free weights and a boxing bag in the barn. Judging by a radio, a water jug and a cast-off sweatshirt, someone used the equipment on a regular basis. Maybe more than one person.

Cheyenne tried imagining what her sister must be feeling, only to shy away from it. She didn't want to consider the implications of what she'd found in her mother's room, especially because she'd destroyed the evidence, and that put *her* on the wrong side of the law, as well.

Dylan's dogs were barking and jumping against the sliding glass door. They knew she shouldn't be there. She paused to stare at them. As a child, she'd pleaded for a puppy. Anita had once allowed her to take in a stray, more by tacit approval than actual agreement. Then she'd dragged Cheyenne away from Albuquerque and made her leave the dog behind.

Cheyenne had often thought about getting a pet now that she was older, but taking care of her mother had become her primary focus. And she wasn't sure her future rental would permit animals, at least not without a hefty deposit.

Maybe someday, she told herself, and tapped the glass. "Hey, boys." She had no idea if they were both male. But they were big.

"You okay?"

She turned to see that Riley had followed her. "I'm fine. Presley's not here. No one is."

"This is where the Amoses live?"

She nodded.

"Not bad. Beats the hell out of where I'm living at the moment." They walked back to his truck together. "Where next?"

"Carl Inera's, I guess." She knew she was retracing Dylan's steps from the night before but something could've changed since then.

Riley took her hand. "Have you told Eve about your mother?"

She hauled cold air into her lungs. "Not yet. I didn't want to ruin the rest of her trip."

"She'd want to know."

"There's nothing she can do about it now. Let's wait until she gets back."

He pulled her to a stop. "Are you sure?"

She nodded. "All I want is to find Presley."

"We'll find her." He seemed confident, but she was beginning to wonder. She couldn't see Presley being able to live with what she'd done.

Cheyenne wasn't sure she could live with what Presley had done, either. Or what *she'd* done to cover it up.

23

Joe was in front of the station, talking to a customer about an oil change, when his father leaned out of the minimart. "Come in here when you're done, will ya?"

Martin called him in all the time. Sometimes he had an idea for some way to improve the station. Or he thought they should hire or fire an employee, like the kleptomaniac Mindy they'd had to let go a couple of years ago. Joe wasn't particularly concerned. After scheduling the oil change, he strolled inside. "What's going on?"

Joyce Weatherby, a local schoolteacher, stood at the register, buying a pack of gum. Martin told her to have a good day and waited until she was gone before responding. "Have you heard the news?"

"What news?"

"Cheyenne lost her mother."

Joe hadn't been aware of that. He hadn't called her yet. He'd been too caught up in making plans with his girls. He was supposed to pick them up in an hour and a half and keep them for a few days. "Who told you?"

"The hospice nurse stopped by to get gas a few minutes ago. She was on her way over with a hot meal for Cheyenne and Presley. She asked me to let anyone who might be friends with them know, so they could get some emotional support."

"Have you called Gail?"

"No, but I will."

He shoved his hands in his pockets. "So Anita's finally gone."

His father gave him a stern look.

"There's no use pretending," he said, and checked the time. His ex was expecting him at seven. Maybe he could talk Cheyenne into driving to Sacramento with him. He could take her and his girls to dinner while they were there. A night out just after her mother had died might not sound very appealing to Cheyenne, but with her friends in the Caribbean her alternative would probably be staying home — alone if Presley had to work. That couldn't be much better.

Besides, he was curious to see how she'd interact with his children. It wasn't like he could cancel his plans. His girls had asked a friend to change the date of her Christmas party so they'd be able to visit Whiskey Creek. The judge had assigned him Christmas Eve and Suzie Christmas Day.

"I'll give Chey a call."

His father was watching him a little too closely.

"*What?*" he said.

"You like her, don't you."

He did. He liked her a lot. "Quit acting so smug," he said, and his father chuckled as he walked away.

When Joe's call came in, Cheyenne silenced her phone. She knew it was rude not to answer. It seemed like she'd been avoiding him all week. Gail tried calling next. But she couldn't talk to either one of them right now. After several hours of searching without success, she was too panicked. She wanted to take a flashlight and comb the woods by the river. Presley loved it down there. During the summer she'd stand and wade in the water and smoke cigarette after cigarette.

Although it was too cold for that at Christmas, especially after dark, Cheyenne decided to go down there, anyway. But first she was hoping to enlist the support of the local police. She and Riley had contacted all of Presley's friends and coworkers. She wasn't sure what else she could do. Driving around, asking anyone and everyone about her sister wasn't producing any results. Presley had left in the dead of night. Not many people in Whiskey Creek were up in the wee hours.

Riley waited in his Explorer as she knocked on Tim Stacy's door. Tim hadn't been the chief of police for more than a few years, but he'd worked for the four-man department as long as Cheyenne had lived in Whiskey Creek, so she'd seen him around. He'd once pulled Eve over when Cheyenne was with her, for accidentally running a red light.

When he answered the door, she could tell she'd interrupted his dinner.

"Sorry to bother you," she said.

"No problem." He wiped his mouth with a napkin he'd carried away from the table and glanced surreptitiously over her head, at Riley. "What can I do for you?"

He listened as she explained the situation, but as soon as she mentioned Presley's name she could tell he was only being polite. By the time she reached the part about her sister taking off, and the fact that she hadn't been seen all day, he was already discounting Cheyenne's concern.

"It's not even eight o'clock," he said.

"But she left in the middle of last night. That means she's been gone for fifteen hours or more."

"*Hours*? Come on, you know your sister's never been as . . . shall we say, stable as you have."

"That may be true —"

"I'm sure she's just trying to cope with her grief," he broke in. "You've both been through a lot. The loss of a parent affects us all differently."

"She's never disappeared like this," Cheyenne said, but that was desperation talking. She knew the second those words came out of her mouth that she'd lost all credibility. Presley had disappeared for *days* at a time. Once, she'd run away for weeks.

This situation was different, though. But only Cheyenne knew why.

No longer in uniform, he adjusted the belt that held up his jeans. "She's got her car, right? She'll come back when she's ready."

"What if she doesn't?"

"If she's not back in another day or so, we'll see what we can do."

"Day *or so*?" she echoed.

"I can't use the city's resources too quickly, Cheyenne. That wouldn't be fair to the taxpayers, now would it — if I were to

393

round up everyone and keep them out all night, on overtime, searching, only to find her drunk in some bar in Sacramento?"

Cheyenne's heart sank. Once again, her sister's reputation was working against her. Cheyenne had battled Anita's irresponsibility all her life and now she was battling Presley's.

Still, she made an effort to convince him. Riley even got out and said he thought something might really be wrong this time. But being gone for less than a full day wasn't considered abnormal behavior, especially for a known drug user.

"I'm sorry," Riley said as they walked back to his SUV.

Cheyenne was too angry to respond.

He opened the door for her. "What are you going to do?"

"I'm not giving up," she said. "You can go home if you want, but I'm not giving up."

"I don't want to go home, Chey, but —" he grimaced "— I left Jacob at a friend's. I need to get back there and collect him. I can leave him at my mom's and come back later, though. I'll do that, okay?"

Warm tears slid down her cheeks. She'd already taken his whole afternoon and most of the evening. But there wasn't anyone else she could turn to.

"That's okay," she said. "Stay with Jacob. He's off school and, for a change, not involved with sports and homework. And it's almost Christmas. I don't mind doing it alone."

Aaron sat on one of the plastic chairs in the waiting room, drinking a Pepsi. Normally when he came in from the back, he got what he wanted and returned directly to the shop. He also left with the others at five o'clock, which he hadn't done today. Dylan got the impression he was lingering because he had something to say.

"So . . . you really like Cheyenne, huh?"

That was it? He wanted to rub Dylan's nose in what had happened last night?

Dylan finished the bite he'd taken of the sandwich Mack had brought him for dinner. He'd stayed at work because he was behind — and he thought it might help him forget Cheyenne. For the moment. "What's on your mind?" he asked.

After downing half his soda, Aaron belched. "Didn't I just tell you?"

"You don't give a shit about my love life. And it's got nothing to do with you, anyway. So is there something else we need to talk about?"

A strange look flickered over his brother's

face. Aaron seemed to struggle to come up with the right words. Then he muttered, "What the hell. Forget it," and got up.

There was emotion in his voice beyond his usual petulance. It caught Dylan's attention, brought him to his feet. "Aaron!"

He turned at the door and stared at him with hollow eyes, as if he couldn't tolerate the pain that was eating him up inside.

"What is it?" Dylan asked, softening his voice.

Aaron's throat worked as he swallowed. He seemed desperate to talk . . . and yet reluctant at the same time.

"Tell me," Dylan prompted.

Rubbing his free hand over his face, he said, "I hate Dad."

This wasn't news. This was merely the warm-up. "Just Dad?"

He dropped his hand. "No. Mom, too."

As the oldest, Dylan had known their mother best. He felt it was his duty to defend her and yet . . . what could he say? He felt as robbed as Aaron did. But, he tried, as usual. "She was mentally ill."

Aaron lifted a hand. "Don't feed me the bullshit you've been giving us ever since it happened. Far as I'm concerned, she took the easy way out. Bailed on us." When Dylan didn't react, Aaron's hand shot out to punctuate his words. "Come on, you have to be angry with her, too! Look how much it changed *your* life."

If only Aaron knew how angry Dylan had been. What did he think had fueled the rage driving Dylan at eighteen? Did he think Dylan *wanted* to get into the cage with some of those fighters? That he hadn't been afraid of the experienced martial artists he'd had to go up against?

He'd done it because it was the one thing he could do to pay the bills when the shop wasn't covering them all.

Rage had saved him, had made him an indomitable fighter. It'd helped that he'd had more at stake than his opponents. But the rage fueling him during those fights was mostly spent. Every once in a while, Dylan experienced a trace of it, enough to remind him what his emotional state had been like, but he'd learned to let go. Learned that he had to overcome the past or the past would overcome him. "Not anymore."

Aaron's jaw tightened. "How did you beat it back?"

Dylan often had difficulty stating how he felt, especially toward his brothers. He'd tried to show them with his actions, by the fact that he'd stayed when he could've taken off. But he wasn't sure he'd ever actually told any of them he loved them. He'd kept a roof over their heads and food on the table, and he'd done what he could to keep them in line. That was more than J.T. had succeeded in doing once he started drinking so heavily. But Dylan had been absolutely inadequate at replacing their mother. They'd missed out on the gentleness and nurturing she could've provided. So Dylan forced himself to speak even though the emotion behind what he said made him uncomfortable, especially in front of Aaron. "I knew if I gave in to those negative emotions I'd lose you."

His brother's eyebrows jerked together. "You mean Mack."

"I mean *all* of you. Do you think I've done what I've done just for him? If that was the case, two mouths would've been easier to feed than five."

After hours, the office felt abnormally quiet. The workday was so loud and frenetic. But this silence seemed even more profound.

"I feel bad about Presley," Aaron said at length.

So that was what had triggered this heart-to-heart. Dylan was relieved to know his brother had some reaction to what had happened besides his usual "I don't give a shit."

"So do I." Dylan felt bad about Cheyenne, too, but he didn't want to get his life tangled up with a woman who was always looking beyond him, always wanting something better. He figured he should steer clear of that emotional crash if he could. Lord knew he hadn't avoided many other pitfalls.

"Where do you think she is?" Aaron bent his can as he turned it in his hand. "You don't imagine . . ." He stopped talking the second his voice cracked.

Dylan felt a fresh burst of concern. "You're really that worried about her? Why?"

"She's gone, man!"

"But it hasn't even been twenty-four hours. You know Presley. It's not exactly unusual for her to take off. She might not surface for days." What he'd seen in Anita's room meant it wasn't quite that simple. But Aaron wasn't aware of that, and Dylan wasn't about to reveal it. Especially because there was still a chance everything could end well. They hadn't heard from her, didn't know for sure what had happened.

Aaron shook his head. "I shouldn't have let her go."

"Wait a second." God, Dylan wanted a cigarette. He hadn't had one all day. But he was still trying to quit smoking, to prove to himself, if not Cheyenne, that he was every bit as good as Joe. "You told me you didn't see her."

Aaron's bad attitude reasserted itself. "It was only for a minute."

"But you said you didn't see her!"

"I wasn't completely honest with you, obviously."

Son of a bitch. "You didn't have a fight. . . ."

"No."

"And you didn't withhold any other information that might've helped us find her?"

"Of course not."

"Then . . . what is it?"

His chin bumped his chest and Dylan's heart began to race. "*Aaron?*"

"When I wouldn't go over to her place she hung up. But she stopped by later. I asked about her mother, but she wouldn't give me a straight answer. She was too upset. She wanted to come in — started kissing me right there on the doorstep."

"And?"

His speech slowed, but he continued. "I felt like shit. So I wasn't interested. She asked me if I had any pills and . . . I gave her what I had and sent her home."

The possibility of an overdose crossed Dylan's mind, as it had before. Only now

400

he had to worry that Aaron was responsible for it. *Shit . . .* "She didn't go home."

"No." He raised his eyes. "But if I had any clue where she did go, I would've told you."

Disgusted as well as concerned, Dylan rounded the reception desk. "What kind of pills did you give her?"

Clearly uncomfortable, Aaron stretched his neck. "I didn't have any pills. I gave her crystal meth."

"*Where did you get it?*"

"Come on, Dyl. It's available, okay? I can get it if I want it. You can't shut down every dealer I know. This is on me."

"It better not be Carl."

"It wasn't Carl. He's terrified of you. He freaks out every time I get near him."

"Good." But Aaron was right. Dylan couldn't threaten every drug dealer in Northern California. If Aaron wanted to get high, he'd find a way. "Was Presley already stoned when she came over?"

"How should I know? I was half-asleep! I didn't give her a drug test."

Dylan pictured what he'd seen inside Anita's room before they came to take the body. He guessed Presley had been on something. She'd probably left immediately after Anita died — confused, upset and maybe coming off her high enough to crave more. So she'd stopped by their house. "How much did you give her?"

"She was so freaked out and upset I just wanted her to leave me alone. I gave her a few points — all I had." He sounded close to tears when he added, "Dyl, I need help."

This admission frightened Dylan as much as all the rest of it. The demons Aaron was fighting weren't ones Dylan could slay for him, so he wasn't sure he *could* help. That was why he'd resorted to threatening Carl. At least it was *something*. "Getting clean starts with rehab. Only you can commit to that. Only you can change your life."

"I know." He blew out a sigh. "You've been trying to tell me for a long time. Maybe if I'd listened . . . Presley would still be here."

Dylan said a silent prayer that this would be a turning point, that he wouldn't lose yet another member of his family. He also prayed that it wasn't too late to save Presley. "I'll do whatever I can to get you what you need."

A wry smile appeared on his brother's lips. "That much I can count on."

Aaron started to leave but Dylan stopped him. "What's love, if not that?"

■ ■ ■ ■

Joe hadn't been able to reach Cheyenne all evening, but he'd enjoyed seeing his girls. They'd admired the tree, just as he'd expected, ordered pizza, watched a movie and sat up talking about Christmas, school, their friends. He was determined to show them a good time while they were in Whiskey Creek. He didn't get to have them all that often, and missed being a full-time father. But concern for the woman he wanted to date had been hovering in the back of his mind all day. How was she taking her mother's death? And who was around to support her, since most of her friends were on that cruise?

He knew Presley was less of an asset than she should be. And Gail hadn't been able to reach her, either.

Once Josephine and Summer were in bed, and his father was home to watch them, he decided to go over to Cheyenne's to see if he could do anything to help.

The stores were closed after ten, so he stopped by the Gas-N-Go to pick up a long-stemmed white rose and a card.

Sandra Morton was working. Slow as it was this time of night, she could've been

sitting on the stool behind the register, reading a book. Instead, she was busy cleaning.
She was one of their best employees. Her
son, Robbie, worked for them, too. He was
young, only eighteen, but he already had a
baby to support.

"Hey!" she said when he walked in.

He smiled. "Wishing you could close early
and head home to that grandbaby of yours?"

"Naw. I'm fine with staying till twelve.
Little Dodge has a cold. Long as I'm here
his mother has to walk the floor with him
instead of me."

Robbie and his wife, who was a year
younger than he was, lived with Sandra. It
was the only way they could make ends
meet while he went to college in Sacramento, since his wife was still in high school.

"She doesn't get up with him?"

Sandra rolled her eyes. "Not if she can
help it."

"Even while she's on break for the holidays?"

"*Any* time."

He didn't envy Sandra the difficult position she was in. No parent wanted his or
her son getting a girl pregnant before he
could even legally drink. "Good thing you
love that baby so much."

She chuckled. "No kidding. The sun rises

and sets on that kid."

He selected a card and a pink rose since they were out of white and removed his wallet. He owned the store with his father, but he paid for everything he bought there, just like anyone else.

"Are you seeing someone?" she asked, eyeing the flower.

"Cheyenne Christensen's mother died today," he explained.

Her smile vanished. "I heard about that. I'm so sorry. Actually, she dropped in earlier and left a note for you. I didn't expect to see you so I tacked it above your work desk. I would've forgotten if you hadn't mentioned her. I swear my mind isn't the same since Robbie had Dodge. That baby's all I think about."

Sandra kept talking but her words dimmed to background noise. Why hadn't Cheyenne just called him back?

"I'll grab it on my way out." He wasn't sure if he'd interrupted Sandra, but he didn't particularly care. She'd talk all day if he let her. After taking his change, he headed into the garage, where his desk languished beneath a pile of work orders and auto parts.

It took a moment for the new energy-efficient lights to come on. When they did, he found a piece of copy paper with his name on it, folded up tightly and stapled shut, tacked to the bulletin board where he'd put up pictures of his kids, the shop calendar, invoices and various "to do" items he didn't want to forget.

After retrieving it, he sank onto his stool to read what she'd written.

Thanks for all your messages today, Joe. It means a lot that you're concerned about me. I've almost called you back several times, but I'm not sure I'd have the courage to come out with what I have to tell you, so I hope you'll forgive me for doing it this way.

First of all, my life is completely upside down right now. I should get my head on straight before I start seeing anyone. More than anything I don't want to mislead you or disappoint you. I've always admired you, will never forget how wonderful you were to me when I first came to town.

Joe couldn't remember being "wonderful." He remembered being angry at how her mother treated her and how his father had cautioned him to stay out of it. But that was all.

So I have to be up front with you. Remember when I said I was a virgin? I was — at the time. I know that wasn't too long ago (uncomfortable laugh goes here) but since then I've slept with Dylan (yes, Dylan Amos). Dylan and I weren't seeing each other or anything; it just happened out of the blue. I'm not quite sure how after thirty-one years! I know this probably isn't what you want to hear, but you've already been through a lot, so before you start to care about me or build any expectations based on what I told you before, I thought it only fair to be as honest as possible.

No matter what happens I will always think of you as a hero.

Cheyenne

"Wow . . ." he breathed, feeling as if he'd just been sucker punched. He'd certainly never seen *this* coming.

"Wow what?" Sandra asked. "Everything okay?"

Joe had been so engrossed he hadn't realized his employee had poked her head into the garage. Trying to rally from the shock, he got up. "Fine. It's just . . . her car needs some work."

"She had to ask me for a stapler to be able

to tell you that?"

He didn't answer, but his silence didn't deter Sandra from speaking again. Nothing deterred Sandra. But he knew she meant well.

"I wonder if she's found her sister."

"Her sister?" he asked, glancing up.

"That's the reason she came here in the first place. She was looking for Presley, said she hadn't seen her all day. Knowing Presley, I wasn't overly concerned. You can't keep track of someone who's hell-bent on destroying herself. But I said I'd keep an eye out. Then she came back a few minutes later with that."

Joe needed to think about what Cheyenne had revealed, figure out how it affected what he felt for her. But now was not the time. Sandra was being too nosy. "Maybe I'll go by and see if Presley's back."

"That would be nice. Presley's troubled, but Cheyenne's sure a great person."

24

Cheyenne's car was gone but Dylan knocked, anyway. She didn't answer, confirming his first guess. She hadn't found Presley. She was still out searching for her sister.

He wondered if she was doing it alone.

Maybe she had Joe, her knight in shining armor, to help her.

Despite his own sarcasm, Dylan hoped she did. He hated to think of her trying to cope on her own — frantic, heartbroken, vulnerable.

He lifted his hand to bang on the door again, just in case he was wrong and she was inside, asleep. It was eleven, certainly late enough for that. She could've left her car elsewhere and had someone drop her off.

The sound of an engine made him turn. The vehicle pulling into Cheyenne's drive wasn't the Oldsmobile or the Mustang, however. He couldn't determine the make or model, but the headlights blinding him were too high for either.

This was a truck — and once he could see it clearly, he realized who it belonged to.

Suddenly, Dylan wanted to be anywhere else, but he forced himself to stand on the stoop and wait until Joe turned off his engine and got out. If he was bringing Cheyenne home, at least Dylan would be able to reassure himself that she was okay.

But she didn't get out of the truck. It was only Joe who walked toward him. "She's not home?" he said, his voice clipped, not open and friendly like it had been at the Victorian Christmas celebration.

Dylan figured it was finding him on Cheyenne's doorstep so late that accounted for the change. He shook his head. "She's not with you?"

"No."

They stared at each other for several seconds, opponents for the first time, a subtle but unmistakable shift. Then Joe shoved his hands in his pockets and heaved a sigh. "She told me about you."

Instantly wary, Dylan narrowed his eyes. "Told you what about me?"

"That you two —" he shrugged, obviously looking for the right words "— were together," he finished with a wince.

Dylan frowned. "Telling you was a hell of a risk to take. But . . . somehow it doesn't surprise me."

Joe stepped closer. He seemed intent on seeing Dylan's face. "Why not?"

"She's been in love with you since she was fourteen, thinks you walk on water. Didn't she tell you that, too?" The jealousy he was feeling leaked into his voice, but Dylan couldn't help it. His chest was so tight he could scarcely breathe, let alone talk.

Joe stopped a foot or so away and toed the dirt between the dead clumps of grass. "She didn't say that, exactly."

"She's wanted you for a long time. So . . ." He met Joe's somber gaze. "I hope you won't let what happened between us get in the way."

A touch of confusion showed on Joe's face. "Something like that's hard to forget, Dylan."

Especially when he'd already dealt with a cheating wife. His background would make it even harder. "I'm just telling you it would be a mistake. What we did didn't mean anything to her. It was . . . an act of desperation, I think. I hit on her in a vulnerable moment."

"So . . . more your fault than hers."

"Definitely." He knew that should be an easy sell. People in Whiskey Creek liked to blame him for whatever went wrong. In high school, he'd deserved a lot of that blame. He'd broken into the school and vandalized it, he'd stolen a car and gone on a joyride, he'd started a bonfire in an abandoned building so they could roast hot dogs and gotten in more trouble for that than the car incident. So maybe blaming him had become a habit. Regardless of the reason, he'd been picked up three different times since then for shit he *didn't* do.

"Nice of you to take responsibility."

Dylan managed a cynical smile. "Yeah, well, I wouldn't want to stand in the way of true love."

Joe jerked his head toward the house. "So what are you doing here now? Hoping to get lucky again?"

Cigarettes. Dylan needed a smoke, but he patted empty pockets. He'd bought a pack, since his brothers had taken his advice and thrown out what they already had. However, he'd subsequently tossed that new pack, too. "I was just trying to check on her."

"Sure you were."

"I don't owe you anything, Joe. If she comes back to me, I'm going to take all I can get."

Joe's voice dropped low. "Stay away from her."

"It would be a mistake to try to enforce that," Dylan said, and walked off before the temptation to leave Joe writhing on his back could get the best of him.

Cheyenne had never been so cold. But she refused to go home to an empty house. She would find her sister first. She hadn't come this far to let her life fall apart now that Anita could no longer affect her.

"Presley!"

There was a movement across the river. She angled her flashlight in that direction, but succeeded only in startling several deer. They bounded away, snapping twigs and crashing through branches.

It took a moment to absorb this latest disappointment. She'd gone down as far as Carl Inera's and was on her way back following the river, but darkness, thick vegetation and rocks, both sharp and slippery, made the journey difficult. She'd already passed the swirling pool Presley favored. But she had to keep searching. She could easily imagine her sister getting high and wandering around out here until she either fell into the river or froze to death.

That didn't explain where her car was.

But Cheyenne had to at least *look* in their own backyard, had to be sure.

"Presley!" She was getting closer and closer to Dylan's house, but she didn't care if he or his brothers heard her. She didn't care about anything except finding her only family. "Answer me!"

She smelled cigarette smoke before she realized she was no longer alone. Stopping not far from Dylan's barn, she closed her eyes and inhaled. That scent reminded her of Presley, but she knew it wasn't Presley smoking out here tonight. She used her flashlight to scan the woods ahead of her until she saw Dylan leaning up against a tree at the edge of his property.

"No luck?" he said, shying away from the light.

She wondered how long he'd been there, listening to her call out. He wasn't even wearing a coat. "No."

When he pushed off the tree and came toward her, she noticed that he was carrying a bottle of hard liquor in one hand and a cigarette in the other. "Joe came over to your place tonight. Thought you'd like to know. If you call him, you might be able to catch him before he goes to bed, get him to come back."

Because it was rude to do anything else,

she pointed her flashlight at the ground, but that made it impossible to ascertain his expression. He looked like nothing except a tall, dark shadow. "How do you know he came over?"

The whites of his teeth flashed in a smile, but she suspected it wasn't a happy one. "We bumped into each other."

Her heart was pounding. She wanted to believe it was due to the physical exertion but knew there was more to it. Seeing Dylan did this to her. "I told him about us."

He drank from the bottle, then wiped his mouth. "So he said."

Dylan's words took Cheyenne by surprise. "*He mentioned it to you?*"

"Point-blank. You went for full disclosure, huh?"

When she folded her arms, hugging herself against the cold, he offered her a drink.

She caught a whiff of whiskey as she pushed it away. "I didn't want to feel as if I'd been sneaking around."

"Gutsy move. Admirable, considering how much you care about him."

Was he being sarcastic? She couldn't tell, but she was now convinced he was drunk. "You need to go inside, Dylan. It's too cold out here."

"You're telling *me* that?"

"You don't have a coat on."

"I don't need a coat." He took a long drag. "I don't need anything."

"Least of all me?"

He didn't respond.

"Come on." She held his arm so she could tug him toward his house, but he jerked out of her grasp.

"Aaron saw her, you know."

She let go of him. "He what?"

"He saw Presley last night."

"That's not what he told us."

He kept smoking but didn't say anything.

"Dylan?"

"Apparently, he wasn't entirely honest." He shrugged.

Mouth dry, she steadied herself by placing a hand on the closest tree. "What happened?"

"He was an asshole to her. Just like you're afraid I'll be to you. Should make you glad you never gave me the chance, huh?"

She couldn't let their personal problems enter into this. She had to find Presley. "Does he know where she is?"

"No. She came by when he was asleep. He didn't want to see her, so he turned her away and then she asked for drugs."

"And . . ."

"He gave them to her. See? You can't

count on an Amos to do the right thing."

But Aaron was as screwed up as Presley. Cheyenne couldn't judge Dylan by Aaron's actions, any more than Dylan could judge her by Presley's.

Again, she thought of the possibility of a baby and felt heartbroken for her sister. She might've felt heartbroken for herself but refused to contemplate whether or not she might be pregnant, too. "He doesn't care about her?"

"The ironic thing is —" he dropped his cigarette and stubbed it out "— I think he does."

He didn't offer an excuse as to why Aaron might've reacted as he had, but Cheyenne could guess. He'd lost his own mother; why would he want to be involved in losing hers?

"They both need to go into rehab."

"Aaron says he's ready for it. I'm taking him down after Christmas."

"Good. It might be his last chance to get his life turned around." She hoped Presley would have the same chance, hoped it wasn't already too late.

"I'm sorry for the way he treated her," he said softly.

"He's the one who should be sorry. Come on, let's get you inside."

"I'm fine!"

"Please?" she said. "I don't want to worry about you, too. I can't . . ." When her voice broke, he tossed away the bottle and stepped up to frame her face with his hands.

She stared at him, waiting for him to kiss her, hoping he would. The way he made her feel when she was in his arms could overcome the pain. But he didn't.

"Go out with me," he whispered. "Just to dinner. I don't pretend to be perfect, or even as good as Joe, but I can love you twice as much. If you don't have a good time, I'll leave you alone."

She wanted his arms around her so badly. Rising up on her toes, she tried to press her lips to his, but he stopped her.

"Just a date. That's all I want."

No, he wanted her to legitimize their relationship. To make it public. She understood what that dinner signified. It would put her at odds with almost everyone she knew. It would also put a decisive end to anything she had going with Joe, if the note she'd left him hadn't already done that.

"I'm obsessed with you," she admitted.

"Then say yes."

She couldn't see his expression, but she could hear the entreaty in his voice, feel the hopeful tension in his body — and couldn't refuse. "Will you go inside if I do?"

"I want to help you find your sister. That's why I came out here."

"It's no use." She swept her flashlight through the trees. "I've looked everywhere."

He took her hand, toyed with her cold fingers, then pulled her to him and rested his chin on her head. "She's going to be okay."

There were no guarantees, but Cheyenne preferred to believe him. She certainly didn't want to face any of the other possibilities. "When do you want to go out?" she asked.

"There's no rush. You can call me when you're ready. I just . . . I want you to give me a chance."

"I'm not a safe bet, Dylan," she said into his T-shirt. "You know that."

He kissed her temple. "I think that's what you're holding against me."

Presley woke in the sleeper of a semi. The man who'd picked her up was driving. She could hear and feel the motion of the truck. But she was naked beneath a blanket so she knew they probably hadn't been on the road for long.

Squinting in the darkness, she shoved herself into a sitting position so she could see who she was with. When she saw it was a man somewhere in his late fifties and that he was obese and terribly unattractive even in the dim light of the instrument panel, she nearly groaned out loud.

"What time is it?" she asked, her voice raspy.

"Nearly two."

She pressed her fingers to her temples in an effort to ease the pounding. "Where are we?"

He used the rearview mirror to look back at her. "Near Phoenix. You hungry? I can stop at a hole-in-the-wall café I know. They cater to truckers so they're open twenty-four hours."

She wasn't hungry. She was never hungry. She just wanted more meth, Oxycontin, pot, *anything* that would dull the awareness dawning on her. "You don't happen to know a dealer in Phoenix, do you?"

"No. I've never done drugs. My wife would divorce me if I did." He winked at her. "But I've got more Jack Daniel's, if that'll help."

She remembered drinking with him hours ago. That was probably the reason she had such a splitting headache. "I've had enough of that."

"Want me to pull over at the next stop? I could give you another massage."

420

The way he smiled at her certainly didn't help the roiling in her stomach. "There's no chance you're a serial killer, is there?"

His eyes widened as if she couldn't possibly have meant that hopeful inflection. "Oh, no! Don't worry. You're the one who wanted to . . . you know. I would *never* hurt you."

The truck rumbled beneath her as she sank back onto the pillow and stared up at the blackness. "That's what I thought."

"You seem disappointed," he said with an uncomfortable laugh.

"I am. Would it be so hard to put me out of my misery? Maybe you could just push me out while we're driving."

"That would *kill* you." He sounded shocked. "I told you I'm not going to hurt you. You're such a beautiful girl. Why would you have a death wish?"

She didn't answer.

"Maybe you're a little crazy, but you're a hellcat in bed. It's been a long time since I've had sex that good. I owe you."

She thought of Aaron and the pain in her head and chest became so acute she nearly blacked out. He was the only one she wanted, but he didn't want her. And now she was carrying his child. She wasn't sure what to do about the situation. She knew she shouldn't be drinking or using. The over-the-counter test she'd taken just after Cheyenne left for A Victorian Christmas with Joe confirmed it. But if she was going to end the pregnancy anyway . . . "I want to get out."

"*What?*"

"Pull over and let me out!"

"I can't do that here! We're in the middle of the Sonoran desert."

"So?" She rested one arm over her eyes. "I'll walk."

"It's too cold outside. And it'd take you hours to get to Phoenix."

She didn't argue. She didn't care enough about anything to put up a fight. Her mother was dead. Her sister wasn't really her sister. She was pregnant. And the man she'd considered her boyfriend didn't give a shit about her.

"Presley?"

Why had she told this man her name? Couldn't he tell that she didn't even want to *see* him? "Yes?"

"Are you okay with Phoenix? Can I let you out there?"

Phoenix was good as anywhere. "Whatever."

Cheyenne checked Presley's room as soon

as she woke up. Still empty. So she went to the front door, hoping her sister's car might be in the drive despite her absence from the house.

Except for the Oldsmobile, the drive was empty, as well. Not really a surprise, despite all her wishing it could be otherwise. There was, however, a rose and a card on the doorstep where the hospice nurse had left a meal last night — a meal Cheyenne had taken in before searching the riverbank but hadn't eaten.

In spite of the cold, she scooped up those small gifts and walked outside to sit in her sister's chair. But when she saw the ashtray perched precariously on the banister, she didn't even bother to open the card, which she assumed someone had left because of Anita's death.

Her phone rang, cutting through the worry that held her in such a tight grip. She'd kept her cell with her every minute since Presley had gone missing. But this wasn't her sister, either. It was the casino, wondering whether or not Presley would be coming in to work later.

Although Cheyenne explained to Presley's boss that their mother's death, which she'd told him about yesterday, was hitting her sister hard, he hardly seemed sympathetic.

He managed another perfunctory, "I'm sorry." Then he told her that Presley would lose her job if she didn't make it in tonight. They were short-staffed and couldn't get anyone else to fill in over the holidays.

Hoping Presley's friend, Carolyn, might've heard from her, or that she could cover the shift and buy Presley some more time, Cheyenne called her.

"Have you heard from her?" she asked as soon as Carolyn picked up. She left the card that she'd found on the doorstep in her lap but held the flower to her nose.

"No, nothing. And I've called her phone a million times."

There was no guarantee Presley even had her cell with her. If the ringing bothered her, she could've thrown it out the window. When she was high, there was no telling what she might do. That was how she'd wound up getting a tattoo depicting wild beasts devouring innocent prey covering one whole arm. "It's a dog-eat-dog world," she'd said when Cheyenne had asked why she'd chosen something so violent.

Cheyenne had just thanked Carolyn for agreeing to cover Presley's shift when a call from Eve beeped through. No doubt Riley had let her know what was happening. Cheyenne had told him not to — Eve couldn't do anything from the Caribbean — but she had to admit it was nice to see that familiar name pop up on caller ID.

"Chey, did you find her?" Eve asked without preamble.

"No."

"I can't believe she'd do this."

"You *can't* believe it or you don't *want* to believe it?"

"You're right. I don't *want* to believe it. Where do you think she went?"

"She could've gone anywhere."

"And here I am, stranded on this damn boat." She made a sound of annoyance. "I asked if I could get off early, but there's no way. I'm stuck until we dock in Puerto Rico."

Cheyenne gazed out across the yard. "Thanks for trying."

"I never should have left Whiskey Creek."

"So Riley told you about my mom, too?"

"He did. He called last night, worried when he came over to help search for Presley and you weren't home."

"He helped me all afternoon. He didn't need to do more."

"He feels bad. We all do."

She studied the flower in her hands. "He must've been the one who brought me this rose."

"What rose?"

"I found it on the doorstep."

"You don't know for sure?"

"Hang on." She propped the phone to her ear with one shoulder while reading the card. "Actually, it's not from him."

"Who's it from?"

Cheyenne might've shied away from mentioning that it was the guy Eve had wanted, except that at this point she was too numb to lie. "Joe."

Maybe Eve was faking it, but she sounded enthusiastic. "That's nice! How do you know?"

"There's a card with it."

"What does it say?"

"It's just your basic sympathy card," she said, but it was much more than that. He'd written that he felt bad for what she was going through and wanted to be there for her. He'd also written that he wanted to talk to her about Dylan.

"So how are things between you?"

"I like him. He's nice."

"That's it?"

She rested her head on the back of her chair. "I'm not capable of any more right now. All I know is that Dylan is the one I want to get naked with." There, she'd said it.

After a slight pause, Eve said, "Chey, Dylan has a certain . . . magnetism. I've felt it. I'm sure most women have. But think about what it would be like trying to maintain a relationship with him, what *he* might be like after the initial excitement. Joe's a family man. He's dependable, steady."

Dylan had raised his brothers. He'd stuck with them regardless of how difficult life became. How could anyone be more of a family man than that? Or steadier?

Still, she knew what Eve meant and couldn't argue. Last night she'd felt guilty for judging him by Aaron's misdeeds, but Dylan's checkered past also spoke against him. "You think what I'm feeling is merely lust?"

"You've never been to bed with anyone but him. Sex has created a bond between you. That's what it's meant to do. But . . . you can't let physical attraction get in the way of what's best for you. Who's more likely to help you build the life you want?"

"How do I know? I can only see so far down the road."

"But if you aren't careful, if you take a wrong turn, you'll wind up at a dead end."

"Isn't that why you have to trust your gut?"

"I think, in this case, it might be smarter

427

to trust your *friends*."

Cheyenne saw Dylan's Jeep coming down the road and jumped to her feet. She knew he could simply be heading home for lunch. He and his brothers went past her place all the time. But he turned in.

"He's here," she whispered into the phone.

"Let me talk to him," Eve said.

Cheyenne lowered her head so Dylan wouldn't be able to see her face. "No."

"I'll be nice."

"You won't. You're too protective of me. You feel my mother's already shortchanged me and you're not going to let anyone else do the same."

"Damn right!"

"See? I'll talk to you when you get off the boat." She hung up as Dylan approached.

"Any word on Presley?" he asked.

Putting her phone on the railing next to the ashtray, she shook her head. "What are you doing home this time of day?"

"Work's over."

"At noon?"

"We closed up early for Christmas Eve."

Cheyenne hadn't realized what day it was; she'd lost track in the haze of recent events. "Oh. Right. I guess it is. Where're your brothers?"

"They went to grab a bite."

"And you didn't go with them?"

He didn't respond. It was obvious he'd come to see her instead. And that made it even harder to resist her feelings for him.

As he climbed the steps, his eyes shifted to the rose and card she'd left on the table. "A not-so-secret admirer?"

"Joe."

"Ah, my competition hard at work."

"He wants to talk to me about you."

"What will you tell him?" He sat on the steps and stared out at the yard instead of looking at her. "You could blame it all on me if you've changed your mind again." He was referring to her promise from last night.

"I haven't changed my mind. I'll tell him the truth."

Twisting around, he glanced back at her. "Which is . . ."

"I can't stop seeing you."

A crooked grin suddenly curved his lips. "I'm sure he'll appreciate your honesty."

"I'm not sure what he'll say."

He patted his pocket as if he wanted to smoke, but didn't pull out a pack of cigarettes. "When is this supposed to occur?"

"I don't know, but . . . he invited me over for Christmas."

Dylan's smile disappeared. "Are you going?"

"It'll be hard to have Christmas without Presley," she said as she sank into her chair.

"Sitting here alone won't help."

"I've got my mother's funeral to plan."

He clasped his knees loosely to his chest. "That can wait, Chey. Presley's coming back."

He said it so matter-of-factly; she hoped he was right. "So you're trying to talk me into going?"

His expression let her know what he thought of that. "I'd rather you came to my place. It's not like any of us do any baking, but . . . we buy that big Christmas dinner from Nature's Way and —" he shrugged "— it's not too bad."

She could imagine how unconventional Christmas might be at the Amoses, but she was used to unconventional holidays. It didn't matter as long as Dylan was there. "*I* could do some baking. That would give me something to focus on besides my worry."

"I wouldn't mind a homemade pie or two."

"Pumpkin?"

"And pecan. But before you start, let's go to the police."

The warm feeling that had come over her at the prospect of sharing Christmas with Dylan vanished. "I tried. They don't care that she's gone."

"They'll care at some point. We have to push them, get them involved. We need the help."

We. It felt so good to have some support, especially *his* support. "Okay. I'll get showered."

He looked up at her when she stood, his eyelids half-lowered in predatory interest. *"Alone?"*

25

She was falling in love. Right in the middle of the worst week of her life. It didn't make sense that she'd lose her heart to this particular guy when she thought she was already in love with the "ideal" man. But it was Dylan's smile that put butterflies in her stomach. Dylan's smell that made her eager to bury her face in his neck. Dylan's touch that left her feeling warm inside. Maybe she was bucking her own better judgment — not to mention the advice of her best friend, who'd never led her wrong — but her heart simply would not cooperate with the idea of staying away from him.

Neither would her body.

As he stared up at her from his seat on the porch stairs, waiting for her answer, she had to ask herself, *Am I really going to give up Joe DeMarco for* Dylan Amos?

But she knew the answer.

"Sounds like Santa might be coming to

my house, after all," she said, and he laughed as she pulled him to his feet.

"What are you smiling at?" Cheyenne murmured above the sound of the water.

They'd barely spoken since they'd undressed and stepped into the shower. They'd been too busy enjoying the sensation of slick, wet skin against slick, wet skin, but when she said this, Dylan moved to shield her face from the spray so they could talk. "I've never seen you naked, not in daylight. It makes me feel lucky."

She blushed, and he nearly drew her into his arms. He loved how honestly delighted she seemed by even the smallest compliment.

"What are *you* smiling at?" he teased.

"I was remembering about that day in the park." She shivered as he bent his head to lick a drop of water off the tip of one breast. "I can't believe you said what you did to me," she continued. " 'You ever want me to show you what it feels like to have a man in your bed, you know where to find me.' Don't you think that was a little bold, Mr. Amos?"

He chuckled as he turned his attention to her other breast. "It worked, didn't it?"

"I'm embarrassed to say it was far more

effective than it should've been."

"No guts, no glory," he said. But that wasn't what he'd been thinking at the time. He'd assumed she'd shut him down no matter what. So he'd acted as if he had nothing to lose.

She laughed as she traced the lion inked on his chest. "What does this represent?"

"My mother was a Leo." She'd called him her lion cub, since he was also a Leo, but he didn't add that.

"And this one?"

"The scales of justice." He tried to kiss her, but she held him off.

"I know that. I want to know why you picked it."

"I'm not entirely sure. It just . . . spoke to me. When I got it, I was determined to make things right."

"For . . ."

"Myself. My brothers. All of us."

"And you did."

"I did what I could."

She caught his face between her hands. "I'm so happy right now. I'm sick with worry for my sister and yet, when I think of you, I'm happy. Is that crazy?"

He was too distracted to have a serious conversation. He couldn't wait to make love to her now that she seemed to feel something for him. But what she'd said was important enough to address here and now, so he stemmed the desire threatening to carry him away. "Not at all, because your sister is going to come back soon, and she'll be fine, so worrying would only ruin your day." He dropped a quick kiss on her lips. "And you're about to get lucky. That makes most people happy."

Closing her eyes, she pressed her cheek to his chest. "I don't think my happiness has anything to do with getting lucky."

He slid his hands down her smooth back to curl around her bottom. Then he hauled her up against him. "You might be speaking too soon."

"I know what I'm saying. How I feel comes from being with you, no matter what we're doing. When we were watching that movie at your place, and I was clear across the room, I couldn't think of anything except getting closer to you, curling up against you."

He smoothed her wet hair out of her eyes. Did she really know what she was doing, picking him? He'd never dreamed *he'd* wind up with her, not over Joe. What if he disappointed her? Or tomorrow she came to her senses? "Joe's a good guy, Chey. He —"

"He *is* a good guy," she interrupted. "He

took the news that I'm sleeping with you so graciously. But . . ."

"But?"

"He isn't you." She brought his mouth to hers and kissed him, openmouthed and hungry.

Arousal, hot and thick, pumped through Dylan's blood. The flat of her stomach brushed against him, making him even harder. "All this enthusiasm from my little virgin?" he murmured against her lips.

"I've got a lot more where that came from." She tried to draw him back for another kiss. Their lovemaking was about to turn from sweet and enjoyable to intense. But before he reached for the condom they'd brought in with them, he wanted to experiment.

"In a minute you're going to love me even more."

"What do you mean by that?"

"You'll see." Pressing her up against the tile, he dropped to his knees and, if his mouth hadn't been otherwise occupied, would've grinned from ear to ear when her hands anchored his head in place and she gasped his name.

Dylan was standing in front of her Christmas tree when Cheyenne, who'd finished getting ready, walked into the living room.

"You don't have any presents under here," he said.

"You don't have any presents under your tree, either," she told him. "You don't even have any decorations."

"We're guys," he said as if that explained it all. "I'm fairly sure this isn't normal for three women, though."

She thought of the gifts she had yet to wrap. The way Presley had put off shopping, she probably hadn't bought any. Chances were, she didn't have the money, but that wasn't unusual. The more she got involved with drugs, the less she cared about anything else. "We're not normal women. And this hasn't been a normal year. Not that we've ever had much to give one another. Do you and your brothers exchange gifts?"

"We do. Now that we're all adults, those gifts just aren't things that can be wrapped. Even if they are, we pretty much leave them in a bag."

She shook her head. "You need a woman over there."

"That's why I'm taking you home." He swatted her behind. "For Christmas decorations and pies and present wrapping."

"I thought it was for sex," she teased.

"That, too."

"After what you did in the shower I'll gladly follow you anywhere." She gave him a saucy smile. "Besides, you still owe me seventeen questions."

He grinned, obviously proud of what he'd accomplished a few minutes earlier. But she couldn't focus on how much she loved the contrast between his tough-guy image and the sensitive heart he guarded so well. She'd just caught sight of the rose and card she'd carried in from the porch earlier. "But first I have to call Joe."

His jocularity faded. "Right this minute?"

"Yes . . . Before we go out in public. I wouldn't want to run into him or . . . or make him feel as if I've made a fool of him."

"He warned me to stay away from you last night."

"He did?" She hadn't thought he'd care enough, not after what she'd revealed to him.

"To be honest, I wanted to warn him off, too. Guys can be territorial."

So could women. She was feeling rather territorial herself. Stepping up to him, she swept a kiss across his lips. "And, of course, you realized you were getting in his way and immediately backed off."

With a chuckle at her sarcasm, he put his

arms around her and rubbed his cheek against her neck. "I knew the two of you had it wrong."

"Had *what* wrong?" she said when he let her go.

His gaze met and held hers. "I knew you belonged with me."

It was hard to believe she'd once found Dylan less attractive than Joe. Now she felt exactly the opposite. "I just have to figure out a gentle way to break this to him."

His smile shifted toward the devilish. "I'd be happy to take care of that for you."

Cheyenne knew he was only joking, but she explained why she felt it was important not to create bad feelings despite that. "He's someone I've always admired, someone who's looked out for me in the past. He's also the brother of one of my best friends. I have to be careful."

He nodded. "Would you like some privacy?"

"Not for my sake, but . . . I'd want the conversation to be private if I were him, so I'd like to give him that."

"I'll go home and make sure someone put the dogs out in the yard. Call me when you're done."

She nodded but couldn't let him leave without a final, lingering kiss.

■ ■ ■ ■

Even with Dylan gone, it was hard for Cheyenne to call Joe. She almost dialed Gail's cell first. She wanted to tell her friend why she was about to do what she was going to do. But she knew Gail would say the same thing as Eve. They'd both try to convince her not to make the "mistake" she was making. They'd say she couldn't trust a guy like Dylan.

But they didn't know Dylan. Surely, if they did, they'd see his better qualities — wouldn't they?

Too tense to sit back, she perched on the edge of the couch and stared into the fireplace, remembering the night Joe had come over and built a fire. She'd been so infatuated with him. She'd thought it was love, but . . . she'd merely been in love with what he represented.

With a sigh, she scrolled through the call history on her phone. She'd received a slew of calls yesterday — people reacting to the news of her mother's death. She'd been too busy searching for Presley to do more than quickly sift through the messages.

But being preoccupied with Presley's situation wasn't the only reason she'd avoided the people closest to her. She'd been afraid of what she might reveal if she talked to them. She hadn't come to terms with the evidence that suggested Anita'd had help dying. . . .

Presley had added one more skeleton to the family closet. . . .

"Why?" she asked, appealing to the empty house. But *why* didn't matter when dealing with her sister and mother. She had to face the reality and cope with it, because there was no changing them. She'd learned that long ago.

Presley could be anywhere. It was that thought and the need to get the police out searching that made her stop procrastinating and call.

Joe picked up immediately. "There you are. How are . . . things?"

"Okay. Thanks for the concern. And for the flower and card. That was thoughtful of you."

"It was nothing. I've been worried."

"I know. I'm sorry. I should've called sooner."

"No problem. Did you find Presley?"

She propped his card up on the mantel. "Not yet."

"I'm sure she'll come back when she's ready."

"Maybe," she said, but how could her sister come back after killing Anita?

"It's a hell of a thing to deal with at Christmas. I can't believe the timing of this. What can I do to help?"

"Nothing. I've looked everywhere. I'm counting on the police to get involved. At this point, they're my only hope."

"That's tough. Waiting must be so hard." He paused. "Is there any chance you're coming for dinner tomorrow? I told the girls you might. They're excited to meet you."

He'd mentioned her to Josephine and Summer? "I would love to meet them, too, but —" she straightened her spine "— I'm going to be at Dylan's, Joe."

Silence. Then, "Does that mean what I think it does?"

Was it a mistake to make this decision *now?* Probably. But she couldn't deny what she felt. "Yes."

"You're officially seeing him."

"I'm afraid so."

She thought he might give her all the reasons she shouldn't, but he didn't.

"Dylan and I have had a professional relationship for years."

Here we go . . . She bit her lip. "And?"

"I've always liked him."

"That's a generous thing to say. I hope . . .

442

I hope there're no hard feelings."

"I feel like I missed out, Chey. I'm not going to lie. But there are no hard feelings."

Suddenly deflated from all the stress, the worry and the secret she was carrying, she rested her head on the couch. "I've always thought so much of you, Joe." She smiled as she fingered the rose he'd left for her. "It's nice to know you're everything I ever imagined."

"I'm here if you need me," he said. "Merry Christmas."

"I can't believe we're at sea when all hell is breaking loose at home." Eve smacked herself on the forehead. "I *knew* I shouldn't have gone."

As usual, Callie and the others had joined her for morning brunch, but they'd eaten so much over the course of the past ten days that no one was very interested in food. Mostly, they nursed their coffees while talking, the same as they did every Friday in Whiskey Creek when they congregated at Black Gold Coffee. Except that Cheyenne wasn't there. Eve was feeling her absence more acutely today than ever.

"You can't blame yourself for taking a trip you planned for two years," Callie said. "I mean . . . I feel guilty, too, but . . . we were well past the refund period by the time we realized that Cheyenne's mother would likely die while we were gone."

"Anita lasted so long," Noah said. "I guess I figured she'd last a little longer. Or somehow go back into remission."

Baxter combed his fingers through his thick, wavy hair. "What could we have done even if we'd stayed? What could anyone do?"

Eve speared him with a look. "I hope you're kidding."

"I wish we were there to support her as much as you do." He spread his hands. "But . . . her mother was going to die either way."

"Her sister is missing, too!" Eve snapped.

Ted turned his coffee cup in his hands. "I'm not sure we could've stopped that, either."

Somehow Ted's weighing in made Eve feel slightly better. He'd always been the academic of the group, the voice of reason. He and Gail had finished at the very top of their class. Eve should've had higher marks herself. If she hadn't been so involved with her high school boyfriend, she might've been able to concentrate.

"I don't think Eve's talking about Anita or Presley," Callie said. "Not really. They've always been a problem, so . . . nothing new there. The real issue is Dylan."

Ted rocked back in his seat. "Maybe she's not that serious about Dylan. Maybe she just wanted to get laid."

The guilt Eve had been feeling reasserted itself. Initially, she'd kept Cheyenne's business a secret. But the more worried she became about Dylan and the relationship that was taking shape at home, with only Riley there to look out for Chey, the less inclined she was to keep it to herself. Despite what she'd said to Cheyenne, it was more natural to share this information, since they all divulged the intimate details of their lives — most of the time, anyway. "Maybe I could believe that if it was a one-time hookup. But it's evolving into more," she insisted. "They've been sleeping together all week."

"The last thing Cheyenne needs is to go through anything remotely similar to what I've been through." Kyle added this. Although he was only married a year, his marriage had been painful from the start. He'd been manipulated into saying "I do," and had never really loved his ex.

"We don't *know* it'll end badly," Noah said.

Eve leaned forward. "You think that if Cheyenne dates someone who parties like

Dylan, it could end any other way? That she won't mind when he breaks some guy's arm because he made the wrong comment to one of his brothers at a bar?"

"Consider this." Callie spoke mostly to the boys. "Would you want your daughter dating someone like Dylan?"

They glanced at one another as if that drove the point home.

Eve shoved her cup away. "We left her on her own during the most vulnerable period of her life."

Baxter grimaced. "She's not a child, Eve," he said, but he didn't speak with much authority. She could tell he felt badly, too.

"She might not be a child, but she *is* going through hell right now and grasping for an anchor. Anyone would grasp for *something* to hang on to if they were in her situation."

"Too bad we couldn't count on Sophia to look out for her while we were gone," Ted grumbled.

"You don't even want Sophia coming to Friday coffee," Callie pointed out.

"But if she has to come, she can at least do her part for the group."

Eve lowered her voice as several other vacationers filed past. "Sophia's got her own problems. Did you see that bruise under her eye before we left?"

"What bruise?" Noah asked.

"The one she was trying to cover up with makeup."

"She must've done a good job of it." This came from Ted. "I didn't notice."

"Because you won't even look at her. And you don't *want* to notice."

"Her injuries don't always coincide with her big-shot husband being in town," Baxter said.

"How would we know? He doesn't check in with us, and there's a lot she won't say. We haven't been all that nice to her."

"We can't be too bad. She keeps showing up, doesn't she?" Ted again.

Callie used a napkin to clean up some drops of cream. "She's lonely."

"Am I supposed to feel sorry for her after what she's done?" he responded.

"Let's not get into that," Eve said.

Noah jumped in next. "I agree. We've been trying to figure out whether or not Skip is abusive for a long time. The thought of it makes me want to break his smug-ass jaw. But unless she speaks up, there's no way to know. And as far as Cheyenne goes, moaning about what we should've done isn't going to help. We're here, and she's in Whiskey Creek. What can we do?"

"Nothing," Eve said. "Not until we get home."

"And then?" Baxter asked.

Callie leaned to the side so a waiter bussing tables could remove their empty cups. "We have to stage an intervention. It might make her mad at first, but . . . we have to do what we can to protect her."

Eve liked this idea. At least it was proactive — if they weren't too late. "Maybe we can get Dylan to see that he has nothing to offer her. If he really cares about Chey, that should be enough to make him leave her alone."

Baxter cocked his head to one side. "Okay . . . and who's going to risk life and limb by telling him to stay away from her?"

"I'll do it," Eve said before anyone else could speak.

"Good." Ted's cup, which he'd refused to relinquish to the young man cleaning the table, clinked on its saucer. "I don't think he'll hit a girl."

Ted's grin told them he was joking, but Eve didn't find his remark funny. "Somebody's got to do *something*."

"Let's just hope we help more than we hurt," Baxter said.

"You don't think it's worth a try?" Eve suddenly sounded unsure.

"Actually, I do. No hell is worse than falling in love with the wrong person."

If Callie hadn't said anything about Baxter's possible interest in Noah, Eve would've dismissed this comment without a second thought. Baxter could be so negative they sometimes affectionately called him Eeyore. But even while she was consumed with Cheyenne's problems, the sour note of desperation and disillusion in his voice struck her as potentially revealing.

"What do you know about love?" Noah scoffed, barking out a laugh. "I've never even seen you date the same girl twice!"

It seemed to Eve that Baxter blanched at this comment. A poignant empathy thrummed in her chest, tempting her to reach out to him. But she knew he wouldn't appreciate that gesture, so she kept her hands to herself while he mustered a tight smile.

"Maybe I've never met the right girl."

Was that because she didn't exist?

26

Cold and windy, Phoenix wasn't the same city Presley remembered from years before. Anita had brought them here during the height of summer. When the temperature had been 116 degrees. Just sitting in a car with no air-conditioning, even after dark, made their bodies run with sweat. Presley would never forget how hard it had seemed just to *breathe*. She'd also never forget Anita leaving them alone shortly after they arrived, telling them she was going off to buy groceries. They'd begged to go along — she couldn't be trusted to come back in the time promised — but were dropped off at the edge of a wide expanse of desert and told to wait in the shade of a dilapidated chicken coop. There, stomachs aching with hunger, they counted fire ants and watched a spider spin a web between two warped boards on the abandoned coop.

After a while, they scavenged for any type

of fruit-bearing tree, hoping to get lucky enough to find a pomegranate tree, because Anita had said she'd found one on her first trip to Arizona. But the earth was so scorched it didn't seem to produce anything more than scrub brush. They didn't dare approach the house that sat off in the shimmering, hazy distance. They knew what Anita would do to them if they got her into trouble by involving other people.

When Anita finally returned more than seven hours later, she had no groceries. She did, however, reek of alcohol and threaten to knock their teeth down their throats if they didn't stop nagging her for something to eat.

Chey was the one who made that day, and all the others like it, bearable. But Presley didn't want to think about her sister. Life was life. There wasn't anything she could do to change it.

The semi driver — Axle, which had to be a nickname but she hadn't cared enough to ask — had provided her with a meal and money to catch a city bus to Sunnyslope, where they'd once lived with a gruff old man in a single-wide trailer. She could see the sun-bleached sign for Palo Verde Mobile Home Park in the distance. That was where she'd first tried meth, and it was the reason

451

she'd come back here. She needed a supplier and this was the type of neighborhood where she'd be likely to find one.

If only her sudden nostalgia for Whiskey Creek wasn't making her so damned heartsick. She stood on the corner of Nineteenth Avenue and Cactus Road, breathing in the exhaust of the bus as it pulled away and staring down the dystopian-looking street of strip clubs, sex shops and XXX video stores, all of which looked abandoned this time of day.

Her family had left this behind when they moved to California. At that point, their lives had changed dramatically for the better, and until this moment, Presley had forgotten just how much her situation had improved in the passing years.

"Hey!"

Startled by the intrusion into her thoughts, Presley blinked and focused on a tall, dark figure standing in the entry of a convenience store. "You a hooker, honey? You looking for a date?"

She could hardly see the man for the glare. But when she hesitated, he came out of the shadows. With short-cropped hair, a clean shave and a wedding ring on his left hand, he appeared surprisingly respectable for this side of town — except for the smarmy smile.

"I could show you a good time," he offered.

Stepping back, she glanced up at the name of the store: Mel's Quickie Grocery. It hadn't been around when she lived here, but the businesses on this street frequently changed hands. "What are you doing?" she asked. "Just waiting for some girl to come by — like a . . . a spider hoping to catch a fly?"

He chuckled softly. "Not quite. My friend owns this place. He supplies me with . . . certain commodities I enjoy. I spotted you as I was coming out and thought you looked like the type who might enjoy them, too."

This caught her interest, as he'd probably expected. "What kind of commodities?"

"Speed? Crank? What's your drug of choice? I can get it."

At this point, she'd take anything. "I'm not picky."

"Then I won't even have to go back inside."

She narrowed her eyes. "What, exactly, do you want in return?"

"Nothing too out of the ordinary. At least not these days. I enjoy a little BDSM. You?"

Pain, especially voluntary pain, wasn't her thing. But he was offering her what she'd come for, and she wasn't sure she'd find a better opportunity. "I'm not into anything *too* controlling," she said to see how he'd respond.

He adjusted his smile in an all-too-obvious attempt to look more sincere. "Fine. A *light* bondage session, then."

An image of Aaron came to mind. He never hurt her, not physically. He made love gently, sweetly, which would come as a surprise to those in Whiskey Creek who liked to think the worst of him. Already, she missed him, wanted to be with him.

But a girl didn't always get what she wanted. Presley had learned that lesson at an early age.

"I'll need some cash. I'm new in town, and I have to find a place to stay."

He pulled a pack of cigarettes from in his jacket and passed her one. "I might be able to help you out with that, too. My girls make good money, and I keep them safe."

So *that* was it. But as long as she got by, did it really matter? "Then our arrangement is more of an audition?"

He lit her cigarette. "I was just looking for a good time, but . . . who knows where the relationship might go from there?"

She covered her stomach with one hand. "I need an abortion."

"Hazard of the trade," he said without batting an eye. "I can arrange it."

Except this wasn't the type of unwanted pregnancy he assumed it was. She loved the baby's father. It wouldn't be easy to go through with the procedure. Her stomach tightened protectively at the mere thought of it.

If only she had another choice. If only Aaron cared about her. Just a little. She was thirty-three. If she wasn't going to have a child now, when would she start?

Probably never. No one knew better than she did how unlovable she was. It was too much to hope for, too much to expect that Aaron would want to be a father to their child.

The stranger motioned to a Lexus sedan that looked as respectable as he did. "Let's go."

"If you suspect you might not have been born to Anita, what about Presley? Do you think Anita could've stolen Presley, too?" Dylan had to admit that Christmas Eve wasn't the best time to talk about this, but he'd been burning with curiosity ever since Cheyenne had first shared her doubts. And they had plenty of time and privacy tonight. Since all the restaurants were closed, he'd made a salad and grilled a couple of steaks for dinner. Now they were enjoying a glass of wine, curled up together on her couch. He'd wanted to take Cheyenne to his house for the evening; he thought the presence of his brothers and all the activity might take her mind off her troubles. But she couldn't stop hoping that Presley would walk through the door, relieve her worries and possibly refute what she believed about Anita's death. That hope kept her anchored to her own house.

"She's most likely Anita's biological child," she said after a few seconds of deliberation.

"Why do you think so? She doesn't look anything like her. No more than you."

She slid her hand under his shirt but the movement was more about comfort and contact than desire. "There was always a certain affinity between them. One that came naturally. One we just didn't have."

He smoothed the hair out her face. "In other words, Presley was Anita's favorite."

"By a long shot. And I couldn't blame her. Presley was far more flexible and forgiving. I don't know why I couldn't be the same. I've often felt guilty about the resentment inside me, but . . . I haven't been able to overcome it. I think it's because she never felt a moment's guilt over how she behaved. If she'd remained healthy, nothing would've changed."

"Do you know anything about Presley's father?"

She leaned forward for a sip of her wine before putting it back on the coffee table. "No more than I know about my own."

"Where did Anita typically meet men?"

"Besides bars? Begging in the streets. At Laundromats. Homeless shelters. Hanging out around sex shops or those peep-show places. Rest stops. Drunk tanks." She twisted her head to smile ruefully at him. "All the places one usually hopes to find love."

He laughed. "God, what a life. How many cities did you live in growing up?"

She settled against his chest. "Too many to count. We never stayed in one place for long."

"Because your mother couldn't find work?"

"She did odd jobs here and there, but they never lasted. She couldn't get along with her bosses for more than a few weeks or months. Or she abused the system — called in sick too often, stole from the till, handled her personal business on company time. More often she wasn't even looking for gainful employment. She was just hoping for a handout or a quick . . . *transaction* so she could get by and keep moving."

How had Cheyenne and Presley coped with such a mother? He'd heard rumors about Anita, of course, ever since they'd come to town. But he hadn't really clued in to what might be going on in their lives, not until recent years when he'd started noticing the pretty blonde next door who wouldn't give him the time of day. Soon after, he learned quite a bit about Cheyenne, thanks to Presley and the things she said during her many visits to his house. "What was she looking for?"

"I wish I could tell you." There was a shrug in her voice. "The grass was always greener somewhere else. She felt the next place would be easier. I quit trying to figure it out once I realized that even she didn't know what she was looking for."

"*Was* the grass ever any greener?"

"Not until we moved here. We were in New Mexico before. It was terrible for us there. Then Phoenix for a brief time, and that was even worse. Whiskey Creek felt like home to me from the very beginning. But she probably wouldn't have settled down, if not for being diagnosed with cancer."

"She could've moved after she went into

remission."

"Presley and I were out of high school by then, and she knew we wouldn't go with her. We were both too happy to have finally put down roots."

"She didn't want to go without you?"

"I think that having us made her feel grounded, needed, connected. And she was older by then, had lost some of the compulsion to keep moving."

"She's never had anyone besides the two of you?"

"No. She didn't come from the best family." She stared up at him. "Can I ask *you* a question?"

He gave her a half smile. "Does this count toward the seventeen?"

"It should. It's a hard one."

She'd been answering some pretty hard questions herself. And after all, turnabout was fair play. "Shoot."

"How do you feel about your father?"

He'd known this would be coming sooner or later. Of course she'd be curious. Anyone would. "That's complicated."

"I think I might understand why."

For a brief moment, Dylan felt the urge to light up but pushed the desire away and finished his wine. "He still writes us regularly."

"I wondered. What does he say?"

"That he screwed up. That he's sorry. That he loves us."

"Do you believe him?"

"I guess. People make mistakes. But . . . he gets out in less than two years. I don't want to reestablish a relationship because then my house would be the first one he comes to, and I'm not sure I can trust him not to climb right back into a bottle."

"Doesn't he own the house and the business?"

"Not anymore. He sold them to me a few years ago. In return I put some money on his books, which makes prison life a lot easier."

"So you've corresponded."

"Not very often. And not anymore."

"Do you think you'll ever write him again?"

"Sometimes I consider it." Her hair slipped through his fingers. "There's something between us, whether I want it or not. And he owes it to my brothers to try to be some kind of father. They're his responsibility, not mine." Even though he'd done his best to carry them in his father's absence.

Sympathy softened her expression. "I'm so sorry for what happened. It wasn't fair to you or your brothers."

It wasn't the unfairness of life that bothered Dylan. He'd come to terms with that. He just wished certain things could be relegated to the past and left there. But no. He'd have to deal with his father again in two years. "I guess you have to learn to roll over the bumps."

She smiled. "That's a good way to put it. I certainly never thought my life with Anita and Presley would end like this. Anita seemed too tough to *ever* die. And Presley . . . I always hoped she'd realize her strengths and make the most of them."

"Do you blame Aaron that she didn't?" She'd indicated as much when he'd approached her in the park. It was partly why she'd resented *him*. At least she'd given him that impression.

"Not really. I wished she'd find someone who had his life figured out, so he could help her. But . . . now that I've seen her with Aaron, I know your brother isn't the cause of her problems any more than she's the cause of his. They identify with each other. That's what draws them together."

"You told me you think Presley's in love with Aaron."

"She might be, but they're both so broken. . . ." She grew pensive again. Another sip of her wine and a shift in attitude signaled a change of subject. "I don't believe Chief Stacy will really do much to look for Presley, do you?"

"He said he'd put out an APB." Dylan wanted to comfort her where he could, but he was hardly convinced that the chief of police felt any need to gather the troops. Stacy said someone who was grieving could do just about anything, even miss Christmas. But at least they'd done their best to get him involved.

"Will that be enough?"

"We have to hope it will." After visiting Stacy's house, they'd gone out looking again, hoping to spot Presley's car, but found nothing.

Several seconds passed. Then she said, "What if I have another mother out there . . . somewhere? What if all this —" she waved a hand around the room "— was never meant to be?"

Then they wouldn't have met. But he didn't say that. "Another mother could be a good thing."

"Or it could be a bitter disappointment," she said. "What if Anita didn't steal me? What if my real mother gave me away? Maybe she was no better than Anita. Worse, because she wanted to be rid of me."

"That's not very likely," he said. "It isn't

consistent with your memories."

"I'm not even sure those memories are real."

Her cell phone rang before he could respond. He watched as she grabbed it, so hopeful, then sagged. Obviously, it wasn't her sister. After hitting the decline button, she tossed it away.

"Who was that?" he asked.

"Eve."

"You don't want to talk to her?"

She curled into him again. "Not right now."

"She's your best friend. And it's Christmas Eve."

"I'll see her when she gets home."

"She's probably worried about you."

No response.

Eve had been out of town for over a week. Why wouldn't Cheyenne be excited to hear from her? "Chey?"

"I'm dealing with enough," she said when she spoke, but he got the feeling it was more than that. She and Eve had been inseparable since high school.

"Commiserating with her might help."

"I'm fine. I've got you."

Did she have to choose one or the other? "You don't want her to know about me," he guessed.

She tucked her hair behind her ears as she sat up. "She already knows."

"And she doesn't approve."

"She needs to see what you're really like."

Would that change her opinion? What if he couldn't win her over? Cheyenne's friends were a large part of her identity. They'd been her surrogate family. He couldn't imagine ripping her away from that support; he was sure she'd begin to resent him at some point if he did.

But he also couldn't imagine the crowd that had always looked down their noses at him suddenly welcoming him into the group, either.

Cheyenne woke up alone. For a second, she wondered if the past couple of weeks had been a dream. She expected her mother to call out for more pain medication, or food, or to be repositioned in the bed, and for her sister to return home from work.

But then she rolled over and smelled a hint of Dylan's cologne on the pillow and remembered making love with him last night. Some of the worst things in the world had happened to her since Eve and the others had left for the Caribbean. But so had some of the best. Dylan pretty much carried that end of things.

Where was he?

Since it was Christmas morning, she figured he'd gone home to see his brothers. But then she heard the front door open and close.

"Dylan?" She stretched as she called his name. Normally Christmas morning meant cooking a big breakfast for Anita and Presley and exchanging what gifts they had. Since coming to Whiskey Creek, it meant getting together with Eve and her family in the evening for a few hours, too. Sometimes Presley came along. More often Presley stayed with Anita or had her own friends over. Yesterday, the Harmons had called to see if she'd be joining them as usual. But she told them she was already committed to having dinner somewhere else.

Dylan stuck his head in the room. He was wearing the same faded jeans and sweatshirt he'd worn last night, along with an endearing grin. A baseball cap suggested he'd dressed without showering, but she liked him as he was, liked the contrast between his dark beard growth and his white teeth. "Merry Christmas."

She gave him a sleepy smile. "Merry Christmas. But . . . isn't it a little early to be up?"

His grin turned slightly sheepish. "Sorry.

Can't help it. I always wake up early. And it was *especially* hard to sleep this morning."

"Because . . ."

"I'm excited about giving you your gift."

"You got me something?" She shoved herself onto her elbows. This wasn't particularly welcome news since she'd been too busy searching for Presley and making funeral arrangements for Anita to even think about a gift for him. "When would you have had time for that?"

"While I was at work yesterday. I did some research on the internet, made a few calls and found *just* what I wanted."

She raised her eyebrows. "Really?"

"*Really.*"

"But . . . I'd rather we waited to exchange presents until I've had a chance to do some shopping myself. I —"

"I'm not expecting anything," he broke in. "Just being with you is enough."

The honesty of that statement, together with the sincerity on his face, touched her deeply. He meant it. "Why me?" she asked softly, turning the question he'd once asked back on him.

When he answered, she could tell he understood. "You fit me perfectly. I've known you would for a long time."

A wave of happiness washed over her.

Amid all the pain and confusion and moral ambiguity she'd been suffering, she'd found someone who soothed every ache and eased every complaint, and he did it just by being *him*. Ironically, he was the least likely person in Whiskey Creek. Would she have given him a chance if she hadn't bumped into him in the park that day?

Probably not . . .

"I'll go and shower."

He made a sound of impatience. "Do you have to? I can't wait."

Who would've guessed big bad Dylan Amos could remind her so much of an eager little boy? But she loved that unexpected, innocent quality.

"Okay, I'm coming," she said with a laugh and started to get up. She thought he'd want her to go into the living room and sit by the tree, but he held up one hand. "Wait right there."

She heard the front door again. When he returned, he wasn't carrying a wrapped present, but he cradled a furry black-and-white bundle in his arms, which he brought over to her.

"A puppy? You got me a *puppy*?" She reached out to take the squirming little animal, but he hesitated before handing it over.

"I need to explain something first."

As she reached out to scratch behind the dog's ears, it tried to lick her hand. She was so ecstatic she couldn't wait to hold her new pet. "What?"

"I was actually going to get a different dog. So if you want, we can take her back. It was just that . . . once I saw her, I couldn't resist."

"Why would I want to do that? She's darling! I've always wanted a dog. What breed is she?"

"Can't say for sure. There's some Akita and maybe Golden Retriever."

Thrilled at having her first real pet, Cheyenne reached for the animal again, but Dylan still wouldn't hand her over. "Can I hold her?" she asked in surprise.

At last, he relinquished the puppy, but she could tell he was watching closely for her reaction. "What's wrong? Why are you —" And then, as she brought the puppy's body against her chest, she knew something was wrong. Setting the animal on the bed, she took a closer look. The dog was missing a hind leg.

Dylan met her questioning gaze. "It's a birth defect. I knew the other dogs wouldn't have any trouble finding homes, but . . . the volunteer who was helping me said this one probably wouldn't be adopted."

Tears gathered in Cheyenne's eyes as she watched the unfortunate puppy use three legs to scamper around the bed. "So you rescued the poor thing." As he'd rescued his brothers when he was only eighteen. As he'd rescued *her*, although she hadn't known how badly she'd needed rescuing.

He thrust his hands in his pockets. "Actually, I'll take her if you don't want her. Then we can find you a different puppy."

"No." She scooped her new pet close and buried her face in its fur. "I love her. She's exactly the dog I would've chosen."

"Seriously?" He seemed unsure.

"You've seen my Christmas tree, haven't you?"

"Your Christmas tree?"

"Never mind," she said with a laugh. "To me, she's perfect."

"I'm glad to hear that." The tension in his body eased and he started to look as happy as she felt. "I bought her a bed, a leash, some food and toys. You should have everything you need." He bent over to kiss her temple. "Merry Christmas."

She looked up at him as he straightened. "There's no one like you, Dylan Amos."

He chuckled. "There are a lot of people in Whiskey Creek who'd tell you they're grateful for that."

The sound of the doorbell interrupted them before she could respond. "Who could be stopping by at ten o'clock on Christmas morning?" she asked.

A shrug said he had no idea, but since he was dressed and she wasn't, he went out to see. Then he called back to her. "Chey, it's Riley."

27

"Why aren't you taking Eve's calls?" Riley stood on Cheyenne's porch, eyeing Dylan, who was in the living room behind her, with no small amount of suspicion.

"A gift from your aunt?" She held her new puppy against her chest with one arm while indicating the sweater he was wearing.

"Yeah. Noni gives me one every year," he replied distractedly.

Cheyenne already knew this. Following Christmas, they wore their worst gifts to coffee. It was a tradition. "What did you do with that purple one from last year?"

His frown became more marked. "You haven't answered my question."

She nuzzled her face against her dog's back. "Eve's only tried to reach me a couple of times."

"So you *are* aware that she's been trying to call."

A twinge of conscience stole much of the

pleasure Cheyenne had been feeling prior to his visit. "Yes, and I've been planning to call her back. It's just that . . . my life has been crazy the past few days. You, of all people, should know *how* crazy."

"That's why she's so desperate to get hold of you! That's why she called me and begged me to come over here even though I was in the middle of opening presents with Jacob."

"I'm sorry she interrupted your Christmas. I'll call her."

"When?"

"Today."

He wasn't satisfied. It obviously bothered him that Dylan was in her house. He hadn't even mentioned her puppy. "Why have you been avoiding her in the first place?"

How did she explain that hearing what Eve had to say about Dylan upset her? That she was already in too deep to back out? That she didn't want her friends, who'd always meant so much to her, to ruin what she was experiencing? And that she didn't want the fact that she couldn't listen to their warnings to destroy their friendship? "She's worried about things she shouldn't be."

"How do you know? How do you know *you* shouldn't be worried, too? You're taking a huge risk, Chey."

472

"By getting romantically involved with someone?" she asked. "I think I'm entitled, don't you?"

"Of course you're entitled. It's just —" he dragged one hand through his hair, causing it to stick up in front "— you're particularly vulnerable right now. Maybe this isn't the best time to be picking someone."

"Did Eve say that?"

"More or less," he admitted. "Although I could've come up with it on my own. You've seen what . . . keeping the wrong kind of company has done for your sister."

Suddenly, the door was wrenched from her grasp as Dylan opened it wider. "Since you're talking about the Amoses, maybe this is a conversation the two of us should be having."

Contrary to Riley's earlier comments about Dylan, when he'd joked around about being frightened of him, he didn't act intimidated now. He seemed resolute, prepared, as if he'd known they might have a confrontation. That was probably the reason he hadn't brought Jacob along. Unless he was in school, Jacob was always with Riley. "Fine, if it'll make a difference."

Dylan's deep voice sounded from above Cheyenne's head. "What kind of difference were you hoping for?"

Hearing Dylan's inflexible tone, Cheyenne decided she couldn't allow this to go any further. "Stop," she said, trying to nudge him out of the doorway. "I don't want this to develop into a fight."

"That's the problem right there," Riley said. "You shouldn't have to worry that an encounter like this could turn violent. Would you be saying the same thing if you were dating *Joe?*"

"I wouldn't have to."

"Exactly!"

"Because you've accepted Joe. You wouldn't be challenging him."

"She's made her decision," Dylan broke in. "You need to respect that."

Riley didn't respond to him. Instead, he locked eyes with her. "Is that true? You won't listen?"

She hesitated. She wanted him and Eve and all the others to understand, but she knew their prejudices were too strong. Dylan's reputation had preceded him and, even though he'd changed, they weren't willing or able to recognize it. "Yes," she finally said. "I care about him. A lot."

"Shit." His shoulders slumped as he glanced between them.

"Please try to understand," she whispered.

"*Understand?*" he echoed.

"He makes me feel things no one else ever has."

"It's called sex, Chey. We've been telling you about it for years."

The flippancy of that remark angered her. "That's not what I'm talking about," she snapped. "Maybe I clung to my virginity a little longer than everyone else, but I'm not naive. I was raised by a crude, foulmouthed woman who often prostituted herself. I've seen things I've never told you about, things that would curl your toes. So don't talk to me as if I'm too innocent to have a clue about life!"

A muscle twitched in Riley's cheek, but he didn't reply right away. When he did, he spoke more softly, as though he was trying to reel in the emotions that were taking charge. "Is there anything we can do to convince you that you're making a mistake?"

She shook her head. It was too late. She'd already made her choice.

"Then we can't help you," he said, and stalked back to his SUV.

"Merry Christmas, huh?" Dylan muttered as he watched Riley drive away.

Cheyenne turned to face him. "I'm sorry you had to hear that."

He pretended it didn't bother him and

475

closed the door. "I haven't led a perfect life. I'll be the first to admit it." But he'd never dreamed he'd regret his mistakes quite as much as he did, never dreamed that gaining the approval of Cheyenne's friends would one day mean so much to him. Even if he'd known, he wasn't sure he would've been able to change his behavior.

"You've done the best you can," she said.

But his best wasn't enough. Despite knowing that her friends would judge him for lighting up — probably use his smoking as proof that he wasn't as good as they were — he wanted a cigarette. Quitting was much harder than he'd ever imagined.

Maybe he didn't have what he needed to make Cheyenne happy.

"What's going on in that mind of yours?" she asked, her eyes narrowing.

He slipped his arms around her and the puppy she was holding and kissed her neck. What would they have been like if they'd led different lives? "Joe's the better man. Maybe you need to hear it directly from me."

She backed away from him. "I don't believe it."

He stared down at her. "You did at one time."

"That was before I got to know you."

"It's only been a couple of weeks, Chey. We could be making a mistake. I could hurt you, or you could hurt me —"

"That's the risk with any relationship. People change. We can only judge by what we feel now."

"Will that be enough to get us through?"

"*I* think so."

"How can you be that confident?" he asked. Her friends weren't even home yet. Just wait until they were. . . .

"Because . . ."

When she didn't finish what she'd started to say, he tilted his head in question.

"I admire Joe. I really do. But . . ." She set down the dog. Then she straightened and her expression softened as she met his eyes. "I'm in love with you."

Dylan had never expected her to make that kind of admission, that kind of commitment. Not so soon. Not when she had so many reasons to feel torn. But it gave him the confidence he needed to believe that maybe, just maybe, they had a right to be together. He'd never felt the way he was feeling at this moment. The craving for cigarettes disappeared. So did the difficulties he'd known since he lost his mother, the confusion and anger inspired by his father, the loss, the betrayal, the lashing out that came as a result and the regrouping in order to cope. The only thing that mattered was that this woman welcomed his kiss, his touch, his imperfect heart.

Cheyenne spent a wonderful morning with Dylan and her new three-legged puppy.

After showering, they took Lucky, which was what she'd decided to name her dog, and walked over to see Dylan's brothers.

It'd snowed in the night, covering the landscape with a thin blanket of white. The river bottoms had never been the prettiest part of town, but they looked beautiful now, as pristine as anywhere else.

For a second, as she gazed down the road that eventually wound to the right, Cheyenne was sorry Anita wasn't around to see the lacy trees. It was so rare that they looked this way. That it was Christmas morning gave this beauty special significance.

Maybe, with time, she'd learn to appreciate the better parts of the woman her mother had been. She hoped so. She wanted more than the dark memories that rose in her mind so often.

Except for Mack, everyone was still sleeping, even though it was after noon. No doubt the Amos boys had partied late and were taking advantage of the chance to sleep in, since they didn't have to work. Even Dylan's dogs didn't come and greet them, so she felt comfortable putting Lucky on the floor.

Glad she didn't have to encounter Aaron right away, she breathed a small sigh of relief. She wasn't sure how she'd react to him, given that she believed him to be one of the reasons her sister ran off.

"There you are." Mack seemed a little forlorn, sitting in front of the TV alone, with no decorations on the tree and no presents underneath. He was only twenty-one, after all. Like the rest of the Amoses, he'd had to grow up fast — but twenty-one was still young not to have the love and support of either parent. Cheyenne felt guilty for stealing Dylan away for so long.

"Hey, you about ready for your present?" Dylan asked.

Mack's reserve seemed to vanish. "Were you trying to make me think I wasn't getting one this year?"

Dylan laughed. "You've never been overlooked before, have you?"

"Santa's never been so preoccupied," Mack teased, winking at her.

She grinned back at him. "Fortunately, your Santa's pretty reliable." Another thing she liked about Dylan.

Dylan marched down the hall, banging on doors as he went. "Hey, you're sleeping Christmas away! Get up if you want your presents!"

Cheyenne watched to make sure Lucky would be okay when Dylan's dogs came bounding out of the bedrooms, but they merely sniffed her, looked at Mack as though asking how they should react to this interloper, then wagged their tails. Once Cheyenne was satisfied that Lucky wouldn't be harmed, she sauntered over to the kitchen and peered in the cupboards. She wanted to start baking. Dylan had assured her they'd have all the supplies she'd need, but he'd never made pies before.

"Where'd that dog come from?" Mack asked.

She turned to see that Dylan's youngest brother had followed her. "She's my Christmas present."

"A deformed puppy? I hope it wasn't from Dylan."

She couldn't help laughing at his horror. "Actually, it was."

"Jeez, he couldn't have gotten you one with all its legs?"

"He picked the one I would've picked," she said simply. She loved Dylan all the more for understanding what would be important to her, but she didn't add that.

"I see. Nice."

She laughed again when he finished with an uncertain "I guess," that indicated he didn't see at all. Then another voice caught her attention.

"Is Presley home?"

The joy she'd been feeling seemed to leak out of her, like a balloon slowly losing its air, as she noticed Aaron, who looked as if he'd just stumbled out of bed.

"I'm afraid not," she said. "Not yet."

"Have you heard from her?" Eyes red, hair wild, he'd obviously passed a very difficult night.

"No."

A confused, hurt expression stole over his face. "Where could she be? She never goes too long before contacting me."

Cheyenne shook her head. She had no answers.

Presley squinted up at the single bulb on the ceiling overhead, in so much pain she could hardly move. Apparently, a "light" bondage session for her new business partner meant whips and chains *and* a few blows from his closed fists. But at least he'd provided some of the best drugs she'd ever had. He'd used a needle. She hated to think it was heroin — she knew how addictive it could be, had always promised herself she'd never go that far — but she had a feeling heroin was exactly what had produced such a magnificent high.

Gingerly, she moved her tongue over her busted lip, listening to find out if the man she'd met outside that ramshackle grocery had returned. He'd been gone for hours, or so she thought. She couldn't say with any certainty. Before he left, he'd given her another shot. She'd been floating in euphoria for God knows how long. As a result, she wasn't aware of who was in the house with her or how much time had passed. She couldn't even tell if it was day or night. She had only one frame of reference: she could remember being driven to an old pueblo-style house that sat on hard-packed dirt with the desert stretching for miles beyond it. The windows had been blacked out, the place had smelled like mildew and there'd been plenty of BDSM toys in the bedroom — along with a video camera.

"Dick?" Her voice sounded more like a croak. But she didn't care. She was trying to remember if Dick was even his name.

No answer. Running water droned in her ear. When she listened carefully, she was pretty sure it was the toilet in the bathroom.

"Dick?" She lifted her head, trying to see if the video camera was rolling, but there was no way to tell. He'd left the overhead light on, but she couldn't see a red indicator on the camera.

She called his name two more times, louder, and tried to move but found that her right arm was still shackled to the headboard. What the hell? How dare he leave her like this? How would she get free?

She was just starting to tug in earnest, despite the pain caused by the slightest movement, when she saw a key on the nightstand. She could unlock herself and leave. But beside it was a syringe containing a brownish liquid and a note that read, "Have a good time while I'm gone. Merry Christmas."

28

The Christmas feast Dylan had bought was tasty despite the fact that it wasn't home-made. And, after running home to get cinnamon and cloves, Cheyenne had managed to bake a coffee cake and an apple pie, which everyone seemed to like. Everything would've been fairly idyllic — as idyllic as could be expected under the circumstances — if not for Aaron's morose mood. His gloom overrode the excitement of the new smartphones Dylan had purchased for each of his brothers. Mack and the others showed a great deal of interest, but Aaron would barely touch his. He seemed preoccupied and upset, and that made it impossible for Cheyenne to forget the reason.

Not long after they ate, she went home. Dylan walked her to the door and promised to come over later but returned to his brothers. She was glad. She felt Aaron and Mack needed his attention. Also, she was planning to call Eve, and she figured it would be better to have some time alone for that.

But even after she and Lucky had gone in and she'd locked up it took her several minutes to work up the nerve. So much had changed since Eve left that Cheyenne had no confidence she'd be able to explain what it all meant.

She tried Presley's number first, but was immediately transferred to voice mail, which suggested the battery was dead or the phone had been turned off.

The same thing had occurred the last hundred times she'd called. With a sigh, she forced herself to dial Eve's cell instead.

"Don't tell me this is my best friend calling," Eve said without preamble.

Cheyenne cringed at her wounded tone. "I'm sorry, Eve."

Silence.

"Did Riley tell you about this morning?"

"Yes. And I can't believe it."

Lucky was sniffing around her feet, trying to climb into her lap. Cheyenne reached down to help her. "I need you to trust my judgment," she said. "I . . . I really need that."

"I don't want to see you hurt, Chey."

"I understand. The fact that you'd give up Joe, the man *you* like, rather than see me with Dylan tells me how sincere you are. But Dylan is a good person. Even if he's not perfect, neither am I. I believe . . . I believe he's the right man for me."

"Wow." Eve sounded shocked. "I've never heard you talk like this."

Her puppy curled up in her lap and laid its head on her thigh. "Because I've never felt like this."

"I have to admit — that threatens me in a whole new way."

Encouraged that Eve seemed to be bending, Cheyenne hurried to reassure her. "You have no reason to feel threatened."

"I don't? You get with Dylan and suddenly I'm not even important enough for you to answer my calls."

"That wasn't it at all. I . . ." She ran her fingers through Lucky's fur, taking solace in the feel of it. "I couldn't bear to hear you tell me not to see Dylan."

"He's *that* important to you? *Already?*"

She smiled, as she did every time she thought of him. "I'm in love."

It took Eve a few seconds to absorb this news. "Oh, boy," she said when she spoke again. "And we were going to stage an intervention."

"Please don't. Don't even try. I need him. Especially now. My life's a mess. I'm still getting my bearings. But I have two things going for me."

"Those are . . ."

Cheyenne felt the wet rasp of Lucky's tongue. "You — and him."

A sniff showed that Eve was crying.

"Can't you just . . . support me even if I'm wrong?"

"Of course. We're best friends." She sniffed again. "If it turns out to be a good decision, I'm here to celebrate with you. And if it turns out to be a bad one —"

"You can say 'I told you so.' "

"No. Then you'll need me even more."

"Do you mean that?" Cheyenne asked. "There'll be no more talk about making the biggest mistake of my life and taking un-necessary risks and . . . and interventions?"

"Riley said an intervention wouldn't do any good, anyway."

"He's right." She tried to lighten the moment with a laugh. "Nothing can save me now."

Emboldened, Lucky stood to lick her face. Cheyenne raised her chin so the dog wouldn't be able to reach the phone, which made her bark.

"What was that?" Eve asked.

Cheyenne urged Lucky to lie down again. "My Christmas present from Dylan."

"He gave you a dog?"

"A puppy."

Eve sighed audibly. "Okay. He wins."

Cheyenne smiled. "You're going to like Dylan. You'll see. All you have to do is give him a chance."

"He has a chance so long as he treats you right."

"That's fair."

Call waiting beeped; someone else was trying to get through. She pulled the phone away from her ear to see who it was and nearly fainted. "Eve, Presley's calling! I've got to go!" she said, and clicked over. "Presley? Where are you?" she asked, her heart hammering against her chest.

"This is Officer Hauck with the California Highway Patrol."

Cheyenne's stomach plummeted. *Please don't tell me my sister is dead.* "What . . . Why do you have Presley's phone?" she asked, her mouth suddenly dry. "She's okay, isn't she?"

"I'm afraid we don't know" came the officer's reply. "We're trying to find someone who might be able to help us locate her."

Nudging Lucky to one side, Cheyenne got up, trying to prepare herself for whatever news she was about to hear. "Because . . ."

"We found her car on Interstate 5. Her

purse, her phone, everything was inside. Except her."

"What if you could figure out where you were born and where you really came from — whether your mother was Anita or someone else? Would you want to pursue it?"

Cheyenne was half-asleep when Dylan posed this question. But he sounded wide-awake, which gave her the impression that he'd been thinking about her situation for some time.

Shifting onto her back, she covered a yawn. "Definitely."

"Even though Anita's gone and you're happy with where you're at in life?"

She was glad he hadn't mentioned that Presley was gone, too. Surely Presley's "gone" wasn't as permanent as Anita's. Since the police had recovered her car, Cheyenne was feeling a resurgence of hope. At least Presley hadn't crashed; they hadn't found a body. And Chief Stacy was finally making some calls. She'd contacted him after hearing from the CHP earlier. Because of where Presley's car had been left, they thought maybe she'd hitchhiked to Los Angeles, which seemed like something she'd do. In the morning, Dylan was going to drive Cheyenne to Los Banos to pay the impound fees and pick up the Mustang.

"I could have a different mother out there. A better one. Maybe even a father or other family. Why *wouldn't* I want to find out about that?"

"Because you'll have to face the resentment and anger of *knowing* what Anita did to you. It won't be just a suspicion anymore."

As she heard rain pelting the roof, Cheyenne felt glad Dylan was here with her. Otherwise, it would be such a lonely sound. Maybe snowy days wouldn't make her melancholy now that Dylan was in her life. "I realize that. But, either way, I need closure. I think everyone wants to be certain of where they came from, don't you?"

Those details might be important to her children someday, she thought, but she didn't say that. She didn't want Dylan to think she was already considering a family. She hadn't had her period since she'd been with him, but it wasn't due yet, which left her hopeful that she wasn't pregnant. She preferred not to deal with that kind of complication so early in their relationship.

"We could hire someone to look into it," he suggested.

"*We*?" Scooting closer, she kissed his whiskered cheek. "I don't have the money, and it's not your problem."

"I'm happy to help."

"I appreciate your generosity, but now that I won't be chained to this house every minute I'm not at work —" and she wouldn't have to contend with her mother daily "— I'm going to make a more concerted effort to do some searching on my own."

"Where will you start?"

Leaning over him, she rubbed her nose against his. "I'll go state by state, if I have to. Send a letter to every single county, asking for my birth certificate."

He held back her hair. "And if Anita changed your name?"

That was a very real and depressing possibility. "I'll know if there's no record of a Cheyenne Rose Christensen being born on my birthday."

"*If* it's your birthday."

"If it's my birthday."

"And then?" he prompted.

Cheyenne toyed with the hair leading down from his navel. "And then I'll call every police department in America. I'll start on the West Coast, since I don't think Anita was ever out East, and I'll ask about any cases they might have involving a missing girl."

His hand slid up her bare back, moving in a gentle caress. "There might be a less tedious way."

The rain was falling harder, and the wind was picking up. "How?"

"If you *were* kidnapped, there's a good chance Presley knows about it."

Cheyenne sat up. "No. She would've told me."

He propped his hands behind his head. She couldn't see his expression clearly in the moonlight streaming through her window, but she could make out the general shape of him. "How old were you when you were wearing that party dress?" he asked.

She knew where he was going with this and didn't like how it made her feel. Doubting Anita was one thing. She'd always doubted Anita. But Presley was a different story. Presley had been her ally, her confidante, the one person she trusted, in certain ways even more than Eve, to have her best interests at heart. They'd made incredible sacrifices for each other over the years — going hungry so the other could eat, taking a beating to spare the other further blows, lying to avoid seeing the other punished. There were some lines they didn't cross, and this would be one of them.

"About four," she admitted grudgingly.

"That would make her . . ."

"Six."

"That's old enough to remember *something*."

She could hear the frown in his voice. "Not necessarily," she argued. "Anita could've told her I was her sister but had been staying with someone else. That would make it seem less remarkable when they 'picked me up.' Anita would've had to invent some excuse, right? Maybe it all happened so smoothly, Presley had no reason to be aware of anything unusual."

"Are you serious? She didn't have a sister and then she did? That's not unusual?"

"You have to understand what our childhood was like, Dylan. People came and went. It wasn't out of the ordinary for us to call men Daddy when we'd known them for less than a week. And the next man who came around? Suddenly, *he* was Daddy, and it meant nothing that the last guy was gone. We called women we'd met five minutes earlier Aunt Whatever. So I'm not sure Presley, especially at six, would find *anything* odd."

He seemed to be choosing his next words carefully. "You've asked her about it, then? What she remembers?"

"Hundreds of times."

"And she always gave the same answer?"

For some reason, Cheyenne flashed back to the night she'd brought up the Amoses after talking to Dylan in the park. At some point in the conversation, Presley had said, "You should've been born in a different era. Or to a Quaker family. Sometimes I wonder where the hell you came from."

The way she'd acted right after that statement made Cheyenne even more uncomfortable now than it had then. But she wasn't willing to admit it, wasn't willing to doubt Presley. Not on this. Presley would know how important this was to her. "Every time."

"So you trust her completely."

"I do."

He raked a hand through his hair. "Then I hate to tell you this, but . . . pursuing the truth might break your heart."

"You don't want me to start digging? You'd rather I just left things as they are?"

"I don't want you to be hurt." He sat up, too. Sounding reluctant but resolute, he added. "Listen, Chey. I had a long talk with Aaron this afternoon."

"About Presley?"

"She was top of the list. I grilled him on whether or not she'd said or done *anything* out of the ordinary in the past couple of weeks. I was looking for details he might've forgotten or considered too inconsequential to mention."

"And?"

"At first, he denied that she'd acted strange in any way. But then he recalled something about a private investigator."

"Crouch."

"That's him. Eugene Crouch."

Her hands clutched the bedding. "What about him?"

"Aaron said she was afraid of him, afraid of what he might do."

"Why?"

"He wasn't clear on that, but one night she was so agitated he was all she could talk about. And the drunker she got, the more worried she became."

Cheyenne thought she had the answer. "Because my mother was always doing stuff that could get us in trouble. I heard Presley refer to Crouch, too. He approached her, looking for my mother, but he wouldn't say why."

"You don't find that odd?"

"Not necessarily." She explained about the hit-and-run that had haunted her and Presley ever since it had happened, and their guess that Crouch's visit had something to do with that.

"But you don't know. You've never talked to him."

"No."

"Maybe you should."

Suddenly, she remembered how secretive Presley had been when Cheyenne had overheard her first talking about Crouch to Anita. She hadn't even admitted that he was a P.I., not at first. When Cheyenne had asked who Crouch was, Presley had said he was just some guy she'd met at work.

Why hadn't Presley guessed, from the very beginning, that it was the hit-and-run and come to her instead of Anita?

"Whatever he wanted . . . it couldn't be about *me*," she said in an attempt to shore up her crumbling confidence.

"Yes, it could," Dylan insisted.

"She wouldn't have told Aaron about Crouch if she was afraid it might get back to me."

"Until very recently, you and I lived in separate worlds. The thought that it could get back to you probably never crossed her mind."

Cheyenne's stomach tightened into a hard knot as she considered his implication. Could she really trust Presley as much as she claimed? Or would Eugene Crouch, someone she would've overlooked if not for her relationship with Dylan, have the answers she craved about the little girl in the party dress and the black patent leather shoes?

29

Most of the next day was spent picking up Presley's car. The impound and storage fees added insult to injury after what Cheyenne had already been through. Her bank account was feeling the strain. She still wasn't sure how she could afford to bury her mother. She'd have to ask the funeral home if she could make monthly payments and put the burial plot on her Visa. That was the only way she could manage it. She'd promised Anita she wouldn't cremate her, even though that would've been cheaper.

At least she had the Mustang. She and Lucky were following Dylan back to Whiskey Creek.

It felt strange to smell the familiar scent of the cigarette smoke that lingered in her sister's car and to wonder if she'd ever see Presley again. It felt even stranger to have her sister's purse and cell phone on the passenger seat. Although she'd been more optimistic about Presley's well-being since that first call from the CHP, her hope was dwindling. She couldn't imagine any woman leaving her purse and cell behind. How could Presley be getting by without them?

The police had searched the contents of her purse — her phone, too, once they'd had the Mustang towed and were able to track down the right kind of charger, since the battery was dead by then. They said there was nothing to indicate where she'd gone. They'd called everyone on her contact list, even Aaron. No one could tell them a thing. There were no airplane or bus tickets, no travel brochures, no receipts in her car or in her email that gave any clue. The last internet sites she'd visited on her cell had no connection to her absence, either.

She must've hitched a ride. That was their best guess.

The question was: With whom? And was Presley safe?

Cheyenne drove as long as she could before pulling over. She hadn't examined Presley's belongings herself, because she hadn't wanted to break down in front of the officers who were handling the transfer of her personal property. She figured there'd be time to see what Presley had abandoned once she'd reached the privacy of her own home.

But she couldn't wait that long. She wanted her sister back so badly she had to go through those items now, in case she found something the police had missed. They didn't know Presley the way Cheyenne did.

After easing onto the shoulder of Highway 88, she cut the engine. Dylan was in front of her. She wasn't sure he'd immediately notice that she'd stopped following him, but that was okay. She could catch up with him later.

"Pres, you've really done it this time," she murmured as she moved Lucky out of the way and picked up her sister's purse.

Presley's ID was in her wallet. Tears rolled down Cheyenne's cheeks as she gazed at it. She wished her efforts to help her sister, to be there for her, had made more of a difference.

Loose change jingled in the bottom of Presley's purse, but there were no bills. She never carried much money. She spent whatever she had, on friends if not on herself.

Besides the coins, Cheyenne found various kinds of makeup, mixed with a host of snack wrappers, notes and old gas receipts. Presley didn't keep her purse any cleaner than her car —

She heard a door shut behind her and twisted around to see that Dylan had circled back. He was walking along the shoulder to her car, coming up on her left.

With a sniff, she wiped her tears and rolled down her window.

"You okay?" he asked.

She managed a watery smile at the sympathy in his voice and nodded.

He slid his hands into his pockets and hunched against a biting wind. The rain they'd gotten last night had stopped, but the wind was stronger than ever. "What's going on?"

"Nothing. I just . . ." She gestured at the items in her lap.

"Were the police right?" He knew they were, of course. But he seemed to understand why she'd feel the need to check for herself.

"Yeah." She was piling everything back inside Presley's purse when a business card fluttered out from a handful of wrappers and other garbage. She almost picked it up and shoved it back in without looking at it. Cheyenne didn't expect Presley's trash to reveal anything useful. But the name on the card caught her eye. Eugene Crouch, Private Investigator.

Presley had told Cheyenne she'd thrown his card away. So what was it doing in her purse? And how had the police missed it or deemed it irrelevant?

Turning so Dylan could see, she squinted up at him.

"Looks like Crouch is going to be even easier to find than we thought," he said.

Dylan wanted to contact the P.I. as soon as they got home from picking up the Mustang, to see if that would confirm their suspicions about Cheyenne's background, but Cheyenne asked him to wait until after her mother's funeral. She said the next week would be hard to get through as it was, especially if Presley didn't come home, and he knew she was right. He needed to give her time to adjust to all the changes in her life. They were hitting so hard and fast.

In the meantime, he had his own challenge to face — preparing Aaron for rehab. And Eve was home from her cruise. She'd called Chey almost as soon as they walked in the door to say she was coming over.

When Cheyenne brought out a wrapped gift in preparation for her friend's visit, Dylan faked a yawn and stood. "Jeez, is it that time already? I'd better head home. See what everybody's up to."

She rolled her eyes at his facetious tone. "Let me guess. You don't want to be here when Eve arrives."

"Why would I mind?" He pressed a hand to his chest in mock innocence. "That confrontation with Riley was so much fun. I laugh whenever I think of it."

She smiled at his antics, so he pulled her into his arms. "Come over later," he said, burying his face in her neck. He loved the smell of her, the feel of her. He was pretty sure he loved *her*. It seemed like he'd always loved her, that he'd just been waiting for her to finally notice him. But it was frightening to acknowledge the strength of his feelings.

"I wish you'd stay and meet Eve," Cheyenne said.

"Eve and I already know each other."

"No, you don't."

"She's convinced I'm pond scum, Chey. I think it would be smarter to wait. Let her settle into the idea that you have a boyfriend first. We'll tackle the fact that it's one she hates later."

"*Hates?*" Cheyenne leaned back to look in his face. "She'll like you, Dylan. She just doesn't know it yet."

"What has you so convinced?"

She took his hand. "*I* like you, don't I?"

"Things have been different since your friends left. We had a brief time when they didn't figure in. Now that they're back . . . you could change your mind."

"Never."

He kissed the side of her mouth, her cheek, her temple. "How can you be so sure?"

"Because I could be pregnant with your baby, and if I am, I'd be okay with it."

He jerked his head up. Was she trying to tell him something? Or . . . "Are you testing me?"

"Testing you?"

"To see if I'd be upset?"

Her chest lifted as she drew a deep breath. "Maybe. There was that one time, at the inn. . . ."

"I know." He'd been worried about a possible pregnancy after that encounter, but he'd lulled himself into believing it couldn't really happen.

"So . . . would you be upset?" she asked.

He thought about it as he ran a thumb over her bottom lip. "No."

"What would you say?"

The image of her, big with his child, brought a flicker of excitement and a wave of possessiveness. Was that how a guy knew when he'd met the right woman? When it was time to settle down? "I'd say, 'Will you marry me?' "

The smile that broke across her face was the most beautiful smile she'd given him yet. "You wouldn't be afraid of making a commitment like that?"

"A little," he admitted. "But there isn't anyone I'd rather take a chance on."

She kissed him tenderly. "I'm glad you propositioned me in the park."

"I'm glad I found the nerve to show up after you called and didn't really say anything," he told her. "I knew if I didn't, I'd probably never have another shot. But knocking on your door that night wasn't as easy as it looked. I never dreamed you'd really let me in."

"I'm not sure how you have convinced everyone you're so tough," she said. "You're a teddy bear."

"Only with you."

They were kissing when the knock came. He was the first to pull away. "Damn. I didn't get out of here fast enough."

She laughed. "It's going to be fine. Stop acting like I'm shoving you in front of a firing squad."

He caught her by the arm as she slipped away. "Just do me one favor."

"What's that?"

"Tell her I quit smoking."

"You think that's going to help your cause?"

"It's all I've got."

Eve wasn't pleased to see Dylan at Cheyenne's house. But not because she was planning to say anything else about him — at least not anything negative. It was more that she'd missed her best friend after being gone so long. She was dying to catch up, and having someone else there felt awkward.

They exchanged Christmas gifts — Cheyenne gave her the Dolci perfume she'd been coveting, and she gave Cheyenne a pretty pearl necklace she'd bought in Martinique — and they played with her puppy, who was darling. But the conversation felt stilted. Although Eve was able to talk to Cheyenne about Anita and Presley, to express her condolences and concern, she couldn't tell Chey what she and Callie suspected might be going on with Baxter. Not with Dylan there. That information was too personal to the group.

Understandably, Dylan didn't seem to be a whole lot more comfortable in her presence than she was in his. She'd never known him to be the nervous type. From what she could remember, he'd always had a big chip on his shoulder, a "you can kiss my ass if you don't like me" attitude. But he was obviously making an effort to be liked now.

They talked about where Presley might have gone, when Cheyenne should hold the service for her mother, how she'd pay for it, if she'd move out of the river bottoms as she'd planned. Eve wasn't surprised that Cheyenne didn't seem so keen on getting a house closer to town anymore. Then, out of the blue, Cheyenne announced that Dylan had quit smoking.

When Eve glanced over at him, he managed a rather pained smile as if he understood that hadn't really flowed into the conversation naturally but was something he wanted her to know. "Better late than never," he added.

Eve resisted a chuckle. This was serious business, no matter how charming that had come off. "It's good to give your lungs a break," she responded. "But I'm more concerned about whether or not you do drugs."

How had she let that slip out? She'd promised herself she wouldn't be confrontational. Cheyenne had begged for her support and she'd come here with the intention of giving it.

Fortunately, Dylan seemed to welcome

the chance to defend himself. Pretending there wasn't an undercurrent was hard for him, she realized. He wasn't the type to fake niceties, and she respected that.

"I don't do drugs. I can't say I've never tried certain substances," he admitted. "There was a time I did, a number of years ago. But I'm sorry about that now."

She narrowed her eyes. "So the rumors are wrong?"

"They don't pertain to me."

Those rumors had come from somewhere but, whether his brothers deserved it or not, he didn't push the blame onto them. Eve got the impression he was too loyal, which eased her mind more than the fact that he'd given up smoking. It showed her that he wasn't willing to hurt others to protect himself.

"You have to judge Dylan on his own merit," Cheyenne chipped in, obviously trying to sell her, too.

Eve told herself to shelve her disapproval and let it go at that, but she had one more question, and she figured she might as well ask it. "And the run-ins with the law, Dylan?"

"All in the past." He raised his hands. "I swear. I haven't been arrested for . . . at least three years. No more fighting." He seemed so earnest Eve couldn't help smiling.

"You really care about her."

He looked her right in the eye when he nodded, but confirmation wasn't necessary. His feelings were apparent in the way he touched Chey, the way he looked at her — even the fact that he was sitting here, putting up with the skepticism of her best friend. A guy like Dylan wouldn't do that for just any woman.

Somehow his devotion made up for what Eve had lost. Maybe her relationship with Chey would never be the same. Eve mourned that and knew she would for some time. But she could tell Cheyenne was happy, and that was more important than anything else.

"She really cares about you, too," she said. "I think that's what has me so scared."

Dylan's smile slanted to one side. "I won't try to cut you out if you don't try to cut me out," he said, and that was all it took to convince Eve she could give him a chance.

"Deal!" she said, and slapped his hand in a high five.

"See? That wasn't so hard," Cheyenne said as she held Lucky back from following Eve outside and closed the door.

"Easy for you to say," Dylan grumbled, but Cheyenne knew he was teasing. Having Eve over had gone better than either of them had expected.

"My other friends will be the same way," she predicted. "They're all good people. Just like Eve."

Her phone rang before he could say anything. She glanced at the clock, wondering who could be calling after ten. She didn't recognize the number. It started with a 408 area code, which corresponded to Phoenix, if Cheyenne remembered correctly.

Maybe it was the police with some word on her sister. But when she hit the talk button, she couldn't get anyone to speak.

"Hello?" she said. "Hello? Is someone there?"

No response.

"Could it be Presley?" Dylan whispered.

"Presley?" Cheyenne said. "Pres, is that you? If it is, say something. I've been *so* worried."

Nothing.

"Please? I miss you! Tell me where you are. I'll come and get you."

Finally, she got a response. "You wouldn't want me back if you knew the truth."

It was her sister, all right. Was she talking

about her involvement in Anita's death? Or Crouch?

"I already know the truth," Cheyenne said, but it was too late. Presley had hung up.

Cheyenne tried to call her back, but all she got was a recording. "This payphone doesn't accept incoming calls."

30

According to the conversation she'd just had with Chief Stacy, the police couldn't do anything to help bring Presley home. She'd left of her own free will. She was an adult. She had the right to leave. But Cheyenne knew Presley couldn't be doing well. She didn't have any money, any clothes, any way to survive. Cheyenne shuddered to think how she must be getting by.

At least she was alive. If only they could find her and take her home before that changed.

She knew putting Anita's funeral on hold while she searched for her sister was a problem. The undertaker wanted to have the service and get her buried. Anita was taking up space in his cooler. He'd said that once. He wouldn't be making much money off the Christensens so he had no reason to be accommodating.

But Cheyenne couldn't even consider

burying Anita until Presley was back to pay her final respects. She saw Presley's participation as a necessary part of her recovery. Presley had to come to terms with whatever happened the night Anita died, even if it meant going to the police to confess that she'd performed a mercy killing.

Cheyenne hated to think of everyone's reaction when news of that came out, but she saw no alternative. She'd confess her role in covering it up, too. Keeping that secret, living in the shadow of it, would be too difficult for both of them.

"How will we find her once we reach Phoenix?" Dylan asked.

They were at the computer, where they'd confirmed that the area code Presley had called from was, indeed, Arizona. They'd arranged for Eve to watch Lucky, and Grady to take Aaron to a rehab facility in Sacramento, so they could leave first thing in the morning.

"She's returned to Sunnyslope, where we used to live. Look at this." She pointed to the computer screen. "I found the location of the payphone she called me from by putting the number in a search engine."

"What kind of neighborhood is it?"

She zoomed in on Google Earth.

"I see," he said with a frown.

"Not so pretty."

His chair squeaked as he shifted his weight. "Do you mind if I tell Aaron she's okay?"

Cheyenne frowned at him. "Does he care?"

"He doesn't want to. He's not emotionally prepared for a committed relationship. But he's been worried. I think this news will help him go into rehab tomorrow."

She wondered if she should tell Dylan about her sister's possible condition. But, again, she couldn't bring herself to share that information. She had no idea what Presley might do if she was pregnant — or what she might already have done. Cheyenne certainly didn't want to make Presley's return any harder. "Of course."

She listened, petting her dog, who'd nudged her leg to be picked up, as Dylan called Aaron on speakerphone.

"Why hasn't she contacted me?" Aaron asked.

Cheyenne wanted to say it was because he'd given her no reason to. That he'd provided nothing for her to hang on to. But she bit her tongue. Aaron had his own issues.

"You sent her away," Dylan said.

"I didn't want to deal with her right then.

That didn't mean I never wanted to see her again!"

Dylan's gaze locked with Cheyenne's. "We don't know what was going on in her mind, Aaron."

She'd needed him, and he hadn't been there for her. Presley had been let down so many times it was hardly surprising that she had no self-esteem.

"Maybe I should put off rehab," he said. "Go to Arizona with you."

"No," Dylan started, but Aaron cut him off.

"I won't be able to concentrate if I'm wondering about her all the time."

Cheyenne broke into the conversation. "You'll be a lot more help to her if you get clean, Aaron. Maybe we'll be fortunate and Presley will follow your lead. She's going to need friends who don't use. Maybe you can be that friend."

"You think I'm capable of it?" he asked.

He was talking to her. That surprised Cheyenne. "I think you could be as wonderful as your big brother. But right now, you're letting everything that's happened to you stand in the way."

"Just because you and Dylan have been able to pull your lives together doesn't mean the rest of us can."

"Yes, it *does*," she said. "If you want it badly enough. I hope that's the case. I hope you'll get clean regardless of what happens to Presley."

"Don't talk like she's a lost cause," he said. "She's not."

"I pray you're right." Cheyenne set her dog down so she could start packing. Finding Presley would be a long shot. Just because she'd called from Sunnyslope didn't mean she'd stay in those nine square miles. But Cheyenne had to take the chance.

The calendar on the clinic's opposite wall had *X*'s through December 28. Where had the days gone? Presley felt as if she'd entered a time warp since leaving home. Even her stint with the semi driver who'd driven her to Phoenix seemed more like a dream. Only the bruises on her body and the busted lip Dick had given her felt real. She'd seen what he'd done to her face when she'd asked to use the restroom, since the house where she'd been staying didn't have a mirror. With a black eye and a swollen mouth, she looked like she'd been in a fight. . . .

"It'll be okay." Dick was sitting beside her wearing the new clothes he'd gotten for Christmas, presumably from his wife. When he wasn't aroused he acted quite normal. Except he'd forced her to wear a dog collar in the car.

On second thought, he wasn't normal. She was just too scared to care about anything other than what was about to happen.

"Presley?" he said.

She blinked, then focused on him. "What?"

"Did you hear me?"

She nodded. She hadn't realized he'd expected an answer to that comment. She wished he wasn't even there. Once they arrived, she'd told him he could drop her off, that she'd call him when it was over. He'd let her remove the collar at that point. But he'd insisted on coming in. He said she needed someone to support her.

She would've liked that someone to be Cheyenne. If she had to go through an abortion, she wanted her sister at her side. It was her first time in this situation. But she had no right to ask for anything from Chey. Not after what she'd done. Not after the lies she'd told.

We aren't even sisters. . . .

"You're spacing out again."

Her eyes cut to her companion. "What did you say?"

"I asked if you were scared."

When? She hadn't heard that. "A little," she admitted.

"A little . . . what?"

Confused, she stared at him until he whispered in her ear. "*Master.*"

"Oh, right." She'd forgotten that part. He wanted the playacting to continue. But with only two other women and one man in the waiting room, it was so quiet she hated to speak. The receptionist glanced up whenever they broke the silence. She preferred to go unnoticed, but the marks on her face made that impossible. Presley had witnessed the woman's shocked reaction when she signed in. She'd mumbled a line about being in a car accident but she wasn't sure the receptionist bought it.

"I don't think she believed me about the accident," she said, keeping her voice too low for anyone else to hear.

"Doesn't matter," he responded. "It is what you say it is."

"I guess."

He leaned closer. "Bottom line, it's none of her damned business. I'm your master, and I can do what I want."

Ignoring that part, because she found it ridiculous, she changed the subject. "Seems like there aren't a lot of women who get an abortion right after Christmas, huh?" She gazed around at the empty seats.

"People are celebrating. They'll deal with their problems later on."

A woman in a white jacket poked her head through a door near the reception area. "Ms. Christensen? The doctor's ready for you."

Dick got up to go in with her. He even took her hand. But Presley jerked away. "I'll be back when it's over," she said. She would not have this stranger, this . . . twisted man witness her most vulnerable moment.

Anger flashed in his eyes. He couldn't insist in front of the nurse and the receptionist. But he pulled her back and showed her the syringe he had hidden in his pocket. "This will be waiting for you," he whispered, and kissed her as if that was what he'd intended all along.

"Do you think Aaron will stay in rehab?"

Dylan glanced over at Cheyenne, who'd been staring at Eugene Crouch's card for several miles. Although Phoenix was a good fourteen-hour drive from Sacramento, they'd decided to take his Jeep so they wouldn't have to rent a car or worry about flights.

He preferred to remain mobile and at the controls of his own vehicle. "He's promised me he will this time, but . . . who knows?"

"Does he write to your father?"

"You're whittling down the number of questions you have left. I hope you know that," he teased.

"What number am I on?"

"You maybe have three left."

"Then this can be one of them."

"Fine. I'm pretty sure he doesn't write."

"He's never said?"

Dylan thought of all the comments his brother had made over the years. If there'd been one common sentiment, it was *I hate Dad*. "In so many words."

"So J.T. doesn't hear from any of his sons."

"Rod's written him once or twice. Grady, too."

"Mack?"

He turned down the radio. "J.T. doesn't seem to matter all that much to Mack."

"Because he sees you as his father."

"He was really young when it all went down," he agreed, slowing as he came into traffic in Los Angeles. With any luck they'd reach Phoenix by ten tonight. That was when Cheyenne felt they had the best chance of finding her sister, anyway.

"Eve called while you were getting gas," she said as he changed lanes.

"At that last stop?"

She nodded.

"What did she want? Is Lucky okay?"

"Lucky's fine. Eve's taking good care of her. She just wanted to tell me she's praying for us." She grinned at him. "And to see if I thought any of your brothers might be fun for her to date."

"*Seriously?*" he said with a laugh.

"I shouldn't have told her you were so good in bed."

"Does she think it runs in families?"

"With the way all you Amoses look, she's willing to take the chance."

He slung an arm over the steering wheel. "No way am I going to let *that* happen."

She adjusted her seat belt. "Me, neither. In case it doesn't work out. But it was a nice thought."

Eve's question, however teasing it was, told Dylan that Eve was trying to accept him, trying to change her prejudice against him. He appreciated that.

"She also said something else, and this has me sort of . . . troubled," Cheyenne said.

"What's that?"

"Do you know Baxter North?"

"That friend of yours?"

"Yeah. The one who wears the expensive suits."

"What about him?"

She bit her lip. "Eve thinks he might be gay."

"*Might* be?" he repeated.

"What's that supposed to mean?"

He could hear her surprise. "He *is* gay. It's obvious. But even if it wasn't, I've seen him with a guy."

Her jaw dropped. "*What?* When?"

"Maybe a year ago."

"Where?"

"I met Manny from the gym and his sister at the Devil's Lair in Jackson for a drink. It was a weeknight, not too crowded. Baxter was there with someone."

"Did he see you?"

"Not at first. Which is why I'm quite clear on what was going on."

"What did he say when he realized you'd seen him?"

"We pretended not to recognize each other. I didn't see any point in embarrassing him. His sex life is his business. But he never touched his date afterward."

"That could've been a friend," she said.

He threw her a look. "I know the difference. What does it matter, anyway?"

"It doesn't. Except that we can't figure out why he wouldn't tell us. Eve thinks it might be because he's in love with Noah."

"Rackham? Hmm. He might be. I've seen

them together, too, although not in that way. Rackham's straight, isn't he?"

"Sure is."

"If that's true, it won't be a pleasant revelation for either of them."

"Exactly why we're worried."

He touched her hand, which was still holding the business card. "You tempted to call Crouch?"

She rubbed the embossing, allowing herself to be distracted. "Every day."

Presley was shaking by the time the doctor walked into the room. The clothes Dick had purchased for her were folded neatly on a chair. She was wearing a paper gown that left her feeling completely exposed.

"Good afternoon."

The doctor was an older woman with gray hair. She seemed kind. Presley told herself a gentle female doctor should put her at ease. This woman looked like someone's grandmother. She leaned against the counter, wearing reading glasses as she perused the forms Presley had filled out. But there were so many conflicting thoughts and feelings whirling through Presley's head she couldn't relax. Her love for Aaron. Desire to keep the baby. Fear that she wouldn't be any better as a mother than Anita had been. That syringe in Dick's pocket. If she could just get through the next half hour, she could escape the fear and pain — forget *all* her troubles. At least until she needed another fix. But as long as she was willing to do Dick a few favors, he seemed happy to supply her.

He was waiting for her with that syringe. Escape was close.

Or was it really slavery? She had a terrible feeling she'd never have children if she went through with this, that she'd drift into obscurity. Already, she could see the track marks on her arm, felt self-conscious enough to hide them from the doctor. Was this what she really wanted to be? A drug addict? Someone who couldn't contribute to life? Who had no one to love and no one to love her?

"Is that your boyfriend out there?" the doctor asked, interrupting her thoughts.

Presley had to clear her throat in order to speak. It felt as if she'd swallowed an orange. "No."

"A friend?"

"More or less," she replied.

The doctor continued to study her chart, then set the clipboard aside. "It appears you've sustained some injuries." She came over to examine Presley's black eye. "Want to tell me what happened?"

Presley averted her gaze. "Car accident."

When there was no response, she looked back at the doctor. Eyes slightly magnified by her glasses, she studied Presley without responding. Then she said, "Are you going to stick with that story?"

Presley bit her lip. "It's as good as any other."

The doctor's fingers curled around her upper arm as a way to gain her undivided attention. "If you need help, I know of a shelter nearby," she said softly. "After we finish here, we could sneak you out. He'll never know where you went."

Presley opened her mouth to deny that it was Dick who'd hurt her. But what was the point in lying? "I — I'm fine." It wasn't as if he'd ever *forced* her to stay. And there was that syringe in his pocket. How could she get by without it?

"You can have a few minutes to decide. Consider doing yourself a favor, giving yourself a chance at a better life."

When tears suddenly welled up in her eyes, she tried to blink them back, but they streamed down her cheeks, anyway.

The doctor bent her head to see into Presley's face. "Is there any family we can call?"

Presley thought of her sister. Cheyenne had always been there for her. But how could she turn to Cheyenne after what she'd done?

"No," she murmured.

"Okay." The doctor gave her a gentle pat. "Just relax. This won't hurt a bit." She encouraged Presley to lie back and place her feet in the stirrups, but a jolt of sheer panic made that impossible. Her heart had jumped into her throat, racing so fast she was afraid she'd pass out.

The doctor paused. "It's a relatively simple procedure."

But her baby — Aaron's baby — would be gone when it was over. That meant she could go back to life as she knew it. But was that really worth the trade-off?

"Are you having second thoughts?" the doctor asked.

Presley pictured Aaron. He didn't care about her, and he definitely wasn't ready for a child. As far as he was concerned, they'd just been having fun, getting high, having sex, laughing. He'd said so, many times, whenever she wanted to get serious.

Raising a child was a lifelong commitment. But she was thirty-three years old. When was she going to grow up?

"Ms. Christensen, I'm getting the impression you don't really want to go through with this," the doctor said.

"If I don't . . . if I decide to keep the baby . . . do you think it'll be okay?"

"You're not even showing, so you can't be very far along. That's good. Are you using?"

She nodded and turned her arms.

The doctor examined the track marks. "You'd have to stop. *Now*. No alcohol, either."

"And then you think my baby would be healthy?"

"There are no guarantees, but I'd say there's a good chance. Certain tests can give us an indication, so you'll be able to make a more informed decision later on."

A good chance . . .

"Take some time to think about it. You can always come back another day."

But what would she do even if the baby was perfect? She wasn't capable of raising a child. Cheyenne might be willing to stand by her, but she couldn't go back to Whiskey Creek. Not for any length of time. She'd be showing in a few months.

"I — I need some help," she whispered.

"Rehab?" the doctor asked since she'd already turned down the shelter.

She needed her sister. To tell Cheyenne the truth about what Anita did. To walk out of here and never look back. To put her heart and soul into loving those around her, loving her baby, instead of destroying herself.

Most of all, she needed to fight her craving for what was in that damn syringe.

"Can I use your phone?" she asked.

31

Cheyenne wasn't sure what to expect when they arrived at the address Presley had given her. It turned out to be an abortion clinic in Phoenix. Since it was well past ten, the clinic should be closed, but there was a light burning inside.

She dialed the number Presley had called her from hours earlier, when they were leaving Los Angeles.

"Hello?" The woman who answered had a thick Mexican accent.

"This is Cheyenne Christensen. I'm here to pick up my sister."

"Wonderful. She has been waiting for you. I will unlock the door."

Taking a steadying breath, she shot Dylan a look that begged his forbearance — she felt because she should go in alone — and got out of the car.

The woman who met her at the door seemed to be in her forties, had dark skin, long black hair and bright, shiny eyes. She introduced herself as Maria Sanchez, the receptionist at the clinic, and thanked Cheyenne for coming.

"I'm so grateful to you for staying with her," Cheyenne said.

A smile curved the other woman's lips. "I could not release her into that man's hands. He is a devil."

"What man?"

"The man who brought her in. When you see her face . . . But she is fine. Do not worry. Her injuries will heal. There is nothing serious."

Injuries? Presley hadn't mentioned that she was hurt. She'd talked about the blonde woman in Cheyenne's memories and what she knew about Anita as if she couldn't wait to get it off her chest. "That's why you stayed? To keep her safe?" she asked Maria.

"What else have we got in life if we do not help one another?" she replied with a shrug.

Cheyenne wiped sweaty palms on her jeans. "That's true. Still, it was very nice of you."

"This way."

She followed Maria through the empty lobby to one of the examination rooms in back, where she saw Presley curled up on her side, sleeping.

"Your sister is here," Maria said, shaking her gently.

Presley awoke with a start, then pushed herself into a sitting position, but that was as far as she got before Cheyenne pulled her into an embrace.

"Thank God," she breathed as Maria left to give them some privacy. "I thought I'd lost you."

"I'm sorry, Chey," she said. "I should've told you from the beginning. I should've told you about Crouch."

What Presley had confessed on the phone earlier hadn't been the shock Presley assumed it would be. "It's okay," she said. "I can see why you were scared."

"I didn't want to lose you."

"I know."

"I'll make it up to you. I promise. I'm going to get clean. I'm going to change my life."

"I'm so glad to hear it." She drew back to look at her sister's injuries. "Who did this to you?"

"I don't want to talk about it."

Cheyenne decided to let it go. Presley was safe now. That was all that mattered. "Fine. I don't want you to worry about anything. Even what happened the night Mom died."

Confusion created lines in Presley's fore-

531

head. "What are you talking about?"

Cheyenne swallowed hard. She didn't want to address this so soon, but they had to get past it. "I saw the pillow, Presley. I saw the blood. And I understand why you might have —"

"Wait." She grabbed Cheyenne's hand. "You think I killed Mom?"

"You didn't?"

"No! She . . . she begged me to. She was in so much pain. She said if I loved her I'd put her out of her misery. And I tried. But . . . when I couldn't leave the pillow on her face for more than two seconds, she got up, swearing and angry, and knocked over the lamp. Then she —" tears caught in Presley's lashes "— fell back. And that was it. She was gone."

Relief surged through Cheyenne. Could this be true? It had to be. Why would Presley lie about the night Anita had died after telling her the truth about the private investigator? She had as much reason or more to continue lying about Crouch. "Then why did you run away?"

"Sandra Morton at the Gas-N-Go told me that someone named Crouch came by, asking about you. I couldn't stand the thought that Mom was dead and, because of him, because he wouldn't go away, I was going to lose you, too. More than anything, I didn't want you to know *I* was the reason you didn't have that other family you've always wanted."

Then there was the baby. Cheyenne smoothed her blouse as she glanced around them. "I see. And . . . I'm guessing you were pregnant."

Presley nodded.

"But you've —" she cleared her throat "— taken care of that?" This was delicate territory, something Cheyenne didn't even want to think about. So she couldn't blame her sister for not answering.

"I'm going to move to Sacramento, Chey. Start over."

"You're willing to leave Whiskey Creek?"

"I have to. I don't want to fall in with the same people. Especially Aaron. He has too strong a hold on me."

Cheyenne tried to imagine her sister living elsewhere. It could work, if she was really ready and willing to give up drugs. "Sacramento isn't that far. Or the Bay Area. We'd get to see each other anytime we wanted. We'll make it work. I'll do whatever I can to help."

"Rehab first," she announced.

Cheyenne agreed with that, too, but she felt duty-bound to tell Presley about Aaron.

"Aaron is already in rehab. He just went in. To a new facility south of Sacramento."

"There's more than one place to get help. I'll go to the Bay Area."

Cheyenne couldn't believe her sister suddenly had so much resolution, that she was willing to make the sacrifices it would take to build a better life, but she didn't want to sound skeptical so she didn't question Presley further. "Let's get you home."

Once Maria heard them in the hallway, she came back to show them out. "Do not forget to take your prenatal vitamins," she cautioned Presley, wagging a finger at her as they stepped outside.

The receptionist's words made Cheyenne's heart skip a beat. "You're still pregnant?" she whispered as soon as they were alone.

Presley's chin came up. "I'm keeping the baby, Chey. I want this child."

Conscious of Dylan, who'd spotted them and was driving across the lot to pick them up, she lowered her voice even more. "Why didn't you tell me?"

"Because I'm not telling anyone."

"Not even Aaron?"

"Especially not Aaron. He's not ready. But I am. I need this — someone else to love, some reason to take care of myself and contribute to life."

"He has a right to know, Presley." If it *was* his child . . . Cheyenne supposed there was that small question.

Presley shook her head. "I don't care. This is the only thing I have, and I'm going to do everything in my power to protect it."

Cheyenne would've argued further, except that her sister was right in at least one respect. Aaron wasn't ready. And, if Presley had gone through with the abortion, there wouldn't be a baby to fight over. "You have to tell him someday, don't you?"

"Maybe, when I think it's safe."

They said nothing more. They couldn't. Dylan was getting out to hug Presley.

"I can't believe you're with Dylan," Presley said. It was late but they were both awake, lying in Cheyenne's bed with Lucky, Cheyenne's new puppy. It had taken them two days to get back from Phoenix, so this was Presley's first night at home without her mother. It felt strange, especially with the dark memories of Anita's final night, when she'd demanded that Presley finish her off.

"I'm in love with him," Cheyenne said simply.

Presley experienced a twinge of jealousy. She so desperately wanted that same relationship with Aaron. But she'd given him up, traded him for his baby. In her mind, it was better to take the sure thing. For a child, her child and his child, she could get clean. "You deserve him," she said when she'd mastered her emotions enough to say the words.

Cheyenne reached for her hand. "It's okay, isn't it? You haven't lost anything, Pres. Now you'll have two people to love you instead of just one."

Dylan had treated her well when they picked her up. He'd always been nice, but there was added kindness in his words and actions tonight. There was also the tenderness he showed her sister. That gave Presley hope she might find a man like him someday, even if it wasn't his brother.

"Do you think you'll get married?" she asked, pulling Lucky closer to her body.

"Maybe." Her sister's smile was barely discernible in the dark. "I'm pretty sure I'd like that."

"Tomorrow night is New Year's Eve. Seems fitting, doesn't it?"

"What do you mean?" Her sister was getting tired, starting to drift off.

"We'll both be living new and different lives in the new year."

■ ■ ■ ■

The weather was beautiful for Anita's funeral, which was held on January 3. So many people came out. All of Cheyenne's friends were there, including a very pregnant Gail and her movie-star husband, Simon. Most of Presley's friends came, too. The Amos boys turned out — except Aaron, of course — in suits, no less. They looked as respectable as any man there, especially Dylan, who'd cut his hair. Joe and his father attended, too, along with the Harmons, the hospice nurse, Marcy Mostats-Passuello, even Chief Stacy. As they lowered the casket into the ground not far from the place where little Mary Hatfield was buried and began shoveling dirt on top, Cheyenne couldn't help but think how grateful she was that Anita had brought her and Presley to Whiskey Creek seventeen years ago.

This was her home. These people were her family.

She could feel Dylan at her side, a constant source of strength. Presley had talked her into taking an over-the-counter pregnancy test before the funeral, and she'd been slightly disappointed to learn that she wasn't pregnant. Seeing Gail's extended stomach and knowing Presley's would soon be the same made her crave a baby, too. But there would be time for children — after she and Dylan were married.

As the mourners came by to hug her and Presley before moving off toward the B and B, where many of them had parked, she could see Clarence Holloway, the undertaker, waiting to speak with her. No doubt he was eager to discuss his bill, but she didn't want Dylan to be around when they did. She knew he'd try to pay for it, and she didn't think it was fair for him to bear that expense.

Excusing herself the moment Eve started talking to him and Presley was preoccupied, she walked over to Clarence. "Thank you for arranging such a lovely service."

He bent his head. "That's what we do at the Holloway Family Funeral Home."

She cleared her throat. "I know I owe you quite a lot of money. I'd like to assure you that I have every intention of paying. Have you decided whether or not you'd be willing to set up monthly installments?" She'd asked him twice before, once just yesterday, but he'd never given her a commitment. He kept saying he'd think about it as if he'd capitulate only if he had no other choice.

"There's no need for that," he said.

What did he mean? She shifted on her feet, feeling awkward and wanting to get this over with before Dylan could join them. "Excuse me?"

He handed her a piece of paper. "I was just waiting to give you this."

"What is it?" she asked, but he didn't answer.

She opened it, and saw the word *Invoice* was stamped across the top. The total for the funeral and burial, written in red, could be found at the bottom: $5,200. It was a fortune to her. But then she saw a zero below that, after the words *Total Due*.

"I don't understand." She frowned at him.

He nodded toward those still lingering at the grave — Gail, Simon, Sophia, Ted, Riley, Noah, Baxter, Callie, Kyle, Eve and a few others. They were planning to go over to the coffee shop together so they could spend some time with Gail and Simon while they were in town. "Your friends split the bill. They've covered everything."

Cheyenne felt her eyebrows shoot up. "But . . . they shouldn't have done that! You shouldn't have let them. This isn't their responsibility."

"They said you'd complain. So they told me to give you this, too."

Stunned, Cheyenne accepted the card he

thrust into her hands. It was a sympathy card, one created by Callie on the computer, with pictures of them as a group in Santa Cruz, San Francisco and Tahoe. Her favorite was the photograph of them at their graduation. They looked so young in their caps and gowns. . . .

The bottom read "That's what friends are for."

"Don't be nervous." Dylan's presence, his support, soothed Cheyenne, but there was no way she could master her nerves. She'd finally garnered the courage to call Eugene Crouch. Now she was sitting in the anteroom of his office in Danville, waiting to meet with him. She had no idea what he might reveal or what that information might mean to her life, which was why she'd delayed scheduling this meeting until Gail and Simon had gone back to L.A. and she'd booked Presley into a rehab facility in Walnut Creek not far away.

"What do you think he'll say?" she whispered.

"That he's been looking for you a long time," Dylan replied.

Cheyenne drew a deep breath. She was so happy now. Was she crazy to risk that happiness by opening a Pandora's box?

The door opened and a tall, gaunt-looking man peered out at her. Despite his height and craggy features, he had a gentle demeanor. She liked him immediately. "Well, hello, Cheyenne Christensen." He smiled. "I can't tell you how glad I am to see you."

"Thank you," she managed.

"Are you ready for this?"

"I hope so."

He came to her and gave her his hand, then turned to Dylan. "And this is . . ."

"My boyfriend, Dylan Amos."

They shook hands, too. "I'm glad you came along." Mr. Crouch indicated his inner office with a jerk of his head. "Let's go have a seat."

Dylan's hand felt warm against her cold fingers as they followed Eugene Crouch and took the seats he offered them.

"I was pleased to hear from you the other day," he said as he rounded his desk.

"It wasn't an easy call to make," she admitted.

"I can understand why. I'm sorry to hear about . . . I guess we should call her Anita. Cancer is a difficult way to go."

Cheyenne didn't know what to say to that. She wasn't sure why he was being so generous toward the woman who'd kidnapped her. She was back to feeling angry again.

Somehow, she could forgive Presley. Presley was as much a victim as she was. But Anita . . . "Is my real family looking for me?" she asked.

"Yes. They have been for some time. They've hired a number of private investigators over the years. They were working with an associate of mine, who tracked Anita to California. Then, at his recommendation, they hired me, since he lives in Colorado."

"Where do *they* live?"

"They're also in Denver."

A place where it snowed . . . "Is that where I was born?"

"Yes, ma'am." He slid a birth certificate across his desk. "I believe this belongs to you."

Her hand shook as she reached over to take a look. She'd wanted that simple paper, a paper most people took for granted, for so long. "Jewel Montrose," she read, and glanced at him. "That's my real name?"

"It was."

Jewel Montrose . . . Cheyenne had no recollection of ever being called that. The sound of it was strange. "Can you tell me about the blonde woman?" she asked. "Was she my mother?"

"You remember Victoria?"

She closed her eyes, conjuring up the image that had confused her for so many years. "I remember her face. She was very pretty."

"She's still pretty," he said when she opened her eyes. "But no longer blonde. I'm afraid that, like mine, her hair's gone gray."

Her attention switched back to the birth date. "This says my birthday is July 5."

"Yes. Is that the one you've been celebrating?"

She shook her head. Anita probably hadn't known her real birthday so she'd given her one — May 15. She was nearly two months younger than she'd thought. At least Anita had gotten the correct year. "Are you *sure* you have the right person?" she asked, feeling more and more unsettled.

"*I* am. You look exactly like your mother. But it would be wise to do a DNA test, just to be sure. It wouldn't be a pleasant experience for you or her to meet and then learn . . ."

He let his words fall off but Cheyenne understood what he meant.

If they connected and then learned they weren't related, they'd both be disappointed. She couldn't imagine what it would be like to feel she'd found her real family at last, only to discover it was a case of mistaken identity.

"Okay," she said. "Does that mean I have to go to a lab? Or . . ."

"Actually, it's much simpler than that. I have the kit right here." He swiveled to get inside a drawer. "We just need to swab your cheek and send it in. I'll be in touch as soon as I have the results."

She followed the instructions he gave her. Then, when he'd placed the swab securely in its vial, she gathered up her purse and stood. "How long does it take to get the results?"

"A few weeks at most."

Telling herself she should save all other questions until this vital piece of information was in place, she started to leave, but her curiosity got the better of her, and she turned back at the door. "Do you know how it happened?"

"How —"

"I was abducted? From where?"

"A preschool located near a park. It was during a blizzard. As the parents were coming to pick up their children, there was an accident in the parking lot. The teacher walked over to make sure no one was hurt and when she turned around, there was one less child lined up against the wall."

"So how did you ever track me?"

"That teacher, a Ms. Grimwald, had met

Anita a few days earlier. Anita had approached her to see if she needed any volunteers in the classroom. Because she smelled of alcohol and wasn't particularly . . . respectable-looking, Ms. Grimwald told her that anyone who had contact with the children had to pass a background check, and Anita immediately backed off. Ms. Grimwald thought her behavior strange enough to mention that incident to the police. Then someone else came forward to say she saw a woman matching that description in a car pulling out of the school the day you went missing. Your mother realized it was the same person she'd hired to help get the house ready for a charity event. Victoria had allowed her to bring her daughter over to play one afternoon while she worked, and in the course of their conversation she happened to mention where you went to school."

"That sounds like Anita — taking advantage of someone who was trying to be nice to her. So my abduction was reported."

"Absolutely. The police had Anita's name, her description and the make and model of her car. Thanks to the fact that she already had a record for minor infractions, they even had a photograph. But they were never able to find her. She didn't go by 'Anita' back then. She kept changing her name, which complicated matters."

"But my family didn't give up."

"No, they didn't give up."

She slid her hand inside Dylan's. "Do I have a father?"

"You do. Walt is sixty this year. He and Victoria are still married and love each other very much."

Dylan's fingers tightened around hers. "Siblings?"

"A younger brother. Victoria couldn't have any more children after that. Fertility issues."

Cheyenne tried to imagine a "Walt" and a younger brother to go with her "Victoria" but couldn't. "I had a bedroom with a canopy bed."

He smiled. "Yes, you did."

The next two weeks passed with agonizing slowness. Cheyenne tried to throw herself into the remodel at the B and B, which was taking longer than expected. She also worked with Gail over the phone, trying to gain the interest of *Unsolved Mysteries*. She wanted to help Eve kick off the inn's upgrades and new name in grand style — with the type of PR that would really attract attention. But the whole time, her mind was on that DNA test she'd taken in Eugene Crouch's office and what might happen once the results were in.

She was at the inn when she got the call. Eve was sitting at the other desk in their small back office, paying bills, but swung around the second she heard Cheyenne say, "Oh, my God!"

"What is it?" she asked as Cheyenne hung up.

"The DNA was a match. My name is really Jewel Montrose. My birthday isn't May 15, it's July 5. And I'm from Denver, Colorado."

With a scream, Eve jumped up to hug her. "I can't believe it!"

"My parents want to meet me . . . er, see me."

"When?"

Her mind was racing. "As soon as I can come. They told Eugene to buy me a plane ticket."

"That's fine. Go this weekend. I can manage here. I'll even go visit Presley."

"This facility doesn't permit visitors for the first month." Cheyenne covered her mouth, then dropped her hands. "Those memories I had, they were right all along."

Eve's eyebrows came together. "Why didn't you ever tell me about the blonde woman?"

"Because I wasn't sure about her. I didn't want to claim I'd been stolen without some sort of proof."

Eve smiled. "Now that you have your birth certificate, we can go to Europe."

"I'm going to hold you to that."

"If you don't marry Dylan before we can get it planned!"

Cheyenne laughed. Except for when they were at work, she and Dylan were together almost all the time. "We could always take him with us."

"Only if he'll bring one of his gorgeous, troublemaking brothers," Eve teased.

"I've got to call him." Cheyenne turned to look for her phone but before she could locate it on her desk, Eve received a call and then she started screaming.

Cheyenne gaped at her, waiting for the news.

"Gail got hold of *Unsolved Mysteries*. She told them that Simon would make a guest appearance on the show if they'll come out here and chronicle the facts of Mary's murder."

"And?"

"They're coming in two weeks!"

Cheyenne had chosen to make the trip to

Colorado by herself. Dylan had been willing to come with her — he said he'd prefer it, knowing how hard this might be on her — but she'd convinced him that this was something she needed to do alone. If Presley and Aaron could continue to brave rehab, she could face her past.

The flight had been crowded and, thanks to the weather, turbulent, but she'd scarcely noticed. She'd been too preoccupied thinking about the people who'd be meeting her at the airport. Eugene Crouch had said that her parents, her brother and his family — meaning his wife and two boys — would be there.

What would they be like? How could they ever regain the years that'd been lost? What would they think of her?

Her brother had been eighteen months old when she went missing. That meant he didn't remember her any more than she remembered him. Would he mind suddenly having a big sister? No longer being an only child? Her abduction must have had a significant impact on his life. Their parents might have become extravigilant, maybe even overprotective.

Or maybe not. It was impossible to say how they'd reacted without knowing them. Cheyenne had spoken to her mother once while they were making travel arrangements. Victoria had sounded excited about seeing her, but they'd decided to wait until they could meet to really talk.

The first thing Cheyenne saw when she reached baggage claim was a small group of people carrying signs.

Welcome Home.

We Missed You.

We Are So Happy to Have You Back.

Thank God!

She saw that none of them had her name written on them. They probably didn't know what to call her. She'd been Cheyenne Christensen for twenty-seven years.

Stopping before she reached them, she studied each hopeful face. Sure enough, her mother was no longer blonde, but Cheyenne recognized those eyes, that smile. The memory of her mother's face was indelibly etched into her brain. Although she didn't recall her father as well, his expression showed just as much eagerness, just as much longing. Even her brother and his family seemed excited.

"Is that her? Is that my auntie?" one of the boys cried, and the whole group hurried toward her, carrying those signs, as well as balloons and presents.

They all looked so well-groomed, so *nor-*

mal, so different from Anita. . . .

These were the people she'd lost.

"We found you at last," her mother said, and they both started to cry.

EPILOGUE

When Dylan came to find her, Cheyenne was sitting outside on the steps of the newly dubbed Little Mary's B and B, watching the snowflakes swirl gently to earth. Because Simon O'Neal's cameo for *Unsolved Mysteries* was being filmed inside, she knew he'd expected her to remain in the middle of things, along with Eve and Gail and everyone else. Getting the inn on TV had been her idea, after all. But she'd wanted a moment to reflect on the past month and all that had happened — and to enjoy the snow.

"What are you doing out here?" he asked.

She twisted around to smile up at him. "Just thinking."

"About . . ."

She patted the step and he sat with her. "My trip to Colorado."

His shoulder bumped hers. "It's cold. You can't think inside?"

"Wouldn't be the same."

"So what about your trip to Colorado? You've only been back a week. Are you ready to go see your family again?"

"I am." She'd had a wonderful visit. Since her return, she heard from her mother every day. "But next time I'm taking you with me. The Montroses want to meet you."

"I'd like that." He bent to look into her face. "Is that all? Or is something else going on? Because you're going to be soaked by the time you go back in and you're missing all the fun."

She smiled into his handsome face. The more she got to know him, the more she loved him. "I heard from Presley this morning."

"How is she?"

"She can have visitors in a few days. She's holding up well."

He grimaced as he glanced at the sky. "I wish I could say the same for Aaron."

"You don't think he'll make it?"

"It's not looking good."

"You've done all you can, Dyl."

He kicked some snow off the step below them. "Let's hope it's enough."

She felt guilty for not telling him about Presley's pregnancy. She wanted to, but Presley wouldn't allow it, and the baby was the only thing that kept her hanging on. It was all she talked about, the motivation behind her desire to get her life in order. Cheyenne didn't dare take that from her.

But the fact that Aaron was Dylan's brother made her feel bad about keeping the truth from him. "Whatever happens with Aaron and Presley . . . we can't let it affect us, okay?" she said.

"What do you mean?"

"We're happy. Whether they make it through rehab or not, what's between them or not between them . . . it's their business."

"Of course." He acted surprised that she'd even mention it, but he didn't know what she knew. She hoped he'd never have to find out. Just because Presley had a baby didn't necessarily mean it was Aaron's.

"I've been wondering . . ."

He kissed the top of her head. "Here we go."

She wrinkled her nose, showing her indecision. "Should I change my name back to Jewel?"

"Do you want to be called by that name?"

"I don't know. I think I've been Cheyenne for too long to make the switch and my family accepts that."

"What about your last name?"

"I definitely don't want to go by Christensen anymore." She'd decided that already. "I'm thinking I'll go with Cheyenne Montrose."

He offered her a sexy grin. "I personally like the sound of Cheyenne Amos."

She blinked at the snowflakes hitting her face. "But that would require you to make a lifelong commitment," she said with a grin.

The commitment didn't seem to bother him. "What if I was willing?"

She sobered. "Are you really ready for that?"

He shifted so he could dig a velvet box out of his pocket, which he handed to her. "I thought I'd do this tonight after dinner, in front of the fire, but . . . somehow this feels right, here in the snow."

It wasn't until that moment that she realized his question hadn't been hypothetical. She turned to gape at him. "You're serious? You're proposing?"

"I've never been more serious." He motioned to the box. "Open it."

Inside, she found a large round diamond set in white gold with smaller diamonds all around the band. "It's gorgeous!" she murmured. "It must've cost you a fortune."

He lifted her chin with one finger and gave her a lingering kiss. "You're worth it. I love you, Chey. You've wanted to move out of the river bottoms for a long time. Let's do it together."

She smiled as the whole world seemed to turn white around her. "But . . . what about your brothers?"

"They can have the house. They're old enough to live without me."

A noise caught Cheyenne's attention. Leaning to the left to see around Dylan, she spotted Eve coming out of the inn. "There you are! Why'd you disappear?"

Cheyenne held up her diamond ring.

"Oh, my God!" Eve grabbed the railing. "He just proposed? You're getting *married*? When?"

Laughing, Cheyenne threw her arms around Dylan's neck. "As soon as possible," she said.